The
Mayan
Codex

The
Mayan
Codex

MARIO READING

CORVUS

This paperback edition first published in the UK in 2010
by Corvus, an imprint of Grove Atlantic Ltd.

This is a work of fiction. All characters, organizations,
and events portrayed in this novel are either products of
the author's imagination or are used fictitiously.

9 8 7 6 5 4 3 2 1

A CIP catalogue record for this book is available from
the British Library.

ISBN: 978-1-84887-710-8

Printed in Great Britain by Clays Ltd, St Ives plc

Corvus
An imprint of Grove Atlantic Ltd
Ormond House
26-27 Boswell Street
London WC1N 3JZ

www.corvus-books.co.uk

For my beloved wife Claudia de Los Angeles,
la guardiana de mi corazón

Mario Reading 2010

AUTHOR'S NOTE

Just as with the Gypsy lore in the first book in my Nostradamus Trilogy, *The Nostradamus Prophecies*, the Maya lore, language, names, habits, and myths depicted in this book are all accurate. I have merely concatenated the customs of a number of different Maya tribes into one, for reasons of fictional convenience. The barbarities perpetrated by Friar Diego de Landa, as recounted by Akbal Coatl – aka the 'night serpent' – have not been tampered with in any way. These horrors happened, and in just the way I have described. The bulk of Maya written history was destroyed in one all-encompassing pogrom.

ACKNOWLEDGMENTS

I've been very lucky indeed in the people who have aided and abetted the production of this book, and this is my opportunity to thank them. Firstly, my agent, Oliver Munson, of Blake Friedmann, who has championed my work – both fiction and non-fiction – for a number of years now, and to whom I am deeply indebted for his dedication, judgement, and endless good humour. Thanks, also, to my publisher, Ravi Mirchandani, for encouraging me both 'onwards and upwards' (to filch one of his favourite catchphrases). Also to my former editor at Atlantic, Caroline Knight, for her wise suggestions on the text, and to Laura Palmer, my present editor at Atlantic's new imprint, Corvus, for making me feel so instantly at home. Thanks, too, to Henry Steadman for his outstanding jacket design for both my recent novels, and to my perennial copy editor, Shelagh Boyd, for her tact, insight, and wisdom in suggesting improvements to the text without alienating its author – a neat trick when one can pull it off! Also to the nameless Maya man who guided me on his *triciclo* around the site at Kabáh, and explained to me so patiently how and when one might hunt iguanas. Finally, deepest thanks must go to my two 'secret sharers': to my wife, Claudia, to whom this book is dedicated, and to my good friend Michèle O'Connell, for casting her invaluable eye over my work-in-progress and always telling it like it is.

EPIGRAPH

Eat, eat, while you still have bread
Drink, drink, while you still have water
A day will come when dust will possess the earth
And the face of the world will be blighted
On that day a cloud will rise
On that day a mountain will be lifted up
On that day a strong man will seize the land
On that day things will fall to ruin
On that day the tender leaf will be destroyed
On that day dying eyes will close
On that day there will be three signs seen on a tree
On that day three generations of men will hang there
On that day the battle flag will be raised
And the people will be scattered in the forests.

From *The Nine Books Of Chilam Balam*
Translated by the author

PROLOGUE

1

–

Le Château De Monfaucon,
Montargis, France
25th October 1228

The young King knelt and prayed a little before the hunt – God, after all, was on his side. Then he and his fifty-strong entourage clattered out of the Château de Monfaucon towards the domanial forest.

It was a blustery autumn day, with fine leaves churning in the wind, and a sufficient edge of rain to dampen the cheeks. The twelve mounted Cistercian monks who always accompanied the King were finding it increasingly difficult to adjust their chanting of the hours to the wind's hullabaloo. The King glared back at them from time to time, irritated at their swooping and swelling.

'You can all go home. I've had enough of your caterwauling. I can't make out a word of it.'

The monks, used to their master's whims, peeled off from the hunt procession, secretly relishing the prospect of an early return to cloisters, and to the roaring fire and plentiful breakfast that awaited them there.

Louis turned to his squire, Amauri de Bale. 'What you said about the wild boar. Yesterday. When we were talking. That it, too, is a symbol of Christ. Was this true?'

De Bale felt a sudden rush of exultation. The seed he had so carefully sown had germinated after all. 'Yes, Sire. In Teutonic Germany the boar, *sus scrofa*, is known as *der Eber*. I understand that the word *Eber* may be traced directly back to Ibri, the ancestor of the Hebrews.' Via a peculiarly convenient false etymology, de Bale added silently.

Louis hammered the pommel of his hunting saddle. 'Who were known as the Ibrim. Of course!'

De Bale grinned. He offered up a private prayer of thanks to the phalanx of tutors who had ensured that Louis was even better educated than his effete sodomite of a grandfather, Philip II Augustus.

'As you know, Sire, in ancient Greece the boar was the familiar of the goddesses Demeter and Atalanta. In Rome, of the war god Mars. Here in France, the boar might be said to stand in for you, Sire, in the sense of encapsulating both valiant courage and the refusal to take flight.'

Louis's eyes burned with enthusiasm. His voice rose high above the wind's buffet. 'Today I am going to kill a wild boar with my axe. Just like Heracles on Mount Erymanthus. God spoke to me this morning and told me that if I should do so, the attributes of the boar would transfer themselves to me, and my reign would see the permanent annexation of Jerusalem, Nazareth, and Bethlehem by the Holy Mother Church.'

De Bale raised his eyebrows. 'By the Holy Roman Emperor, you mean?'

'I mean by me.'

De Bale found himself temporarily at a loss for words. This was getting better by the minute. The King had even made the suggestion himself. He checked out the horsemen surrounding them – yes, they'd heard the

2

King all right. He could almost hear the surreptitious tightening of sphincters as the King's entourage realized they were to hunt for wild boar – and not deer – that day.

De Bale glanced across at the King. At sixteen, de Bale was a full year older than Louis. Physically, he was already fully formed, whilst the King, at fifteen, was only incipiently pubescent. In terms of height, however, Louis towered over de Bale by more than a head, and he sat his horse with the confidence of unchecked youth.

'*Dente timetur*,' said de Bale.

'*Rex non potest peccare*,' riposted the King.

The King's entourage burst into spontaneous applause. Even de Bale found himself moved by his monarch's elegant *jeu d'esprit*. He bowed low in his saddle. De Bale had simply intended to protect his back – *dente timetur* was a well-known Latin expression for 'you'd better watch out for the teeth'. But the King had countered with *rex non potest peccare* – 'the king cannot sin'. By the most delicate of hesitations, however, between *potest* and *peccare*, Louis had transformed the phrase into 'you cannot sway the king, wild pig'.

The pun had been so magnificent that de Bale was briefly tempted to ignore his orders and spare the King's life – where else but in France could you find a fifteen-year-old king with the wit of a Peter Abélard? But a wise man thought twice before antagonizing a kinsman as powerful as Pierre Mauclerc, Duke of Brittany. De Bale was nicely caught between the Plantagenet rock and the Capetian hard place.

He eased his horse closer to the King's, then darted a look back over his shoulder to see how the other squires were taking his arrogation of the King's attention. 'I know where you can find one, Sire. He's a monster. The biggest tusker this side of Orléans. He's four hundred pounds if he's an ounce.'

'How's that? What did you say?'

The fool's been praying again, thought de Bale – he should have been born a priest and not a king. If he carries on like this they'll have to sanctify him. Either that, or he'll finish up the bloodthirstiest, most vainglorious, most self-acclaiming tyrant since Nero.

As if in echo of his secret fears, de Bale's very own version of a solemn prayer flashed, uncalled for, through his head. 'May it please you God that after what I am about to do, this whoreson doesn't end up as a martyr, and I a disembowelled, disjointed, discombobulated regicide.'

De Bale bowed in belated response to the King's query, a sickly smile plastered across his face. 'I'd actually been reserving him for myself, Sire. My servants . . .'

'How can you reserve him for yourself? All wild boar belong to the King. Who do you think you are?'

De Bale flushed. God protect me from men who are my masters, he mouthed to himself. He was already beholden to Mauclerc, and here he was crossing swords with his other liege lord, Louis IX, whom Mauclerc wanted dead. De Bale could feel his brain spinning on its axis. He groped around for the right approach – the right way to jump.

'The animal is well outside the royal forest, Sire, and therefore legally mine. And I have not killed him yet. I merely instructed my people to build a wicker barricade around his lair, and to keep him in place with a charivari. I know he's in there. I just haven't seen him. I was going to dedicate him to Our Lady and then slaughter him. They say he has twelve-inch tusks.'

'Twelve-inch tusks? Impossible.'

De Bale knew his man. He shrugged, and looked away into the distance.

'Then he's the Devil, not a boar. Four hundred pounds, you say? And twelve-inch tusks? He's an impostor. It's inconceivable that our Lord Jesus Christ should be reflected in such a monster.'

De Bale edged in for the kill. 'That could be so, Sire. You are doubtless right.' He crossed himself with an extravagant gesture, almost as if he were sprinkling holy water over an invisible assembly. 'What more suitable opponent, then, for a Christian king?'

2

—

It took the King's party five hours to reach the de Bale manorial forest. Spare horses had been called for, and de Bale had ordered food, and a pavilion to be set up, just outside the monster's bower. He had also sent ahead to excuse his tenantry from their work for the day, ensuring himself the widest possible audience for what he trusted would be an earth-shattering, realm-transforming event.

When the King eventually rode in from the St Benedict marshes, five hundred of his eager subjects fell to their knees in welcome.

'Would you care to rest first, Sire?' De Bale caught his steward's eye. The man bowed, indicating that everything was in place for the King's comfort. 'Or shall we get straight to it?'

The King was staring out over the wicker enclosure. His face was ashen.

He's losing his nerve, thought de Bale. The poor fool's had five hours to think about the thing and he's losing his nerve. 'May I be your champion, Sire, and axe the porker on your behalf?'

Louis threw his leg up and over the pommel of his saddle. A servant skittered around the horse's croup, making a table of his back so that the King would not need to dirty his boots. 'Did God speak to you this morning, too, Amauri?'

'No, Sire. Of course not. God only speaks to kings and to popes and to the Holy Roman Emperor.'

The King grunted. He beckoned to his equerry. 'Bring me an axe. I shall kill this boar, and then we shall eat.'

De Bale offered up a fervent prayer of thanks that none of the King's mature advisors had bothered to attend the hunt. True to form, the whole lot of them were off scheming and plotting with the Queen Mother. He had the field entirely to himself.

He raised his gauntlet, signalling to his venerers that they might begin the drive. They, in turn, motioned to their flaggers, who transmitted the order through to the waiting beaters at the far end of the covert.

'The boar might emerge at any moment, Sire. May I suggest that you take up your position?'

The King stepped through the gap created for him in the wicker barrier. Ahead of him was a deep clump of thorn and withies. A channel had been cut through the mass of vegetation, via which the boar would, in theory, be funnelled.

De Bale raised his chin to one of his men-at-arms. The man threw him a pike. De Bale took his place to the right of the King, and a little behind. 'I will only intervene, Sire, should your first blow be deficient.'

'You will not intervene. My first blow will not be deficient. God has spoken to me. I am his anointed vessel.'

De Bale bowed his head in ostensibly reluctant surrender to the King's wishes. The King would not see the movement, but everybody else would. 'So be it, Sire.' He leaned on his pike and waited.

Soon a clamour could be heard over the peak of the hill. The *battue* had begun. De Bale had ordered the approaching line of beaters to march at no more than one-yard intervals – the last thing he wanted was for the boar to double back and eviscerate one of his own men instead of the King.

'Sire, remember to keep your legs together when you strike.'

'What are you talking about?'

'A boar scythes upwards with his tusks in order to disembowel his victim. If you keep your legs together, Sire, you will be protecting not only yourself but also the future of France.'

Louis burst out laughing.

Good, thought de Bale. Yet more evidence to the surrounding witnesses that all is well between me and the King. And if he keeps his legs together, the fool is that much more likely to botch his stroke.

A crash came from the underbrush, followed by a howl of excitement from the crowd. A boar burst out of the funnel of thicket and made straight for the King.

'Not that one, Sire.'

De Bale sprinted forward and speared the boar with his pike. The animal shrieked and fell on its back, kicking with all four legs. De Bale waved to his venerers, who ran forward, slit the pig's throat, and dragged it away. A pungent scent lingered after the carcase.

'Less than two hundred pounds, Sire. Your boar is more than twice that size.'

Louis's eyes were wide. He seemed transfixed by the still steaming blood-pile left by the slaughtered animal.

Come on, de Bale muttered silently to the King's back. Don't lose your nerve now, man. You'd never live it down. People would make up songs about you. You'd go down in history as Louis the Weak. And fate would no doubt dictate that you'd live to be a hundred years old.

There was a communal moan. A white hart had emerged from the plantation. The hart fell back a little on its haunches, and then sprang through the line of venerers, cleared the wicker fence in one bound, and galloped off into the surrounding woodland.

De Bale allowed a string of expletives to trickle silently out under his breath. 'It is a white hart, Sire. Its presence signifies that your goal is unattainable. We may as well go home.' The words stuck in de Bale's craw. But the symbol was so specific, and the significance of the white hart so well known to everybody, that it would have been folly for de Bale, given his status as the King's host, not to have acknowledged it.

'*As the hart panteth after the water brooks, so panteth my soul after thee, O God.*' Louis readied his axe. It was clear that he intended to prove both de Bale – and the hart – wrong.

There was a shriek from the back of the approaching line of beaters. Then a hullabaloo of voices. It was clear that someone had been gored.

The King was looking everywhere at once, his face livid in the sudden flare of the sun.

The boar emerged from the extreme flank of the thicket, red streamers hanging from its tusks.

At first the King did not see it. But the enraged boar – the first of the pair to taste blood – now saw the King. It glanced towards the line of venerers. No gaps there. Then back towards the King, who was surrounded by nothing but air.

The boar charged, twitching and flapping its snout to rid itself of the tangle of intestines obscuring its vision.

The King saw the boar and drew himself up. He stretched the axe back and waited.

'Run at him, Sire! You must run at him!' De Bale had not the remotest idea why he was trying to help the King. He wanted the man dead, for pity's sake, not transformed into a legend.

The King began a lumbering trot towards the boar, his axe raised for the kill.

The boar jinked, and swept his tusks sideways at the King.

The King screamed and fell.

The boar twisted, and started on his second pass.

Without stopping to think, de Bale rushed towards the King, slashing downwards in the direction of the boar's path with his pike. The pike sliced through the boar's shoulder. Arterial blood jetted in a crimson fountain over the King's recumbent body.

The blow had shattered the pike's shaft, leaving de Bale with only a slivered piece of wood in his hands.

The great boar was crawling towards the King, intent on finishing what it had started.

The venerers were approaching, daggers drawn, their mouths agape in shock.

De Bale saw all of this as if in slow motion. It was clear that he had only one choice left.

He threw himself onto the boar, grabbing its razor-sharp tusks with his hands. His last conscious memory was of the knife blows of his venerers raining down beside his head.

Amauri de Bale, Count of Hyères, spent the next sixteen years of his life in involuntary exile from the Court.

The Queen Mother, Blanche de Castile, had never forgiven him for what she saw as the encouragement of her son, the King, to commit an act whose folly was only outweighed by its pointlessness. The fact that de Bale had saved the young King's life at considerable risk to his own counted for little in the Queen's estimation – although it had undoubtedly protected de Bale from a regicide's agonizing death by quartering.

The King had been forbidden by his mother ever to communicate with de Bale again, and he had acceded to this request out of duty and affection for his mother, whilst stopping just short of agreeing to the actual administration of a formal oath.

But the King was a profoundly pious man, and renowned throughout Europe for his sense of fair play. Over the years of their enforced separation he had become increasingly convinced that Amauri de Bale had been marked out by God to save him from the machinations of the Devil. And furthermore that the great St Benedict boar, far from assuming the guise of one of the very symbols of Christ, had in fact been Lucifer himself.

In the late summer of 1244, and following a near mortal illness, King Louis, to his mother's horror, had unilaterally declared his intention to take the crusader's vow. After considerable soul-searching, and with the guidance of his confessor, Geoffrey of Beaulieu, and of his chaplain, William of Chartres, it was decided that it would be impossible for the King to take the cross without first acknowledging God's part in his decision. And this, in turn, could not be done without recognition of some sort for the man who had clearly been chosen by God Himself to protect the King from the Devil.

The problem was further aggravated by the fact that a number of the King's squires – many of whom, sixteen years on, were now holders of important Offices of State – had clearly heard the King, that morning back in 1228, explaining to Count Amauri de Bale that he, Louis, *Rex Francorum* and *Rex Christianissimus*, Lieutenant of God on Earth, Lord High Protector of France (the Eldest Daughter of the Church), had been personally instructed by God that if he ever wished to secure the permanent annexation of Jerusalem, Nazareth, and Bethlehem to the Holy Mother Church, he must first go out and kill a wild boar with his axe.

Thanks to his ever more profound understanding of the scriptures, the King – and via the King, his counsellors – now understood that God had had a further and less obvious motive in mind that day. And that this motive involved the selection of Count Amauri de Bale to be the King's sole champion. To act for him and on behalf of him, in other words, in the gratification of God's wishes.

As a direct consequence of this fact, and in the teeth of the Queen Mother's vigorous disapproval, the King issued a formal summons to de Bale to present himself at the Basilica of St Denis, next to the tombs of the King's father, Louis VIII, and of his grandfather, Philip II Augustus, on the exact day, and at the exact moment, of the sixteen-year anniversary of his God-driven intervention.

4

At first Amauri de Bale had been tempted to avoid what he suspected was a trick invitation by impulsively volunteering to serve in the army of Frederick II, Holy Roman Emperor. But he knew that if the Queen Mother truly wanted her revenge on him, she could reach him in Germany just as easily as she could have reached him at any time during the past sixteen years within the tenuous security of his chateau and estates.

That he owed his life – and the non-severance of his extremities – to the King's grace was in little doubt. De Bale shuddered to think what the Queen Mother would have ordered done to him had he not changed his mind at the very last moment and leapt in to save the King's life. His – on the face of it – perverse decision that day had not been prompted by any unlikely eruption of random human charity, however, but rather by a trained warrior's reactive instinct, twinned with the sudden realization – triggered by the King's sublime *jeu d'esprit* – that Louis might yet prove to be a credit to France, rather than merely another Capetian burden on its soul.

The upshot, of course, had been that de Bale had fallen foul of the Duke of Brittany, with all that that entailed in terms of loss of influence, a less advantageous marriage, and a dramatic narrowing of his political ambitions. But he had decided, in the general scheme of things, that this was the lesser of two evils – Mauclerc was bad, but the Queen Mother was awful.

De Bale knelt, therefore, before the King's father's sarcophagus, his head bowed, his forearms resting across his single upraised knee, and waited for the King's pleasure. His entire life had consisted of a series of often impulsive gambles, and he now felt a fatalistic sense of his own insignificance in the magnificent new *Rayonnant* Gothic setting of the St Denis Basilica.

The King, flanked by his confessor, Geoffrey of Beaulieu, and his chaplain, William of Chartres, watched de Bale from the lee of one of the twenty statue columns adorning the portal of the Basilica's west façade.

'Look,' said the King. 'It is Our Lady.'

The two counsellors fell back, staring at their King. 'We see nothing, Sire.'

The King turned to them. 'You see nothing?'

'No, Sire. We see nothing. What do you see?'

The King turned back in the direction of his father's crypt. 'I see Our Lady, the Mother of God, raising my champion's cloak and laying it tenderly across his back so that he should not take cold.'

The two men covered their faces with their hands. Then they fell to their knees and prostrated themselves on the flagstone flooring of the nave.

The King, after only a brief hesitation, strode towards the kneeling figure of the Count.

De Bale heard the King's approach, but chose not to look up. The King's words had carried to him through the echoing Basilica, and de Bale understood that, at this exact moment, his own and his family's future was being decided forever.

He felt the tip of the King's sword touch him on the back of his right shoulder. 'You saw the Devil, de Bale?'

'I did, Sire.'

'And you protected the King?'

'With my life, Sire.'

'And you will always protect the King?'

'Always, Sire.'

'And this realm of France?'

'I and my family, Sire. Throughout eternity.'

'Then you shall be my Corpus Maleficus.'

Louis turned away. He raised his voice, so that it echoed throughout the Basilica. 'I have the Bishop of Reims to crown me. The Bishop of Laon to anoint me. Langres to bear my sceptre. Beauvais my mantle. Chalons my ring. And Noyons to bear my belt. I have the Duke of Normandy to hold the first square banner, and Guyenne to hold the second. I have Burgundy to bear my crown and fasten my belt. I have the Count of Toulouse to carry my spurs. Flanders my sword. And Champagne my Royal Standard. But who do I have to protect me from the Devil? Who to be my champion?'

De Beaulieu and de Chartres had risen up from their prone positions. Both men recognized a *fait accompli* when they saw one. 'You have the Count of Hyères, Sire.'

Louis nodded. 'The Count of Hyères is now the thirteenth Pair de France. My father's and my grandfather's bones are witnesses to this fact. Bring me the Seal and my crusader's cross.'

PART ONE

1

Le Domaine De Seyème,
Cap Camarat, France
Present Day

Ex-Captain Joris Calque, grateful recipient of the Police
Nationale Française's early-retirement plan for officers
injured in the line of duty, had long ago accepted that he
was built for comfort and not for speed.

It was for this reason that he had bribed a notorious
local poacher to build him a camouflaged hideout on a
hill overlooking the present-day Dowager Countess of
Hyères's private estate on the St Tropez peninsula, almost
exactly 765 years after the events at the St Denis Basilica.

The hideout came complete with battery-operated
fan, blow-up armchair, and high-density, polyurethane
insulated, safari-style picnic box. From his eyrie on the
opposing hillside, the newly retired Calque intended
to monitor the comings and goings of the group of
individuals he now knew as the Corpus Maleficus, and,
in his own time, to secure proof of their involvement in
the death of his lieutenant earlier that same year.

Calque had done his homework well. He had spent
the first fortnight of his retirement trawling through the
records of the Bibliothèque Nationale de France and the
French National Archives at Fontainebleau, researching
everything he could about the history of the de Bale family.

And he had come to a number of inescapable conclusions.

Firstly, that the de Bales had managed to thrust their fingers into just about every slice of religious, political, civic, administrative, governmental, socio-religious and socio-political pie that France had contrived for itself – or had contrived *on* itself – since the early Middle Ages. And secondly that, almost without exception, the de Bales had abused whatever power they had thus managed to grasp.

Across a span of nearly eight hundred years, the de Bales could count three marshals, one seneschal, and two constables of France amongst their number. They had bought archbishoprics, infiltrated the college and orders of the Cardinalate, and even manipulated popes, without ever having quite achieved the papal tiara themselves. They had started wars and engendered riots. They had conducted massacres, espoused revolutions, and incited assassination attempts. They had weakened kings and queens, suborned dauphins and minor princelings, seduced foreign princesses and even, on one occasion, a Mademoiselle de France. They had fomented bastards, and undermined the principles of fair play at every opportunity. Far from protecting France from the Devil, the de Bales appeared, at every opportunity, to have eagerly encouraged her towards his fold.

The history of the de Bale family, via even the partial records available to Calque through the exclusively public sector access open to him, showed a family so intent on the pursuit and enjoyment of power, that it had ultimately ended up so diluting itself and dispersing its seed that, by the time of the Great War, it had lost virtually all influence. Lord Acton, thought Calque, had hit the nail squarely on the head with his 'power tends to corrupt, and absolute power corrupts absolutely. Great men are almost always bad men.'

This had led to a situation where the last remaining direct holder of the de Bale name had found himself – via the misfortunes of war – incapable of procreating and of continuing his direct line, whilst at the same time being titular head of a fast diminishing cabal that was unravelling itself at the speed dirty water flushes down a drain.

Nearly thirty years later, in the age-old way of such things, and in one final, desperate grasp at life, this elderly man had then procured himself a much younger woman, of lesser lineage, perhaps, than his own, but who was possessed of that inestimable compensation – a greater fortune. The family of Geneviève Odilonne de Moristot had been more than happy to trade her youth, her beauty, and the astonishing fortune she had inherited thanks to being the only daughter of a minor nobleman with a phalanx of elderly female relatives widowed in the Great War (and now gradually dying off in their coddled eighties and nineties), for a countship, a marquisate, and one of the oldest names in France.

The fact that the de Bale line could not be continued in the direct fashion that might have been expected had proved no hindrance to the new Countess. Using the example of Italy, in which the *per se* continuation of great names often takes precedence over strict genetic purity, and of France's very own '*Maman toujours, Papa peut-être*' – 'Mummy always, Daddy only perhaps' – dictum, she had persuaded her elderly husband to allow her to adopt thirteen children from her family-funded nunnery orphanage.

When Calque had first confirmed that this number was true, he had reared back from the microfiche newspaper he had been reading just as if a poisonous spider had landed in front of him and flashed him her claws.

But upon further consideration, he had begun to see the logic behind the Countess's actions. What better way

18

to rebuild the Corpus's influence? She had had both the money and the leisure – thanks to her extreme youth in relation to that of her husband – to use it. If one accepted that the nature/nurture debate was something of a moveable feast, what better way to gain power over your adopted children than by the use of titles, influence, and, last but by no means least, virtually unlimited funds? The old Count had chosen his partner well.

So was Achor Bale simply the exception that proved the rule? As far as Calque could tell, he had been the only one of the thirteen children adopted by the Countess old enough for his character to have been significantly formed before the fact. Was he the simple one-off freak that he seemed, and that Calque's Commandant insisted he was? Or had all the Countess's children been similarly groomed? Freed from the pressures of bureaucratic interference by his premature retirement, Calque now intended to find out.

The jobbing farmer on whose land Calque had planted his semi-permanent encampment had been easy enough to persuade. Before vacating his desk at the 2ème Arrondissement, Calque had contrived to mislay his Captain's badge and shield amongst the maelstrom of his boxed-up belongings. He had been a police officer for thirty years. Calque reckoned that the desk sergeant, embarrassed at having to say farewell to a man he had taken orders from since he was a wet-behind-the-ears rookie, wasn't going to quiz him any too closely about the loss.

In the event all Calque had needed to do was to promise to drop the badge and shield off the next time he visited his old friends at the precinct. It was with exquisite satisfaction that Calque had noted the desk sergeant solemnly ticking off the box marked 'Identification Returned' on his retirement checklist. He had plans for that badge, the first of which was to use it to silence the farmer.

Calque hadn't been that badly injured, of course, in the car accident the Countess de Bale's adopted son, Achor Bale, aka the 'eye-man', had contrived on him and his assistant, Paul Macron, earlier that summer. But Macron's brutal death at the hands of Bale a few days later had damaged more than merely its victim – it had undermined Joris Calque's rock-solid sense of his own vocation.

It wasn't that he mourned Macron unduly, or even felt guilty about his death – the man had been a bigot, for God's sake, and as thick as a navvy's bicep. It was more that he had lost the urge to explain himself anymore to superior officers who were both younger than himself, stupider than himself, and seemingly incapable of seeing or imagining anything beyond the confines of their own little time capsules.

This new breed of men and women infesting the upper echelons of the police department had no earthly sense of history – no earthly sense of what was seemly or appropriate in terms of their behaviour. When Calque had told the Commandant of his initial suspicions about the Countess and her baker's dozen of adopted children – Calque had briefly been tempted to call them by the more accurate medieval term of a 'Devil's dozen' but had thought better of it – the man had as good as laughed in his face.

'Achor Bale was a freak. A one-off. What do you think? That someone as respectable as the Countess of Hyères – who must be seventy if she's a day – has been grooming a family full of killer orphans to fulfil her late husband's 800-year-old sworn duty of protecting the French Crown from the Devil? Captain Calque, this may come as a surprise to you, but there *is* no Devil. And there is no French Crown any more, either. The last King of France was Louis-Philippe. And he was got rid of in

20

. . .' The Commandant had hesitated, a vague sense of betrayal suffusing his face.

'They got rid of Louis-Philippe in 1848. But he wasn't the last King of France. He was the last King of the French. The last reigning King of France was Charles X. You've heard of him, surely?'

'You're skating on very thin ice here, Captain.'

'I know that the Countess was running Bale while he was cutting his murderous swathe across France. That she had ordered him to harry the American, Adam Sabir, and his two Gypsy friends, Alexi Dufontaine and Yola Samana, to death. That she was convinced Sabir knew the identity of Nostradamus's Third Antichrist. A secret the Corpus Maleficus needed to secure if it was to continue with its sworn duty of protecting France from the Devil.'

'Pah.'

Calque was fleetingly tempted to throw in the information Sabir had vouchsafed him, in the strictest confidence, about the possible existence of the Second Coming, but decided that discretion was the better part of valour. The situation already sounded terminally far-fetched. Why aggravate the issue even further? The Commandant was probably an atheist anyway – he was certainly incapable of any significant degree of lateral thought. 'Achor Bale took his orders directly from the Countess, his mother. That makes her an accessory before the fact. In fact I would even go so far as to say that she was a joint principal.' Calque realized that he might be stretching the point a little. 'A great deal more than a simple conspirator, anyway.'

'Have you any proof of that?'

'He called her from the Maset. When he was in trouble. He asked her if he could come home. She told him to finish the job. To kill Sabir.'

21

'No he didn't. He spoke to that butler of hers. . .' The Commandant ransacked his memory, unconsciously pandering to Calque's notorious pedantry. ' . . . Millefeuille.'

'Milouins.'

'Milouins then. And Milouins replied to him partly in German. He used the word *Fertigmachen*. Which could have any number of meanings. From "go away and off yourself, you murderous bastard", to "let's make an end of it here and now". But Bale never spoke to the Countess personally – the evidence that the order came from her is purely circumstantial. But we've already been over this, Captain.'

'I've seen that hidden room at the Countess's house, Commandant. I've seen the document she keeps in there. The one that mentions a secret society called the Corpus Maleficus.'

'But the document was indecipherable. Written in an unknown code. You've acknowledged that much yourself. Damn it, man, the thing was dated 1250. What earthly connection can it have with a crime committed today?'

'It wasn't dated 1250. It was post-dated 1228. We know this because it contained the non-coded signatures and seals of three men crucial to King Louis the IX's realm. One man, Jean de Joinville, would have been four years old at the time of the signing. An impossibility, of course. So the document was clearly enacted retrospectively – possibly in appreciation of an act whose real significance was only recognized later.'

'For pity's sake, Captain. We all know about your absurd pretensions to a classical education – you made Paul Macron's life a misery with them. You've no way of knowing this, but a week before his death Macron put in an informal complaint against you for psychological harassment.'

'Psychological harassment?' Calque wanted a cigarette badly, but, thanks to the new ruling, he knew that if he dared to light up, his superior would probably call in the Paris Fire Brigade to put him out with a hosepipe.

'We persuaded him that it was in his own best interests to shelve the complaint. Your long service with the department still counts for something, you see. But the complaint can easily be resuscitated – even from beyond the grave – and all the more damaging for that. However, we are straying off the point. From here on in you will leave the Countess and her children alone. Do you understand me? The case is over. Bale is dead.'

'You mean she's too well-connected to tangle with?'

'In a nutshell, Captain? Yes.'

It was at that exact moment that Joris Calque had decided that his injuries from the car accident were a good deal more severe than he had ever let on. A stumble or two in the office, followed by a full-on fall had been quite enough to start the ball rolling. He had then found difficulty remembering simple things. Been forced to acknowledge to the Chief Medical Officer that he had been suffering from blackouts ever since the accident, and that he had recently been entertaining thoughts of suicide because of his guilt at Paul Macron's death.

The whole process had proved surprisingly simple. He had only had five more years to serve out anyway until forcible retirement – in the event they had been glad to be rid of him. Clear up the office. Out with the unregenerate males. Bring in new blood.

Calque had left the building without so much as a backwards glance. The icing on the cake had been that his ruinous-to-maintain ex-wife would now be deprived of her legally sanctioned monthly tranche of his pay cheque. Because he had been invalided out of the service with full honours and an unblemished record, and had, in consequence, been deemed incapable of functioning at 100 per cent of his usual competence thanks to the injuries – not to mention the post-traumatic stress – he had suffered whilst on active duty, the State would now be taking up a significant portion of the financial slack on his behalf. And the State, as Calque knew only too well, didn't go in for guilty consciences.

Grinning to himself, Calque leaned back in his blow-up armchair and focused his binoculars onto the front entrance to the Countess's house. He had been watching the place, day in, day out, for five weeks now. The routine had become a way of life for him. He had banked everything on his belief that the Countess would quite naturally have sought to maintain a low profile for a month or two after her adopted son's death. No muddying of the waters. No gathering in of the clan. And so far he had been proved right.

But Calque had known that it wouldn't last. The woman was reptilian – as cold-blooded as a coral snake. It was inconceivable that she shouldn't contrive some sort of revenge on Adam Sabir for the killing of the demented Bale. And Sabir had proved on more than one occasion how blind he was to any potential danger.

So Calque had decided to spend the early part of his unanticipated retirement doing what he had always done best – protecting the public. Except in this case the public consisted of precisely one individual, the errant American writer Adam Sabir. And the forces of law and order were no longer officially sanctioned, with the full panoply of the State's legal mechanisms backing them up, but merely consisted of one overweight, overeducated, and terminally underfunded former policeman.

Why was he doing it? Boredom? Sour grapes? Resentment at the truncation of his decreasingly high-flying career? None of that. The truth was that Sabir had touched a surprisingly sensitive nerve in the usually unsentimental Calque with his mysterious tales of the Second Coming and of the rapidly approaching Armageddon predicted in the 52 lost verses of Nostradamus – verses that Sabir had managed to memorize before his final reckoning with Achor Bale. Calque's intellectual vanity had been aroused – and his latent republican ire had been triggered – by the Countess's inbred assumption that she and her aristocratic ilk would always win out in the end.

This new, knight-errant version of the formerly cynical Joris Calque had attended Achor Bale's funeral, therefore, and had noted with satisfaction the absence of Bale's twelve remaining brothers and sisters. Only the Countess and her near-ubiquitous personal assistant, Madame Mastigou, had bothered to turn up.

But the Countess would have to convoke them at some point. Bring them up to scratch. And the telephone or the internet just wouldn't do – far too many loopholes and opportunities for covert surveillance. That meant that her children would have to return to the Domaine de Seyème – and to the secret room one of his officers had unexpectedly discovered behind the library – in person. That was where the Corpus Maleficus held its meetings, wasn't it? That was where they hatched their schemes?

And that was where Joris Calque had illegally hidden a voice-activated tape recorder whilst he was busy conducting his entirely legal search of the Countess's house nearly eight weeks before.

2

The recently entitled Abiger de Bale, Chevalier, Comte d'Hyères, Marquis de Seyème, Pair de France, *primus inter pares*, bundled his twin brother ahead of him up the steps of the TGV. 'Go on, Pollux. Move your arse.'

'Stop calling me Pollux. My name is Vaulderie.'

'All right then. I'll call you Vaulderie from now on. Vicomte Vaulderie. How's that? Now you sound like a sexually transmitted disease.'

The twins threw themselves down in opposing seats in the first-class carriage. Vaulderie kicked out at a cushion. 'Why should I be a mere vicomte when you're a fucking comte? Why should you be the one to snaffle Rocha's title?'

'Because I was the last one to emerge from our mother. That's the Napoleonic Code for you. Last out, first conceived. Enlightened primogeniture, *mon pote*. Christ. Just think. If it wasn't for King Clovis, our fallen angel of a sister would have inherited instead of me. She's two years older. *Maltho ti afrio lito.*'

'What the hell does that mean?'

'Salic Law, dummy. Male primogeniture. It's what saved our bacon.'

'No. The other bit.'

'It's the only full sentence left in Old Frankish. "I tell you. I free you. Half free." Complete gobbledegook, of course. Be thankful you've got a title at all. If Rocha hadn't let that pig of a policeman loose off a shot at him, you'd have remained a commoner all your life. Now you're a real vicomte you can flash your *chevalière* ring at all the girls and their pants will automatically fall down. Just like I've been doing for years.'

Vaulderie launched another kick at the seat cushion, but harder this time. 'It's not fair. If we'd been born in England, I would have been the senior of us two. First out is considered the eldest there.'

'Lucky for me we weren't born in England, then. We'd have had an idiot as head of the family.'

The brothers, despite the fact that they were all of twenty-five years old, began to wrestle. Watching them, the off-duty railway security inspector – who was availing himself of his free first-class travel privileges – thought yet again how lucky France was to have a Republic. It was always these young blue bloods, off for the weekend, who caused the most trouble on his trains. He could see their signet rings flashing as they fought for control of each other's throats.

'That's enough. I'll have no rough-housing here.' He eased his way up the central aisle and flashed his badge at the boys.

Both young men straightened up and smoothed back their hair. 'Sorry, Colonel. It won't happen again. We were only mud-larking.'

The inspector was rather taken aback. He had expected trouble. These two had all the earmarks of their class. Absurdly well-cut hair. Double-breasted grey flannel suits that fitted them like a second skin. Not an ounce of excess fat on the pair of them – fencing, probably, or some exclusive tennis club with a five-year waiting list. When he looked at them more closely, he was astonished to realize that they were identical twins.

He shrugged, not a little disarmed by their unanticipated courtesy. 'I won't take your names this time, as we're nearly at my destination. You're lucky – you've both got off more lightly than you deserve. But remember.' He pointed above his head. 'There are security cameras on this train.'

'Yes. We noticed those.' The boys grinned at each other, as if in echo of some telepathic joke.

The inspector hesitated, tempted to say more – to make his mark on these gilded hooligans. Then he shrugged a second time and moved back down the aisle. He was due off at the next station anyway. In twenty minutes' time he would be home with his wife. Why complicate matters?

'Shall we?' Abiger gave his brother a playful nudge with the toe of his shoe.

'Are you crazy? We'd be forced to change trains. We'd be late for Madame, our mother. She might even ask us what we were doing that was so important we missed the beginning of her gathering.'

'Oh come on, Vau. Live dangerously for once. We're too old to be thrashed with a wooden clothes hanger anymore. Anyhow, I'm head of the family now.'

'Madame, our mother, is head of the family. You're merely its technical figurehead. And a plug-ugly one at that. That much I'll acknowledge.'

Abiger de Bale lurched forwards as if he intended to trigger a rematch of their wrestling competition – but then, with the movement only half-completed, he changed his mind. Grinning, he allowed his gaze to slide away from his brother and follow the line of the inspector's retreating back. 'That worm insulted the CM, Vau. I say we do it.'

For twenty-five years Vaulderie had followed his brother's lead in everything. Gone everywhere he had gone. Even taken his punishments for him. It was far too late to turn back now. With the death of Rocha de Bale, their adopted brother – the man now known to the outside world as the murderer, Achor Bale – everything had changed. What had been hidden was now open. What had been obscured was now set to be revealed.

The Corpus Maleficus would finally be taking its rightful place as the driving force behind a new order.

Vaulderie gave a defeated sigh. 'I say we do it too.'

3

—

At first, after leaving the train, the boys worked in a zigzag formation behind the inspector's back. That way, if the man had a car, one of them could break away from the stalk and procure a vehicle, whilst the other could mark the direction taken and keep in touch via his cell phone.

But the inspector didn't have a car. It soon became obvious that he lived within walking distance of the station – a railwayman through and through. Instinctively, intuitively, the boys decided not to take him en route. Far more sensible to deal with him at home, well out of the eye of the storm. Far more fun to wait.

At one point the man stopped. He cocked his head downwards and to one side, as though he were listening to something passing underneath him. The boys froze in their respective positions, visible, but not visible, maybe fifty metres behind him. In their experience, marks never turned around. People simply didn't expect to be followed – not on a suburban street, mid-afternoon, in *la France profonde*, with mothers collecting their children from school, and yellow postal vans busy on their last collection of the day.

The boys converged again when they saw the inspector hesitating at the communal door to his apartment block

– feeling for his keys – tapping his pockets for cigarettes. Would he turn at the very last moment and head for the *Bar/Tabac* on the corner? Have himself a quick snifter before facing his wife? In that case both twins knew that they would be forced to abandon the hunt and head back towards the station.

For despite all their bravado, each, in his own way, feared Madame, their mother, as they feared nothing else on earth. She was like Agaberte, daughter of the Norse god Vagnoste, who could transform herself from a wrinkled old crone into a woman so tall she could reach up and touch the sky – a woman who could overturn mountains, rip up great trees, and dry up the swollen beds of rivers. Abi and Vau's childhood had been spent entirely in her thrall, and no power on earth could entirely break her dominance of them.

The inspector reached forward and unlocked the door. Now the boys were hurrying, not wishing to be faced with an unknown, untested lock. Vau caught the door just before it clicked to, and Abi slid through the crack his brother made for him, one eye fastened on the stairs above him.

Shoes in their hands, they padded up the concrete stairwell behind the inspector. How could people bear to live like this? Money and power were there to be taken. All you needed was the nerve.

The inspector was stepping into his apartment – calling out to his wife.

Abi reached out and touched him on the arm. 'Colonel. A word.'

4

Some years before, the brothers had had a series of telescopic, lead-weighted, fighting batons designed and made for them. Eight inches long, the batons fitted comfortably inside the forearm sleeve of a jacket, where they were secured in place by the simple expedient of a loop and a double button.

Although principally made of rubber, the batons were not able to pass through a metal detector by dint of their lead content, and therefore had to be transported separately on an aeroplane as part of hold baggage – or secreted, for instance, inside a travelling fishing-rod case, where they could be passed off as fisherman's priests. By train and by car, however, they were perfection itself. Once liberated from their housings, the batons extended with a simple flick of the wrist to a total of two feet in length, retaining more than enough rigidity to guarantee a quite remarkable hand-to-target action.

They would kill, of course, if used aggressively, but their principal function was defensive – they were designed as pacifiers. In ten seconds a man could be crippled, his legs worse than useless, by the simple expedient of a scything stroke behind the knee. The twins, being two, found this the best resort in all but the most extreme of circumstances. One would monopolize the target's attention whilst the other struck him from behind. It had never failed them. A frightened man on the floor, one leg unmarked but useless, was a very different animal indeed from an angry man in possession of all his physical faculties.

The inspector curled up in the foetal position at the entrance to his apartment and began to dry retch, like a cat attempting to bring up a fur ball. His wife came hurrying out of the kitchen, where she had been preparing their supper. Vau gave her two for good measure, one behind each knee. She dropped to the floor and then stretched out, like a postulant at some Easter confraternity ceremony.

Abi closed the door. He and Vau dragged the couple through into the lounge.

Vau switched on the television. 'Gas explosion or double suicide?'

The inspector tried to raise himself from the floor. Vau flailed him behind the other knee. 'Silence. You will both remain silent, faces to the ground. Do you understand me?'

The woman was unconscious – shock, probably. The boys were used to people responding in disparate ways. Women were particularly vulnerable to sudden explosions of violence, whereas men would often struggle, requiring further pacification.

Abi snapped his fingers triumphantly. 'No. No. Listen. I've got another idea. Kill two birds with one stone.'

'How's that?'

'Wait for me here. I won't be more than ten minutes. A surprise.' Abi was staring out of the window now, his expression speculative. He snapped the baton shut and secreted it back inside his sleeve. He had scarcely even broken into a sweat.

5
–

Abi had passed the Jaguar Sports on their way in from the station. The car had captured his attention even then, as it had seemed so out of place in a street full of Peugeots, and Renaults, and six-seater Fiat run-arounds. A pimp's car, probably, or the vehicle of some chancer who had made it good and couldn't tear himself away from the old neighbourhood. Perhaps the owner was visiting his elderly mother?

It took Abi less than a minute to bypass the alarm system. He had been breaking into cars ever since his early adolescence, and considered it one of his primary skills. During their teen years, Madame, his mother, had arranged for him and Vau to serve as apprentices to one of the best auto thieves in the business. It was something he was infinitely grateful to her for. It had given him power.

He drove the car to the front of the inspector's apartment building and triggered the trunk mechanism. Vau was watching from the inspector's window. Abi mouthed a few words and pointed to the trunk. Vau nodded his head.

He emerged, less than a minute later, supporting the inspector like a man will support his drunken friend after a night out on the town.

Abi had closed the trunk by this time, and was holding the passenger door open, with the seat pulled forward. He checked around, then nodded. Speed was of the essence in such cases – any hesitation could prove fatal. Neither he nor Vau appeared on any police records, and he intended to keep it that way. 'Get in there. Keep your head down.'

The inspector stretched himself flat down across the well. 'What about my wife? What are you doing with my wife?' His voice shook. One hand snaked down as if to feel for any damage to his knees.

'Don't worry, Colonel. She's coming along for the ride too.'

Once they were safely out of town, Vau stopped the car, and they transferred the inspector and his wife to the trunk. It was a tight fit, but it seemed unlikely the pair would actually suffocate. Both parties had wet themselves, which saved the brothers the trouble of having to stop somewhere en route for a leak break.

Vau caught his brother's eye. He gave a speculative chuck of the head. 'I know exactly what you're thinking. But we'll never make it. You can't beat a TGV. Those things average more than three hundred kilometres an hour.'

'Three stops. They have to make three stops. Then they have to cut their speed radically along the coast. I'll give you a thousand Euros if we make it to Madame, our mother's, twenty minutes before our allotted time.'

'Done. You want to take the wheel?'

'No. You're a better driver than I am.'

Vau fishtailed the car out onto the highway, in the direction of the nearest autoroute toll booth.

6

They made it to the Cap Camarat lighthouse with fourteen minutes to spare. Below them the rocks loomed white in the glow of the waxing moon.

'Jesus, Abi. You don't mean to bung them off here? We're only a few kilometres from the house.'

'Look.' Abi held out an unfamiliar cell phone. 'It probably belongs to the pimp who owns this car.'

'So what?'

'So what? So everything. We get them out of the trunk, give them the keys, and let them take off.'

'Are you crazy?'

'But not before we've phoned a place in South Africa I know of and arranged a movie download – the damned thing will take hours and cost thousands. Then we bury the cell phone down the side of the seat. After that we phone the *flics* back in Saint Evry, and check up on what we claim is our stolen car – the one that we called in a few hours ago. Don't they remember taking the call? Maybe it was someone else on duty? There'll be a record of it, anyway. Then we tell the *flics* that we just remembered that there's a cell phone in the car, and give them the number and the server. Then we leave the rest to them.'

'I still don't understand.'

'Come on, Vau. The *flics* check on the cell phone. They find that the line is conveniently open. They can then pinpoint the car to within about three metres, give or take. So they swoop down and reel these two losers in.'

'But then they'll tell the *flics* about us.'

'Oh really? That they were kidnapped and forced to drive three hundred kilometres by two guys the inspector talked rough to on the train? That they were then calmly handed back the stolen car keys, and, to celebrate, they began to download a child porn movie? When the *flics* get through with them – if they ever get through with them – Monsieur *et* Madame L'Inspecteur will still have the pimp to reckon with. And his dear old mother lives just down the road from them, remember? And they've just run up an uninsured bill of three thousand Euros on the pimp's cell phone, and got him branded a paedophile to boot.'

'Christ, Abi. That's genius.'

Abi used his own cell phone to call up a local taxi. 'You're right. It is. Why bother to kill people when you can simply ruin their lives with a little creative imagination?'

7

—

Geneviève de Bale, dowager Countess of Hyères, stood on the steps of the Chateau de Seyème and watched as her adopted twin sons descended from their taxi. They were the last of her children to arrive, and she was marginally displeased.

'You were due in at 8.10.'

She leaned towards her personal assistant, Madame Mastigou, who consulted her brooch watch and mouthed the correct time to her.

'Abiger, you are twenty-five minutes late. I had expected you to join me on the steps to greet your brothers and sisters. You are the new Count now. As I am a widow and you are still unmarried, it would have been proper for you to have welcomed the family at my side. Instead, I have had to stand here alone.'

Abi kissed Madame, his mother's, hand, and touched it to his forehead. Then he took up position a step or so below her on the stairs. 'Vaulderie and I had a little business to attend to. You would have approved, I promise. Please forgive me.'

On the opposite hillside, Joris Calque fiddled with his night glasses, cursing the gibbous moon and the clouds that were obscuring it.

36

The Countess bent over and kissed her eldest son on the crown of his head. Vau hurried expectantly towards her, but was rewarded by a simple one-handed cupping of the face. He gave his brother a 'nothing ever changes' look, and hurried inside.

'Of course I forgive you, my darling.'

The two of them – mother and adopted son – stood staring out into the surrounding gloom for a few moments, as though an invisible cine camera were recording them for posterity.

Then Abi took his mother's arm and they followed Madame Mastigou back inside the house.

8

Calque threw himself back on his inflatable armchair and felt around for his cigarettes. Normally, at this time of the evening, he would never have dreamt of lighting up for fear of giving away his position – but today's events were just cause for celebration. He was in with a fighting chance again.

The butler, Milouins, had been the first to emerge from the house at around four o'clock that afternoon. After a short pause to sniff the air, he had begun to rake the courtyard into something approximating Zen spirals. Then one of the footmen had appeared with a bucket and a squeegee mop to wash down the stone steps. Finally the gardener had entered unexpectedly from stage right and had attempted to snatch the rake back from Milouins – an altercation ensued, which the gardener lost.

The gardener had then retreated without his rake, scuffing the once immaculate gravel behind him as he went. The footman, plainly recognizing on which side his bread was buttered, had jettisoned whatever remained in his water bucket in the direction of the gardener's retreating back.

Calque made a swift mental note to ascertain the gardener's identity as a prelude to approaching him for indiscreet information about the household setup – disenchanted domestic servants, embittered spouses, and disinherited relatives had always formed a major part of his stock-in-trade.

After the initial flurry of preparatory activity there had been a pause of three hours, during which Calque had dozed off on six separate occasions – he had been on the job since early that morning, and was not in the first flush of youth. At about eight o'clock, during a gap between dozes, the Countess had appeared on the steps with her assistant, the ever-elegant Madame Mastigou, at her side. A certain amount of clock consulting had then gone on. At 8.15 the first of a total of five separate cars had drawn up in the driveway.

Each car had then disgorged its occupants, each of whom had gone up to the apparently immovable Countess to kiss her hand and to receive a series of four kisses – two on each cheek – in return.

Then the cars had retreated, leaving the Countess and Madame Mastigou to contemplate the abandoned courtyard like the final guests at a Wagner evening.

Not long afterwards a local taxi had lurched into view, and two men had emerged from its maw. The deteriorating quality of the light had made it impossible for Calque to make out the men's faces – either one or both of them appeared to be the exception to the Countess's rule on stasis, however, for she actually moved a step or two towards them in welcome, implying that they were marginally higher in the pecking order than the other arrivals.

One of the men had then disappeared inside the house, leaving the Countess and the other man standing in a pool of light halfway down the entrance steps.

By the time Calque had succeeded in refocusing his night glasses, the pair had turned around and gone inside.

9
—

Madame Mastigou sat with her pen poised over a sheet of finely milled Florentine writing paper and waited for the Countess to break her silence.

There was a palpable sense of expectation in the hermetically sealed assembly room. This was the first time in five years that all the Countess's adopted children had been brought together in one place, and Madame Mastigou could sense the tension behind her employer's otherwise frozen countenance.

The butler, Milouins, had been delegated for guard duty outside the hidden door in the library, and one of the footmen was acting as outrider in the salon, ensuring that no one could make their way through the household's *cordon sanitaire* unannounced. Inside the secret chamber the Countess stood at the head of the table, with her children, in strictly descending order of seniority, taking up the remaining seats to her right and left.

They ranged in age from a mature twenty-seven, in the case of Lamia de Bale, the oldest girl, to around eighteen, in the case of Oni de Bale, the youngest male – a virtual giant, nearly seven feet tall, with the trademark red eyes and unpigmented skin of the true albino.

Abiger and Vaulderie, being the oldest males present, and therefore in legal receipt of the countcy and viscountcy through agnatic primogeniture, had been allocated the two senior seats, despite being two years their sister's junior. At the very end of the table, a chair had been left empty. In front of it lay a sword, a signet ring, and a velvet brocade sash in memory of their brother, Rocha.

To the clinically detached eye it would soon have become apparent that each of the Countess's adopted children was graced with some defining mark or characteristic that separated them from the herd.

The oldest girl, Lamia, had a prominent strawberry birthmark that spread across half of her face – seen from one side, she was beautiful, whilst from the other side her beauty was disguised by what, at first glance, appeared to be a piece of blood-soaked surgical gauze. Her younger sister, Athame, was dwarfish in stature, with tiny hands and feet. Berith, the young man sitting below her, had a harelip. Rudra de Bale limped as the result of an untreated club foot, and Aldinach de Bale was a natural hermaphrodite, something which only manifested itself in the marked delicacy of some of his movements – in reality there were times when it suited him to dress as a woman, and other times as a man.

Further down the line came Alastor de Bale, who suffered from cachexia, a wasting disease that made his near neighbour, Asson de Bale, appear even larger than his 22-stone frame would normally warrant. The 21-year-old Dakini de Bale had preternaturally long hair, which framed a face that seemed frozen in a sort of malevolent rictus, and her twenty-year-old sister, Nawal de Bale, suffered from hirsutism, which gave her the visage of an animal.

Each of the thirteen children had been told, since earliest childhood, that they had been marked out in this way by God as a sign of His especial grace. As a result they each bore their affliction not as an affliction, but more as a mark of special selection. The Countess had also explained to them that, thanks to the prevalence of a certain sort of guilty sentimentality in much of the twenty-first century's increasingly decadent populace, they might even be able to use their afflictions to divert suspicion from themselves – and out towards innocent parties – in the event of a crisis.

Glancing about the room, the Countess could barely disguise her satisfaction. It was at her direct instigation that her husband had resuscitated the almost moribund Corpus Maleficus. The first time he had described the cabal to her – and his family's inextricable link to its aims over a history spanning nearly eight hundred years – had been just a few days before their marriage. The Count had sounded almost apologetic, as if he had been forced to summon up a hoary old skeleton from the family vaults in order to forestall his future wife learning about it from other, less well-intentioned, sources.

The Countess – the accustomed recipient, since early childhood, of the complete attention of her extended family thanks to her position as sole inheritrix of both her father's and his distaff relatives' extensive fortunes – had realized its glorious potential at once. She could feel herself moving, inchmeal, from one non-carnal embrace to another, infinitely more preferable one. Before this moment she had merely sensed, thanks to her father's subtle hints, that she would be investing in something more than simply a name with her fortune, but she hadn't realized exactly what she was buying into. Now she knew for certain. 'You can't let something like this just die.'

Her elderly fiancé had smiled. 'How can one resuscitate a skeleton? The outer body and epidermis began to expire alongside the final vestiges of the age-old aristocratic order after the disasters of the Great War. The inner body, along with its vital organs, finally perished alongside my manhood, on Monday the third of June 1940, during the German bombardment of Paris. Do you remember Jean Renoir's film, *La Grande Illusion*? The characters played by Pierre Fresnay and Erich von Stroheim? The Old Guard aristocrats recognizing each other, and realizing that they had both reached the end of their usefulness? Well Renoir was right. We are tired and irrelevant.'

The Countess had turned on him, revealing for the very first time the inner fire that drove her. 'Von Stroheim was not an aristocrat, but the son of a Jewish hat-maker. Fresnay's father was a Huguenot, and therefore a hater of Catholics. And Renoir's father was a hack painter who depicted his women as if they were made out of marzipan. Who are such people to tell you that your class is doomed?' She turned on him. 'I won't have it. A man doesn't need a functioning member to be a man. An institution doesn't need the sanction of the State to give it weight. The flower of France's chivalric tradition should not need the permission of its inferiors to celebrate its past achievements and prepare its future triumphs.'

The Count had continued smiling. 'Future triumphs? For reasons that are entirely beyond my control, it seems that I am to be the last in my line. More than a thousand years of history will die with me, my dear. Where are these future triumphs you speak of going to come from?'

And so she had told him – told him of her plans to adopt a new generation of soldiers for the de Bale cause. Told him of the true extent of her fortune, and what they could both achieve with it. And gradually his face had started to light up. His expression to change. 'You really think this is possible? I am an old man.'

'But I am not. I shall represent you. Represent our family. Fight for our status as hereditary peers of France.'

'Why? Why should you do this?'

She had hesitated for some little time, almost as if she had no answer to his question. Then she had turned to him, taken his hand, and placed it above her heart. 'Because it is my destiny.'

It was only later, and well into their marriage, that the Countess had realized just how elegantly the Count had steered her towards exactly the conclusion he himself had so fervently desired.

10

So. It was time. The Countess laid aside the document whose ancient codification had caused so much trouble to the inquisitive police Captain – what had been his name? Clique? Claque? – the one who had so dogged her footsteps in the run-up to the death of her eldest son earlier that summer. She knew its entire contents by heart.

'Who are we?'

'We are the Corpus.' Her children responded as one.

'Which Corpus?'

'The Corpus Maleficus.'

'And what do we do?'

'We protect the realm.'

'And who is our enemy?'

'The Devil.'

'And how shall we defeat him?'

'We shall never defeat him.'

'And how shall we unseat him?'

'We shall never unseat him.'

'So what is our purpose?'

'Delay.'

'And how do we procure it?'

'By serving Christ's dark shadow.'

'And who is that?'

'The *antimimon pneuma*. The counterfeit spirit.'

'And what is his name?'

'The Antichrist.'

'And how do we serve him?'

'By destroying the *Parousia*.'

'And what is the *Parousia*?'

'He is the Second Coming of Christ. He is the brother of Satan.'

'And how shall we know Him?'

'A sign will be given.'

'And how shall we kill Him?'

'He will be sacrificed.'

'And what shall be our reward?'

'Death.'

'And what is our law?'

'Death.'

'And how shall we achieve it?'

'Anarchy.'

'And who are our brothers and sisters?'

'We shall know them.'

'And who are our enemies?'

'We shall know them.'

'And who is the Third Antichrist?'

'We shall know him and guard him.'

'And who is the Second Coming?'

'We shall know Him and kill Him.'

The Countess made the reverse sign of the cross, followed by the reverse sign of the pentacle, just as her son, Achor Bale, had done just a few short hours before his death.

'And Holy is the Number of the Beast.'

The children intoned the answers to the Countess's questions with their eyes turned up into their eyelids – as they spoke, their hands also made reverse crosses, reaching from their crotch back over to the nape of their necks. This was followed by the sign of the six-sided pentacle, also from the direction of the lower to the upper body.

When the invocations were over, the Countess walked the length of the room to stand behind Achor Bale's empty chair. She kissed her fingers and laid them tenderly on the hilt of his sword. 'You all realize, of course, that Rocha's death occurred as a direct result of investigations he was undertaking on behalf of the Society?'

There was a generalized intake of breath.

'It was at my instigation that he followed the man Sabir. It was at my instigation that he intervened following Sabir's discovery of the lost verses of Nostradamus. He died fulfilling his duties to the Corpus.'

Abiger glanced across at his brother. He was scarcely able to keep the grin off his face. He knew what was coming.

'A spy in the apostate Nostradamus's household – a spy in the pay of one of the noblest of your ancestors, Forcas de Bale – alerted his master to the verses' potential contents. The Count was already on his way down to Agen when news reached him of Michel de Nostredame's death. When he arrived, the verses had already been dispersed and the seer buried. It took nearly 450 years for the verses to reappear. We in the Corpus have long memories. An oath is an oath for us. Once bound, always bound.'

'Once bound, always bound.' The children whispered in echo of her words.

'Abiger . . .' The Countess turned towards her eldest son. 'The time has come for you and your brother to travel to America. You will identify the man Sabir. First, you will extract the secrets of the prophecies from him in whatever manner you may deem appropriate. Then you will take revenge for the murder of your brother. Is that clear?'

'Perfectly, Madame.'

The Countess turned towards her eldest daughter. 'Lamia, you did not make the reverse cross. Kindly make it now.'

Lamia's hand crept towards her throat. The rufous complexion marring one side of her face turned, if anything, a deeper red.

'I am waiting.'

'I cannot do it, Madame.' Lamia shook her head.

Her brothers and sisters stared at her like dingoes alerted to a kill.

'Abiger. Escort your elder sister to her room. She will remain there until she is able to offer a suitable explanation for her behaviour. Apprise Milouins of the situation. The rest of you may take the blood oath. You will be told when you are needed.'

Oni de Bale glanced down at his mother from his great height. 'Do we others continue with our work, Madame?'

The Countess turned away, motioning to Madame Mastigou, who was cleaning a small ivory receptacle. Then she turned towards her dwarfish daughter, Athame, a sufferer from Ellis–van Creveld Syndrome. A polydactyl, Athame was unconscionably dexterous with all of her twelve fingers. 'Athame. Live up to your name.

You may do the necessary cuts for the blood oath.'

'Yes, Madame.'

'Mother?'

'I heard you, Oni.' The Countess turned and laid a light hand on her youngest son's forearm. She glanced up into his eyes, her neck forced back against the collar of her elegantly tailored 1950s Dior suit the better to take in his span. 'Always continue with your work. That is the way to please me. Stir, stir, stir. Keep the broth moving. Never let the commoners rest at ease. The Devil is a hungry angel – he will come calling if we don't forestall him. That is your primary job.'

'Yes, Madame.'

'And, Oni.'

'Yes, Madame?'

'Soon, I may have a more specific use for you. You must hold yourself in readiness for that.'

Oni hunched down and kissed his mother's hand.

The Countess noticed Lamia hesitate on her way to the door. 'Have you anything to say to me, my child?'

It looked for a moment as if Lamia would speak. Then she shook her head and followed her brother quietly out into the library.

11

At precisely 9.30 the next morning, Joris Calque watched from his camouflaged hiding place as the battery of chauffeur-driven cars returned to collect their clients. He counted them off, one by one.

'That leaves three of them still inside the house. Two males and a female, if I am not mistaken.'

In the lonely weeks that Calque had spent ensconced inside his eyrie, he had occasionally drifted into the habit of talking out loud to himself. He was well aware of this new tendency, but didn't, as yet, feel that he was in imminent danger of turning into one of those ubiquitous males – and they were always males, weren't they? – who stride up and down the pavements of their home town mouthing off to imagined companions.

If he ever did slide into such a public form of idiocy, Calque hoped that he would have enough wit left to wedge a cell phone speaker in his ear, thereby protecting himself against the very forces of public order to which he had for so long subscribed.

His main problem now wasn't incipient dementia, however, but rather to retrieve the – hopefully – brimming voice-activated tape recorder from the Countess's inner sanctum.

He stood up and glanced around his eyrie. So. His time here was over.

He wouldn't miss the chemical toilet, the smell of stale tobacco, or the curious quality of light that filtered through the gaps in the camouflage netting. But he would miss the birdlife, and the sightings of badgers, rodents, rabbits, deer and foxes with which he had wiled away the more tiresome hours of his vigil. He decided, on the spur of the moment, to bequeath the entirety of his hidey-hole to the poacher who had set it up. That would save him the trouble of carting everything back to his car. It would serve to cover his back-trail rather nicely, too.

Calque's experience told him that he didn't stand a cat-in-hell's chance of getting into the Domaine to retrieve the recorder himself. He was neither young, suicidal, nor particularly eager to see the inside of any of the prisons to which he had consigned so many felons, child-molesters, and murderers in the course of his detecting career.

But there was one possible alternative to professional suicide. And Calque made up his mind to explore it without further delay.

12

Calque watched as Paul Macron's cousin put the finishing touches to a louvred shutter. The man was aware of him, that much was obvious. But it would have been unrealistic of Calque to expect an ex-Foreign Legionnaire to come running just because a captain – strike that, an ex-captain – of police showed up at his workshop. At least it would give him time to have a cigarette.

Just as Calque was preparing to inhale, he saw Macron gesticulating at him with his sander from across the *atelier*.

'Put that fucking thing out. This isn't a country club. There's enough dry wood stacked up in here to smoke a whale.'

Calque gave a sickly smile and crushed the as yet unsavoured cigarette and its accompanying match out beneath his foot. He should have expected that, too. Macron's cousin had no reason to view him with anything other than disdain. Paul Macron had been killed on his watch, and it was only luck, and Adam Sabir's suicidal bloody-mindedness, that had allowed the police to put a line under Achor Bale's killing spree.

Aimé Macron went over to a sink in the corner of the workshop and started on the laborious rigmarole of washing his hands, his face, and the back of his neck. Calque could see Macron weighing him up in the pin-up plastered mirror above the basin.

Calque didn't move. He was weighing Macron up, too. Deciding whether to trust him with information that, in the wrong hands, could send him to prison.

'You're not a *flic* any more, are you?' Macron was moving towards Calque now, scrubbing at his neck with a towel, his eyes hooded.

Calque was fleetingly tempted to brazen the thing out – pretend he was still on the force – flash his purposefully mislaid badge – but he thought better of it. 'No. I'm not. How did you guess?'

Macron shrugged. 'I was in the Legion for twenty years. I can tell when a man has power by the way he carries himself. You don't have power any more. If you were still a *flic*, you would have breezed in here and interrupted my work, knowing it was your fucking right. But you waited for me to finish instead. Cops aren't usually that fastidious.'

'*Touché.*' Calque was impressed despite himself. He instantly changed tack, and approached Macron from a different direction to the one that he had initially intended. 'You remember me, don't you?'

'How could I forget? You brought us the news of Paul's death.'

Calque squirmed inside, each word like a touchpaper to his policeman's soul. 'You helped me that time. You gave me valuable information about Achor Bale. About his time in the Legion.'

Macron squinted, as if something he had not understood had just been made blindingly clear to him. He lit a cigarette.

Calque made a face.

Macron grinned. 'Yeah. I was just bullshitting you back there about the fire hazard and the cigs. Have one of mine.'

Calque cocked his head questioningly. 'Why the change of attitude all of a sudden?'

'Do you really want to know?'

'I really do. Yes.'

Macron snorted smoke through both nostrils. 'Because you're not a *flic* any more. I like you better this way. They kick you out because of Paul's death?'

'Indirectly.'

'Fuckers. It wasn't your fault. If it had been, you wouldn't have made it past the front gate.'

'I suspected that.' Calque lit the proffered cigarette.

The two men stood staring at each other, smoking.

'So what do you want, Monsieur l'ex-Capitaine?'

'Want?'

Macron scrubbed his fingernails across his razor-stropped head. 'Don't fuck with me, Inspector. You haven't come around here to see how I'm getting on. Or to chew the fat about all those happy times you shared with Paul. Neither of you could stand each other.'

Calque could sense himself about to go on the defensive – he wrestled the instinct down. 'You're right, Macron. I need more than information this time. I need your help.'

Macron allowed himself the ghost of a smile. 'Paul's killer is dead. What do you need *me* for?' His face changed expression. 'You need someone nobbled, don't you? That's it, isn't it? And you remembered that good old Aimé Macron was on the prison register for GBH, and maybe he hadn't forgotten some of his old tricks in the years since they let him out?'

'It's not that.'

'Then what is it?'

Calque felt like a fool. What was he doing here, talking to a compete stranger about breaking the law, after spending his entire working life as its bondservant? He swallowed. Might as well get it out. What did he have to lose? His pension? It was hardly enough to keep him in toilet paper. His good name? What was that worth in this brave new world they called France? His integrity? He'd lost that when he'd trousered his badge back at the station. 'Do you have any ex-Legionnaire friends who are firemen? Down St Tropez way, maybe?'

'Firemen? Are you serious?'

Calque flicked his cigarette into the puddle of water left over after Macron's frenetic ablutions. 'Perfectly.'

13

——

Abiger de Bale sat on the bed across from his sister.

Lamia de Bale had her back to him, and was staring pointedly out of the window.

'I've never liked you, Lamia. I've always considered you the weakest link in our family chain.' Abi threw himself back on the bed and lay there, staring up at the ceiling.

Lamia turned towards him. 'Why not kill me then? That's what you're good at, isn't it? Just like Rocha. Both of you, born killers.'

'I only kill vermin. You should view me like a terrier, trained to kill rats. I'm sweet when you get to know me. Cuddly, even.'

'Get out of my room. You're dirtying my bed.'

'I'm waiting for Milouins. He's coming up to take over keeping an eye on you.'

'I don't need keeping an eye on. What do you think? That I'm going to betray you all?'

Abi shrugged. 'What's to betray? We all work separately. None of us has a record of any sort. If you said anything, nobody would believe you. What we do makes no logical sense, unless one understands the Mysteries.'

'What Mysteries? You don't actually believe in a Second Coming, do you? Or the emergence of the Third Antichrist?'

'Of course not. But Madame, our mother, does. And she holds the purse strings.'

Lamia shook her head. 'So it's just an excuse, then? For you and Vau?'

'No. Vau really believes in all that hogwash too. I do it for the fun of it. He does it out of conviction. The result's much the same.'

'You make me sick.'

'Why? The others all believe it too.' Abi grinned. 'Gather together a bunch of freaks. Then brainwash them from birth. Tell them they're special – that they've been handpicked by God, and that everyone else is inferior to them. Then shower them with money and privileges. Works every time.'

Lamia glanced towards the open door. 'If Madame, our mother, heard you talk like this, it wouldn't be me whom she imprisons.'

'But she won't ever hear me talk like this. I'm not going to kill the golden goose. Do you think I'm insane?'

'I refuse to answer that.' Lamia hesitated. Against her better instincts she allowed herself to frame the question uppermost in her mind. 'What do you think she will do with me?'

Abi laughed. 'If I were you, I'd change my tune. Fast. That way you won't need to find out.'

'What do you mean?'

'I don't know why I'm telling you this, because it's not to my advantage in any way to do so. But you are my sister. Even if not by blood.' Abi sat up straighter on the bed. 'Do you know what I would do if I were her?'

Lamia took a step towards him. 'Tell me.'

'I'd ask someone like me to kill you.'

Lamia stopped. The unmarked side of her face turned deathly pale. 'Is that what you've been sent to do?'

'Me? No. You'd be dead already. I wouldn't have bothered warning you either. We've got a jellyfish plague out in the bay. I'd simply have dumped you out there, in the middle of the biggest school of lashers I could find, and dragged you around on a rope and a life-ring. Everybody would think you'd been caught out swimming. Enough jellyfish stings, and you go into anaphylactic shock and drown. It's happened hundreds of times. There are no EpiPens out at sea.'

She stared at him. 'Why? What's so vital about now? What could possibly be important enough to kill your own sister for?'

Abi shrugged. 'I'd have thought it was obvious. This is the moment our family has been waiting eight hundred years for. Madame, our mother . . .'

A voice at the door interrupted him. 'Yes, Abiger. You are right. Madame, your mother, does think that this is the moment the Corpus has been waiting eight hundred years for.' The Countess swept in, accompanied by Milouins and Madame Mastigou. She inclined her head first towards Abiger, and then towards her daughter. 'But Niobe did not kill her own children, did she, Lamia? It was the immortal gods who decided on *their* fate.' She glanced around the room, her eyes strangely unseeing. 'You will remain here at the house for the foreseeable future. Or at the very least until such time as you can convince me that you've seen reason. Milouins will see that you are adequately looked after, and he and the men will watch over you in shifts. You will take your meals with me of course. That will give us time to talk. Aside from that you may use the library and the games room. But not the telephone or a computer. Do you understand me?'

Lamia's eyes flared briefly. Then she lowered her gaze in acquiescence. 'Perfectly, Madame.'

'This is all highly inconvenient, you understand? I have more important things to think of.'

Abi, who had sprung to attention the moment his mother had entered the room, flashed his sister an old-fashioned look.

The Countess turned towards her son. 'Abiger. You have your orders. You and your brother are no longer needed here.'

'No, Madame.'

'Do you have adequate funds?'

'Ample, Madame. As you are well aware.'

'Then don't let me down.'

14

—

'Yeah. I know a fireman. He works in Draguignan, though. Not in St Tropez. He's a communist. Wears red underpants. Is that any good?'

Calque closed his eyes. I must be insane, he thought to himself. Why am I doing this? I should be in Tenerife, living in one of those long-let apartments they lease out at peppercorn rents to the silver-haired brigade for the winter. I could play dominoes every morning with retired bank managers and redundant civil servants, and then flirt over the lunchtime *apéritif* with their wives. I wouldn't even notice when the infarct took me. And my terminally uncommunicative daughter would only find out her father had finally cashed in his chips when they brought her my medals and the accompanying life-insurance cheque on a velvet-covered tray.

'I'm afraid that won't do.' Calque hesitated. 'I'll be frank with you, Macron. I owe you that much. I need to get inside a house. A well-guarded house. I need to retrieve something I left there some months ago. Something that involves your cousin, and the people responsible for his death. It occurred to me that if a fire alert were called in – by a concerned citizen, say – everyone inside the house would be forced out while the firemen were checking around inside. I would pay the man for securing this article for me, of course. And I can assure you that it would not be a case of theft. The article belongs to me already. No one else even knows of its existence.' Calque's voice trailed off. Brought out into the open like that, his idea sounded lame in the extreme.

Macron opened a cupboard concealed in a far corner of the workshop. He brought out a bottle and two glasses. 'Pastis?'

Calque was on the verge of saying that he was on duty, when he realized that he wasn't. 'Gladly.'

The two men avoided each other's eyes as they sipped from their glasses.

Macron allowed his gaze to wander around his workshop. 'Took me two years to build this place up from scratch. Can you believe that? Summon up a reputation. Get in some regular trade.' He took another sip of his drink. 'I'm on the up now. Might even think about getting married. Breeding some hoppers.'

Calque put down his glass and prepared to leave. The game was up, and he knew it.

'Wait.' Macron tipped back his head. 'You see all this?' He pointed to his carefully tiered stock. 'Each piece is best-grade hardwood. Over 95 per cent yield. Quadruple A. I get all my lumber from an ex-Legionnaire who lives out near Manosque.'

'Manosque?' Calque couldn't work out where Macron was headed. Was the man deaf? Hadn't he heard anything Calque had said?

'Manosque. Yes. The man's a marvel. He gets me anything I need. Doesn't matter what sort of notice I give him. Totally reliable.' Macron pointed with his chin. 'That's his card. Pinned up on the wall over there. You can scribble his name down in your notebook. Say you come from me when you speak to him. Tell him Aimé L'OM says *marche ou crève. Droit au but.*'

Calque hunched his shoulders questioningly. 'Lumber? You get your lumber from this man?' He wanted more. Some assurance that he wasn't being led up the garden path.

'Good luck. I hope you get back what you lost.'

Calque sighed. He wrote down the woodsman's name in his notebook.

Macron hesitated, still reluctant to commit himself – still reluctant to trust a *flic*. 'That cousin of mine, Captain. The one the eye-man shot. Your associate. He was a little *Front National* shit. That *métis fiancée* of his is well rid of him.' He slugged back the remnants of his pastis. Then he looked Calque straight in the eye. 'But his mother. My uncle's wife. The one who collapsed into her husband's arms when you told her the news about her son. She's a woman in a million, that one. I think the world of her.'

15
—

Lamia de Bale glanced out of her bedroom window. It was midnight. The house was finally asleep.

Outside her door she could hear Philippe, the footman, resetting his chair on the tilt.

Her first idea had been to switch on the radio. Get him used to the music. But everybody knew that she never listened to music. The little pervert would come straight in to check what was going on out of sheer curiosity. And then he would probably try to inveigle her into bed, as he'd attempted to do on at least three separate occasions in the past year. And this time she was vulnerable. Not his employer's daughter any more, but a prisoner, with no rights of her own. It wasn't worth the risk.

She picked up the bundle of sheets, went into the bathroom, and closed the door.

First, she switched on the shower. Then she took the pair of surgical scissors out of the first-aid kit, and began slicing the sheets into strips.

I can't believe I'm doing this, she intoned to herself. What if I fall? What if I break a bone? They will kill me.

When she'd finished dissecting the sheets, she began the laborious task of twisting and knotting them together. At one point she switched off the shower, and padded through into the bedroom, making sure to switch on the lamp by her bed and turn off the main light, just as she normally did.

Then she tiptoed back into the bathroom and continued with her task.

When she had the sheets knotted together to her satisfaction, she measured them out against her forearm. Their length came to about ten metres. She hoped it would be enough.

Her room was on the third floor of the house, over the courtyard. Once she was safely down, she intended to make inland for Ramatuelle. She knew where Monsieur Brussi, the taxi driver, lived. She had known him all her life. Even though Madame, her mother, had confiscated her purse and credit cards, surely he would agree to take her somewhere – anywhere – on credit?

She unlatched the window, and sifted the knotted sheets through her hands. She'd taken the precaution of tying a hairbrush to the bottom sheet, and she hoped, in this way, to be able to gauge, even in the dark, how much further she would need to drop if her makeshift rope didn't stretch all the way down to the ground.

When the sheets had reached their full extent, she began swinging them from one side to the other, as gently as she was able. The hairbrush struck something a glancing blow.

Lamia stopped her swinging, and listened, one hand cupped behind her ear. After a minute's intense concentration, she relaxed. She had learned two things. The first was that there was no one stationed down in the courtyard. The second was that there was a further potential ten-foot drop between the opened shutter that she had just struck with her hairbrush, and the ground.

She attached the free end of the knotted sheet to the central section of her bedroom window. There. Now she'd lost another foot in length. She'd have to drop down maybe eleven feet in the darkness. She racked her brains as to whether there was anything below her that might fall over and give her away. How stupid she had been not to have checked the whole area over while it was still light.

With a final, bemused glance at her room, Lamia eased herself out of the window. She was about to leave everything she had ever known behind her. Security, family, tradition, and emotional ties. For twenty-seven years she had been living a monstrous lie.

The real truth about her life, together with the true motives of the cabal that had adopted her – a cabal to which she had unwittingly and unthinkingly transferred all her loyalties – had only dawned on her following the publicity surrounding her brother's death. If what she had been doing was by order of the Corpus Maleficus, then just how damaging had all the pathetic little courier jobs – which were all that Madame, her mother, had seen fit to allocate her over the years since her majority – actually been? How much damage had she inadvertently foisted on a society ignorant of the extent – or even the existence – of its own guilt? Now, at last, she would be able to enter the real world unencumbered by any of the baggage of the past.

Using her feet as clamps, Lamia eased herself gingerly down the knotted line. She was fairly fit in terms of her age – tennis, yoga, and the occasional dance class had been her staples – but she was prone to vertigo, and she found herself thanking Providence that she had been forced to conduct her stunt in the dark.

Once, halfway down her ersatz rope, and feeling herself in danger of freezing in fear, she had twisted the sheets violently around one wrist until the interrupted blood flow had forced her to gather her wits together and continue on with her descent.

Finally, after what felt like half an hour but which had, in practice, been no more than a three-minute descent, she encountered the hairbrush with her feet. Carefully, she eased herself all the way down until she was hanging off the extreme end of the knotted line.

Then, without allowing herself to think, she let go.

Her plan was to strike the ground running. Instead, she took two lurching paces and fell to her knees. Instantly, every light in the courtyard switched on. Lamia twisted onto her back, her face contorted in shock. This was new. Madame, her mother, had never thought to safeguard the house with automatic security lights before.

Lamia scrambled to her feet and began to run. Perhaps, when she was out of the courtyard, the lights would switch themselves off? Perhaps, if no one had been watching, they would think that a deer had wandered in from the surrounding fields and triggered the sensor?

The front doors of the Domaine burst open and Milouins emerged. He was carrying a shotgun.

Lamia struck out with all her might for the gap between the garage and the stable block. If she could only make it beyond the outbuildings, she might be able to lose herself amongst the vines.

Milouins threw the shotgun aside and started after her.

The instant he began to run it became obvious to Lamia that she stood no chance at all of evading him. He ran like an athlete, his hands pumping high above his hips, his face in a rictus of concentration.

Lamia looked wildly around. Then she stopped, and fell back against the wall, holding her heart. She watched Milouins approach with her head down, sucking in air, like a feral, tethered mare, facing up to the man who intends to master her.

'You'll come with me, Mademoiselle.'

Lamia shook her head.

Milouins took her arm just above the elbow. When she attempted to struggle, he changed his grip so that he was holding both of her arms straight behind her back, where he could exert any pressure he chose against her shoulder sockets. 'Please, Mademoiselle. I have no wish to hurt you. I've known you since you were a little girl. Walk quietly with me. I'd be beholden to you.'

Lamia let out a sob of frustration. She nodded her head.

Milouins relaxed his grip. He contented himself with walking two paces behind her, confident in his ability to catch her once again should she attempt to flee.

The footman who had been guarding Lamia's room skittered down the steps at the front of the house, the leather soles of his shoes echoing off the marble cladding. He stopped and made a face at Milouins as the pair came abreast of him. 'The old woman will massacre me for this.' He scowled at Lamia. 'I hope she gives you to me to do over. I'll stick a plastic bag over your head so I won't have to look at you.'

'Shut up,' said Milouins. 'And go and wake Madame la Comtesse.'

'She's up already. The burglar alarm must have gone off in her bedroom when you came through the front door without neutralizing it.'

Lamia, Milouins, and the footman stood in the hall, looking up towards the stairs.

The Countess, in her dressing gown, and accompanied by a similarly clad Madame Mastigou, was descending the staircase to meet them.

'What shall we do with her, Madame?' Milouins looked marginally uncomfortable, like an axe-man at a royal execution who is suffering from a sudden onset of *lèse majesté*.

'Do with her?' The Countess came to an abrupt halt. 'Get Philippe to tie her up, feed her a sedative, and then

62

lock her in the Corpus chamber. That way we can all get some sleep. There are no windows in there to tempt her towards further recklessness. I shall decide on her future in the morning.'

16
—

Ex-Sergeant-Chef Jean Picaro – twenty years in the Legion, ten years banged up in La Santé prison for armed robbery, eight years on the outside as a procurer of hard-to-access items to the criminal fraternity – scratched his clean-shaven head with fingernails worn down by years of automatic habit. A former sufferer of bread scabies, which he had contracted at La Santé during a particularly pernicious period in its history, Picaro had found it physically impossible to rid himself of his fifteen-year-old anxiety tic whenever he entered periods of high stress.

And it was most definitely stress that he was feeling now. One thing was certain – to all intents and purposes he was looking at a straight in-and-out affair. So why was he sweating? And why was he scratching his head like a chimpanzee with mange?

At first he had been minded not to take the job at all. It went against the grain to deal with ex-*flics*. Shit sticks – and old shit sticks the worst. But the man came recommended by Aimé Macron. And Macron had saved Picaro's life in Djibouti when he'd fallen foul of an Afar brigade leader in a convoluted deal involving drugs, women, and a consignment of FAMAS assault rifles which had somehow gone missing from the Legion warehouse.

The *flic* had further undermined his objections by coming straight out and offering him 1,500 Euros on the nail, and a further 1,500 down the line, to liberate a personal item belonging to him from inside a house on the Cap. The deal didn't even involve a break-in. The *flic*, as *flics* do, had secretly palmed and wax-pressed a backdoor key while conducting an investigation inside the house two months before. Picaro had even been given a detailed map of the layout, showing the position of the library and of the concealed doorway leading to the room containing the object. A piece of cake, surely. But something was still bothering him.

He played his torch over the map. He'd been watching the back of the house for over an hour now, and everything seemed quiet. No dogs. No automatic lighting sensors this side of the property. The *flic* had even explained to him where the alarm system and circuit breakers were, and how best to de-activate them. The whole thing was a fucking dream. But in Picaro's experience, dreams had a nasty habit of jolting you awake when you least expected it.

He flicked some imaginary skin from the collar of his jacket.

Right. Either you do it or you don't, Legionnaire.

Picaro rose to his feet and padded down towards the *buanderie*.

17

Picaro stood inside the back door and sniffed. He didn't know how or why, but sometimes you could smell the presence of people, even rooms away from you. It was some atavistic instinct, he reckoned, from mankind's earliest times as a cave dweller. Enter an empty cave which you meant to occupy yourself, and before you settled down in front of the fire it was a smart idea to make sure that no one else, man or beast, felt they had a prior claim.

Satisfied, Picaro padded up the concrete stairway that led to the back of the hallway. After neutralizing the alarm system within the stipulated two minutes, he cracked his torch and checked his map one final time. A left, a right, and then another right, and he should be in the library. Then a few steps across the room to the bound set of *La Vie Parisienne* – the *flic* had even set down the exact number of volumes there were in that particular run – and hey presto, open sesame.

Picaro cast a quick glance up the stairs as he passed through the hall. Despite the multitude of houses he had broken into during the course of his life, Picaro still couldn't stop himself fantasizing about his own particular nightmare – that of an Alsatian – it was always an Alsatian – bounding noiselessly down the stairs, dewlaps flapping, saliva jetting into its mouth at the prospect of a piece of Jean Picaro's thighbone.

Giving a little jump to settle his gooseflesh, Picaro eased himself through the doorway of the library. Jesus. He was getting too old for this. What did he need 3,000 Euros for, anyway? His bank account was heaving. He owned his house outright. His son was apprenticed to the best electrical engineer in the business, and he had vowed to die rather than ever to go back to prison again. So what the hell was he doing it for? Habit? Addiction to the kicks? Or just because it was one of the few things he could still do well?

He bent down and felt around for the catch that the *flic* had told him was hidden under Volume Three of the collected periodicals.

A door, hidden in the bookcase, flicked open. With a cautious glance over one shoulder, Picaro stepped inside the concealed room.

'*Putain de merde*!' he mouthed to himself, his eyes widening in horror.

The unconscious figure of a woman was tied to a chair in the very centre of the assembly table. Her head had fallen at an angle, and as Picaro played his torch across her, he saw that one whole side of her face was covered in what appeared to be a thin sheet of congealed blood.

18

Ever the professional – and ever mindful of his 3,000 Euros – Picaro felt around under the table for the *flic's* precious tape recorder. Exactly two metres to the right of the master chair, taped up inside the skirt, at the exact angle of the joist and the cross-brace. Yes. There it was. Picaro pocketed it.

He hesitated, and then made briskly for the door. What business was the woman of his? He'd done what he came here to do. He was already running late because of his previous caution. Why complicate matters? This way, he could get out of the house before daybreak with no one the wiser.

His gaze travelled inexorably back to the woman. What the hell had they done to her? Maybe she was dead, even? But no. He could see her breathing by the light of the torch.

As he played the light across her body, a memory came back to Picaro from his time at La Santé prison. A young lad, mixed race, not more than nineteen years old, who had fallen foul of one of the methamphetamine gangs. One day the gang had waited for him in the showers – for sooner or later, as Picaro had tried to explain to the boy, the bad guys always get you. What the hell else did they have to do with their time? But the boy had been too young and too cocksure to listen to him.

This one they'd condemned to a *tournante* – a gang rape. When Picaro found the boy, they'd left him tied to a chair, with his head through the seat, his belly over the backrest, and his hands and feet strapped to the legs – that way he would be available for anyone else to use who happened along.

At first Picaro hadn't understood what he was looking at. It was like when his son had emerged, balls first, from his mother's womb. Picaro had fallen back, his face ashen, shouting, 'Christ, what's that?'

'It's his testicles, Monsieur,' the midwife had told him. 'They swell up in a breech birth, because the legs are stretched back over the head.'

When he'd seen the state of the young man's anus, Picaro had vomited. Then he'd untied the boy, straightened him out as best he could on the cold floor of the shower room, and gone to fetch the *toubibs*.

They'd stitched him up good, but the boy had never been right again after the attack. One day, about six months later, he'd cut off his own balls with a piece of broken glass.

Sighing, Picaro moved back to the table. Taking out his Opinel, he cut the cords binding the young woman to her chair, eased her towards him, and let her fall across his right shoulder.

With a hitch of his arms, he settled her weight more squarely. Then, feeling all kinds of a fool, he started back across the hall.

No point closing the door behind me now, he thought to himself. I might as well leave a fucking paper trail.

19

Picaro laid the woman gently on the rear seat of his car. He stood back and looked down at her in the cold glow of the interior lights. What he had imagined in the darkness of the sealed room to be blood, now proved to be nothing more than a strawberry birthmark. Poor bitch. She'd have been pretty without that. Sometimes you wondered what God was thinking of.

Picaro sprung back her eyelids and checked her pupils. She was doped – that much was obvious. He was briefly tempted to tie his chamois leather duster around her eyes so that she couldn't identify him if she woke up – but with his present run of luck, she'd probably panic on awaking and cause a car wreck. Best to leave things be for the time being.

He'd arranged to meet the *flic* at the old parking place behind Pampelonne beach. A twenty-minute drive at the outside. He'd simply dump the female and the tape recorder on him, get the rest of his money, and then scram. The *flic* could sort her out. That's what *flics* did, wasn't it? Sort things out?

Three times on the drive to Pampelonne Picaro wondered whether he wouldn't do better just leaving her on the side of the road. She hadn't seen him yet. She hadn't seen the *flic*. Why complicate life when you didn't need to?

But the image of the girl tied to the chair in the centre of the table haunted him. What had that boy's name been? The one in the prison? Chico? Chiclette? Something like that.

Stupid to put the chair on the table. What if the girl had woken up and thrown herself to one side in a panic? She could have broken her neck and paralysed herself. People could be dumb sometimes.

He saw the *flic* waiting for him in the curve of the headlights. Well. Here goes. What a man will do for three thousand smackers.

Picaro pulled up beside Calque. He got out of the car and looked around. Well. No unexpected reception committee. That was a good first sign.

'Did you get it?'

'Of course I got it.' Picaro eased the tape recorder from his pocket and handed it to Calque.

Calque palmed him the remaining fifteen hundred.

Picaro jerked his thumb back towards the car. 'I've got something else for you, too. No extra charge.'

Calque flinched, as if someone had fired a dried pea at the back of his neck. 'What do you mean?'

Picaro opened the back door of his car and stood waiting for Calque to join him. They both stared down at the girl.

'Don't worry. She's not dead. Someone drugged her and tied her to a chair. They left the chair on the table in that secret room of yours. I thought at first that it might have been one of those sex things – you know, a bondage thing, when they pop amyl nitrate and then half suffocate themselves in an effort to increase their kicks. But one look at her face told me otherwise. I thought about leaving her there, but I just couldn't do it. She hasn't seen me and she hasn't seen you. My advice would be to abandon her here. But she's your problem from here on in. Agreed?'

'Agreed.' Calque had total control of himself again. He was already busy working out the possible ramifications of this new development.

'Want me to move her, or will you?'

'You'd better move her. I'm not in the best of health.'

Calque watched as Picaro eased the girl across the back seat towards him.

'What's that on her face? Is she injured?'

Picaro held the girl's head up towards the light as if he were exhibiting a vase to a potential buyer at an auction house. 'No. Birthmark. It's a fucking shame, isn't it?'

Calque recognized the girl's facial disfigurement at once. She had been one of the members of the first party to arrive at the house – the party which had preceded the arrival of the two men. She had to be one of the Countess's daughters, therefore – one of the Devil's Dozen. But what could she possibly have done to turn the Countess against her? Either way, he desperately needed to talk to her.

At that exact moment, Lamia opened her eyes.

Picaro raised his hand, ready to rabbit-punch her before she could catch a glimpse of his face.

'No. No. Wait!' Calque hurried forward. He scrabbled in his pocket and held out his badge. 'Police,

Mademoiselle. For your own good, do not look around. I'm going to ease you out of the car.' He took her face in his hands. 'Keep looking at me. Don't look around. Trust me.'

Lamia was still dopey. She stumbled forwards and fell against Calque's chest, her knees buckling.

Calque nodded at Picaro.

Picaro jumped into his car and slewed away. The back door slammed shut of its own accord as he revved up through the gears.

20

Philippe Lemelle had been one of the Countess de Bale's footmen for eighteen months now. It was the single longest period in his life that he had ever held down a job, and he was beginning to get itchy feet. Something good needed to happen, or the old cow wouldn't see his trail for dust.

Lemelle's father and his grandfather had both worked for the old Count, and it was this fact, and this fact alone, which had secured the slow-witted and low IQ'd Lemelle the job. As a result, Lemelle was fully conversant – or so he fondly thought – with all the Corpus's aims and aspirations. If it wasn't for the butler, Milouins, who was clearly jealous of his good looks and his success with women, Lemelle was firmly convinced that he would have risen far more rapidly in the Corpus hierarchy, with the Countess using him for something just a little more onerous than the cleaning of people's rooms and the mounting of guard duty on her disfigured bitch of a daughter.

Lemelle felt personally humiliated by Lamia's escape during his watch, and his sense of humiliation was further compounded by Milouins's triumphant recapture of the stuck-up bint just a few seconds after she'd touched down in the courtyard. He derived belated comfort from the fact that it was to him, and not to Milouins, that the Countess had reassigned Lamia after the escape fiasco. Madame la Comtesse had clearly marked him out from the herd, and intended him for higher things.

From the very first moment that he had seen her, fourteen months before, during a brief visit on the occasion of her mother's birthday, Lemelle had found Lamia sexually attractive – despite, or perhaps even because of, the strawberry birthmark that marred her face. After all, as his father used to say, you don't stare at the mantelpiece while you're poking the fire.

As a result he had taken an unusually keen pleasure in knotting her to her chair, and forcibly dosing her with twice the regulation measure of tranquillizers. He was beginning to regret his final sadistic flourish, however, which had seen him balancing the now unconscious woman on top of the council room table for reasons which, in retrospect, eluded even him. In fact the memory of his stupidity had positively begun to haunt him. What if she woke up in a panic, fell off the table, and broke her stupid neck? That would complete Milouins's triumph over him, wouldn't it? The Countess would have every reason to bury him alive.

Lemelle threw on a few clothes and padded furtively downstairs. The stillness of the sleeping house was oddly comforting to him, for ever since childhood Lemelle had been prone to passages of voyeurism, and night time – with its secrets, and its recondite laws, and its infinite promises of concealment – held deeply stimulating associations for him.

The in-built connection between darkness and sexual promise now provided Lemelle with his next brainwave – with Lamia dosed up to the eyeballs on tranquillizers, what possible harm could there be in paying her something more than just a fleeting visit? If he was caught, he could always claim that he'd simply gone downstairs to check on her welfare.

For the fact remained that when Lemelle wasn't working, sleeping, or eating, he was busy constructing elaborate sexual fantasies about any real-life women he happened to encounter. And ever since he had first heard of people using roofies to drug women so that they would neither resist nor remember anything that occurred, Lemelle had dreamed of getting hold of the stuff and using it as a means of self-empowerment. And if he couldn't get his hands on the date rape drug Rohypnol, surely a double dose of Temazepam was the next best thing?

Even a cursory glance at Lemelle's computer would have thrown up thousands of images from rape, BDSM, and sleep-attack websites. Here was his chance to turn fantasy into reality. If Lamia was still out cold, he could do whatever he wanted to her. The thought turned his legs weak with anticipation. He patted the digital camera in his jacket pocket. It would serve the bitch right if she found out in a month or so's time that she was unexpectedly pregnant by her mother's footman – and that if she decided to cut up rough he could take his revenge by plastering pornographic pictures of her all over the internet. She'd have to notice him then, wouldn't she? She'd have to come to terms with him then. And Christ, how he'd make her suffer.

Lemelle's first hint that his future plans weren't going to run quite as smoothly as he expected came at the library door. It was wide open. And the Countess's standing orders were that every unused door in the house be kept tightly sealed unless the room was actually in use. In fact the bastard Milouins set such store on pleasing the Countess on this subject that it would have been more than Lemelle's job was worth not to double-shut the damned thing after he'd trussed the woman up and stuck her on the table like Quasimodo. Shutting doors had become an automatic part of his make-up – rather like a man who runs around the house switching off unnecessary lights.

The Corpus chamber door was wide open too. A wave of nausea leached through Lemelle's body. If the woman was gone a second time, he'd get the blame for that too. That was as clear as day. He'd lose his job. Even his mother wouldn't be able to protect him this time.

Lemelle eased himself around the open door. Lamia was nowhere to be seen. Her chair lay upside down on the floor, next to the council table. Lemelle picked up one of the discarded ropes and thumbed its end. It had been cut – clearly cut. So the bitch had got someone in to help her. Lemelle could already hear the triumph in Milouins's voice when this new disaster came to light.

'Twice? You let her go twice? We told you to tie her up and dope her, for Christ's sake. What did you do, Lemelle? Give her a double espresso?'

Lemelle hurried through the empty house, his eyes searching for anything remotely out of place. Yes. Here was another door left wide open. Lemelle descended towards the *buanderie*. He could already feel a current of colder air playing against his forehead. Should he call Milouins and tell him what had occurred? Of course. That would be the smart thing to do.

Lemelle took out his cell phone and glared at it. He was near the back of the house now, looking out over the fields. As he watched, some car headlights cut a circular swathe across the vineyard.

Lemelle thrust the cell phone back in his pocket and hurried around to the servant's garage. In the fantasy world Lemelle had constructed for himself, heroes didn't fritter away their second chances. As he passed the gunroom he helped himself to Milouins's precious Mossberg 500 pump-action shotgun and a box of twelve-gauge cartridges.

Whatever route they intended to take, Lamia and her white knight would have to pass within half a kilometre of the front of the property. This meant that Lemelle would have ample time to get the estate Land Rover out, douse the headlights, and follow on behind.

Fuck Milouins. This time around, he'd get the woman back himself.

21

—

Twelve minutes into his pursuit of Picaro's car, Lemelle's cell phone started to vibrate. The shock of it nearly launched him out of his seat.

He glared down at the lighted screen. It was Milouins. Best answer it then. He wasn't on the strongest ground.

'Yeah?'

'What the blazes is going on? I heard an engine start up down in the garage.'

Lemelle ground his teeth together and hammered silently at the steering wheel.

'Lemelle? What's happening? Out with it.'

While Lemelle was still debating what to say, the car he was following turned unexpectedly down the track towards Pampelonne beach. Lemelle thought for a moment, and then pulled off the road. He backed the Land Rover just inside a stand of trees and cut the engine.

'Answer me, Lemelle – I know you're listening.'

Lemelle made a violent arm gesture at his cell phone. Then he switched it on to hands-free, and threw himself back in his seat. 'The girl. Lamia. She's bolted again.'

'I can see that. I'm standing in the library.'

'Listen to this, then. She had help. One man. I was just in time to see them getting into their getaway car. So I borrowed the Land Rover. I've been following the two of them ever since they left the house.'

There was a brief silence. Well thank me, you bastard, thought Lemelle.

In a pig's ear.

'Where are they now?'

'The guy must be an idiot. He's backed himself into a corner. He's just headed down the cul-de-sac at Pampelonne. You know. The road to the beach. There's no possible way out but back past me. Because I can't see that shit-heap of a car of his ploughing off around the point through the sand.'

'Does he know you're following him?'

'Of course not. I held way back with my lights off. There's no way he can have seen me.'

'What if he's simply dropping the girl off?'

'Oh come on. That's bullshit. Why would he drop her off down there? The place is as good as abandoned this time of year. He'd get the fuck away, that's what he'd do. He's made a mistake, that's all. He'll be back past here in five minutes. Then I'll have him.'

'What do you mean, you'll have him?'

'Just that. I borrowed your shotgun too.'

Milouins's voice crackled through the speaker. His tone was urgent. 'Don't even think of it, Lemelle. If Lamia is in that car, and she gets hurt . . .'

'Wait. Wait. I think I can see his headlights coming back. Yes. Yes. I'm sure of it.' Lemelle broke the connection as fast as he could, a wolfish grin on his face. There were no headlights, of course. But there was also no way he would allow that bastard Milouins to queer his pitch again. This time he would do the job himself. It was still dark. There were no houses around. No one to see what happened. He had the whole fucking place to himself.

Lemelle eased himself out of the Land Rover and slammed the door. He fed eight cartridges into the Mossberg and then positioned himself behind a nearby tree. He was only ten yards from the road. The bastard who took Lamia would have to pass right by him when he returned from the beach after realizing he'd taken a wrong turn. Lemelle would simply spring out from cover and take the guy's tyres out – after that he could do over the engine or not, depending on circumstances.

Lemelle could already taste the crump of lead as it bit into sheet metal – already feel the power the shotgun would give him over the two passengers in the car. Christ, how he'd make them grovel. There was no danger in all that, surely? When it was all over, and he'd had his kicks, he'd head back in triumph to the Domaine with his prisoners.

'I'm returning your daughter to you, Madame la Comtesse. No. No problem at all. Just doing my job.'

Lemelle's fantasy world had switched to overtime.

22

Jean Picaro was relieved to be rid of the girl. There had been something uncomfortable about the whole affair – as if it were tainted in some way. Devil-struck. It didn't make sense to leave a woman tied up and doped like that, in a sealed room, stuck up on top of a table. What sort of a maniac would do a thing like that?

Privately, Picaro had made up his mind that this would be his last ever job. His wife and son were secure, his business, on the surface at least, was legal – or if it wasn't strictly legal, at least it didn't involve breaking into people's houses and kidnapping sex victims.

He was too old for the action stuff now. Didn't crave it. He'd experienced enough of that to last him a lifetime, and he didn't want any more. His conscience was clean. He could have left the woman behind, but he hadn't. While that didn't make him a hero, it didn't make him a total villain either.

He saw the stationary Land Rover first. Then he caught a flash of movement from behind the tree. He was already travelling faster than was strictly wise, thanks to his relief at getting away from the *flic*.

As a Foreign Legionnaire, Jean Picaro had spent the formative years of his life being trained to look out for – and to counter – ambushes. And he was still hyper-keyed up from the break-in, and angry about the way the woman had been treated, with its revocations of what had happened to the boy at La Santé.

He didn't even need to think.

As the man raised his shotgun, Picaro wrenched the steering wheel over to the left and headed straight for him.

The man's mouth dropped open in shock. He didn't even have time to fire off a single shell.

Picaro's car careened off a ridge of earth and struck the man mid-thigh. The man's face and chest slammed down onto the bonnet, the shotgun skittering off to one side.

Picaro backed up and made a second pass over the man's body. No point leaving witnesses. This one wasn't going to blab to the *flics* if Picaro could possibly avoid it. There would be no more prison for him.

Leaving the engine running, Picaro stepped out of the car. He gathered up the Mossberg, checked it for damage, and threw it onto the back seat.

Then, without so much as a backwards glance at his victim, he got into his car, manhandled it back onto the road, and headed off in the direction of Ramatuelle.

23

Milouins arrived at the scene twelve minutes later.

He saw the Land Rover straight away, and marked its position. No sign of Lemelle, though.

Milouins hesitated, debating with himself whether to ignore Lemelle entirely and continue on towards the sea, or rope him in as back-up. But the fool was right about one thing. There was only one possible route back from the beach. Lamia and her chance abductor – because there was no conceivable way in Milouins's mind that her kidnap could have been pre-planned –

had no choice but to come back past here, if they hadn't done so already.

And this time of morning, who else would be using the beach road? It wouldn't do to meet them on the narrow road coming back from the beach. Best to wait here and follow them with his lights off – just as Lemelle had done from the house – when they eventually came back on by. Find out where they were heading. Who was behind the whole thing.

Checking in every direction, Milouins pulled his car off the road, facing back towards St Tropez. Where was that stupid bastard Lemelle hiding himself? He'd have his guts for garters.

It was then, with the dawn slowly breaking in the eastern sky, that he saw the body.

'*Oh, putain.*'

Milouins glanced up and down the road. Nothing was moving. It was five o'clock in the morning, and the holiday season was over. Builders and maintenance men wouldn't be about for another hour or so at the very least.

He moved across to Lemelle, his gaze focused away from the body and towards the beach road, watching for traffic.

He ducked down and pressed a finger against Lemelle's carotid artery, his gaze still fixed on the road.

Then he took a deep breath and looked down.

Whoever had done Lemelle over had done him good. His head looked as if it had been laid open with a baseball bat. He had bled from the chest cavity, but the blood flow had staunched itself, and strings of coagulated gore lay scattered across his belly, his groin, and the surrounding tussocks of grass. If Milouins had wanted to, he could have reached in past Lemelle's shattered breastbone and plucked out what remained of his heart.

Milouins dry-retched. Then he stood up and glanced over at the Land Rover. Only one thing to do.

Still gagging, he hefted Lemelle in both arms and manhandled him across to the vehicle. The man reeked of shit from his ruptured bowels. Milouins threw open the cat-flap and windmilled Lemelle in over the lower tailgate. Then he hunched down behind the Land Rover and vomited up his supper.

With Lemelle safely tucked inside the vehicle, Milouins set about covering the body with some sacking and a scattering of loose straw. Then he tidied himself up as best he could with a horseman's wisp made from the remainder of the straw. When he was done, he refastened the tilt and went to look for his Mossberg.

A ten-minute search produced a grand total of three unused cartridges that had probably been ejected from Lemelle's pocket when the vehicle – and Milouins now accepted that it had to be a vehicle – had hit him. But no Mossberg.

So either Lamia and the man who had rescued her had clean escaped, or Milouins's original hunch still held, and her abductor had dropped Lamia off at a secondary vehicle, fallen foul of Lemelle on the way back out, and driven straight at him.

Lemelle, being Lemelle, had no doubt brandished the shotgun menacingly at his intended victim before actually getting around to firing it. That's what the tracks told Milouins, anyway – and Milouins was a man who always believed the evidence of his own eyes.

Milouins glanced down at his watch – 5.20. And the rapidly stiffening Lemelle was obviously in no hurry to go anywhere.

Milouins checked back down the road again, one forearm clamped to his nose in a vain effort to obviate the smell that still permeated his clothes. Either Lamia and her St George were long gone, or she was still down there, cash on delivery. What did he have to lose by backing his hunch? He'd either lost them, or he hadn't. If they came back down the road he would follow them – to hell and back if necessary. If not, he would go back to the Domaine and arrange Lemelle's secret burial.

Satisfied that he had cleaned up the area and secured Lemelle's body, Milouins got back inside his car and settled down to wait.

24

Incongruous in his ten-year-old charcoal-grey *Le Bon Marché* suit, Calque sat in the sand, his knees spread, staring out to sea at the gradually emerging dawn. The woman, covered in a tartan blanket from the back of his car, lay motionless beside him.

The sudden opening of her eyes had proved to be a false alarm – a purely automatic reaction to the change of light. She was still doped out, her mouth partly open, her hands turned back on themselves as if she were trying to fend off the attentions of an overactive pet.

Calque lit a cigarette. Scrunching his eyes against the smoke, he fished the tape recorder out of his pocket and reversed the spool. Then he hit the play button and held the recorder up to his ear.

The recorder was sound-activated – meaning that the moment it identified a sound within a radius of maybe three metres, it would start itself up. The tape would then automatically turn itself over after forty-five minutes, and cut off for good after ninety. Calque noted with satisfaction that the full ninety minutes appeared to have been used.

The first noise Calque heard was that of a vacuum cleaner. The tape switched itself on and off a dozen or more times as the vacuum cleaner moved in and out of focus. Calque reined in a desire to fast-forward the tape. He had time. No one knew he was here. And the sea was calming in its way.

Half an hour in, he picked up his first voices. Calque shrugged out of his jacket and draped it over his head, creating a mini echo chamber. Two men were talking. Calque recognized the voice of the butler, Milouins, and someone whom he assumed to be one of the footmen – for it was clear from Milouins's tone that he was addressing a subordinate. The two men seemed to be preparing the room for a meeting. As Calque listened, Milouins told the footman to lay on the wax polish with a will. A series of bumps followed.

'The bastard is cleaning the table,' Calque said to himself.

More bumps.

'He's moving chairs. The bastard is moving chairs.'

Another ten minutes went by and the tape auto-reversed. Still cursing, Calque began to fast-forward. Nothing. Just bumping, banging, and the occasional word between Milouins and the footman he was ordering about.

Calque switched off the tape recorder, replaced it in his jacket, and let the jacket slip down around his shoulders. He threw back his head as if he were about to howl at the moon. Five weeks. Five weeks of waiting and watching, and for what? A ninety-minute tape recording of two men cleaning a room.

He was past it. That was clear now. He had finally lost the plot. The Service had been right to green-light his early retirement. He was nothing but a liability. A dinosaur.

He looked down at the woman.

The dawn was up and her face was clearly visible now. She was watching him, her eyes wide open in shock.

Calque fought the temptation to plunge his hand back inside his jacket pocket and drag out his purloined badge for the second time. Why aggravate the situation? If the woman decided to prosecute him for kidnap, the fact that he had attempted to masquerade as a serving police officer would doubtless secure him a good two-to-three years' extra prison time. Think what a field day some of his recidivists would have with him inside. They'd tattoo his eyeballs with a screwdriver.

'You're free to go, Mademoiselle. I want you to understand that. I'm not coercing you in any way.'

Lamia raised herself up on her elbows. After staring silently at him for what seemed the better part of sixty seconds, she allowed her eyes to drift away from Calque's face and off towards the horizon. 'Where am I?'

'You're at Pampelonne Beach. Near St Tropez. It's just after dawn.'

Lamia sat up, shrugging the blanket away. She stretched her hands out in front of her, as if she still expected to find them tied up. 'What am I doing here?' She glanced across at Calque. 'And who are you?'

'Ah,' said Calque. 'You want to know who I am?' Once again he found himself on the cusp of declaring that he was Captain Joris Calque, Police Nationale, 2ème Arrondissement, Paris. Instead, he muttered, 'If you will forgive me, Mademoiselle, I will withhold my name until the situation we are in establishes itself a little clearer.'

Lamia began to laugh. 'Are we really in a situation?'

Calque shrugged. He felt like digging a hole in the

84

sand, laying himself face down in it, and inviting the woman to fill it in. 'In a manner of speaking. Yes.'

The smile stayed on Lamia's face. 'Have you kidnapped me? Or have you saved me? Make up your mind, please.'

Calque unslung his jacket from about his shoulders and replaced it carefully over Lamia's. 'It's cold, Mademoiselle. This is the time of day when the body is at its most fragile.'

Lamia reached across herself and touched the flap of the jacket. 'If you're a kidnapper, you're not a very good one. You've left your gun in your jacket pocket.'

Calque gave a small bow. It was clear that the woman was inviting him, for the second and last time, to lay his cards on the table. 'It's not a gun but a tape recorder, Mademoiselle. A tape recorder that I secreted illegally in your mother's house some months ago, whilst I was still a serving police officer.'

Lamia pinched the jacket closer around her shoulders. 'Ah, yes. The intellectual policeman. I've heard all about you. You're the man my mother says harassed my brother into an early grave.'

Calque could feel himself bridling. An early grave? A psychopath like Achor Bale? Best place for him. He stopped marginally short of expressing his feelings in words, however, for he was still trying to second guess the woman's intentions – just as she was attempting to gauge his.

He cleared his throat, measuring the level of his tone against the distant sound of the sea. 'You were tied up and doped when my associate found you. Am I right in assuming that my admission about bugging your mother and your siblings has not distressed you quite as much as it might have done under other circumstances? That you might even . . .' and here Calque felt perversely tempted to burst out laughing ' . . .be alienated in some way from the rest of your family?'

Lamia gave Calque his jacket back. 'Could we discuss this someplace else, do you think? Over a coffee and a croissant perhaps? I haven't eaten anything in fifteen hours.'

Calque shrugged on his jacket. He could smell the woman's scent on his collar, and it disturbed him. 'Of course.'

'And my name is Lamia.'

The sudden volte-face wrong-footed Calque. 'Lamia? That is certainly an uncommon name.' He vainly tried to conjure up who or what Lamia had represented in Classical mythology. Had she been the one whose tongue Jupiter had torn out in a fit of pique to prevent her giving the game away to Hera about one of his many affairs? No, that had been Lara. Or was that Laodice? So it was true, then. His brain was definitely going. 'My name is Calque. Joris Calque. Ex-Captain in the Police Nationale.'

'Well, Ex-Captain Calque, do you have any aspirin on you? I have a splitting headache. And your associate – for you mentioned an associate, didn't you? – appears to have overlooked my handbag in his headlong rush to kidnap me.'

25
—

Lamia emerged from the unisex washroom at the back of the fisherman's café near the Pointe de la Pinède. She had scrubbed her face and fluffed out her hair with her fingers, but the corrugations in her slacks were more terminal. She bent down, yanked at the slacks one final time, and then gave up.

Calque saw some of the early morning regulars watching her. Despite the catastrophic blemish on the side of her face, she was still a self-evidently handsome young woman.

Calque stood up as she approached his table. 'I thought you might have run away. Or gone to call the police. You would have been perfectly within your rights to do so.'

'I know that.'

'So why didn't you?'

Lamia sat down. She stared at Calque, her eyes unwavering. 'Because you offered me your jacket when you thought I might be cold.'

The waiter interrupted to bring them their café-crèmes and a metal basket of croissants.

Lamia looked up at him. 'Do you have any aspirin?'

'Yes, Madame.'

She pinched two of her fingers together. 'Two? With a glass of water? I'd be eternally grateful.'

Calque saw the waiter's eyes hovering anywhere but on the woman's strawberry birthmark. He felt an unexpected rush of pity for her – almost as if she were his daughter, instead of the pathetic, alienated girl who truly fulfilled that role, and who, terminally brainwashed by her termagant of a mother, hadn't been able to bring herself to speak to him for the past fifteen years.

Lamia pecked at her coffee. 'I suppose you've got everything on that tape machine of yours? The full record of what took place in the Corpus chamber? Or did you hide your recorder in the kitchen by mistake?'

Calque thrust his sentimental nature resolutely to the back of his mind, where it belonged. He took a preparatory breath – something he always did when he was about to tell an untruth to someone he was questioning. 'To answer your questions in reverse order, Mademoiselle – no I did not leave my recorder in the kitchen. And yes I do have a full record of what went on.' The lie sat uneasily with him for some reason, and he could feel the strain telling on the muscles below his eyes.

For Joris Calque had always been susceptible to women – it was a fact that he had been obliged to live with during his thirty years as a police officer. But he was not so naive that he didn't realize that women, at their worst, could be just as lethal as men. Look at the Countess. And here he was, calmly chatting away to the woman's daughter as if she were a work colleague – or his next-door neighbour.

He forced himself to remember that he was still dealing with a potential accessory before the fact. A woman who might even be a joint principal in the *actus reus* committed by Achor Bale against his subordinate, Paul Macron.

'So I've no need to explain anything to you, Captain?'

'No.'

Lamia prodded at her croissant, but didn't make any further stab at eating it. 'So what are you planning to do about it?'

Calque dipped his croissant in his coffee and transported it to his mouth, one hand automatically protecting his shirt from drips. 'What do you suggest?'

Lamia took the glass of water and the two aspirin from the saucer the waiter was offering her. Still watching Calque, she tossed back the pills and swallowed the water. 'You could alert the police, for a start.'

The waiter flinched, then backed away, as if he had inadvertently wandered too close to an open fire. Lamia gave him an absent-minded smile of thanks.

'The police?' Calque laughed. 'I'm something of a *persona non grata* with my ex-colleagues at the

88

moment. And you must know that tape recordings do not constitute evidence. They can be doctored too easily.'

Lamia massaged her temples, as if she felt that this might serve to speed up the aspirin's effects. 'But you knew that before you started, Captain Calque. You must have made some contingency plans?'

Calque sat up straighter in his chair. 'Contingency plans? How could I make contingency plans when I didn't know what I was about to hear?'

Lamia stared at him quizzically. 'And Adam Sabir? What are you going to do about him?'

Calque could feel his fragile house of cards beginning to topple. 'I'm going to phone him up, of course, and bring him up to date.'

'Phone him up? Bring him up to date? Are you quite mad? Bring him up to date about what?'

Calque tipped back his head and closed his eyes.

Lamia sighed. 'You don't know anything, do you, Captain? You're merely grasping at straws. Was there anything on that tape of yours at all?'

Calque allowed his head to snap forward. 'Oh yes. I have a good hour-and-a-half's worth of material.'

'Material? What sort of material?'

'Your meeting. Two days ago.'

'Then you know what I was doing in the room where your mystery associate found me? Why I was doped and tied up?'

Calque felt as if he were sucking on a lemon and trying to blow through a trumpet at the same time. 'Of course.'

Lamia stood up. 'Then you don't need anything from me, do you, Captain? I thank you for your frankness. Would you kindly do me a further favour and call me a taxi? And I would appreciate the loan of a few *sous* until my bank opens and I am able to inform them about the loss of my cards. I will write you an IOU if you so desire.'

26

Calque followed Lamia out onto the street. The early morning rush hour had started, and the buzz and swish of passing traffic merely added to his sense of frustration. 'What are you going to do, Mademoiselle? Where are you going to go?'

'What possible concern can that be of yours?'

Calque was briefly tempted to come clean and admit that his tape recording was useless. To follow his hunch that the woman was genuine. Perhaps she really had rebelled against her mother and all that she stood for? But thirty years of ingrained caution, in which Calque had lived by the rule that you never, ever, offer information to your opponent that he might one day use against you, overrode his better instincts. 'Please let me drop you off somewhere. It's the least I can do in the circumstances.'

Lamia shook her head distractedly. She was on the look-out for a taxi, and already seemed to have blanked Calque out from her consciousness.

Calque's cell phone rang. He received a call so rarely that at first he only looked around vacantly, as if the call belonged to someone else. Then he slapped his jacket, and began to rummage in his pockets.

Lamia had seen a taxi, and was beckoning it towards her.

Calque pressed the receive button and raised the cell phone gingerly to his ear, as if he feared that it might be about to explode. 'Yes? Calque here.'

'It's Picaro.'

Calque flinched. What the hell was Picaro doing, calling him up in a public place? Their business was over. The whole sorry fiasco had cost him 3,000 Euros that he could ill afford, and had provided him with precisely zero information, and a resentful woman eager to wipe his dust off her shoes as fast as humanly possible.

'Listen, Captain. Don't ask me why I'm doing this. But I can't let you walk into a shit storm with a leaking umbrella.'

Calque was concentrating all his attention on Lamia. A taxi had stopped directly in front of her. She caught Calque's eye and made a money movement with her fingers. 'What? What are you talking about, Picaro? What shit storm?' Calque raised a placatory hand and started across the road towards Lamia, the phone still clamped to his ear.

'You've heard of a *shamal*, Captain? That's what the desert Arabs call a five-day, three-thousand-foot-deep sandstorm. The type that's so fucking powerful it can strip the skin right off your face. Well this is a *shamal* of a shit storm.'

'Picaro . . .'

'Listen. On the way out to the main road. After I'd delivered the woman and the tape recorder. A man was waiting for me. An armed man.'

'A what?'

'You heard me, Captain. I'm not going to repeat myself. This man I'm speaking about. He must have gone to check on the woman, realized she was gone, and followed me from the house. He came at me with a pump-action shotgun. So I had to kill him.'

'You killed him?' Without realizing it, Calque had switched back into police mode. He patted at his jacket in a vain search for his notebook.

'Look, Captain. I don't want this coming back at me in any way. I've a wife and son to think of. I've thought about it, and I think you owe me that much.'

'How did you kill him, Picaro?' Calque had abandoned the search for his notebook. What was the point?

'I smashed into him with my car. He was going to put out my lights. I had no choice in the matter.'

'And the shotgun?'

'Already disposed of.'

'Where did you leave him?' The taxi driver was shrugging his shoulders at Lamia, and pointing to his meter.

'In the brush. By the side of the road. Did you see a parked Land Rover when you drove away from the beach?'

'Yes. Yes, I did. And another car. An empty blue Renault. Parked close up nearby.'

Picaro froze. 'Captain. There was no blue Renault parked when I left there. The area was clean. I'm getting off the phone right now. And you. You'd better look to your own arse.'

27

Calque reached Lamia in three strides. He held up a placatory hand to the taxi driver, and drew her to one side.

'We have a problem. The man who got you out of the house has just telephoned me. He ran into one of your mother's people on the way back from the beach. The man came at him with a shotgun, and he was forced to kill him. As a result, we were almost certainly followed here.'

'But that's impossible . . .'

'We don't have time for this, Lamia. I'll explain later. You know your mother better than I do. You know what she and her people are capable of. Will you do as I ask?'

Lamia allowed her eyes to search across Calque's face. She nodded.

'Get into the taxi. Now. I'm going to give the driver the address of my hotel in Cogolin. You must go there. I shall follow along behind in my car. At some point you'll see me turn off the road. Don't change the driver's instructions. I must know where to find you. My hunch is that we are dealing with only one man. He will follow me, because I present the greatest threat to him. And if he doesn't follow me and follows you instead, I will know where to come to find him. Do you understand what I am saying?'

'Yes.'

Calque leaned across and gave the driver his instructions. He handed Lamia some Euros.

'I'll catch you up. Don't worry. Take a room at my hotel under the name of Mercier. Then lock your door until I come. Have you got that?'

He backed off before she could change her mind. Without looking around, Calque made for his car. He got in, started the engine, and pulled into the traffic fifty metres or so behind the taxi. There were three cars between him and Lamia. None of them was a blue Renault. Calque glanced into his rear-view mirror.

The Renault was five cars behind him.

Calque's belly tightened with fear. He wasn't an action man. Never had been. He had always left that to the young – to people like Paul Macron. Which is why Macron was dead, and he was still alive. The thought ate into him like acid.

Now his only priority was to protect the woman. It was clearly his fault that she was in this situation, and he must do his very best to extricate her. He mustn't fail her the way he'd failed his assistant.

Five kilometres down the road, at the Cogolin Plage roundabout, Calque veered off to the left, onto the La Croix Valmer road. The blue Renault followed him.

Calque made the sign of the cross. He knew that his only chance now was to use his intelligence. Outflank his opponent. Think laterally. If he couldn't achieve that, the man would simply force him off the road at a suitable spot and do away with him.

He must keep the man guessing. Force him to hold back.

Calque hung a left towards Gassin. That would make the man think. Was Calque heading back towards Pampelonne? Or to the Countess's house?

Calque accelerated up the steep hill towards the village. The road beyond Gassin was a winding one, and little used at this time of year. If the man was to make his move, he would doubtless make it there.

Calque was counting on the man's innate curiosity to stay his hand. It was a thin edge to trust your life to, and Calque could feel the anxiety eating away at him. He had no weapon in the car. No possible means of self-defence. His heart was weak, and a lifetime of heavy smoking had ensured that his lungs would be of little use in a crisis.

The blue Renault closed in on him. They were well out of Gassin, now, and heading into the hills towards Ramatuelle. They couldn't be more than five or six kilometres from the Countess's house. Surely the man would hold his fire for a little longer?

Calque saw a car ahead of him, and speeded up. There was safety in numbers. People instinctively tried not to shit on their own doorsteps if they could possibly avoid it. And certainly not with witnesses present. The man behind him had already had one body to deal with – two would prove something of a crowd, surely?

The extra company appeared to have put the blue Renault man off his stride. Calque saw the car behind him drop back again. Perhaps he still thought that Calque was unaware of his presence?

Now they were approaching Ramatuelle. Calque sent up a brief prayer that the motorist in front of him was not intending to stop off for a newspaper or for his morning cup of coffee. He felt an overwhelming affection for the anonymous little man he was following – curious how it was possible to love a complete stranger.

The man continued on out through the village with Calque clinging to his tail like a pilot fish. They were barely three kilometres from the Countess's house now, and Calque began to feel an upwelling of confidence in his own judgement. He had called the thing correctly. The man driving the blue Renault had obviously been in touch with the Countess, and she had told him to hold off and see what Calque intended.

Now it only remained for Calque to keep his head – before inserting it directly inside the tiger's mouth.

28

With one hand still on the wheel, Calque felt inside his jacket pocket and retrieved the tape recorder. He flipped open the lid of the tape compartment and extricated the cassette. He wedged the tape recorder behind the passenger seat cushion, and placed the cassette on his lap. Then he felt around for his cell phone and placed that beside it. He owed that much to Picaro. It wouldn't do to have the Corpus scrolling back through his recent calls and identifying who it really was who had snatched Lamia.

The blue Renault was still pulling flotilla duty fifty metres behind him.

Two kilometres to go until they reached the Countess's house – had he left it too late? Had fear eaten into his brain and frozen his intelligence?

Calque saw an S-bend three hundred metres ahead. That was it. This would be his last chance. The man in the blue Renault would almost certainly close up on him as they neared the Countess's house.

As he approached the bend, Calque triggered the off-side electric window and stepped on the gas. It would take the blue Renault a split second to respond to the move and match his speed. That would be enough to carry Calque into the blind part of the corner, temporarily out of sight of both the car in front and the blue Renault behind him.

As Calque rounded the crest of the corner, he tossed the cassette and the cell phone through the open window, his eyes searching feverishly for landmarks in the underbrush at the side of the road. Then he punched the window button, and used his engine braking, and a rapid downshift through the gears, to slow the car back down – he wanted no tell-tale flashing of red lights to mark what he had done.

The blue Renault was sitting directly on his tail now. Calque recognized the butler, Milouins, in the driving seat. So it must have been one of the two footmen that Picaro had killed. Butlers. Footmen. Calque wondered what century the Countess imagined she was in. Hadn't she heard of the Revolution? Had the woman no shame?

The entrance to the Domaine de Seyème was fifty metres ahead on the left. Calque fought back a last-minute impulse to accelerate away from the blue Renault and try to avoid his impending fate – but that would mean overtaking the car in front on a blind corner, and dealing with a vengeful Milouins if he happened to survive the manoeuvre. No. The Countess was a better bet. He might be able to bluff her. Milouins, on the other hand, had always struck him as the sort of man who shot first and asked questions afterwards.

Calque switched on his indicator and prepared to turn. Marvellous. Here he was, naked and out in the open, voluntarily putting himself in the enemy's hands. How was it possible? If he'd tried to botch the thing on purpose, he couldn't have contrived a more humiliating ending for himself. All they had to do now was kill him – in as tactful and non-intrusive a way as possible – then plant him in his car, and deposit the car on top of Picaro's hit-and-run victim. He could just imagine the Countess's relish at describing what must have taken place to the police.

'We knew the ex-detective was stalking us. That he somehow blamed our family for the death of his assistant. That it had become an obsession with him. So I sent one of our people out to reason with him – we

97

didn't want to waste any more police time, you see. But the man must have been mad. He simply drove at my footman in a rage – then, when he saw what he had done, he killed himself.'

That would tie in nicely with his purported breakdown, wouldn't it? He could imagine the *Nice Matin* headlines. EMBITTERED EX-COP GOES BERSERK.

Talk about an own goal . . .

Calque drew up in front of the Countess's house. Milouins pulled the blue Renault across the entrance to the courtyard behind him, effectively sealing him in. Calque sighed, and rested his head back against the seat restraint. The Corpus certainly wasn't beating about the bush.

Calque reached across and checked that the empty tape recorder was sufficiently well concealed behind the passenger seat cushion. Then he climbed slowly out of the car. No point in locking the damned thing. They'd simply bust in the window.

The last time he'd stood in this courtyard had been with Macron, two months before, with the full force of the French judicial system at their backs.

Now here he was again. Alone.

29

Calque sat on a porter's chair in the hallway, and waited. Six feet away stood the Countess's surviving footman. Calque cracked the man a supercilious smile. The footman drew one finger slowly across his throat, and then pretended to gag, with his tongue dangling out the side of his mouth.

Well. It was communication of sorts.

Twenty more minutes went by.

Calque began to speculate on how the Countess would decide to play it. Would she offer him a cup of coffee first, like she did last time? Play the Grande Dame? Or would she calmly order Milouins to smash in his teeth with a *matraque*?

Calque cursed himself for having played so cravenly into the Countess's hands. No one but Lamia knew what he was engaged upon. And there was no one else who could be remotely relied upon to explain to the authorities what he'd been up to these past six weeks. Picaro? Aimé Macron? Neither one was the sort of man who easily volunteers information to the police. And what did they have to offer, anyway? Hearsay. Pure hearsay.

Calque sensed that he was about to become a victim of the very *loi du silence* he had striven against all his working life. He hadn't even had the nous to bring Adam Sabir back into the loop. No. He had wanted to play it smart, and spring everything on Sabir at once. Prove what a clever man he was. Vainglory. That was what was going to do for him. The fatal hubris of the inadequate soul.

Milouins poked his head out of the salon and indicated to the footman that he should bring Calque inside. He was dangling Calque's tape recorder like a yoyo from his right hand.

Strike one for the Corpus, thought Calque. I hope to hell they don't torture me. That would be the final straw. It would never occur to them that I know precisely nothing.

The Countess was sitting in her customary seat, near the fireplace, with Madame Mastigou perched at her right shoulder, dictation pad at the ready.

Milouins positioned the tape recorder on the glass-topped occasional table in front of her as though it were a platter bearing John the Baptist's severed head. Then, with a toss of his chin, he indicated that Calque should sit down.

'Are you quite recovered from your previous injuries, Captain Calque? Madame Mastigou reminds me that you had been involved in a car accident when last we met. Alongside your assistant, Lieutenant . . .'

'Lieutenant Macron. Yes. The man your son killed.'

The Countess's eyes flared – the effect was like a dying bonfire receiving a sudden rush of cold air. 'Please leave my son out of this, Captain Calque – my emotions on the subject are still very raw. It might act to your disadvantage.'

Calque could feel the Countess's anger burning into him from across the room. He had the sudden, discomfiting conviction that the woman might actually be mad, and that no one in her entourage dared make the first move to have her sectioned. Working for the woman must be akin to being a senior Wehrmacht general in the final years of Adolf Hitler's Thousand Year Reich.

The Countess drew herself up. It was clear by her attitude that she intended to cut directly to the chase. She pointed to the tape recorder. 'You, or one of your associates, broke into my house early this morning. I assume that it was not merely to kidnap my daughter?'

Calque stared at her. What was the point of talking?

'Milouins, where did you find this tape recorder?'

'In the Captain's car.'

'And what sort of tape recorder is it?'

'A voice-activated tape recorder, Madame.'

'Which means?'

'Which means that it will switch itself on and off according to the volume of incoming sound.'

'Instantly?'

'It will respond to any sound whatsoever, Madame, yes. And it is designed to overrun. Meaning that once it has been triggered, it will continue to record for a certain period, even if the sound cuts off.'

'Have you discovered its original place of concealment?'

'Yes, Madame. Beneath the table in the Council Chamber. The marks of the electrical tape with which it was attached to the table are still clearly visible. They are also visible on the recorder.'

'And the tape reel itself?'

'The cassette, Madame? Nowhere to be found.'

The Countess turned to Calque. 'That was clever of you, Captain Calque. That idea you had to hide the tape recorder in your car, where it would almost certainly be found. A cynic might go so far as to construe that you wished for it to be discovered. Why would that be, I wonder?'

Calque shrugged. His throat felt drier than a grain extractor.

'Then I'll tell you. Milouins has explained your machine to me in all its intricacies. As you can see, we know where it was hidden, and also when it was hidden, for logic dictates that you must have concealed it, illegally, during the search your policemen made of my house in May. Given this limited time frame, we have come to certain conclusions.'

Here we go, thought Calque. Bang goes my chance to bluff my way out of this.

'Milouins cleans the Council Room at least once a month. No one else goes in there. Just him and a footman. So he conducted a little test while you were waiting outside in the hall. Play the tape, Milouins.'

Milouins retrieved a cassette tape from his pocket and placed it in the machine. He turned the volume to high and pressed play. The sound of a vacuum cleaner resonated throughout the room, followed by voices, and the bangs and crashes of moving furniture. Every now and again the tape would cut off and then start again, following a short period of silence. Madame Mastigou continued busily writing on her shorthand pad.

Calque knew what it felt like to be caught red-handed, with your fingers in the till. He must never again underestimate these people. And the Countess was not mad – that would have been too convenient. She was insane, with a hefty leavening of lunacy.

'There. Interesting, isn't it? I merely asked Milouins to recreate the exact sounds he would have made last week, whilst preparing the room for use. It is clear from his demonstration that you will have succeeded in recording nothing of any conceivable interest either to yourself or to the police, Captain Calque, on the ninety minutes of magnetic tape that you had at your disposal. If you had, you would have thrown the entire machine out of the window of your car, rather than just the cassette tape inside it.'

Calque decided to attempt a bluff anyhow. 'I still have Lamia. And you have a murder you need to hush up. Even you can see that two people from the same household dying in violent circumstances within a few months of each other might stretch the bounds of coincidence. We ought to be able to come to some sort of accommodation, surely? I have considerable influence left on the force.'

The Countess glanced across at Madam Mastigou. Madame Mastigou consulted her brooch watch and nodded.

'You misunderstand the situation, Captain Calque. My daughter, Lamia, will be back with us very shortly. At this exact moment two of my other children are entering your hotel in Cogolin and demanding to see their sister.

She will leave with them, because she is a dutiful girl, and does not wish to vex her mother.'

Calque could feel the colour draining away from his face.

'I own the main taxi service in the St Tropez peninsula, Captain Calque. In fact I own a considerable part of the peninsula itself. I invested a small part of my fortune in the local economy after my marriage – and very profitable it has been. You forget, perhaps, that my husband's family have been Counts of this area for nine hundred years? Milouins simply called in the cab number and received an instant reply – the police and the tax authorities require each fare to be routinely logged within a central registration system, as you well know, so the process was a simple one. And Cogolin is hardly Siberia. What did you think? That you were dealing with amateurs?'

'And the body? Out at Pampelonne?'

'What body is that, Captain? My footman, Philippe Lemelle, has bipolar disorder. He has already absconded without leave three times during his present period of employment. Once he even sold all his possessions, including his car, to the first man he came across. Milouins came upon him living rough in Mandelieu. We took him back that time. In fact we've been very tolerant indeed with him – his family, after all, have been working for us for generations. But he was nevertheless given formal warning that if he absconded again, he would lose his job. That now appears to have happened.'

'That's bullshit, and you know it.'

'Not according to our local doctor. Or to Milouins. Or to Monsieur Flavenot, our company registrar. I can assure you of that.'

'I have access to the blood-stained car that killed him.'

'Oh, please, Captain. Whoever drove that car also broke into my house and kidnapped one of its occupants

– not to mention killing an innocent man via a hit-and-run. If we wished to pursue this matter, it is you and your associate who would find yourselves caught in the crossfire, not I. I think you will find, upon further reflection, that our interests coincide in this matter.'

Calque's ears had begun to hum with tension. 'What are you holding me for, then? You know everything. You control everything. I must be a massive irrelevance to you.'

'You chose the word "irrelevance", Captain, not I.' The Countess stood up. 'And we certainly aren't holding you. You came here of your own free will. You may leave here equally freely. We have nothing more to say to one another.'

Calque rose to his feet in automatic echo of the Countess's movement. What was it about the woman? Was it her impermeable self-belief? Perhaps if you were truly convinced that whatever you undertook was automatically rubber-stamped by God, then you also believed that the rest of the world's idiots would play along with your fantasy? 'May I have my tape recorder back?'

'Perhaps you would like us to indemnify you against the loss of your cell phone, too? There are limits even to my patience, Captain.'

Calque hesitated, still not sure whether the Countess truly intended to let him go free. He took a tentative step towards the door. When no one made a move to stop him, he headed swiftly in the direction of the hall. He was briefly tempted to crook his arm obscenely at the ghoulish footman, but thought better of it. Perhaps this was all some outrageous bluff, and the minute he left the Countess's presence they would manhandle him down the cellar stairs and start in on him with their rubber hosepipes?

He allowed the thought to fester inside him all the way to his car. Perhaps they'd tricked that up instead? Sawn through the cables? Drained the brake fluid? Set a bomb to go off on a trembler mechanism the moment he broke through the fifty-kilometre-an-hour mark? Christ knows, they'd had enough time. Calque felt like a *gallus* gladiator, forced to exit through the gates of the Circus Maximus at the tip of a spear in order to appease the bloodthirsty expectations of the crowd.

It was gradually dawning on him that he had pitched himself against an organization so complete in its self-belief – and so hermetic in its identity – that no single man could ever hope to match himself against it.

Puffing with relief, Calque climbed into his car and started the engine. His hand trembled as he put the car into first gear. With his foot still braced on the clutch pedal, Calque reached across for the crocodile-skin cigarette case his wife had given him when they were first married. Miraculously, it had somehow evaded the divorce settlement. He scattered its contents like chaff onto the passenger seat. Palming the nearest cigarette, he speared it between his lips. For some reason he had considerable difficulty matching the tip of the cigarette to the glow of the cigar lighter.

No one followed him out of the courtyard. No one followed him to the junction with the main road. Mystified, Calque turned right, towards Ramatuelle. No. There was definitely no one on his tail.

He pulled over into the first available lay-by and got out. First he lay on the ground and checked the underside of the car. Nothing. No sign of tampering. Then he looked in the engine compartment. Clean as a whistle. He felt around beneath the seats. Then he went around to the back of the car and checked there, paying particular attention to the exhaust pipe. Finally, he eased up the spare wheel cover. If the Corpus had bugged him or booby-trapped him, they'd certainly concealed their work well.

Calque got back in the car, readjusted his seat, and set off again. Twenty yards into the journey his body gave a convulsive shudder, like a horse shucking off rainwater. Calque hammered the steering wheel in sheer frustration at his lack of physical self-control. He simply must pull himself together. He daren't fritter any more time away appeasing his unfounded fears. He had to retrieve his cell phone at all costs. Adam Sabir's home number in America was concealed somewhere within its maw, and Calque's first priority must be to warn the man that the Corpus was still on his case.

For Joris Calque had learned one valuable thing from his conversations with the Countess and with Lamia – and it had come to him more or less by default. The Countess had spoken about everything under the sun during their discussion – everything but Sabir. The man's name hadn't even figured. And yet Sabir was the very first person Lamia had asked him about when she'd regained consciousness after her doping.

Calque hadn't spent the better part of his life interrogating people for nothing. He knew for a fact that the questions people left hanging – and the obvious names that they omitted during formal police interviews – were invariably of more significance than the ones they voluntarily allowed to surface.

The one thing he wouldn't be doing when he got his cell phone back would be to try to interest any old friends in the Police Nationale about the curious disappearance of Philippe Lemelle – the Countess had figured it right. Jean Picaro had put his neck on the line to help the girl, and later to warn Calque that the Corpus was on to him – and Calque knew a multitude of so-called law-abiding people who wouldn't have done half so much for a man they hardly knew, or for an unknown woman who had nothing whatsoever to do with the job they were being paid for.

Picaro had asked him to go easy as a personal favour on behalf of his wife and son. And Picaro was a two-time loser – meaning that the next occasion he was sent to prison, he would stay there for good. No parole. No time off for good behaviour.

Though it pained Calque's soul to let the Countess wriggle off the hook, it was better, sometimes, to let sleeping dogs lie.

30

_

Calque sat in his car, watching the entrance to the Hotel de la Place at Cogolin. It was twelve o'clock. The lunchtime traffic was just building up. He'd tried to contact Sabir three times on the way back from Ramatuelle, but the phone at Sabir's Massachusetts' home simply rang in an endless, useless litany.

What would he have said to Sabir, anyway? Watch your back, man? How would Sabir go about doing that? Hire himself a bodyguard? Call in the FBI? Or he could have advised Sabir to take off on an extended holiday. Which was even more pointless. Calque had the Countess's measure now – the woman was implacable. When and if she ever decided to revenge herself on the man who had killed her son, mere geography wouldn't act as a deterrent.

In the event Calque didn't have a single shred of evidence to place in front of Sabir – just a hunch that Sabir felt the same way as he did about the Corpus. That Sabir, of all men, wouldn't believe that the Corpus's ambitions had died down there in that cesspit alongside Achor Bale. No. Calque was convinced that they still wanted what Sabir had. They still wanted the prophecies.

Now, with the benefit of hindsight, he realized what a fool he'd been not to trust the girl from the outset. He might at least have got something concrete out of her – some clue as to the Corpus's true intentions to compensate for his fiasco with the tape recorder. Instead, he'd held back, like the obstinate policeman he still was, and more or less gifted her back to her family. He could feel the frustration eating away at his guts like arsenic.

All Calque's case notes were up in that hotel room, together with Sabir's private address, and his detailed annotations about the last conversation they'd had together, including the tantalizing clues Sabir had given him about the 52 lost prophecies – out of Nostradamus's original 58 – which specifically dealt with the run-up to what may, or may not, prove to be planet earth's final Armageddon. It had never occurred to Calque to conceal them. He'd been running the show – not the Corpus. Or at least that's what he'd thought. Now it looked very much as if the hound had become the quarry.

Calque stepped out of the car. His eyes raked the surrounding area. Across the way, a small queue of people was steadily making its way into the adjoining restaurant section of the hotel. Calque felt his stomach turn over with hunger.

He strode across to the hotel entrance and sidestepped through the revolving doors. The concierge wasn't at his post. Perhaps he, too, was having his lunch? Like any normal person at midday.

Calque scanned the hotel message board. His room key was no longer in place. He had been half expecting that, of course, after the Countess's hints, but still he found himself having to fight off a strong desire to break into a trot and head straight back out into the street.

Some deep-seated part of Calque's make-up was still resisting the thought that the prophecies might have any value whatsoever beyond the purely commercial. How could a man born half a millennium ago be expected to predict an accurate series of events 450 years in the future? No rational person could entertain such an idea. Adam Sabir had been in a post-traumatic state, and still recuperating in hospital, when he had told Calque of Nostradamus's prediction of the 52-year run-up to the Great Change in 2012. Third Antichrists? Second Comings? The whole thing was insane. Calque wondered whether he wasn't suffering from the early onset of senile dementia. That would explain why he had temporarily suspended all rational judgement and allowed Sabir and the Gypsies to get so deeply under his skin.

But belief or non-belief was no longer the point. Crimes had been committed. People had been killed and injured. Incipient dementia or not, Calque's sole remaining purpose in life must be to stop the commission of yet more crimes. He owed his late assistant that much, surely? He owed Paul Macron the courtesy of a significant death.

31

Calque ignored the box elevator and made his way laboriously up the stairs. He hesitated for a moment at the threshold to his room. Then he reached down, twisted the handle, and threw the door open in one fluid movement. What was the Corpus going to do? Bushwhack him? Shoot him in a public place? They'd already had their chance at him, and passed on it. He obviously wasn't that important to them.

The room was immaculate.

With a burgeoning sense of hope, Calque hurried across to his suitcase and threw open the lid. All his notes were gone.

'*Merde*! *Putain de merde*!'

Calque slammed the lid of the case. He had grown up under the tutelage of a Protestant mother and a Catholic father, both of whom had instilled in him their very own – although occasionally contradictory – versions of correct behaviour. As a result he rarely swore. What was the point in shutting the stable door after the horse had bolted? But today was something of an exception.

What terminal lunacy had encouraged him to leave his notes in his hotel room? And why had it never occurred to him to use the hotel safe? Too darned inconvenient, that's why. If Calque had ever bothered to subscribe to something as mundane as the concept of low self-esteem, he would have been forced to admit to feeling gutted. As it was, his brain simply jerked up another gear and into overdrive. And the first thing on his sparkling new agenda would be to find out all he could about what had happened to the woman.

Leaving his door wide open – after all, what did he have left for anyone to steal? – Calque retraced his steps down to the lobby. The concierge was back in his usual place, no doubt digesting after his lunch break. Calque cut straight to the chase.

'Did my assistant, Madame Mercier, register with you this morning? She was due to arrive here around breakfast time.' He allowed the man a brief flash of his illegal badge to further drive home his point.

The clerk looked about him in so secretive a manner that even if Calque had not been watching out for it, he would have been hard-pressed not to suspect that the man had some hidden agenda. 'Madame Mercier, you say?'

'You heard me.'

The clerk swallowed. He looked as if he were fighting some internal battle with himself, and losing. 'I have to ask you something first. It's very important.'

Calque felt like giving the man an open-handed clout around the head. Instead, he nodded encouragingly, his lips fixed in the rictus of an artificial grin. 'Go on then.'

'How many croissants did you eat for breakfast this morning?'

Calque's mouth fell open. He was briefly tempted to reach across and grab the clerk by the scruff of his neck and shake him like a terrier does a rat – but in the present circumstances that might have proved counter-productive. Instead, Calque fixed his eyes on the clerk, leaving the man in little doubt that he would not take kindly if his question masked some vague attempt at a practical joke. 'You're serious? The important question you have to ask me is how many croissants I ate for breakfast this morning?'

The clerk nodded. 'Yes, Sir. That's the question the lady told me to put to you.'

111

Calque rolled his eyes. He willed himself to cast his mind back to earlier that morning, and not to throttle the clerk. 'Let's be surgically precise here. I ate three. Or rather, two and three-quarters. Two of my own, and one of Madame Mercier's that she inadvertently abandoned, unfinished, on her plate. Does that satisfy you?'

The clerk scrabbled underneath his counter and came up with an envelope. 'Then I've been told to give you this, Captain.'

Calque lunged for the envelope.

The clerk clutched it against his chest, a canine expression on his face.

Calque grunted. He rummaged around in his pockets and handed the man a ten-Euro note.

The clerk hesitated, as if he were briefly considering holding out for more. Then he handed Calque the envelope.

'Did anyone else ask for Madame Mercier?'

The clerk shrugged. 'If they had, I would have asked them the same question I asked you. And if they had answered correctly, I would have given them the envelope. Madame Mercier gave me the strictest possible instructions.'

Yes. And a fifty-Euro tip with my money, you snivelling little bastard, thought Calque.

Calque retreated to the lift, just as if he were contemplating an imminent return to his room. Once out of sight of the front desk, however, he tore open the envelope. All it contained was a single line of writing and an initial.

8, 7, 11, 13, 12, of where we sat this morning. Your jacket.
L

Calque leaned back against the wall. What now? Another trap for him to stumble into? Perhaps the Corpus was having difficulty reading the handwriting on his case notes? Perhaps they wanted to invite him back to the Domaine to make sense of all the material they'd pilfered from his hotel room? It would be a simple enough thing for anyone with a semi-normal IQ to work out where he and Lamia had been sitting that morning. After all, the Corpus had staked out the place with cold-blooded efficiency, had it not? And the road to the beach was a cul-de-sac – meaning it led to a single, specific destination. The whole thing was scarcely nuclear physics.

Calque shrugged, and began to work out the riddle in his head. He decided that he had little choice, in the circumstances, but to follow where it led him.

PAMPELONNE PLAGE. Eighth letter N. Seventh letter O. Eleventh letter P. Thirteenth letter A. Twelfth letter L. NOPAL. What was that? Some kind of Mexican cactus, no? Or was it a seaweed? Definitely Mexican, anyway. So what was there likely to be that was Mexican in a town like Cogolin? A restaurant? That was the most likely answer. Or maybe a shop that sold Mexican goods? But more likely a restaurant. Lamia wouldn't have had a long time to think up her plan, and she would have been under considerable pressure. She would have made the answer as obvious as possible in the time left to her.

The concierge was obviously for sale to the highest bidder, so no point asking him if there was a Mexican restaurant in town. Calque might as well take out an ad with Radio Free Europe.

Calque made up his mind. He headed towards the rear of the hotel. This time he expected to be followed. If the Corpus had truly failed to get their hands on Lamia, then he was the obvious person to lead them to her.

Calque breezed out of the hotel's rear exit. He accosted the first passer-by he saw and asked the man the way to the nearest police station. Disinformation. That was the name of the game.

With the address of the gendarmerie safely to hand, Calque walked briskly up the street, looking neither to his right nor left. Let the bastards stew in their own juice. They'd obviously let him go for a reason, and that reason was that they'd failed to get Lamia back. Now they were expecting him to lead them to her. Well, he'd soon show them that they weren't about to have everything their own way.

Calque walked boldly up the gendarmerie steps and straight to the main desk in the lobby. 'Good morning, Sergeant. My name is Captain Joris Calque, Police Nationale, retired.' He proffered his entirely legal and above-board retirement warrant card – it wouldn't do to flash the illegal one by mistake.

The *pandore* behind the counter stood up and saluted. 'It's a pleasure, Captain.'

Calque returned the salute. So I've still got what it takes, he thought to himself. You can take the policeman out of the service, but you can't take the service out of the policeman. 'I'm staying up the road, at the Hotel de la Place. I just thought I'd drop by and leave you my card. I have a feeling your Commandant and I know each other from way back.'

'Shall I call him, Captain? I'm sure he'd be pleased to come out and see you.'

'No. Please don't do that. I'm already running late. And I'm sure the Commandant is very busy. I was just passing by on my way to lunch. I'm going to eat at the Nopal. I'm right, aren't I? It's just up the road?'

'The Nopal?'

'A Mexican restaurant, yes. Chillies. Enchiladas. Things like that.'

The desk sergeant grinned. 'No, Captain. That's the Esposito. It's the only foreign restaurant in town. But

114

it's got a bar attached to it that's called the Nopal. You'll find it just off the Place de la Liberté. But I wouldn't recommend either of them. The Largesse is much better. Proper French food. Try their *pot-au-feu*. Madame Adelaïde has been using the same recipe for thirty years. And none of us regulars have complained yet. Tell her Sergeant Marestaing recommended you.'

'Ah. That's it. The Esposito. But we are to meet in the bar first. I knew I would get the name wrong.' Calque allowed a wistful smile to invest his features. 'I have no choice in the matter of where I eat today, Sergeant, as I'm invited. But I shall try the Largesse for certain tomorrow, on your personal recommendation. But tell me. Could I possibly use your toilet while I'm here? I have prostate troubles. Need to go every couple of hours. You know how it is?'

The *pandore* nodded, as if he did, indeed, know how it was. He directed Calque up the corridor.

'Can I go out the back way when I'm finished? Save myself a walk?'

A telephone rang on the *pandore*'s desk, conveniently redirecting the man's attention away from Calque. 'There is a rear exit, yes, Captain. Please feel free to use it.'

'Thank you, Sergeant. I will.' Calque felt curiously satisfied following their exchange, as if he had proved to himself that he could still take the initiative. Still cut the mustard.

Once out in the daylight again, Calque's demeanour underwent a subtle transformation. He stopped three times before he reached the corner of the street to make sure that no one was following him. He wasn't about to make the same mistake twice in one day. He wasn't about to lead the Corpus back to Lamia.

With any luck, whoever had been tailing him would be fully taken up with communicating to the Countess

115

that Calque was still tucked cosily away inside the gendarmerie – no doubt spilling the beans about the dead footman. Disinformation. Disingenuousness. Deceit. The three D's. His late lamented mentor, Maurice Edard – an old-school policeman who had cut his milk teeth in the good old pre-1966 days when the Police Nationale was still the Sûreté – would have been proud of him.

Calque grinned as he imagined the bedlam back at the Domaine. The Countess would be ordering the decks cleared pretty fast if she thought the police might be about to pay her an unexpected visit.

32

By the time he arrived at the Esposito, Calque was 99 per cent certain that he hadn't been followed. He had doubled back on himself twice more since his first flurry of activity, confined himself to side streets only, and he had even done a Humphrey Bogart – minus Dorothy Malone, unfortunately – in a second-hand bookshop.

When Calque reached the restaurant he didn't linger by the menu board, but plunged straight in. He didn't really expect Lamia to be waiting for him. In fact it was far more likely that the message was a false trail laid by the Corpus in an attempt to provide themselves with a fallback position – in case he eluded them the first time, say, or in case he had been professional enough to actually bother hiding his notes, rather than simply to leave them in plain view, like the very worst sort of greenhorn. But what else could he do but take the note at face value? It was the only way he could think of to remain in the game.

Lamia was sitting with her back to him, in one of the private booths. Calque's heart gave a lurch as he saw her. It astonished him to realize that he had been genuinely concerned for her safety. I must be getting soft in my old age, he thought to himself. First I go into mourning for my racist worm of an assistant, and now I'm acting like a bleeding heart for the sister of the very man who killed him.

He sat down in front of her, facing the door, his expression studiously immobile.

Lamia looked up at him. She held his eyes for ten seconds, and when he didn't respond, she quietly slid a packet of papers across the table towards him.

'My notes?'

She nodded.

'I didn't dare to hope.' Calque's features relaxed, like those of a Chinese shar-pei dog. 'How in God's name did you do it?'

Lamia shrugged. 'I knew, the moment you gave the taxi driver the name of your hotel, and mentioned the fictitious Madame Mercier in front of him, that my mother would know all about it within twenty minutes – that we would both be fatally compromised. She owns half of St Tropez, Captain. She has feelers everywhere.'

'I know. I spoke to her.'

Lamia's eyes widened. 'You . . .'

Calque reached across and squeezed her hand. 'The notes, Lamia. How did you manage to get the notes? I can explain all the rest of it later.'

Lamia's expression lightened momentarily. 'The taxi journey gave me time to think things through – to work out where we were most vulnerable. When I got to the hotel I pretended to the concierge that I was your mistress. He didn't bite at first – I mean, who in his right mind would want someone like me as his mistress?' She thrust herself back in her chair, as though she were challenging Calque to contradict her – to negate the reality of her face. 'But then I gave him the rest of your money as a sweetener, and he handed over your key. It's curious how easily men believe us women when we talk of sex.'

Calque inclined his head politely. In reality he was desperately embarrassed at the sudden vulnerability she had shown about her birthmark. But he found it impossible, in the present circumstances, to summon up a suitably gallant riposte. 'And my notes? You read them?'

Lamia turned quickly away.

'Listen. That was not an accusation. I want you to read them – in fact I desperately need your help.'

Lamia turned back. 'So you believe me?'

'Yes. I believe you. I lied when I told you about the tape recorder this morning. I got nothing, absolutely nothing, from that idiotic stunt I pulled – apart from the drone of a vacuum cleaner, and the occasional crash of moving furniture.'

Lamia snatched one hand to her face, as if she were about to stifle an outburst of the giggles.

Calque pretended not to notice. 'In point of fact I'm no further forward with anything. I might as well have spent the past five weeks windsurfing in Hawaii for all I've managed to achieve.'

'You? Windsurfing? Surely not?' Lamia allowed her hand to drop slowly back towards the table. It was a strange movement, akin to the shucking of a veil. Almost as if she were voluntarily revealing herself to him for the very first time. She tilted her head fractionally to one side to indicate that she was no longer jesting. 'Why should

I help you, Captain? Why should I betray my family to someone I only met a few hours ago?'

Calque sat back in his seat. 'No reason. No reason whatsoever. You've already helped me way beyond any capacity I may have to repay you, simply by keeping my notes from the Corpus. If you were to get up and leave now, I would still be infinitely grateful to you. There would be no blame attached to anything you've done.'

Lamia's eyes scanned Calque's face, as though searching for clues to a long-standing and elusive mystery. 'What are you expecting of me?'

'I want you to tell me what you can of the Corpus's plans.'

'So you do want me to betray my family?'

'Just as they've betrayed you. Yes. I won't lie to you, Lamia. I believe the Corpus to be evil. And furthermore I believe your mother to be a person with no moral scruples whatsoever. Someone who would not hesitate to use any means necessary, including murder, to get her own way.'

Lamia watched him, one hand splayed across her chest, as if she had temporarily lost control of her heart rate. 'How much do you already know? About my mother, I mean. About her role in the Corpus Maleficus.'

'Assume I know nothing.'

'What particular question do you want to ask me?'

'A simple one. What went on in that room when you all met?'

Lamia still seemed to be weighing him up. 'The people you saw. Entering the house. You know they are all my brothers and sisters?'

'I deduced that much, yes. And your mother as good as confirmed it to me.'

Lamia shook her head. 'I still don't understand why she let you go. You say you saw her? It seems impossible to me.'

Calque waved away the waiter. He hunched towards her across the table. 'I'm a senior ex-policeman, Lamia. Riverbanks collapse when unexpected things happen to senior ex-policemen – islands are washed away. Your mother was convinced she already had you back under her control. She thought she had my notes. Why muddy the waters further? I don't think she rates me very highly.'

'Then she's a fool.'

'It's nice of you to think so – but I don't believe it for an instant. But if she has made a mistake about me, then she has made exactly the same mistake about you.'

Lamia turned her face away from him again. It was obviously a well-rehearsed, if entirely unconscious, movement. Almost as if she wished to give her interlocutor a rest from having to look at her blemish – or to give herself a rest from having to bear the weight of other people's disenchantment. Just for a moment it was possible for Calque to imagine that she was merely a beautiful young woman – that she didn't have a monstrous birthmark splayed, like a palm print, across the intimate confines of her cheek.

Then she turned back to him, her eyes challenging him for a reaction. 'You guessed right about me, Captain. Some time ago I decided that I wanted nothing more to do with my mother's machinations. The other night it all came to a head. I'd spent weeks building up enough courage to tell her the truth about my feelings. Stupidly, I decided to do it in front of my entire family. At a moment when they were all expecting me to formally renew my allegiance to the cause the de Bales have been single-mindedly dedicating themselves to for nearly eight hundred years. It wasn't what you might call good timing.'

'And what is your mother machinating? What is this

cause that unites different generations of the same family over centuries of time?'

Lamia hesitated. 'The man. Sabir. He's your friend, is he not?'

Calque shook his head. 'I swore I'd be honest with you, Lamia. I'd be lying if I said Adam Sabir was my friend. We connected, briefly, at a low point in both our lives. He took pity on me, after the death of my assistant, and shared some information with me that he is probably now regretting he let slip – probably because he was doped up with morphine at the time. That's the full extent of our relationship. That's as far as it goes.'

'Then why are you still interested in him?'

'Because I think he holds the key to something your mother, and through her, the Corpus, wants.'

'And you believe in this Corpus?'

'I think your mother does. And I believe her to be a very rich, very powerful, and very evil, woman. I also believe that it was she who was directly responsible for my assistant's death. And if she was, I intend to make her pay for it. I owe that much to his family.' He hesitated, then allowed his gaze to drop. 'And to myself.'

Lamia followed him with her eyes. She hesitated for a moment, still watching him. Then she took in a quick breath, which was almost a gasp. 'You're right, Captain. You've been right all along. My mother was directly responsible for your assistant's death. She admitted as much to us the other night.'

Calque lurched forwards, his face alive. 'I knew it. So I haven't been wasting my time?'

Lamia shook her head. 'Far from it, Captain. But the information won't help you. And it certainly won't save Sabir.'

'What do you mean "save Sabir"? What are you talking about?'

Lamia held Calque's eyes with her own. 'My twin brothers left yesterday for the United States. Under my mother's direct orders.' She glanced down at her watch. 'By now, Adam Sabir will be dead.'

PART TWO

PROLOGUE

1

At first you thought it was simply another earthquake. There had been three in the past few days, and you had become used to them by now.

It always went the same way. First, your stomach unexpectedly turned over. For a second or two, you were frozen to the spot, wondering what had happened. Then, if you were unlucky enough to be caught inside your hut, you might have the presence of mind to look upwards. If the oil lamps were swinging, you knew it was an earthquake, and you hurried outside, the ground swelling and bloating underneath you, until you could find somewhere safe to sit that wasn't directly under a tree, a telegraph pole, or any masonry. Then you watched your hut to see if it would fall down.

When the earthquake was over, you would walk back towards your hut, the aftershocks making you feel ever so slightly nauseous. Then you would remember to thank God that the earthquake was only a small one, and that the epicentre was a few hundred miles away on the other side of the country, and you would force yourself back to work.

But this was no earthquake. When you concentrated, you realized that the shaking and trembling of the floor of your hut was also accompanied by a deep rumbling sound. You ran outside and you looked across the hills. One hundred and ten kilometres away from where you lived, the great volcano, 5675 metres high, pierced the sky. You had looked at it every day of your life. All through the year, snow coated its pinnacle, despite the near-tropical climate in which you lived. You had heard that it was still active, but everyone knew that it had not erupted for more than a century and a half. The two great volcanoes four and a half hours further west from you regularly smoked, polluting the atmosphere, or so you had heard, with the smell of sulphur, shit, and rotten eggs. But your volcano had always seemed dormant by comparison. Resting. Unhurried.

Now a massive cloud encircled the familiar peak, blotting out the sun. Even from one hundred kilometres away, you began to catch the smell of sulphur on the air. Soon, you sensed, it would be all pervasive, like the smell of a rotting animal in the underbrush.

You followed the course of the eruption in bewildered wonderment. And as you stood there watching, volcanic ash and tiny balls of mud, about a quarter of an inch in diameter, began to patter around you like hailstones. In the distance, thick clouds of black, white, and blue roiled up from the vent, shot through with eerily silent bolts of lightning, as if someone had inadvertently switched off the sound on the village television set.

You had never thought that this would happen in your lifetime. As guardian of the codex – just as your father, and your grandfather, and your great-grandfather had been guardians of the codex before you – you had been preparing for this event for 163 years. Ever since the last eruption.

Your family's only task during that period had been to make sure that no one discovered the location of the cave that housed the codex, or tampered with its contents.

That task was completed. Now, your second, and greater, task would begin.

And that task involved a journey to the south. A journey for which you were terminally unprepared.

2
-

The Tanyard, Stockbridge,
Massachusetts

For some months, now, Adam Sabir had been unable to complete a full night's sleep inside his own house.

As soon as he began to drift off, the nightmares would return, and with them the claustrophobia that had tormented him since early childhood, when some schoolmates, as part of a Halloween prank, had bound and gagged and then locked him inside the trunk of his professor's car, in imitation, or so he later learned, of a scene from a horror flick that was currently doing the rounds at the local drive-in movie houses.

The professor had discovered Sabir three hours later, his gag chewed to a pulp, moaning, hallucinating, and half out of his head with fear. Sabir had spent the rest of that semester at home and in bed, alternately chain-reading for comfort, and then throwing up as a result of the tranquillizers his psychiatrist was forced to prescribe him for whenever the street doors of his parent's house needed to be shut and bolted.

In true prep school tradition, Sabir had found it impossible to squeal on his tormentors. But years later, as a journalist, he had taken his revenge on them in a manner reminiscent of Alexandre Dumas's *The Count of Monte Cristo* – he had built them up, in other words, each man in his turn, and had then proceeded to tear them down again in an avalanche of failed vainglory.

But the fear of enclosed spaces still lurked in his psyche like a recurring nightmare – only a thousand times exacerbated by what he had experienced earlier that summer, in France, in the cellar of an abandoned house in the French Camargue.

Over the past few months, Sabir's cycle of disrupted sleep had always followed the exact same pattern. First would come the hyper-realist dreams, in which he was back in the cesspit again, deep in the cellar below the Gypsy safe-house in the French Camargue. In these dreams he was up to his neck in raw sewage, his head bent backwards to protect his mouth, his forehead tight up against the lid of the cesspit, which Achor Bale was sliding shut across his face.

Then came the dreams of dreams, in which Sabir revisited the hallucinations he had experienced whilst sealed inside the cesspit. Hallucinations in which his arms and legs were torn off, his torso shredded, his intestines, lights, bowels, and bladder dragged out of his body like offal from a butchered horse. Later in the dream a snake would come towards him – a thick uncoiling python of a snake, with the scales of a fish, and staring eyes, and a hinged skull like that of an anaconda. The snake would swallow Sabir's head, forcing it down the entire length of its body with convulsive movements of its myosin-fuelled muscles, like a reverse birth.

Later, Sabir would become the snake, its head his head, its eyes his eyes. It was at this exact point in the dream that he always awoke, his body drenched in sweat, his eyes bulging from his face like those of a startled cat. He would throw on his dressing-gown and hurry out into the garden, where he would stand, gulping in fresh air, and cursing Achor Bale and the perniciousness of posthumous effect.

The rest of the night would be spent in his father's old Hatteras hammock, in the garden house, with the veranda doors thrown open to the elements, a single blanket draped over his quasi-foetal shape. He had tried switching to a sleeping bag, but the bag's innate constriction had seen him thrashing around like an emergent chrysalis, desperate to disentangle its body from the pupal shell before serving as some passing bird's *hors d'oeuvre*.

On this particular evening the dream had come to him with more than its usual vigour and destructive force. Sabir was perilously close to hyperventilating by the time he made his way across the lawn and into the garden house.

Rationally, he knew that it made no earthly sense for him to persist in trying to sleep in the main building. What was the point, when he would simply come rushing out again, three hours later, gasping for air? But some obstinate part of himself refused to give up on the attempt to live an ordinary life.

He privately feared that once he abandoned all pretence at living inside – once he gave up fighting, in other words – his claustrophobia would enter the obsessive-compulsive stage, dooming him to a downward spiral of psychoanalysis and soporifics.

For that was the way his mother had gone. A steady, inexorable descent towards drug dependence and enforced hospitalization. It had destroyed his father's life, and it had come close to destroying his own.

Recently, Sabir had begun wondering if he wasn't hell-bent on repeating the family pattern?

3
—

'I like small town Americans,' said Abiger de Bale. 'They're so fucking trusting.'

The twins were sitting in their rental car, watching the outside of Adam Sabir's house. They had been in the United States for a little less than twelve hours, and already they had identified their mark.

'What do you mean, trusting?'

Abi wound his seat back to the prone position, so that his silhouette would no longer be outlined against the street lights. He glanced over at his brother. 'I'm pretending to be a tourist, right? I ask them things, right? In the American idiom. Things like "you got any celebrities in this town?" Then they give me a list. Including Norman Rockwell, and Daniel Chester French, and Owen Johnson, and Mum Bett – oh, and that guy who wrote the bestselling book on Nostradamus's private life. And because the writer is the only one on the list who isn't dead yet, they tell me about *his* private life. That he can't keep a woman. That he lives alone. That his mother went mad. Stuff like that. And all without me, the tourist, needing to ask anything at all. Try the same thing in France, and it'd be like attempting to crack a stone wall with the tip of your nose. How did you do?'

'Pretty much the same.'

'You see? I like these Americans.'

Vau cast a quizzical look at his brother. 'You don't think they'll remember us?'

'Lighten up, Vau. Nobody ever saw us together. So they'll just assume we're one and the same person. And the *Amis* can't recognize accents, anyway. They never travel abroad. They'll think we're Canadians.'

'I still think we ought to take him away somewhere. Not do him here.'

'Don't worry about that. I've got a better idea. Sabir's been behaving strangely lately. People around here are starting to think he's taking after his mother. We'll play on that.'

'How?'

'Wait and see.'

4

Adam Sabir's 'Berkshire Cottage' style home was set well back from the Stockbridge Main Street, in grounds totalling a little more than an acre and a half – or roughly the size of a baseball field.

The ultra-discreet street lights cut a fragile arc across the front lawn, but they fell just short of the main part of the house, which was consequently shrouded in darkness. The back garden, in which Sabir's summerhouse-cum-writing-hut was situated, stretched for a further fifty feet towards a thick stand of trees, which marked the extreme boundary between Sabir's property and next-door's smallholding. The rear of his demesne was bounded by a small white picket fence, whilst the front of the house lay directly open onto the street, as if its original nineteenth-century occupants had not wished to mar the vista of its rolling lawns with anything as common as an enclosure.

At a little after two o'clock in the morning, Abi and Vau emerged from their car, checked up and down the street, and then moved swiftly across the floodlit lawn until they were swallowed up by the darkness surrounding the main house.

Once at the rear of the house, Abi made his way cautiously up the veranda steps and tested the back door. It was open. He grinned at his brother. 'Jesus Christ, Vau-Vau. This idiot doesn't even lock his door at night. Do you think he knew we were coming?'

'I don't like this, Abi. No one in the United States leaves their house door open at night.'

'Well Mr Sabir does. And I, for one, am most grateful to him for the courtesy.'

The twins edged their way through the door. They stood in the back hall, staring up at the main stairs.

Abi covered his mouth with his hand. 'You saw him earlier, didn't you? You're sure of that?'

Vau echoed the movement. 'Clear as a bell. His bedroom is the last room on the right, below the gable window.'

'And no one else here?'

'No. He was alone. And behaving like a lone man. You know. Pottering around. Tinkering with stuff.'

Abi shrugged. 'Crazy. Crazy to leave your door open. What is the man thinking of?'

The brothers made their way to the base of the stairs. Halfway up the staircase they stopped and listened once again, but the house was silent as the grave.

'The bastard doesn't even snore.'

'Perhaps he's not asleep?'

'At 2.30 in the morning? So why are his lights off?'

'Okay. Okay.' Vau stopped outside Sabir's bedroom door, one hand on the handle.

Abi stood a little away from him. Without a sound, he unhitched the telescopic fighting baton from his sleeve. Then he nodded.

Vau threw open the door.

Abi sprinted towards the bed, landing with his legs splayed, the full weight of his body concentrated on where he expected the sleeping man to be. 'Christ, Vau. There's nobody in here.'

'You're kidding?'

Abi disentangled himself from the bed covers and cracked on his torch. 'This bed's been slept in, though. It's still fucking warm. Go and check the bathroom. Then we'll do the rest of the house.' Already, without knowing why, Abi was getting the sense that the house was deserted.

'He's not in the bathroom either.'

'Are you sure you didn't see a car leave while I was sleeping? Are you sure he didn't see us?'

'Hell, Abi. Of course he didn't. I would have told you. His car is still in the garage.'

'Maybe he went for a walk? Maybe he creeps across the boundary fence every night and porks the next-door-neighbour's wife?'

Vau shook his head. 'No. I watched him prepare for bed. I even used the binoculars to make sure it was him. The curtains were wide open all the time. The man doesn't seem to give a damn that anyone who wants to can look in on him.'

'Let's check downstairs, then. Perhaps he's got a study? Or maybe a dressing room with a spare bed in it?'

Vau made a face. 'Dressing rooms like that are for men who want a break from their wives. Like Monsieur, our father, remember? Sabir hasn't got a wife. He lives alone.'

Ten minutes of frenetic searching convinced the brothers that Sabir wasn't anywhere in the house.

Abi threw his head back and exhaled through his cheeks. 'Right. Let's do something constructive. Let's find if he's written anything down. At least that way we won't leave empty-handed.'

'What are we going to do then?'

'Burn the place down. That'll bring him running.'

5

—

Sabir had almost succeeded in dozing off when he saw the study lights go on in the main house. For a split second he refused to believe his eyes. Then he eased himself out of the hammock and stood, still rocking with tiredness, on the extreme edge of the lawn and just beyond the arc thrown by the lights.

His house was being burgled. That much was clear. At first the thought caused him some bemusement. What was he going to do? Who was he going to call? His cell phone was up in his bedroom, and he was standing in his back garden, in pyjamas and bare feet, on a chill and windy October night. I mean, how dumb can you get?

Weapons? He didn't have any. What an idiot. He didn't even have a pair of carpet slippers to hit the burglars with. And he couldn't see himself bearding potentially armed men with a garden rake.

He was just beginning to move away from the house and towards Main Street when some instinct stopped him in his tracks. Perhaps it was the memory of another night, five months before, when he had huddled down behind a sand dune in the Camargue and watched a similar house, once again in total darkness save for the opalescent glow from a fragile circle of candles.

That time, the candlelight had been outlining the hooded figure of his blood sister, Yola Samana, as she teetered precariously on a three-legged stool with a noose around her neck, whilst a dispassionate Achor Bale sat in the invisible shadows and watched her as he might have watched a staked-out lamb during a midnight tiger hunt.

Either way, the sudden unwanted echo of the recent past was enough to make Sabir pause in his flight and rethink his position. He edged back towards the summer house wall, hissing nervously through his teeth. He could clearly see the shadows of two men reflected off the ceiling of his study. Burglars? The heck with that. Burglars didn't walk around their victim's house switching on the electric lights. CIA? FBI? IRS? Who the hell else gave themselves the right to come visiting honest citizens in the middle of the night?

With a sudden, intense conviction, Sabir knew exactly who the men were, what they were looking for, and why they were looking for it.

It was at this point that he remembered his father's old shotgun. Ever since his childhood it had been kept in the understairs wine cellar, hanging upside down by its trigger guard on a meat hook. Sabir hadn't moved a thing in the house since his father's death three years before – there had never seemed any point. So if the trigger guard hadn't rusted away in the interim, the shotgun would presumably still be there.

Sabir's sudden focus on the shotgun and on the sanctity of his family home served to pull him together and renew his courage. If these men came from the Countess, as he suspected they did, he had no choice but to confront them. They were his problem and his problem alone. He was damned if he would scuttle off down Main Street in his pyjamas at three o'clock in the morning and go wake up his neighbours.

Sabir had one ace up his sleeve, however. He knew from his time as a journalist on the *New England Courier* that Massachusetts had draconian burglary laws – armed burglary carried a minimum fifteen-year jail term, and even unarmed breaking and entering could fetch you five. And he was willing to bet that whoever the Countess had sent would have come armed.

As he headed for the cellar he began to rehearse in his mind just how the thing might conceivably play out.

6
–

Vau straightened up from his perusal of Sabir's study and turned towards his elder brother. 'Sabir must keep everything locked away in his head. There's nothing of any interest in here.'

'Did you really think there would be?'

Vau shrugged. 'To tell you the truth, I didn't think anything. As far as I'm concerned, we just came here to revenge ourselves on Rocha's killer.'

'Ever the foot soldier, never the captain, right?'

'You can laugh at me all you want, Abi. But I know where I stand in the general scheme of things. I'm grateful to Madame, our mother, and to Monsieur, our father, for adopting me. I'm grateful for the title I've inherited, and even more grateful for the money that goes with it. Cleverer people than me can work out strategies and interpret prophecies and delay the coming of Armageddon – or whatever the hell it is we're meant to be doing. Me, I just obey orders.'

Abi sprawled back against Sabir's desk, his arms spread to support his weight. He looked his brother up and down, a smile playing at the corners of his mouth. 'I suppose you're going to tell me now that you're a happy and contented man?'

'Happy? Contented? I don't know about that. But there's one thing I do know.' Vau hesitated briefly, as if gathering his thoughts together after a long hiatus. 'I'm going to confess something to you, Abi. Something that you may not give a damn about. But I'm going to tell you nonetheless.'

Abi cocked his head to one side encouragingly. He was clearly enjoying himself.

Vau snorted in a lungful of air, as if he was readying himself for a hundred-metre free-dive. 'You are the only person I truly care about in this world, Abi. The only one. And that's not because you're anything special – don't ever think that. But because we're viscerally linked. You're my twin. We were even connected together, or so they tell me, when we were born. Plus you're brighter than me, Abi, I give you that. And quicker. But you won't ever find anyone else truer to you than me, if you were to search for a thousand years.'

'The master of the nonsequitur strikes again.' Abi mimicked being squashed up against a wall by an unwanted admirer. Then his face became more serious.

'Why are you telling me this, Vau? And why here?'

'Because I worry about you, Abi. I think you're beginning to like all this too much. I think you're really beginning to believe that you're something special – something over and above the norm. That moral laws don't apply to you any longer. You're becoming like Rocha, in other words. You're becoming a freak. I mean look at us. We're standing here in a foreign country, in someone else's house – a house that we're on the verge of torching, for pity's sake – lit up like fucking Christmas trees. And you seem to think it's all fine. That there's something normal about this.'

Abi made a full circle on the spot – widdershins – his hands flapping in mock veneration like a cartoon guru. 'But it is normal, Vau. Can't you see the beauty of it?'

'Beauty?'

'Yes, beauty. Let me lay it out for you, *pendejo*. Let me read you a lesson from the Good News Bible.' Abi mimicked flicking open the pages of a book. 'Monsieur, our father's, distant ancestors were given a holy gage by France's greatest and most venerated king – a king the Vatican later turned into a saint by popular acclamation. This gage was to protect the French realm from the Devil. So far so simple, no? But the gage wasn't designed to stop with the king's death. No. It continues on to this day.'

'According to who?'

Abi sighed condescendingly. 'According to you and me. The fact that the rest of society is out of step with us – that France is no longer a monarchy – that none of these atheistical idiots believe in the Devil any more – all that is entirely irrelevant.' Abi was grinning. 'It's the others that are the freaks. The people who refuse to act. The walking fucking victims. The sorts of people who have never moved across into no-man's-land and plundered somebody else's herd.' Abi pointed at his brother. 'We're the hunters, Vau – you and I. And they are our prey. We've been set free thanks to St Louis's edict. That's all the moral justification we'll ever need. Now bust that chair up and stack it over here. We need to get a blaze going.'

Sabir had heard enough. Ammo or no ammo, he wasn't about to allow these maniacs to set fire to his father's house.

He had scrabbled in vain through the wine cellar for the remotest sign of a box of cartridges. The shotgun had been in place, though, just as he remembered it. If he wanted to save his family home from destruction, he would simply have to use the empty weapon as a deterrent. The two of them couldn't exactly stare down the barrels and check to see if they were loaded, now, could they?

He kicked open the study door and brought the shotgun up to bear. He had understood the men to be twins from their conversation, but he was still unprepared for the uncanny resemblance between the two of them. It was like staring into the shards of a shattered mirror.

The one called Vau was already in the process of levering off the semi-circular back of his father's favourite library chair.

'Drop that chair. You're not setting fire to anything.' Sabir kept his back firmly against the door. He had privately decided that if either of the men made an aggressive move towards him, he would simply throw the shotgun at them, turn on his heels, and leg it as fast as possible out of the house.

Both men froze in place. The one called Abi was the first to relax and acknowledge him.

'I suppose you expect us to put our hands up? To go and stand over by the wall, like they do in the movies?'

'I want you to lie down on the ground. Then I want you to unhitch your belts, and push your trousers down around your ankles.'

'Christ, Vau. The guy's gay.'

'Just do it. From this range, I can cut you both in half without even needing to switch barrels.' Adam Sabir raised the shotgun and aimed it directly at Abi's head. It was becoming increasingly obvious which of the two was in charge.

The twins dropped slowly to their knees. Making a show of their reluctance, they unbuckled their belts, pushed their trousers down, and stretched out on the floor. 'What are you going to do now, Sabir? Rape us?'

'The cons at Cedar Junction can do that. In fifteen years' time you'll be able to write a book about your experiences. It'll be a sure-fire bestseller. You can call it *Shafted By The Penal System*.'

'You hear that, Vau? This guy's got a sense of humour. I suppose this means you're going to call in the cops?'

'What do you think?'

'Look. We only came here for information. We're not even armed. If you give us what we want, we'll leave you in peace.'

'You've got to be joking.'

'At least tell us who warned you we were coming? Because somebody warned you. There's no way you just happened to be out of your room and in possession of a shotgun the exact moment we came by.'

Sabir hesitated. Now that the twins were safely down on the ground, he wasn't sure how best to finagle himself out of the situation he found himself in. 'Nobody warned me.' He edged further into the room and sidestepped towards the telephone.

'Bullshit. We saw you go to bed. We've been watching this place for the past twelve hours. Somebody warned you.' Abi turned towards his brother. 'Hey, Vau. I know who it was. It was that pig of an ex-policeman. The one who kidnapped Lamia. The one Madame, our mother, says tried to bug our meeting and failed. But how did he know we were coming over here?'

Vau met his brother's gaze. Then he looked away.

'It was that bitch of a sister of ours, wasn't it? I should have killed her when I had the chance.' Abi got up off the floor. He pulled his trousers up and tightened his belt as though Sabir were no longer in the room. 'Get up, Vau. I've got all the information I need. This bastard's not going to shoot us in a month of Sundays. He hasn't got the balls for it. And I'm not waiting patiently here with my trousers around my ankles while he summons up enough courage to call the cops.'

'Don't move another step, de Bale.'

'Go fuck yourself, Sabir.' Abi sidestepped towards the door. 'You saved your house. Be satisfied with that. Shame, though. I enjoy a good blaze. But it'll have to wait for another day. We'll take a rain check on this one.'

Sabir stood with the gun still trained on Abi. He couldn't think what else to do.

Vau went to join his brother at the door.

'Look. Now you can get both of us again with just one barrel. But you'd have a hard time explaining it away, wouldn't you? And you'd have an unpleasant bit of rearranging to do before the cops got here. That sort of thing takes a cooler head than yours.'

'What are you talking about?'

'What do you think? The back door was open. You even let us in yourself. No sign of breaking and entering anywhere. And as you can see, we aren't armed.' Abi had slipped the fighting baton back inside his sleeve ten minutes before, after finding the bedroom empty. 'No. What really happened was we travelled all the way out here to the United States just in order to forgive you for our brother's death. To reach closure on it for our family. The Yanks love all that psycho stuff. But you turned crazy, like your mother, and threatened us with a shotgun. Just think how that would play out in a court of law – especially as it's common knowledge that you were suspected of murder, and on the run from the French police, just five short months ago. Cops have long memories, Sabir. Shit sticks. And there's no stink without shit.'

Sabir snatched at the telephone. What else was there to do? Pull the trigger on an empty chamber? If there'd been any slugs in his shotgun he might have let them have it, if only for the crack about his mother. But as things stood, he could only watch them back out of the door while his finger tapped out three random numbers on the telephone keypad.

As soon as the twins were downstairs and he heard the back door safely slam, Sabir pressed down on the receiver button, cancelling the call.

He wouldn't be calling any cops on this particular watch.

7

Sabir stood at his bedroom window and watched the twins get into their car, fire up the engine, and roar away from the kerbside with predictably screaming tyres.

He turned around and tossed the useless shotgun onto his bed. Then he lay down beside it and closed his eyes. God, if he could only sleep. Instead he lay awake, the adrenalin rush triggered by the implicit violence of the last fifteen minutes slowly leaching out of his system.

One thing he knew for certain. From now on his house would be as good as dead to him. That much was obvious even to an imbecile. Maintaining a fixed station like this, with Achor Bale's twin brothers on his trail, would make him more than merely vulnerable. It would confirm him as suicidal.

No. The only thing for it was to get on the road and keep moving, taking any information he needed with him in his head. Curiously, the thought of going on the run again didn't worry Sabir overmuch. In his mind he was a thousand miles away from Stockbridge already.

Much to his surprise, his investigation of the 52 lost Nostradamus quatrains had moved on by leaps and bounds in the past few weeks, to the extent that he was becoming increasingly eager to test out his new theories in the field. Maybe, just maybe, he could squeeze a book's worth of material out of the thing without giving anything crucial away.

Sabir realized that only by publishing a rigorously expurgated version of the prophecies – with his own tentative suggestions as to their significance – could he protect both himself and the future of Alexi and Yola's unborn child. He would, in effect, be conducting a damage limitation exercise in expedient disinformation.

When Captain Joris Calque of France's Police Nationale had visited him in hospital all those months ago, the man had not come bearing a punnet of grapes. He had come on a fishing expedition for reasons as to why the Countess's eldest son, Achor Bale, had been pursuing Sabir and his two Gypsy friends, Alexi Dufontaine and Yola Samana, halfway across France with such a murderous and single-minded intensity.

At first, Sabir had refused to enlighten him. Then Calque had reminded him of the sacrifices made by his late assistant, Paul Macron, and by the seriously injured Sergeant Spola in an effort to keep Sabir and his friends alive. Sabir had been forced to acknowledge that Calque had played fair by both him and by Yola and Alexi. At least according to his lights.

Reluctantly, he had taken pity on the man. He had begun by explaining how he believed that Nostradamus's 52 lost quatrains constituted a 52-year rundown towards the date of a possible Armageddon. And that in his opinion the 52-year cycle had begun in 1960, leading to a possible end date circa 2012. And that this end date corresponded as near as dammit to the Mayan Great Change, which was predicted, according to the Maya Long Count Calendar, to occur on 21 December of that same year.

He had gone on to explain how each quatrain in the cycle appeared to point towards the events in just one specific run-up year. The list, in its entirety, covered the first French nuclear test in Algeria, the serial end of the French and British Empires, the Berlin Wall, Yuri Gagarin's trip into space, the Kennedy brothers' assassinations, the Chinese Cultural Revolution, the Arab/Israeli Six Day War, the US Defeat in Vietnam, the Cambodian Genocide, the Mexico City Earthquake, the First and Second Gulf Wars, the 9/11 Twin Towers Disaster, the New Orleans Floods and the Indian Ocean Tsunami.

According to Sabir's theory of Nostradamus's intentions, as each event unfolded just as the seer had predicted, the exact end date of the cycle would, in consequence, became ever more firmly fixed in people's minds. This would then enable the world's population to come to terms with what awaited them and – if at all possible – do something about it. This part of Nostradamus's master plan had not worked out quite as the seer intended.

Instead of being one amongst millions in on the secret, Sabir was now the only man on earth who knew that the prophecy earmarked for the present year purported to describe the location of a new visionary who would either confirm or deny the End Date – a person capable, like Nostradamus, of seeing into the future and channelling the information found there. Only this person could tell the world what awaited it – regeneration or apocalypse.

The final-but-one prophecy in the 52-year cycle went on to describe the birth and identity of the Second Coming and his symbolic role against the Antichrist. It described how the knowledge of the birth of the Second Coming would dilute the Antichrist's power, and make him vulnerable. And how this knowledge would gather together both believers and non-believers in a tidal wave of righteousness combating the forces of evil.

This information Sabir kept rigorously to himself. There clearly had to be a reason why Nostradamus had given his prophecies to the Gypsies for safekeeping, and that reason was that the Second Coming, ergo the *Parousia*, was due to be born of the direct line of the guardians of the prophecies.

This child was now on the way, and Yola, Sabir's blood sister, was to be its mother. She had conceived the child on the beach at Cargèse, in Corsica, after her notional – although entirely voluntary – kidnap by her long-time sweetheart, Alexi Dufontaine. Yola had confided to Sabir that she had conceived the child at the exact moment she lost her virginity, just as a flight of ducks had cast their shadow over the mating couple. Later, after Alexi had symbolically plucked out her eyes – Yola had used the Gypsy euphemism for female sexual ecstasy when describing the event – a male dog had run up to her on the beach and had licked her hand. This was how she knew their child would be a son.

More than four centuries before, Nostradamus had given the Samana family the location and safekeeping of the prophecies precisely in order to protect them from the prophecies' unintended consequences. The fact that the *Parousia* was to emerge from the most hated, reviled, and discriminated-against portion of the world population – people with no clear land of their own, and no clear identity beyond that which they carried with them – would form a necessary part of the supranational healing process. The Gypsies were a nomadic people, shunned and sidelined by virtually all established cultures. Always the optimist, Nostradamus must have reckoned that if the world were ever to accept a saviour from amongst such a company, it must first – almost by definition – have learned the virtues of tolerance and inclusiveness.

Sabir shook his head in despair. It was clear that the world simply hadn't come that far yet. Forbearance and inclusiveness were as far off the agenda as they had been in Nostradamus's time. People paid lip service to ideas of colour-blindness, religious tolerance, and fair play, but if ever their own little bailiwicks were threatened, they very swiftly reverted to racial protectionism and national isolationism – 'strangers out' still seemed to be the motto *in extremis*. As a result of this, nothing on earth would ever get Sabir to divulge Yola's true identity and whereabouts, and through her, the identity of her unborn son. Not to Calque. Not to anybody.

The penultimate prophecy in the cycle went on to describe the Third Antichrist – a being who would, if nothing was done to prevent him, trigger 2012's final holocaust. That, too, needed to be kept secret.

But Sabir had to have something to sell to his publishers and the public at large. A suitable hook on which to hang his story. Or what old-time comedians would have called a shtick.

The safest bet seemed to consist of the narrative of his search for the unique visionary Nostradamus had spoken of in that year's prophecy. A person apparently so in tune with the matted web of time that they could disentangle its threads and read the future from them.

If this person existed then Sabir would find him. And to heck with the Countess, the Corpus Maleficus, and the de Bale twins.

8

Sabir straightened up from checking underneath his three-year-old Grand Cherokee. The garage had been locked tight. He didn't think there had been any way that the twins could have gained access to his vehicle.

Still, forewarned is forearmed. Both Achor Bale and the French police had used electronic tracker systems during their pursuit of Sabir and his friends in France. Sabir had never encountered such systems before that time, but he would certainly not overlook them again. He needed his car to get to the airport, and he needed that car to be clean. The last thing he wanted was for the twins to dog his trail all the way to Saudi Arabia.

He locked and alarmed the garage door behind him and trudged back towards the house. Since the events of the night before he had taken to carrying the shotgun with him wherever he went, trusting that his neighbours wouldn't think he was partly off his trolley, and call the cops. He'd worked out a possible cover story to deal with that eventuality – something about a rogue opossum that had been eating through his telephone wires – but he hadn't had cause to try it out on anyone yet, as none of the neighbouring householders appeared to have noticed his new, military-style incarnation.

Once inside the house he flung a few articles of clothing into a carryall, and gathered up his emergency reserve of travellers' cheques, his credit cards, his passport, and his cell phone charger. Then he stowed the shotgun back on its meat hook in the wine cellar, sealed the house as tightly as he was able, and started back towards the garage.

Halfway there he slowed down, ready to run again. A car was parked outside the garage door, completely blocking the entrance. There was no way on earth the gate could be swung up and over, as it was designed to be.

Sabir looked swiftly behind him. Surely they wouldn't come at him here, out in the open?

The driver's door of the car opened, and a familiar face appeared over the lip of the roof-rack.

Sabir dropped his carryall. 'Captain Calque. Jesus H. Christ. You almost gave me a heart attack. I thought it was the twins again. What the heck are you doing here?'

'The twins?' Calque stepped away from the car, his facial expression taking on a new urgency. 'The twins have been here already? And you are still alive?'

Sabir flashed Calque a look. 'As luck would have it.' He picked up his carryall and continued walking. He glanced inside Calque's car. It was empty. 'This an official visit of some sort? Tidying up loose ends?' Sabir was trying hard to make his voice casual. He didn't want Calque interfering in his plans. Muddying the waters. Queering his pitch for the new book.

Calque allowed his gaze to play up and down the road. He, too, was now busy playing a part. 'No. I took early retirement. I was invalided out of the service. I'm working on my own time now.'

'You? Invalided out? That surprises me. I'd have thought they'd have had to tie you to a stretcher and wheel you out of your office in a straitjacket before that ever happened.' Sabir cocked his head to one side. 'What are you doing here, anyway? Are you on vacation? Come to see the fall colours, perhaps? And so you just dropped by to see me for old times' sake?' He hesitated, frowning. 'Christ, Calque, you're not really a leaf peeper, are you?'

Calque shook his head. The sarcastic undertones in Sabir's voice were unmistakable. He realized he'd have to cut straight to the chase or risk losing him. 'No. I'm not a leaf peeper, as you so charmingly put it. I came out here to warn you, Sabir. About the twins. And there didn't seem to be any other way to do it except in person. I assumed, you see, that you would prefer I didn't contact you through the local constabulary.' Despite his best efforts, Calque had shifted back into police mode again. 'Why don't you leave your damned telephone switched on, man? And why don't you answer your messages? You must have a death wish.'

Sabir gave a non-committal shrug. Privately, he was more than a little taken aback by Calque's tone. 'It's a long story. Basically, I can't sleep at night. So during the day I leave everything switched off so that if I do manage to drop off to sleep, the fucking telephone won't fucking wake me up.' He hesitated. 'If this isn't an official visit, Captain, what is it? And how come you already know about the twins?'

Calque chucked his chin in the direction of his car. 'Get in and I'll tell you.'

9

'The White Horse Inn? You're staying at the White Horse Inn?'

'Why is that so strange?' Calque was concentrating on his driving – he was clearly unused to a manual gear change.

'Don't you realize you'll be paying fall rates?'

'Fall rates? What are those?'

'Christ, Calque. Didn't you hear anything I said to you back there in front of the garage? It's when the inns and guest houses pump up their prices for the leaf peepers coming in to see the fall colours. You pay maybe 75 per cent over the usual odds.'

Calque shrugged. 'It was not my idea. It was that of my companion.'

'Your companion? You've come out here with a girlfriend?'

'In a manner of speaking. Yes.'

Sabir shook his head. He screwed himself nervously around in his seat.

'It's all right, Sabir. We aren't being followed.'

'You're sure of that?'

'I'm a professional. I've been watching all the way. Anyway, it doesn't matter. We'll stick to the public rooms. We just need to talk, that's all.'

The two men got out of Calque's car. The ride to the inn hadn't taken them more than eight minutes *in toto*.

Sabir nodded to the desk clerk as they walked through the lobby.

'They know you here, then?'

'Calque, I've lived here all my life. I was born maybe three miles down the road.'

'It's nice to belong someplace.' Calque's attention was somewhere else, however. He had seen Lamia seated on one of the lobby sofas, near to an open fire. 'Come with me. I want you to meet someone.'

When he first caught sight of Lamia's face Sabir flinched backwards, as though he'd inadvertently stumbled into an electric fence.

Calque turned towards him, shocked. 'You two already know each other?'

Lamia was staring down at the floor. She was clearly mortified by Sabir's reaction to her.

Sabir took a deep breath. 'No. No. We've never met. I'm sorry. It was a bit of a shock.'

Lamia looked up. The undamaged part of her face was still flushed from the effect of Sabir's reaction. 'I know I'm not pretty to look at, Mr Sabir. But few people respond to me in quite the way you did.'

Sabir could feel Calque's critical gaze eating through the small of his back. 'It's not your face. Please don't think that.'

'Then what is it?'

Sabir shook his head. 'I've seen you in a dream. I know it sounds crazy. But it's true.'

'I'm sorry?'

Sabir turned entreatingly towards Calque. 'Maybe the Captain hasn't explained to you what happened to me earlier this summer? There's no reason why, I suppose.'

With a downward thrust of his arm, Calque indicated that Sabir should sit. He was glaring at Sabir as though, given half the chance, he would gladly have smashed one of the hotel chairs over his head. 'May I introduce Lamia de Bale? Adam Sabir.'

Sabir didn't sit down. He simply stood and stared down at Calque. 'De Bale? She's one of the de Bales? Jesus Christ, Calque. Are you out of your mind?'

Calque made another sharp movement with his hand. 'Do I look as though I am out of my mind? Do I look as though I am subject to sudden sharp rushes of blood to my brain? Mademoiselle de Bale has been of extraordinary service to me in recent days. She has, as it were, fallen foul of the rest of her family. Her life, like yours, is in imminent danger. So please sit down and make a pretence, at least, of being civilized.'

Sabir dropped onto the chair behind him. He couldn't take his eyes off Lamia's face. 'I'm sorry. I've heard of you. Heard your name mentioned. I know who you are now.'

Lamia let an embarrassed hand flutter in front of her cheek. 'Well that's all right then. Would you like me to veil myself, perhaps? Like a Muslim woman? Then you wouldn't have to stare at me quite so hard.'

Sabir shook his head violently. 'I'm sorry. Desperately sorry. But it's not what you're thinking. Ever since early this summer – ever since I was involved with your brother . . .'

'Ever since you killed my brother, you mean?'

Sabir glanced away. To a third party it might have looked as though he were searching for an elusive waiter. But Sabir was merely trying to regain his sang-froid. To stop the sudden rush of panic that threatened to overwhelm him. To regain some measure of control over the still visceral memories of what Bale had done to him.

He turned back and met Lamia's gaze full on. 'Ever since I killed your brother, yes. That's technically true. I did kill him. If I hadn't killed him, he would have killed me. Where I come from that's called justifiable homicide, Mademoiselle de Bale.'

'My name is Lamia, not Mademoiselle de Bale. And believe me, Mr Sabir, I don't blame you in any way at all for killing my stepbrother. He was a rabid dog. And I hated him for it.'

Sabir felt as if he were floundering in an unfamiliar ocean, far out of his depth, in a rapidly encroaching riptide. 'I'm sorry. Really sorry that it had to end that way.'

'I am not.'

Sabir stared desperately at Calque. He no longer had the remotest idea what was expected of him. Or why Calque had brought him into this mess.

'Your dream. You were telling us of your dream, Sabir.'

Sabir tried to gather himself together. 'Yes. Yes I was.' The words came out explosively, like a sneeze. 'Ever since I was in the cellar. Or in the cesspit rather. Ever since I thought that I would suffocate to death, in other words, I have been having these dreams. Well, they're nightmares, really. In which I'm quite literally torn apart.' Sabir's voice trailed off. He was making no sense and he knew it. 'And then my head is eaten by a snake. Then I become the snake.' He had begun to sweat. 'It's crazy. I really can't describe it. But I have them pretty much every night. They're so bad I can't sleep. That's how come your twin brothers didn't get me when they broke into my house last night. I get claustrophobic – so most every night I check out of the main house and go over to sleep in the summer house. It's open out there. I can see the sky. I can breathe.'

'You mean they entered the house when you were already outside? In the garden hut?'

'Yes. Crazy, isn't it? I even left the back door unlocked. Later, when they switched on a light, thinking I wasn't anywhere about, I managed to get the drop on them with my father's empty shotgun.'

'You managed to get the drop on them? With an empty shotgun?' Calque seemed to be having difficulty conjuring up a sufficiently lurid image of the event. 'You held up the de Bale twins with an empty shotgun?'

'You see, no one can tell whether a shotgun is empty or not. It's not like a revolver, where you can see the shells. Or lack of them.'

'I understand the constitution of a shotgun, Sabir.'

'Well, anyway, as part of this dream I see a woman. She has her back to me. You've got to imagine that I'm the snake by now, and I'm approaching her. My mouth is hanging open. I'm going to take this woman's head in my mouth, just like the snake did with me. Then at the very last moment the woman turns around. And she has your face, Mademoiselle de Bale.'

'You mean exactly? With my birthmark? With my blemish?'

'Yes. She has a blemish, if that's what you want to call it, just like yours. At first I thought it was blood. All along, really, I've thought it was blood.'

'And now you realize it isn't?'

'Yes. Now I realize it isn't.' Sabir looked down. He understood only too well how badly he had hurt the woman. That he had damaged her in some invisible way. In his head, though, he was still torn between his horror that she was Achor Bale's sister, and his fascination that she seemed to have rejected the de Bale camp and joined the side of the angels – e.g. him and Calque.

'And what happens to this woman who looks so much like me? In your dream, I mean.'

Sabir closed his eyes. Then he opened them again and stared directly at Lamia. 'She opens her mouth – wider even than the snake was able to open its mouth – and she swallows me whole.'

10

'Saudi Arabia? You can't be serious?'

Sabir threw himself back in his chair. 'You bet I'm serious. I've looked into this every which way there is to look, and the quatrain seems to point directly there.'

'Would you be prepared to share your logic with us?' Twice, now, Calque had reached for his cigarettes, and then replaced them in his pocket after reproving glances from the inn staff.

Sabir glanced at Lamia.

She caught the glance, and made as if to stand up. 'Would you rather I left the room? I can fully understand if you still don't feel, despite Captain Calque's assurances, that I am an entirely trustworthy companion.'

Sabir waved her back down again. 'Stay right where you are.' He caught Calque's eye and shrugged. 'There's no way you could possibly know this, but before I got the drop on your brothers, I listened in on their private conversation. A full couple of minutes of it. And together with what they told me later, it soon became clear to me that they think you betrayed them, Mademoiselle de Bale. In fact they think that – via our friend Calque here – you warned me directly about their coming. And that, to put it mildly, they don't like you for it.'

'But she did.' Calque squirmed forward in his seat. 'That's exactly what she did do. She told me of her brothers' mission. In good time for me to warn you. If ever you'd bothered to pick up your phone, that is, or taken an interest in your messages.'

'*Touché*, Captain.'

'And I've not told you how I found her yet. What her family were about to do to her.'

'You don't need to. Her brothers' words were good enough for me. You can't fake attitudes like that. Mademoiselle de Bale is welcome to sit in on our conversation if she wants to.' Sabir was aware that part of him was endeavouring, via a studied politeness, to compensate the woman for his blundering faux pas about her face and the disturbing content of his dream. Another part of him recognized that Calque had obviously committed himself to her in some way – heck, didn't he have an errant daughter hidden away somewhere? Maybe she reminded him of her? – and that he still owed Calque.

'Why did you let the twins get away? They were in your house illegally. Why didn't you simply call the police?'

Sabir shook his head. 'They were playing with me. They knew I wouldn't shoot. They brazened it out, making it clear there'd been no breaking and entering of any sort. That I didn't have a leg to stand on in terms of the cops. Then, when they'd worked out to their satisfaction how I'd managed to avoid their little trap, they left.'

'You let them leave? Just like that?'

'What was I going to do, Calque? Toss the shotgun at them? If you ask me, they're holding fire until they can corner me somewhere private and wring out everything I know. When I haven't got a shotgun in my hand, maybe.' Sabir shrugged. 'Things might pan out a little differently that time.'

11

'Sabir was warned, Madame. I'm certain of it. The American knew we were coming. He was hiding outside the house with a shotgun. When we switched on the lights, thinking he was no longer there, he knew exactly where to find us.'

'You think Lamia warned him? Through Calque?'

'I'm convinced of it.'

'Why didn't he involve the police, then?'

'He was scared to, Madame. We had entered his house through an open door – he slipped up on that one. Given that fact, and the existing relationship between our two families, he would have been hard put to accuse us of robbery. I think we can call this first round something of a stalemate.'

'What are you going to do now, Abiger?'

'We've flushed him out, Madame. He will go on the run now. We must follow him.'

'Have you tagged his car?'

'Impossible, Madame. He has it sealed up tight. And the garage is alarmed. When he leaves, he will leave fast.'

'And Lamia?'

'She is here with the policeman. They are all three sitting in the public rooms of the White Horse Inn. We can't even get close.'

'Will you be able to follow him?'

'Of course, Madame.'

'Abiger, you are talking arrant nonsense. Two men cannot follow a man twenty-four hours by twenty-four. It's an impossibility. And once you've lost him, he is lost for good. I am sending your brothers and sisters over to help you.'

'But, Madame—

'Be quiet, Abiger. I want to know exactly what he does, and why he is doing it. It's not enough simply to deal with him any more in the way we discussed previously. There's more involved. We've got Calque to deal with too. So all eleven of you will conduct a full surveillance on the three of them – if they split up, all well and good. If they stay together, even better. I want to know everything they do – everywhere they go. And I shall decide when it is the right moment for you to strike, Abiger, not you. Have I made myself clear?'

There was a brief hesitation.

'Have I made myself clear, Abiger?'

'Yes, Madame. But I'm still running this operation, aren't I? I'm still in charge?'

'Until I decide otherwise. Yes, Abiger. You are.'

12

At first, you were lucky. The travelling went well. A man taking chayotes down to Veracruz gave you a lift in his truck. Through Orizaba and Cordoba, as far as La Tinaja. He dropped you off there, and you stood on the Tierra Blanca road for three hours, hoping for another lift. But no one stopped. Everyone was going the other way. Towards the volcano. In order to see the free show, you supposed.

It was then you began walking. You had money for food, but not for buses. But there was no hurry. The volcano had done its worst. No one had been killed. A number of villages close to the summit had been damaged, some by lava, some by dust, but the people had had ample time to evacuate, even when on foot. Now the State had promised to rebuild their homes. All this you had heard on the radio of the truck.

The State was indeed a powerful thing, you said to yourself. When things went badly, it was the State which put things right. You did not fully understand this, nor how the State functioned, but you suspected that its benevolence was, as it were, inbuilt. That things had always been like that.

You clutched the thin cotton bag that held the codex to your chest. You were hungry. In the excitement of the eruption, and of knowing that you had a job to do, you had forgotten to eat. Now you stopped at a roadside shack and bought some tacos. You ate half the tacos immediately, and secured the remaining ones in a piece of rough paper for later. You suspected that you might have to sleep out in the open, and for this you would need energy.

You drank some Coca Cola for your stomach, and because, amongst your people, it was sometimes offered as a gift in the church. Somewhere, far back in your mind, you wondered how you would manage to live when you reached your destination, and the little money you had was exhausted. You had never been outside your own province before. What if there was no one there to welcome you? What if you were not expected? Perhaps, then, you should ask the State for help? But you did not know how to contact the State, or how to communicate with it. Perhaps, being all-powerful, it would try to take the codex away from you? Which would leave you with no function. With no reason to live.

No. You must keep away from the State. Something would arise. Someone would recognize you. The protection of the codex had gone on for far too long, and for far too many generations, to mean nothing at all.

13

'Why are you doing this, Sabir? Why are you still sticking your neck out in this way? What's in it for you?'

Calque had an unlit cigarette dangling out of his mouth. He had come to a grudging understanding with the staff of the inn that he wouldn't, under any circumstances, actually light it, but simply suck on it for the taste of the tobacco. Lamia had had to do the translating for him, because Calque's mastery of the English language was marginally inferior to that of the average first-grader.

'But I thought you knew? I'm in it for the money.'

'Bullshit.'

'Look, Calque. You'd better get one thing straight. The only reason I responded to Samana's ad last May was because I thought there was a book's worth of material in it. I write books. And I live off the money I make from writing them. I've put nearly six months of work into this project already. It's cost me the ability to sleep for more than two hours at a stretch. It's cost me part of my ear. And it's turned me into a killer. Beyond that, I've been chased and intimidated and shot at, and an attempt has even been made to bury me alive. People have threatened to castrate me. I've had knives thrown at me. An effort has been made to burn down my house. The French police, in the guise of your good self, have even had me on their Most Wanted list. I think I'm entitled to some comeback after all that – some sort of a quid pro quo. And I am finally beginning to figure out a way to get it.'

'Saudi Arabia, you mean?'

'Listen. The prophecy talks of the eruption of a "Great Volcano". A man, "Ahau Inchal Kabah", lives in the country of this volcano. This man is capable of looking into the future. Through him, the world will know whether 21 December 2012 will bring the feared Armageddon, or the beginning of a major new spiritual era.'

'Why Saudi Arabia?'

'It sounds simple. But it's taken me weeks to work out. The key word is "Kabah". This obviously relates to the Kaaba, or the House of Allah – the most sacred site in Islam. I mean the spelling is pretty much exact, isn't it, give or take an extra a at the beginning and an h tacked on at the end? The Kaaba building is more than two thousand years old – meaning Nostradamus would certainly have known of it. And every Muslim, wherever they are in the world, turns towards the Kaaba when they pray. Next we have "Inchal". The Muslims traditionally call the Will of Allah, Insha'Allah – pretty close, wouldn't you say? With all that in hand, I went to check on what Nostradamus calls the "land of the Great Volcano". I immediately found another link to Saudi Arabia. I now believe the Great Volcano to be the 5,722-foot-high Harrat Rahat, which last erupted in 1256, its lava flow travelling to within three miles of the holy city of Medina. Many think that this volcano is the actual location of Mount Sinai. Exodus 19:18 describes it as "And Mount Sinai was altogether on a smoke, because the LORD descended upon it in fire: and the smoke thereof ascended as the smoke of a furnace, and the whole mount quaked greatly".'

Calque glanced across at Lamia. Then he turned to Sabir. 'Has this volcano erupted recently?'

Sabir made a face. 'Not in the last 950 years, no, it hasn't. I acknowledge that. But then some scholars think Mount Sinai is actually Mount Bedr – or Hala-'l Badr.'

'I suppose that one has erupted?'

Sabir was beginning to lose his temper. 'No. No, it hasn't. Not yet.'

'But you're living in expectation?'

'Well, Nostradamus can't be expected to get everything right, can he?'

'And the word "Ahau"? What about that?'

'I can't get a handle on that one. It doesn't seem to be an Arabic word at all.'

Calque glanced back at Lamia. 'Shall we tell him? Shall we enlighten our intrepid researcher? Who obviously doesn't bother to listen to the news, just as he doesn't bother to answer his telephone?'

Lamia returned Calque's look. 'Why tell him? We don't need him any more. Probably better that we let him swan off to Saudi Arabia, as he intends – that way he can draw my brothers after him, leaving us free to head down to Mexico unmolested.'

Sabir was looking from one to the other of them as if he suspected that he was the victim of some elaborate practical joke. 'Mexico? What are you people talking about?'

'Seriously, Sabir. Are you a complete technophobe? Have you really not listened to the news for the past few days?' Calque had chewed his existing cigarette into a pulpy mash. He snatched the opportunity to replace it with a fresh coffin nail.

The clerk behind the front desk did a quick double take, and then studiously avoided looking in Calque's direction, through fear, Sabir supposed, of triggering an embarrassing confrontation with his only non-English-speaking guest.

Sabir sensed that he was being set up for a fall – he remembered Calque's intellectual vanity from their last meeting, and did not relish a return performance. 'Who the heck are you calling a technophobe, Captain? I seem to recall your refusing to use a cell phone on more than one occasion, much to the frustration of your second-in-command.'

'My question remains the same.'

Sabir drew himself up. 'Okay. You're right. I haven't been following the news these past few days. I've been in a bad place in my head. And I've been working way too hard on my Saudi Arabia theory. I really don't see why you guys are so fired up about Mexico, though, just because "Ahau" is a Maya sun god. Anyway, that's Ahau-kin. Or Kinich Ahau, depending on context. You see. I've done my homework there too.'

Calque settled back in his chair, unlit cigarette dangling, a Cheshire Cat grin on his face. 'If you'd bothered to turn on your television set for just two minutes in the past twenty-four hours, you couldn't have avoided seeing that the Pico de Orizaba, otherwise known as the Volcán Citlaltépetl, has just erupted. We saw the news report on the plane coming over. I would say that that is your Great Volcano, not the Harrat Rahat or the Hala-'l Badr. Wouldn't you?'

'Popocatépetl and Iztaccihuatl are the two great volcanoes of Mexico. Everybody knows that. Why should this Orizaba hill transmogrify into the Great Volcano just because it's picked this particular moment in history to erupt?'

'Why?' Calque raised an eyebrow. 'Because it dwarfs the other two volcanoes, that's why. Orizaba is over 5,600 metres high – that's nearly 18,500 feet to you Yankees.

162

That makes it seven hundred feet higher than its nearest rival. And it *looks* like a volcano, man. It sits there, just like Mount Fuji, looking exactly like a great volcano should – I mean with a caldera, and snow on its peak, and a sneer on its face. Except that it's more than 6,000 feet higher than Mount Fuji, and it's a stratovolcano, just like Mount Mahon, Mount Vesuvius, and Stromboli. And it knocks your two Saudi Arabian volcanoes into a cocked hat.'

'All right, Calque. I'm impressed. You've earned your kewpie doll.'

'My what?'

'Forget it. It was just a turn of phrase. But you got one detail wrong, Calque. Mount Fuji's a stratovolcano too.' Sabir became aware that Lamia was glaring at him, as if the grilling he was undergoing constituted some sort of indefinable test. He instantly regretted the stratovolcano jibe. He'd been trying to score cheap points off Calque in an effort to cover up his embarrassment at being so spectacularly wrong-footed. And now Lamia knew about his insecurities as well. Well, there was nothing like a critical female audience to cement a man's public humiliation. 'What about Inchal and Kabah, then? What of them?'

Lamia stood up. 'Give me five minutes.' She walked across to the desk.

Sabir raised an eyebrow. 'What's that all about?'

Calque shrugged. 'Search me.' He mashed his latest unsmoked cigarette onto the tabletop in front of him and reached for another.

14

Lamia sat down beside the men. During her absence, Sabir had ordered coffee, and now she busied herself 'being mother', an elusive smile hovering about her face.

'Well who's going to be the first to ask, then?' Sabir was still feeling slightly sick that he might, at this very moment, have been jetting off towards Saudi Arabia, if Calque and Lamia hadn't happened by.

There was silence. Calque and Lamia sipped their coffee.

'Okay. I'll admit it. I ballsed-up. I was on the total wrong track. But I still don't get the "Inchal" bit. Or why "Kabah" doesn't apply to the Kaaba.'

Lamia glanced up. 'I've just been using the hotel's internet connection. I typed in "Kabah". With an h. Just as you tell us it's written in Nostradamus's prophecy. Number two on the list of Google hits, after the Kaaba, takes you straight to Kabáh, a Maya site down in the Yucatan. Kabáh means "strong hand", or, in its original form, Kabahaucan, a "royal snake in the hand". The place is famous for the Codz Poop – the Palace of the Masks – in which hundreds of stone masks dedicated to the long-nosed rain god, Chaac, stretch along a massive stone facade. Chaac, if you don't know it, is also the god of thunder, lightning, and rain, and he is considered capable of causing volcanic eruptions with his lightning axe.'

'Jesus.' Sabir had always known he possessed a single-track mind. But his recent inability to think laterally constituted something of a record, even for him.

'The word "Inchal" was harder. At first, I only came up with a place in India, with no link at all to the Maya.

In the end I decided to play around with it a little, and came up with "Chilan".'

'And what the heck is a Chilan when it's at home?'

'It's a Maya priest. The word actually means an "interpreter", a "mouthpiece", or a "soothsayer". The Chilans were responsible for teaching the sciences, appointing holy days, treating the sick, offering sacrifices, and acting as the oracles of the gods.'

'Holy shit.'

'And Chilans traditionally wore the "Ahau", which is the Maya sun belt. The word also means "Lord" in Maya. So Nostradamus's phrase "Ahau Inchal Kabah", and his insistence that this person, blessed with the ultimate gift of prophecy, lives in the land of the "Great Volcano", is so far from implying a place in Saudi Arabia, that it almost beggars belief how you could ever have allowed yourself to be so disastrously sidetracked, Mr Sabir.'

Sabir leaned forward and placed his head in his hands.

Calque squirmed deliriously in his seat. 'Don't tell me, Sabir. You haven't been sleeping recently. Your brain is not functioning to quite its usual standard.' The ex-policeman was enjoying himself. He was behaving as if he had somehow magicked Lamia out of his jacket pocket and presented her, in triumph, to a wildly applauding gallery.

'Don't rub it in, Calque. You're beginning to sound like Svengali.'

Calque glanced towards Lamia. 'What do you think? Shall we let him travel with us? Or shall we go it alone? We have all the material we need.'

'Oh really?' Sabir sat up straighter. 'You've got everything you need?'

Calque hesitated for a moment. 'Yes. I think we have.'

Lamia rolled her eyes.

'You've got the full text of Nostradamus's quatrain, have you? Including the key indicator of where to look for this man once you get to Kabáh?'

Calque fiddled with his unlit cigarette.

'Well you don't need me any more, then, do you?' Sabir stood up. 'But if you should happen to change your minds, you can probably catch me any time within the next half hour. My house. A silver Grand Cherokee. After that I'm gone. Out of here. *Capeesh*, wiseasses?'

15
—

Sabir didn't pull off his 'leaving in a snit' stunt. He was dealing, after all, with two companions to whom – due to either familial or professional habit – compromise was a *sine qua non*.

Whilst he refused point blank to cough up the key part of the quatrain that referred to the actual whereabouts of Nostradamus's Ahau Inchal Kabah, he did agree that the three of them might, at the very least, pool their resources and travel together. It had become blindingly clear to him, over the past few hours, that three minds were a heck of a lot better than one.

'I vote we fly down to Cancun, and then hire a car from there. That way we can be there in less than a day.'

Lamia and Calque exchanged glances.

'What is it? What am I missing this time?'

'You're missing my twin brothers.' Lamia glanced across at Calque.

Calque nodded his head in agreement. 'Airports are our worst bet. They're too easy to monitor. Flight plans and passenger lists are easily obtainable, if one has either the money or the connections. And Lamia's brothers have both. Plus these days most hire cars come with either satellite navigation systems or inbuilt trackers. Meaning that they can be followed, and their exact whereabouts pinpointed. Hire companies do it to protect their investments.'

'So what are you saying?'

'That we ought to go in your car. And that we ought to drive down.'

'Drive down? Jesus. Do you know how long that would take? It's better than three thousand miles. And I'm probably underestimating.'

'Are we in any hurry? Is there a deadline for this thing?'

Sabir shrugged. 'No. I suppose not.'

'And we will be three. To share the driving.'

Sabir nodded. 'There is that. But it sticks in my craw to base our plans on the probable antics of a couple of high-class hoodlums. Sorry, Lamia. But you know what I'm getting at, don't you?'

Calque intervened before Lamia had time to answer. 'Ever since I've known you, Sabir, you've manifested one fatal, but nevertheless entirely consistent, flaw. You've always underestimated your opponents. It's almost a sickness with you.' Sabir tried to break in, but Calque overrode him. 'I don't know anything about these boys beyond what Lamia has told me, but that's enough to give me pause. They are Achor Bale's brothers, in the name of God. They come from the same nursery. They've suckled at the same diabolical teat.' Calque was getting into his stride. 'Unlike Lamia, they have never had doubts

167

about their vocation. They know what they want, and they are prepared to do whatever it takes to get it. I spoke to the Countess two days ago. I was in her presence, Sabir. She is without doubt the most terrifying human being it has ever been my misfortune to meet. She's worse than any politician, in that she *knows* she's right – she doesn't just act out the role, she *is* the role. You killed her son, man. You alone have the information that she and the Corpus Maleficus seek. Take my word for it – the Countess is going to allow nothing, Sabir, but nothing, to get between her people and you.'

16

'Madame Mastigou has arranged the flight plans, Abiger. Your brothers and sisters will be arriving at New York's JFK airport in eight hours' time. They will each have a rental car at their individual disposal. You will keep in touch by cell phone. I will suggest to the others that they buy pay-as-you-go, to avoid any public record of their calls. They can contact you from the airport and you can exchange numbers. Then you and Vau must dump your old phones and buy new ones too.'

'What if our trio head north?'

'Then you will head north after them, and your brothers and sisters can catch up with you later.'

'You're assuming they are going to travel by car.'

'No I'm not. But if they're taking a plane, they won't

leave from a local airport. Calque's no fool. He knows that airports have gaping holes in them in terms of security. Sabir will try to shake you first. Then he'll aim for a hub airport with a lot of traffic. Somewhere like O'Hare, Baltimore, or Boston. Trusting that he can lose himself in the crowd.'

'Wouldn't it be better for us just to take them all here? Ambush them nearby? I can't see Sabir carrying his shotgun with him in the vehicle. Too risky. We could bundle them off to a deserted barn somewhere and sweat them for the information we need.'

'No. Sabir's been forewarned, thanks to your and Vau's mistake. He'll have covered his tracks already. Destroyed all written documentation. The man has a memory like an elephant, or so I understand from certain sources in America that I've paid for information about him.'

'Ah. I see.' His mother had wrong-footed him again. Abiger could feel the resentment eating away at his guts.

'In addition, I think it extremely unlikely that he will have told Lamia and Calque any more than he feels they need to know. So he's still our primary link to the whereabouts of the Second Coming. And to the possible identity of the Third Antichrist. The man carries it all about with him in his head. If he's backed into a corner he's perfectly capable of sacrificing himself for some perceived greater good – he's just that sort of bleeding heart. Remember what he did to my darling Rocha? The man's morbidly claustrophobic, but still he managed to figure out a way to get back at Rocha and kill him. He looks soft, but he has a core of steel. No, I'd rather he leads us inadvertently to wherever he is going. It's better like that.'

'If you say so, Madame.'

'I say so, Abiger.'

17

'Are they still behind us?'

'They're still behind us. And making no attempt whatsoever to hide themselves.'

The trio had just passed through Scranton, and were now on the thruway towards Harrisburg, heading south.

'What if we head towards Miami, and not towards Texas, as we decided? There must be a ferry of some sort from Florida to Campeche? Or to Veracruz? Or even to Cancun?' Calque was feeling irritable. He had come to a grudging understanding with Lamia and Sabir that every hour, on the hour, he could crack open a widow and smoke a cigarette. But he needed more than one cigarette an hour to feel like a human being. He glanced surreptitiously at his watch to see if his hour was up. 'It would save us three days' driving.'

'And it would set us up as sitting targets. While we move, we're safe.' Sabir glanced over his shoulder. 'Smoke your damned cigarette, Calque. You may not realize it, but you're kicking the back of my seat about eighty times a minute.'

'Oh, I'm sorry.' Calque speared the window button with his finger. 'I do get nervous when I'm thinking things through.' He lit his cigarette and inhaled deeply. 'And I'm thinking things through now.' He allowed the cigarette smoke to trickle luxuriously through his nostrils. 'So what are we going to do tonight?'

Sabir turned to Lamia. 'You tell me your brothers won't give up without a fight?'

'That's an understatement.'

'Then what do you think they are waiting for? Why are they holding back?'

'Just as you said. While we're moving, we're safe. But the minute we stop, we're vulnerable. And we're particularly vulnerable at night. I assume you don't intend to sleep in the car?'

'No. Of course not.'

'Then it seems we have only one choice.'

'And what is that?'

'We have to lose them before we bed down for the night.'

Sabir snorted.

'It's three in the afternoon. By nine o'clock this evening we'll be well beyond Harrisburg. If we don't intend to drive all night, we'll have to come up with a plan before that.'

'Great. Any ideas anyone?'

Calque had finished his cigarette. He threw the used butt out of the window. His face wore a placid expression, as if he had just taken a hit of raw opium, and not a toke or two of flue-cured Virginia tobacco. 'I have a plan.'

Sabir glanced in the rear-view mirror. The twins' car was keeping station a steady third of a mile behind them. 'Okay. Give.'

'Ah. Your elegant American expressions. How poorly they translate into French.'

Sabir understood what Calque meant. Translate most American expressions into French and they sounded abrupt – lacking in politeness. French was a language in which requests, and even orders, were customarily couched in velvet. Sabir decided to wind Calque up a bit. 'Esteemed Captain Calque. Mademoiselle Lamia and I would very much appreciate hearing your proposal to rid us of the unwanted attentions of Mademoiselle Lamia's mortiferous twin brothers. In addition, any light that you

171

may be able to shed on their possible future plans would be very welcome indeed. Suffice it to say . . .'

'Sabir?'

'Yes?'

'Shut up.'

There was an amused silence in the car while Calque gathered his wits about him. 'All right. I have my plan. I am ready to give it to you.'

'Excellent. What is it?'

'It involves taking three separate motel rooms. One for you. One for me. And one for Lamia.'

'And to heck with budgetary constraints?'

'Sabir, you are not endearing yourself to me by this levity.'

'I'm sorry.'

'We take three motel rooms. We enter them, leaving the car out front. But not for long. Soon I exit from my room and get into the car. I drive off. Now, because I am not important to them, the twins will continue watching the two remaining motel rooms. Sabir must then go and knock on Lamia's door. She must let him in. Her brothers will draw the obvious conclusions. Am I correct?'

'No. You are not correct.' Lamia was curled up on the front seat, her stockinged feet tucked beneath her. 'My brothers are fully aware that my love life is close to non-existent. They tease me endlessly about it, in that endearing way they have. The idea of my having an affair with Monsieur Sabir within a day of meeting him would strike them as so preposterous that they would probably come barging straight in simply out of curiosity.'

'Oh.' Calque seemed just a little nonplussed, as if one of his fondest illusions had just been shattered. 'You really have no love life to speak of? That is outrageous for such a beautiful woman as yourself. I cannot understand it. The men you encounter must be blind.'

Lamia reached behind herself and felt for his hand. Calque brought her fingers lightly to his lips.

'So what were you imagining for after Lamia came to my room? Beyond the fake sex, that is?'

'I was going to suggest that you both exit via a back window, leaving the lights still on and the door locked. With a 'Do Not Disturb' sign on the door handle. Then you both make your way to a pre-arranged rendezvous – a certain number of streets down, say – where I pick you up. Leaving the twins watching a series of empty motel rooms. We drive on for another hundred miles – on minor roads, of course – and only then do we stop for the night.'

Sabir looked at Lamia. 'Apart from the sex idea, it isn't bad. I like the bit about Calque taking off in the car, leaving both of us back at the motel. That makes sense. Why don't we both just climb out of our rooms independently, and forget Calque's Gallic notions of romance?'

'We'll have to find an old-school motel with through rooms.'

Sabir glanced across at Lamia. 'What do you mean, "through rooms"?'

'Rooms with back windows. Most modern motels aren't built like that any more. And they have central parking, anyway. We need an old-style motel, where you park right outside your room.'

Calque leaned forwards. 'We could do a tour around before we register? Check the layout of the grounds? That's not so strange, is it? No one would guess what we were looking for.'

'You know, I think it's worth a try.' Sabir glanced at Lamia. 'What do you think?'

'I think Captain Calque is what they used to call "a born gentleman".'

173

18

Abiger de Bale glanced at his watch. 'It's getting late. How far are the others away?'

Vaulderie consulted his cell phone. 'I have text messages from Athame, Berith, and Oni, saying they are heading in our direction. Our paths should cross within the next hour. The six others can't be far behind.'

'Good. Three is ample.'

'Why is that?'

'Because Sabir is going to try to slip the net before nightfall.'

'How do you work that one out, Abi?'

Abi shrugged. 'I should have thought it was obvious. Put yourself in their position. They can't reasonably bed down in security knowing that we are outside watching them. They will fear that we will damage their car. Or set a tracker on it. Maybe even break in on them. That's their weak spot.'

'They won't all be sleeping in the same room?'

'They'll be fools if they don't. And barricade the door to boot. Once they split themselves up and go independent, they are inevitably weaker. They can be picked off one by one.'

'So what do we do?'

'Nothing. We let them give us the slip.'

Vau sighed. 'I don't get it.'

Abi glanced across at his brother. 'By the time they settle in for the night, we will have at least four cars following them – three of which they won't recognize. So we two stay close up front. Make ourselves even more obvious than we have been doing. When they try whatever trick they eventually decide on to give us the slip, we let them think that they have got away with it. Athame, Berith, and Oni can position themselves on every road leading away from the motel. When Sabir drives past them in his beautifully visible Grand Cherokee, they will follow him, not us. They then tell us where they are going, and we join them. Only we'll have changed our car by then. With any luck, all nine of us will have met up by that point. We then take it in turns to follow them, jockeying positions every twenty minutes or so, so that they never get to see the same car twice. Madame, our mother, has made it clear that we are not to interfere with them in any way whatsoever until they have reached their final destination. If they take a plane, we follow them. If they continue by road, we follow them.'

'And what about Lamia? What if she recognizes us?'

'From now on everyone will wear baseball caps. Baseball caps and sunglasses. That way we'll look really American. Oni can pin his hair back under his cap and use some tanning cream – he'll look strange, but from a distance, he won't look like an albino.'

'And us?'

'We tag along behind. Way back. So that the three of them never have a chance to see us again. And we keep in touch with the others by cell phone.'

'Are you sure they're going to try and make a break for it, Abi? Are you certain?'

'Dead certain.'

19

Calque climbed back inside Sabir's Grand Cherokee. He spent a little time adjusting the driver's seat forwards and upwards to meet his requirements. Then he stared at the gear shift. It was manual. *Putain de merde*. He had a feel around to work out what trick Chrysler had engineered to protect their reverse gear from inadvertent triggering. When he was satisfied that he had mastered it, he backed the car carefully out of the parking lot.

Next time, he thought to himself, we must think ahead – place the car facing out. For a possible quick escape.

No sooner had he formulated the thought than he shook his head wildly to and fro. What am I thinking of? What am I doing? I could be in France now, having dinner at *La Reine Margot* – *cassoulet*, followed by cheese and a *tarte tatin*. Washed down with half a litre of *Brouilly* and a *café-calva* to follow. Instead, here I am sitting in a strange car, in the northern part of the United States, and all I have inside me is the distant memory of a Wendy's hamburger and so-called French fries, bought on the trot at a drive-thru so that we wouldn't be vulnerable for more than six static minutes to the attentions of Lamia's twin brothers.

Calque drifted onto the main drag. He looked neither to his right nor his left, counting on his peripheral vision to mark the twins' car and to warn him of the lights of any oncoming vehicles. Yes. There they were. Parked right across the road from the motel, where they could cover the way out and all three motel rooms from the same tactical spot. Calque told himself that the very next time that he and his friends stopped for the night they must definitely split themselves up in different geographical locations. That was the obvious answer.

He slapped the steering wheel in irritation. No. That wasn't the answer. That wasn't a clever idea at all. What they should really do is share a room. There was security in numbers. He wondered what Lamia and Sabir would think of that? Calque was aware that he was lamentably prone to snoring. His late assistant, Paul Macron, used to nudge him awake when they were in the car together, solving the problem like that. Maybe, now that no one was looking over his shoulder, he could buy himself a mask? Surely the Americans would have something on the market to deal with his problem? The last thing he wanted to do was to keep on reminding Lamia that he was in late middle-age, and more than a little out of condition. A man could rely on his wit and intelligence to captivate a woman during the day, but a little more finesse – not to mention *realpolitik* – was required, unfortunately, at night.

Not that Calque wished to seduce Lamia – far from it. She was thirty years his junior, and very nearly the same age as his daughter – the whole idea was grotesque. But it was clear that she needed protecting from Sabir's continual litany of gaffes. The man was as unaware of the effect of some of his statements as a six-year-old child. Take that nonsense at the White Horse Inn. No Frenchman would have blundered in like that and drawn attention to the catastrophic blemish on a woman's face in the first few moments of their acquaintance. No. It would take an American to promote such a faux pas.

Calque knew that Sabir had had a French mother, but he privately decided that she must have become Americanized very quickly indeed for a *rustre* such as Sabir to be the end product of her childhood educative influence. When it came down to it the man was as

177

American as apple pie. His maternal French blood was clearly little more than an accident of history.

When Calque finally emerged from his daydream, it was to the realization that the twins were not following him. They had remained on station at the motel, just as he had anticipated.

Calque consulted his watch. Yes, the time was right. He made a left, and then another, until he was on the road parallel to that on which the motel was situated. Then he counted four blocks off in his head, following which he hung another left. Yes. This was it. This was the road they had agreed on after consulting the town map kindly provided by the motel management. Lamia and Sabir would be leaving their motel rooms by the back window about now. He was to give them twenty minutes to make their way the four blocks that separated them from the car.

He let the engine run. Best be prepared. There was always the chance that the twins would intervene early. In that case he must be prepared to hurry back to the motel and do what he could to save the situation. Call the police if necessary. Interpose himself between the twins and their victims. He laid the cell phone he had borrowed from Lamia carefully on the seat beside him.

Then he shook his head. What was he thinking of? He had never been a scrapper or a scrimmager – he simply wasn't cut out for the rough stuff. In fact he found all physical exertion antipathetical in the extreme. Throughout the entire extent of his police career, Calque had never needed to unsheathe his pistol, far less use physical force on anybody. He had always had a plethora of willing – and more or less able – assistants for that.

Lancelot du Lac he was not.

20

'Whatever's going down is going down.' Vau touched Abi on the shoulder.

Abi, as usual, was taking his sleep where he could. Ever since they were children he had mastered the art of dozing off in the most extreme of circumstances. Once, even, he had fallen asleep in the midst of a burglary. It had been a test run, engineered by their mentor, Joly Arthault, at the instigation of Madame, their mother. Vau had looked around for his brother, only to find him curled up on a sofa in the corner of the living room of the house they were robbing. He had protected his brother's back on that occasion, too, just as he had done on a thousand other occasions during the course of their childhood and early adolescence.

The twins watched Calque get into the Grand Cherokee, adjust his seat, then back out towards them.

'Look at him, Vau. The bastard's pretending we don't even exist. His head's frozen in place. He didn't even check if there was any traffic coming. If we didn't know he was planning something, we'd sure as hell know now. Doesn't he realize that people who are plotting stuff should behave and act normally? Not like robots. You'd think a policeman would have a little more sense.'

'What would we have done? If we hadn't had back-up?'

'I'd have got out of the car and stayed here, and you'd have followed him.'

Vau nodded. 'Oh, I see. That way we could keep them all under surveillance.'

'That's it. But now we merely stay here and let him think his little plan is working. I've just heard from Rudra and Aldinach. So that means we now have five people in place to shepherd them through when they try to make their break for it.'

'What will they do? Climb out of the window?'

'Yes. You saw them checking the place out when they first arrived. They were making sure there was a potential rear exit. As we speak, they are probably bundling their belongings out the back, and dodging and ducking their way out of the rear car park. If I had a warped sense of humour, I'd be tempted to take a turn around the periphery of the motel, just out of spite. See two trails snaking out from underneath a car, and you'd know for certain they'd pissed themselves.'

21

Sabir dropped his carryall out of the window, and eased himself through after it. Then he waited for Lamia to do the same thing. He was tempted to reach forward and help her as she struggled out of the window, but something prevented him. He still felt raw about his initial blunder about her face, and he sensed that she was, unsurprisingly, not entirely comfortable with him yet.

'Please. Can you help me?'

Sabir hurried forward. He put one hand on the small of Lamia's back to steady her, and then half lifted, half carried her, away from the window. She touched the ground very lightly, almost as if she had flown out of his arms.

He glanced down at the ground, disturbed at the effect the close physical proximity to a woman was having on him. For the split second that he been carrying her, he had become more than a little aware of the swell of Lamia's hips, and the ultra-feminine contour of her buttocks beneath her thin cotton slacks. Now his eyes made their automatic tomcat journey back to her breasts. He could feel himself beginning to salivate. Jesus Christ. Who'd be a man? It was like being harnessed to an out-of-control lawnmower.

Lamia straightened up and smiled at him.

He felt the smile somewhere in the region of his back pocket. Women, he thought to himself. They always know just how to turn it on. It's a sort of inbuilt instinct. A 'look at me, I'm here' sort of instinct. He smiled back despite himself, more susceptible to the feminine than he cared to admit. 'Come on, we'd better get out of here before they cotton on to what we are doing.'

Sabir grabbed Lamia's bag alongside his own, and started to edge around the parked cars. Now I'm even carrying her bag, he said to himself. Fantastic. Like an on-the-make schoolboy carrying his girlfriend's schoolbooks.

They made their way to the outskirts of a nearby motor court, and ducked in between the parked cars.

'We'll cut through here, and then down a block, so that there's no chance at all of them seeing us. Then we cross three blocks over and up a block – Calque ought to be waiting for us.'

'My brothers aren't as stupid as you seem to think they are, Monsieur Sabir.'

'Adam. Please.'

'Adam.'

'I'm sure they're not, Lamia. But what are they going to do? If they haven't followed Calque, it means they're stuck waiting in front of the motel. If they've followed Calque, we aren't any the worse off than we were before.

181

It's six of one and half a dozen of the other.'

'I suppose so.'

'I know so.'

22

The hermaphrodite, Aldinach de Bale, was the first one to see the Grand Cherokee.

'I've got them. They're heading north out of town.'

'Then follow them.'

'It's already in process.'

Aldinach pulled into the stream of late-night traffic heading out of Carlisle, Pennsylvania. At the very last moment, the Grand Cherokee swung across the oncoming traffic flow, and switched its heading to south.

'They're heading south now. They've switched lanes on the highway.'

'For Christ's sake don't follow them. Oni's facing in the right direction. They can't help but come past him. He can pick them up from there. We must let them believe they've given us the slip. We want them relaxed and at ease.'

Aldinach continued on the way he was going. Only when he was a mile or so down the road, and well out of sight of the Grand Cherokee, did he switch lanes and head south too. He had a sudden, amusing picture in his head of one of those cable-channel helicopter camera shots of an endless trail of cars following the as yet unaware silver Grand Cherokee.

He wondered idly what sort of journey Sabir had in store for them. It looked like south. And Aldinach liked south. He liked the heat, and the opportunity to dress as a woman. In the north, he stuck to his masculine identity, because it seemed more appropriate. But in the south, he was very definitely a girl.

23

'That's it. We've lost them.' Calque was rather keen to pass the driving over to Sabir, but didn't quite know how to engineer it. He desperately needed a cigarette, and didn't fancy driving a monster like the Cherokee with only one hand on the steering wheel.

'Do you want me to take over the driving?'

Calque grinned. 'That would be excellent. Excellent. And do you think, now that we're finally clear of the twins, that we could stop somewhere for some real dinner? I don't know about you, but my stomach is reminding me every instant that it has not eaten since approximately two o'clock this afternoon.'

'Great. We'll stop at a Wendy's.'

'No!' It was almost a scream. A cold sweat had broken out on Calque's face. 'I'm sorry. I didn't mean to shout. But surely, if we park around the back, we could find a nice little family restaurant, serving local, homemade food.'

Sabir looked at Calque as if he had taken leave of his senses. 'It's eleven o'clock in the evening, Captain. And we're in the United States. People eat at seven o'clock here. You'll be lucky to find even a diner open at this hour of the night.'

'A diner. A diner, then.' Calque had a sudden mental image of a whole series of 1940s Hollywood films in which either Robert Mitchum or Humphrey Bogart sat in one of these so-called diners, eating homemade pie with coffee.

'Okay. A diner. But it'll still mean a burger and fries. You realize that?' Sabir understood Calque's recalcitrance only too well, but he had decided to enjoy himself a little at the Frenchman's expense. He hadn't entirely forgiven Calque for humiliating him in front of Lamia over the matter of her birthmark, and for being so damned cute with his theories on the land of the great volcano.

'A burger and fries? You cannot be serious? This is grotesque.'

'Don't worry, Calque. Things will pick up when we get to Mexico. You'll be able to last another three days or so on a typical US diet, won't you?'

Calque gave him a sickly grin. 'Three days? On burgers and fries? I might last, but my liver will not.'

24

At first you had a good run of it. Two lifts in as many hours. The first to Loma Bonita, in a feed truck, and the second as far as Isla Juan. Then the lifts dried up.

You slept that night in a roadside coffee plantation, under a banana tree. You wrapped yourself in your mother's *rebozo*, which you had brought along in the absence of any other form of portable sleeping cover. You kept your machete clasped tightly to your side, in case you encountered a rabid dog, a snake, a rat, or a black widow spider.

You slept well, despite the cold. In the early morning, when you woke up, you had no idea where you were, nor exactly how far it was to the Palace of the Masks. Someone you asked had told you six days. But then when you had asked them if that was by bus, or by car, or by horse, they were unable to answer you. All you knew was that you must head south – south all the time – keeping the coast always on your left. When you were near Campeche, then that would be the time to ask. Someone would doubtless point you in the right direction then.

You had grown up believing in a greater power – a power which you served, and which you therefore obeyed, as any servant should. This power would protect you if it chose, and it would allow you to die if that was its will. *Asi es la vida.* 'That is how life is.' Pointless to fight against it. Pointless to argue.

What you were doing now was at the behest of this power. Your family had been chosen to guard the codex. Your grandfather told you how the original guardians – the ones who had saved the codex from the vengeful ignorance of the Spanish priests – had ultimately paid the price with their lives. He had told you, too, of how his father had come by the codex from the hands of a dying man. How he had been forced to promise this man, upon pain of damnation, that he would protect the codex, and not give it up to the Spanish. Or else they would burn it, as they had with all the other great books of the Maya priests.

'But I am not Maya,' your great grandfather had said. 'I am part Totonaca and part Spanish. I understand nothing of this. We do not even believe in the same God as you.'

'There is only one God,' said the dying man. 'And everyone believes in Him. It is only the names that differ, and that cause strife.'

'But when must I take it? And to whom?'

'You, or your son, or your grandson, or even his son, must wait until the great volcano blooms once again with fire. That will be your signal. Then you must take the codex from this cave and travel south, to the Palace of the Masks. A sign will be given to you there.'

'But where is this palace?'

'In Kabáh. Near Campeche. I will draw you a map in my blood. This you will pass down alongside the codex. There is a sign on it. See? I have drawn it here. It will be recognized.'

Now you took out the map and laid it carefully on the earth in front of you. You had finished your remaining tacos long ago, and your stomach felt empty, as if a worm was gnawing away at it.

Sucking on a stone to conserve your saliva, you followed the line of dried blood with your finger. How far were you down the line now? One thumb? Two thumbs? If you were two thumbs down the line, as seemed most likely, then you had eight thumbs left to go. That meant another four nights on the road.

You reached inside your pocket and retrieved your small bag of pesos. You had many coins, but they were almost worthless. Some scrumpled notes. You straightened them out on the map. Three hundred pesos. Five 50s, two 20s, and a 10. It would simply have to be enough.

You leaned forwards and looked at the sign. It was a snake – yes – it had to be a snake. Its mouth was wide open, and it seemed to be swallowing the head of a man.

What sort of person would recognize such a thing?

For the very first time since you had begun your journey, you began to feel fear.

25

Sabir couldn't sleep. He glanced over towards Lamia's bed. Then towards Calque's. No sound. They were both fast asleep.

The three of them had finally decided that it was better not to split up and make themselves more vulnerable than absolutely necessary. Despite being the one to make the initial suggestion, Calque, for reasons best known to himself, had finished up looking the most uncomfortable with the arrangement, whilst Lamia, who might reasonably have objected to the idea of bundling with two grown men, appeared to have taken the whole thing in her stride.

Sabir had seen the sense of it too, but he had soon become worried that if he underwent another of his nightmares, as he did most nights, he might cry out, or throw himself off his portable camp bed, and thus wake everybody else up. He had allowed this thought to niggle at him for so long now, that he couldn't manage to doze off at all.

Eventually he got up and padded outside. He sat on the ledge of the walkway outside their room and leaned back against a pillar. The night was cold, but not oppressively so. He breathed in deeply, and then sat looking up at the night sky.

They'd been incredibly lucky to give the twins the slip back in Carlisle. Almost miraculously so. Sabir could imagine the twins at this very moment, checking out every motel within a fifty-mile radius of the town in the vain hope of picking them up again. But the trio had travelled more than a hundred miles further south this time, and had slipped off the main expressway toward Harper's Ferry in a further bid to muddy the waters.

They had then found themselves a down-at-heel motel run by a Punjabi family, who seemingly hadn't minded registering them at two o'clock in the morning, and neither had they objected to the fact that two mature men and a considerably younger woman wanted to share a room together. Perhaps such a thing was normal down here in West Virginia? The Punjabis had simply searched out an extra child's bed and had set it up for Sabir underneath the window.

The door behind him opened, and Lamia emerged, clutching a blanket around her shoulders.

Sabir straightened up. 'Hi. Can't you sleep either? Join the club.'

Lamia waved him back down again. She sat down beside him, and snuggled herself further inside her blanket. 'Calque has started snoring.'

'Oh.'

'It's really quite loud. Is he married, do you think?'

Sabir burst out laughing. 'Divorced, as far as I know. Maybe that's why?'

She made a face. 'I thought about nudging him, but then I realized I was so wide awake that it would simply guarantee that two of us would be deprived of sleep, and not just one. Then I saw that your bed was empty too.'

'Well you know all about me. I was scared I would wake up screaming, and start a riot.'

She laughed. 'Well. We're not doing too well so far, are we? As a team?'

'Oh, I don't know. We've lost your brothers. We're a few hundred miles closer to where we want to be, and we're amongst friends. Things could be a whole lot worse.'

Lamia glanced across at him. 'We've only lost my brothers for the time being. You realize that?'

Sabir nodded. 'Yes. I do realize that.'

'Somehow they'll find us.'

'At this particular moment I can't quite work out how. But I'm more than happy to work on that assumption. At least it will serve to keep us on our toes.'

Lamia began to relax, as if she had abruptly decided to disengage herself from an unwanted weight. 'Not much worries you, does it, Adam?'

Sabir shrugged. 'Not sleeping worries me. These nightmares worry me. Offending you worries me. But not much else.'

'What do you mean, offending me?'

Sabir turned towards her. 'When we met. What I said. How I said it. My drawing attention to your face. I didn't mean to do that. That was just dumb of me. Calque was right to call me a hick.'

'You're not a hick. I understood what had happened. Why you did it.'

'Then you're a better man than I am, Gunga Din.'

'What? What is that? What is Gunga Din?' Lamia was cocking her head to one side, like a bird dog, a half-smile on her face.

Sabir noticed, once again, just what a beautiful woman she was. Despite the blemish. Despite her awareness of it. There were moments, and this was one of them, when she seemed to forget all about her face and relate to him person to person, rather than as a wounded woman to a damaged man.

'It's a movie. Well, it's a poem, really, but everyone remembers the Hollywood movie they based on it. Cary Grant is an English colonial soldier, alongside Douglas Fairbanks Junior and Victor McLaglen. They're on the Indian Frontier, and they get involved in all sorts of shenanigans. Then, at the end, they are all going to die, and their water boy, the lowest of the low, who's called Gunga Din, saves them, at the cost of his own life. As Gunga Din lies dying, Cary Grant says this to him: "You're a better man than I am, Gunga Din." That bit comes straight from the Kipling poem.'

'You're a strange man. Do you love movies so much?'

Sabir shook his head. 'It's more than that. They're a passion with me. I guess I had what you might call a lonely childhood. No brothers and sisters. Intellectual father. Crazy mother. Movies and books were what I had in lieu of normal family affection. They defined my life. I could escape into them whenever I wanted. The only thing my father ever did with me was take me to the movies. He wasn't into baseball, or team sports, or anything like that. But every week, without fail, he would take me along to the Lenox Club for their movie matinee. The old guys that ran the matinee would wheel out a screen. Then they'd set up the old projector, with the giant 16mm reels. We'd watch *Henry V*, *The Charge of the Light Brigade*, *Captain Blood*, *Robin Hood*, *The Lives of a Bengal Lancer*. Heck, those old guys were more English than the English. If you looked closely enough, you could see their Harris Tweed coats steaming gently in the afternoon heat.'

'You're crazy. You know that, Adam?'

'What? Crazy for talking to you like this?'

She turned abruptly away. 'I didn't mean that.' Then she accorded him a compensatory glance. 'But crazy for doing what you are doing. For risking your life this way. You could be happily roosting back at your father's house, writing obscure books about the cinema. All you'd need to do would be to publicize what you found out in France. That way you would be safe.'

'Would I? Do you really think your family would believe me? Believe that I had published everything I know?'

'Why ever not?'

'Because they know I know things, Lamia. Things I can't tell anybody. Things that I can't publicize.' He suspected for a moment that she was going to ask him to dot the i's and cross the t's – use the unexpected intimacy that had sprung up between them to wheedle information out of him. A woman's curiosity, and all that twaddle. But she didn't.

Instead she stared him straight in the eyes. 'You want to take this all the way through to the end, don't you?'

He pretended to consider her question, but he already knew the answer. 'I've got no choice in the matter. These nightmares. They're something to do with it. But it's not only that. I'm changing, Lamia. Changing inside. I can't really describe it. But something happened to me down there in that cellar in the Camargue. Something that I still don't understand. I find myself drawn to things. Almost as if I had experienced them before, and now need to revisit them to fully understand their significance.' He shook his head. 'No wonder you think I'm crazy.'

'You're making no sense. Yes. But I don't think you're crazy. I was wrong to say that.'

'And you? Why are you tagging along with us? It can't be for protection. For Captain Calque and I are probably of less potential use to anybody in that department than, well, than Laurel and Hardy.'

Lamia burst out laughing. 'Laurel and Hardy. That's it. That's who you are. The two of you. Laurel and Hardy.'

191

'Thanks. Thanks a bunch.'

Lamia's face became serious again. 'Why don't you have a woman of your own, Adam? What are you? Mid-thirties? You're even quite handsome in an off hand, Dean Martin kind of a way.'

'A Dean Martin kind of a way? I look like Dean Martin?'

'Yes. A little. And someone else. Some 1930s film actor I can't remember. But it will come to me later. I'm certain of that.'

'W. C. Fields?'

She punched him lightly on the arm. 'But I'm serious, Adam. Most men have settled down by this time. Started a family. Yet you are living in a far bigger house than you can ever use. With a beautiful garden. In an exquisite part of America. Why aren't you married? What's wrong with you, Monsieur Sabir?'

'I suppose you're going to ask me now if I'm gay?'

'No. I know you're not gay.'

'Oh yeah? And how do you figure that?'

'By the way you responded earlier this evening when you helped me climb out of the window.'

Sabir could feel himself flushing. 'Oh come on. I just hefted you for a split second. You might as well have been a sack of grain.'

'I don't think so. French women understand such things. I'm not saying you're attracted to me. Don't think that. But a woman knows when a man responds to her as a woman. Gay men don't respond that way. You're way straight, as the Americans say. So answer my question.'

Sabir laughed. But he was actually caught mid-way between embarrassment and awkwardness. He wasn't used to women speaking to him in this way. Part of him liked it, and part of him wanted to be a million miles away. 'It's about my mother, I suppose.'

'With men it usually is.'

Sabir rocked back against the pillar, surprised, once again, at Lamia's directness. 'It's not what you think. Not the usual, I mean. During the better part of my adolescence and through into my twenties, my mother was always ill. I mean mentally ill, not physically. It got so bad sometimes that she had to be taken off to a clinic and tranquillized for weeks at a time to prevent her from committing suicide. It destroyed my father's life. And I suppose it destroyed part of mine, too. I couldn't bring anyone home, you see. And somehow it felt like a betrayal if I went with girls my mother would never get to meet. She wanted to be normal, Lamia. Desperately so. But there was something – some short circuit in her brain – that didn't allow her to be. I went to college like everybody else. Had a few short-term affairs. Minor things, that didn't mean anything. But I could never hold a woman. There was something detached in me – something damaged. When my father died three years ago, I was a 32-year-old man still living for the better part of the year at home.'

'And your mother?'

'Oh, she finally succeeded in what she'd been trying to do for half her lifetime. I was twenty-five, maybe twenty-six, when she took the Nembutal and slit her wrists. I was the one that found her. She did it like Seneca the Younger – in the bath. Only she left the taps running. The blood-stained water came cascading down the stairs like a waterfall. A heck of a way to go. As always, she involved everybody.'

'But you loved her?'

'I loved her and I hated her. Does that answer your question?'

Lamia put out a hand and squeezed his arm, but Sabir jerked unconsciously away from her, as if there was something he feared in her touch.

193

26

The trio drove all of the next day, right along the line of the Appalachian Mountains and down into Alabama. They each took it in turns to share the driving, and both Lamia and Sabir managed to doze a little when it was their turn to take a break.

Calque had attempted to persuade Sabir that civilized people didn't stuff themselves full of eggs, bacon, and waffles at breakfast time, and then snack their way through the day until they ran up against the stone wall of a gargantuan, seven-o'clock dinner. Instead, they started off in the continental fashion, on the strict understanding that they had a good lunch to look forward to, with a light supper to bring things to a satisfactory conclusion.

'This time I shall choose the restaurant. We are not being followed. We don't need to use a drive-thru. It is not required that we sit in the car and stink it up with inadequately fried food.'

Neither Lamia nor Sabir felt it appropriate to draw attention to Calque stinking up the car with his cigarettes – something which he was doing on an ever more regular basis. Neither did Lamia mention Calque's snoring. She was aware of a certain unexpected fragility in him – a fragility that verged on narcissism – and she was also aware of his susceptibility both to her and to the opinions of her sex.

During lunch – for which Calque had unexpectedly found a family-run restaurant near Knoxville which specialized in hickory-smoked baby back ribs, served with corn bread and pinto beans, but, lamentably, no wine – she questioned him about his wife and daughter.

Calque sighed, and stared down at his plate, as if it held within its purview some symbolical key to the human condition. 'My wife wished, from the very first moment that she met me, that I had been a businessman and not a policeman. She managed to convince herself – without, I should add, any encouragement on my part – that I would eventually subscribe to her wishes and switch professions. We would then be able to live a comfortable, bourgeois existence, in a respectable Paris suburb, and take our holidays on the Ile de Ré, just as she and her family had done for the past two generations. I let her down in this, just as I let her down in everything else. We had a daughter. At first this daughter seemed fond of me. I would take her to the flower market, and to the Jardin du Luxembourg to float her sailing boat. When my wife realized how fond I was of this little girl, she understood that her opportunity for revenge had finally arrived. She spent the better part of twenty years alienating my daughter from me in every way she could contrive. I fought back, of course, but a man who works full time, and long hours, in a sometimes brutalizing profession, has a weakened armoury. Eventually, my daughter married, and left home. Now, when I telephone, her husband speaks to me, but not her. Without the presence of my daughter, my marriage seemed even more of a sham than I had originally suspected. I therefore divorced my wife, effectively ruining myself in the process. This is only justice. If a man is a fool, he deserves to be treated like a fool. I was, and am, a fool. But now that I am older, I can look back on my folly and smile. Before, I could only weep.'

Sabir and Lamia stared speechlessly across the table at Calque. Never, in the time that either one of them had known him, had he opened up even remotely about his private life. He might have been a lay monk for all they knew. Now he had spread out all his dirty linen for them to witness, and they didn't know quite how to respond.

'It's a shame they don't serve wine here,' said Sabir. 'I could do with a glass or two myself.'

Lamia glared at him as if he had just overset a saucepot on her dress.

Sabir swallowed, and tried to redeem himself. 'Calque, that's terrible. You mean your daughter won't even speak to you any more?'

This time Lamia aimed a kick at his shin under the table.

Calque, however, appeared not to have heard him. 'Everything is fine now, though. I have taken early retirement from the police force. I have become obsessed with the after-effects of my final case. I have spent the past five weeks sitting in a camouflaged hideout on a hillside in southern France. I have ruined myself afresh by bribing a criminal to break into Lamia's mother's house and retrieve a tape recorder with nothing on it. I have come to America – a land of which I know nothing, and care to know even less – a land where people seem to subsist on fried food and takeaways – and I have made it my own. I have been pursued by madmen, and I have evaded them. I am surrounded by my friends.' Calque dipped his corn bread into the baby rib sauce and ate it with every impression of relish. 'Life is treating me well, in other words. Far better than I deserve.'

Sabir had a quizzical expression on his face. He glanced across at Lamia. 'Is he joking? Or is he being serious?'

Lamia smiled. 'He is being serious. Only he has a very French way of making his serious point.'

'What? A sort of zigzaggy kind of a way? A down-hill-and-over-dale kind of a way? An up and down a few lurching by-ways and around a few blind corners kind of a way?'

'Yes. That is it. That is it exactly.'

Calque had gone back to eating, seemingly unmoved by the remainder of the conversation.

It was as if he had laid his cards on the table, just as pre-arranged, and now it was up to everybody else to decide just what they were going to do with them.

27

All had been going well for the Corpus until their extended caravan arrived in the small town of Wakulhatchee, just south of Tuscaloosa, Alabama, at around nine p.m. on an unseasonably hot Friday night.

It had been a long day's driving for the ten-car, eleven-person ersatz surveillance team. A day whose effects were exacerbated both by the continual need for caution, and by the inevitable wear and tear caused by the obsessive twenty-minute rotas that Abi had insisted upon despite the fact that the trio they were following in the Grand Cherokee appeared to have not the remotest idea that they were still being watched.

Even during the trio's lunch break – when it might have appeared reasonable for the team to stand down and take it easy – Abi had refused permission for any of his brothers and sisters to take time off for anything more than a snack. 'You can relax this evening. When they're static. We'll only need two people at any one time to watch them then. So the rest of you can go off and get some R & R.'

'Which two are going to watch them?'

Abi could see storm clouds looming. He put on his most placatory voice. 'Vau and I will take the first four-hour shift. We're the freshest. And the pressure's been off us all day. The rest of you can draw lots for who's next in line. Those four hours ought to give you all the time you need to get some food and drink inside you and lighten up a little. If our trio decide on a late outing we'll call you and tell you whereabouts they're headed. We don't want you all to crash into each other like ninepins. If Lamia catches sight of any of us, we're done for. They'll bolt again, and this time they'll make damned sure they're not followed. No. We need to keep them sweet and unaware.'

For their part Calque, Lamia, and Sabir had found another of their Olde Worlde – read terminally run-down – motels, on the very edge of town. This one was managed by a Polish family – and they, too, barely raised an eyebrow at their guests' unconventional sleeping arrangements.

After watching the trio check in, Abi and Vau settled down to watch the entrance to the motel from 150 yards down the street. They were driving a different rental from the one they had been using in Massachusetts – a vehicle that had not been within sight of the Cherokee all day.

'How do you think it's going?' Vau asked his brother.

'In a word? Shit.'

Vau sat silently for a while. 'I don't get you, Abi. We've still got them under surveillance. The whole family are here to support us. What is there to complain about?'

'Inactivity. That's to complain about.'

Vau raised his eyebrows in disbelief.

'Oh, come on, Vau. You know very well who you're dealing with here. Our bunch of siblings are used to getting everything they want whenever they want it. They either buy it or they grab it off someone else. That sort of freedom acts like an inbuilt dynamo. Now we're asking that same bunch of anarchists to rein themselves in and conduct a sort of interminable holding operation. Heck, Sabir could be intending to drive as far as Brazil for all we know. Which is fine for him – he owns his damned vehicle. But what do we do? Somehow, at every border, we're going to have to dump the rentals and fetch ourselves new ones. Without losing our marks.'

'But why should we be crossing borders? They might be heading down to Florida.'

'Florida? Haven't you looked at your map recently? We've just driven along the fucking Appalachian Mountains – we're heading for Texas.'

'Well. Texas, then.'

'What's beyond Texas?'

Vau thought for a moment. 'Mexico, I suppose.'

'Don't you think they might be heading for there?'

'Why?'

'Anything happen there in the past few days? Anything out of the ordinary?'

Vau thought again. Then he shook his head. 'No. Not that I heard of.'

Abi settled himself further down in his seat and closed his eyes. 'Jesus.'

28

The place was called Alabama Mama's, and it was situated on the far opposite edge of Wakulhatchee to the trio's motel. It was basically a parking lot with a corrugated iron building pitched into the middle of it.

The corrugated iron had originally been painted rust red, but over the years the patina had changed until it had now come to resemble a sort of inverted, badly limed-up, coffee pot.

At ten o'clock on a Friday evening the car park was still mostly empty, so the sudden arrival of a phalanx of New York registered rentals didn't do more than flurry the waters. A few odd looks were cast in the Corpus's direction – they were, after all, quite noticeable – but nothing untoward either occurred or suggested itself.

Of the nine siblings who entered Alabama Mama's that night, Athame was a virtual dwarf, with tiny hands and feet, Berith had a harelip, Rudra limped in an extrovert manner on account of his untreated club foot, Alastor was spectre thin from the effects of cachexia, Asson was enormously fat, Dakini had hair which grew down below her buttocks framing a face frozen into a sort of malevolent rictus, Nawal suffered from hirsutism, Oni was a seven-foot-tall albino, and Aldinach was a true hermaphrodite.

Of these, Aldinach was the most ordinary looking, as he/she had decided to be a she tonight, given the heat and the sub-tropical climate that ensured that even at nine o'clock in the evening – and freakishly, even in October – the ambient temperature was well above thirty degrees. Inside the club it was hotter still, with the slowly churning ceiling fans barely ruffling the overheated air.

Aldinach had therefore chosen to wear a thin seersucker cotton dress, cut low to show off her small, but perfectly formed, breasts. She was wearing red patent leather 'fuck-me' shoes with five-inch heels, and the sheerest stockings she could find. She had her hair down – when she lived as a man she commonly wore it in a pigtail – and her fringe now curled inwards to flatter and give weight to her heavily lashed eyes. Aldinach refused to enter the club alongside her brothers and sisters, but came in separately, by a side entrance, and took her place alone, at the corner of the bar.

The barman did a double take, and then shook his head in amazement. Despite twenty years spent working in clubs and bars and dives of all persuasions, it still astonished him what women were capable of contriving when they were 'in open season'. He stood for a moment admiring the sight, and speculating which of his regular clients would be the lucky man tonight. Because someone was going to be the lucky man. That much was darned certain.

'I'll have a margarita.'

'Frozen? Or on the rocks?'

'Frozen.'

'Wise choice. Do you want salt around the rim?'

'Yes.'

The barman busied himself with the makings. 'You from Louisiana?'

'Yes.'

'I knew it. I picked up your accent straight away. Lafayette?'

'Lake Charles.'

'Well I'll be damned. I got close, didn't I?'

'You've got an ear. I'll give you that.'

The barman placed a paper mat in front of Aldinach, and set the margarita on top of it. 'Now you try that. Then tell me if it isn't the best damned margarita this side of the Sierra Madre.'

Aldinach sipped the margarita. Then she cocked her head and smiled.

'I told you. I used to work down in Cancun around the Easter break. At the Hotel Esmeralda.' His expression changed abruptly. 'Look. Tell me if I'm out of line here. But you do realize what sort of a place this is?'

201

Aldinach shrugged. 'I have a vague idea.'

The barman glanced towards the main door. 'Well it ain't what you'd call genteel, if you take my meaning.' He hesitated. 'Look, lady. I like you. Strikes me you're a cut above the usual sort of moppet props up this bar. Plus you've got good taste in booze. If I were you, I'd drink up and head on out again. Try the Hummingbird up the road about two miles. I dearly hate to drive away custom, but you don't deserve the sort of riff-raff we get in here. Now take a look at that table of freaks over there.' He nodded towards the far edge of the dance floor, where Aldinach's brothers and sisters had pushed together three separate tables to make one. 'There's trouble if ever I've seen it. Like waving a red flag in front of a bull. The sort of rednecks we get in here on a Friday night will take the mere existence of that bunch as an insult to their manhood. Our clientele ain't much into "special needs". I don't know who they are – an idiot's works outing, maybe, or escapees from the funny farm – but I wouldn't want to be in here when the Skunks get through with them.'

'The Skunks?'

'You don't want to know. Believe me, lady. You don't want to know.'

29

—

Skip Dearborn had been grand master of the Skunks chapter of the Birmingham Hells Angels for nearly twenty years now. In that time he had raped, killed, tortured, stolen, grafted, skimmed, blackmailed, and kidnapped his way through the better part of Southern Alabama, without ever having done any prison time to speak of. Others had suffered in his place. As far as Skip was concerned, that was only just.

He was the smartest and the meanest looking sonofabitch on the block – why shouldn't he benefit from his smartness and his meanness? There would come a time when someone else stole his crown, but that time wasn't looming anytime soon. And in the meanwhile Skip exercised *droit de seigneur* over any women stupid enough to want to associate themselves with his chapter, and had pick of the crop as far as loot, drug money, and any passing pussy was concerned.

Heck, he was like a lion in charge of his pride. He had the shiniest bike, the most patches (he sported Red Wings, Black Wings, the Dequiallo, and even an ultra-rare Filthy Few shoulder blaze), the smoothest leathers, and the foulest body odour of any of the males in his war party. What did he care? Who was going to argue with him? Who was going to cause him any grief? He had a steel plate in his skull, a rivet in one arm, a punctured lung, scars on his back, shoulder, and neck, a perforated eardrum, and occasional tinnitus, which made him very irritable indeed.

Tonight, the tinnitus was real bad. And the only thing that made the tinnitus halfway bearable was either a fight, or pussy, or both. That way, he was able to forget about the hissing in his ears for a pleasurable hour or two.

This particular Friday night he was surrounded by an assorted mob of what the Hells Angels termed hang-arounds, associates, and prospects. Wannabes, in other words, amenable to just about whatever Skip chose to throw at them. A lot of the main chapter members had taken to avoiding Skip's company on a Friday night, either because they were getting too old, or too comfortable, or didn't want their women outraged by anyone other than themselves. This pissed Skip off, and he was prone to take his revenge in unexpected and inventive ways.

Running the hang-arounds was one of his neatest tricks. Most of them were so desperate to join the One Percenters (the 99 per cent of remaining bikers being considered law-abiding – what the Angels sarcastically called 'Citizens'), that Skip could just about do what he wanted with them. Aim a hang-around at a bunch of Citizens and let him loose – that was Skip's motto. Then he'd stand back and watch the mayhem. Get in a lick here or there with a sawn-off pool cue. Smash a few knife-hands. All good fun and games. No one got killed. No one got seriously hurt – unless you called a few lost teeth, a broken nose or two, and maybe a cracked rib, pain.

Skip's newest trick consisted of spraying people with triple-action pepper spray when they least expected it. One shot in the eyes, and you could do what the hell you wanted without any danger of a comeback. Tonight, Skip had a can of pepper spray, a sawn-off pool cue, a Kau Sin Ke Chinese fighting chain, and a switchblade in his armoury. The tinnitus was getting so bad that he had to grind his teeth together to counteract the sound – it was like being tied underneath a damned waterfall in Yellowstone Park. He desperately needed an outlet – some way of switching his attention to outside his head.

He flung Alabama Mama's main door wide open, and strode in, followed by his little coterie of hangers-on. It was early yet. Far too early for any real fun. So Skip intended to hit the mescal for an hour or two, and then take whatever happened in through the door. What he wasn't expecting was that his evening's entertainment would already be in situ.

Skip allowed his eyes to trail lazily across the dance floor. Sweet Jesus. Who were the bunch of freaks huddling together around a far-off table? He was so surprised at the sight of them that he even stopped for a moment to stare as if in wonder. As if he'd witnessed some minor sort of miracle. Then he saw Aldinach at the bar.

'She's mine,' he said to the hang-around nearest him. 'Go fetch.'

The barman came hurrying over towards the assembled Angels. 'Skip, no trouble tonight. You hear me? Last time around you almost got me canned. Drinks on the house, huh? Tequilas all round. How's about that?'

'Mescal. And beer chasers.'

'Sure, Skip. Anything you say.'

The Angels sat down. Skip watched the hang-around angling towards the woman at the bar. Asshole. What was he doing? Fishing for cut-throats?

'You. Miss. Care to have a drink with us?' Skip's voice was loud – stentorian even. As if he was shouting orders down a communications tube.

Aldinach stood up. She looked around with her head canted to one side, as if she wasn't quite sure the yell had really come from Skip's table. 'That would be very nice.'

The hang-around had only just reached her. Now he drew back in horror. What was the slit thinking of? Was she blind? He had anticipated a little local difficulty in persuading her to come across to the Angels' table. A straight no, maybe, followed by a 'fuck off'. He had then intended to try a little wheedling, upon which he would have headed disconsolately back and left the whole thing up to Skip. Let the motherfucker harvest his own pussy.

Instead, the woman gathered up her drink from the bar and accompanied the hang-around voluntarily across the floor.

The barman met them halfway. He raised his eyebrows dramatically when he caught Aldinach's eye, and then shook his head, as though abrogating all further responsibility for his former client. He didn't say anything, because he didn't have a death wish.

Skip got up and offered Aldinach a chair. His manner was studiously polite. Rather like a man who intends to lull a companion into a false sense of security, before snatching the chair away just as they sit down.

He could scarcely believe his luck. What was the slit thinking of? Did she like rough trade, maybe? Was she out for a Friday night she would never forget? And what did he care?

'You want a shot of mescal?'

'No. I'd like another margarita.'

'Coming up.' Skip yelled across at the barman, who waved a hand in weary acknowledgement.

Aldinach looked around at the table of Angels. 'You're all dressed alike. Are you members of some club, perhaps?'

Skip grinned. 'You could call it that. The "share and share alike" club.'

'Oh, really? I have never heard of that.'

'My name's Skip. What your name, sweetheart?'

'You can call me Desiree.'

'You French or something?'

'I'm from Louisiana. Lake Charles.'

'Should have guessed.' Skip hesitated. 'By the way you dress.'

'Do you like the way I dress?'

'Jesus Christ. Do you get this dame?' Skip glanced around at his hangers-on. He was beginning to look ever so slightly nonplussed.

'You haven't answered my question.'

'Sure. I like the way you dress. I like it fine.'

Aldinach stood up. 'I must go to the powder room. You'll wait for me, won't you? You won't go away?'

Skip nearly let his chair tilt all the way over. He could hardly feel his tinnitus any more. There was no way on earth he was going to pass up on this broad. 'You go right ahead, honey. We'll all be here when you get back.'

Aldinach weaved her way amongst the tables. As she passed close to her brothers and sisters she smiled, and raised one questioning eyebrow. Oni glanced quickly across to the Angels' table and shrugged.

'Those freaks bothering you, sister?' Skip was standing up now. He could feel a sudden knot in the pit of his stomach.

'Yes.' Aldinach turned around. 'They have said a disgusting thing to me. And that you Angels are pussies.'

Oni sighed. He looked across at his brothers and sisters. 'Abi will be angry with us if we do this.'

Berith shrugged. 'Who cares?'

Oni glanced across at Rudra, Alastor, and Asson. 'You three on?'

Nawal nudged him. 'What about us girls?'

Oni smiled. 'You can mop up after us.' He stood up and turned towards the Angels.

'Hey boys,' Skip said. 'The fucking circus just came to town.'

30

It was an uneven fight. The hang-arounds didn't really have their hearts in it. The main problem was that no one had tanked up yet on beer and mescal and crank. The Skunks weren't honed. They had no edge to them.

The fat guy, and the thin guy, and the harelip guy, and the guy that limped, all moved one way, and the albino giant just came straight at them through the tables. Drinkers scattered in every direction. The female freaks circled around the outside of the fight like barracuda, watching for an opening.

Each of the freaks drew fighting batons from their sleeves. Seeing this, a few of the hang-arounds began to lose heart.

The albino reached them first. Christ, but he was fucking enormous.

Two of the hang-arounds drew knives, to sort of puncture his morale, but he just swept over them with his fighting baton, cracking the head of one, and smashing in the other man's teeth.

By this time the four other male freaks had hit the ground running. Batons were swirling and swishing through the air. Bones were cracking – hang-arounds were screaming.

Skip ducked under a table, hoping to get a chance to cut someone's hamstring, but two of the female freaks caught sight of what he was doing and piled chairs and tables on top of him, until he was completely covered by a fretwork of steel tubing.

Aldinach stood by the bar, one eye on the barman, the other on the fight.

'You with these people?' the barman said.

'Never met them before in my life.' Aldinach glanced towards the main door. Customers were exiting through it in droves. 'Do you think anyone will call the police?'

The barman shrugged. 'Your guess is as good as mine. But I figure not. Sort of clients we get don't find cops copacetic.'

'Are *you* going to call the police?'

'What for? How often do I get to see the Skunks getting their hides furrowed?'

Things were quieting down now. Most of the hang-arounds had either fled or were stretched out on the floor or across the bar furniture.

Aldinach minced across the floor towards the mayhem. The eight Corpus members turned towards her as one.

'Skip,' she said, in a high, girlie little voice. 'You under there?'

Oni cleared the tables and chairs that were piled up above Skip Dearborn's huddled form. He had adopted the foetal position, same as you do when you are attacked by wild dogs.

Skip emerged from beneath the wreckage and stood up. He was holding his switchblade and the can of pepper spray out in front of him as if they were some sort of lucky charm – a string of garlic designed to ward off vampires. He looked around at what remained of his merry band of men. 'Shit.'

'You going to use that?' Aldinach approached closer.

'This was some kind of set-up, wasn't it? You're all in this together? You knew this was going to happen before we even came in. You people suckered us. You ain't no fucking Desiree.' Skip raised the pepper spray.

Aldinach snatched a fighting baton from Nawal's hand. Before Skip was able to respond, she brought the baton down across his knife hand, smashing the bone. Then, as he bent down to grab his wrist, she smashed him across the back of the neck, snatched the can of pepper spray, and blasted him full in the face.

Skip pole-axed to the ground like a discarded shirt.

'Heck of a date,' said Aldinach, as she and her siblings started out of the building.

31

Calque, who was driving, and not relishing his silent passengers, turned up the volume on the radio. 'Listen to this.'

An announcer was describing the previous night's mayhem at Alabama Mama's.

Sabir, who was trying to get some sleep after yet another disturbed night, groaned. Lamia, who had somehow managed to curl up and fall asleep on the back seat, didn't respond.

'Look what we've been missing. We've been staying in the wrong part of town, apparently. A gang attack. Two groups of Hells Angels tearing into each other. Fourteen people taken to hospital. Redneck heaven.'

Sabir straightened up. He knew he wasn't going to get any sleep from here on in. 'What do you know about rednecks, Calque?'

Calque hitched his chin. 'I know a lot about rednecks. The Polish man at the motel even told me two redneck jokes.'

Sabir pretended to reel backwards. 'But you can't even speak English. How could you possibly communicate with him?'

'It is simple. He is a Pole. A civilized man. A European. He speaks French.'

Sabir sighed. 'Can you remember them? The jokes, I mean.'

Calque appeared to be deep in thought. 'Yes. I think so.'

'Well tell me them, then. If I can't sleep, I might as well be entertained.'

Calque pursed his lips, his eyes furrowed against the morning sunlight. 'The first one goes like this. A redneck from Alabama dies. But fortunately he has left a will. In it he leaves his entire estate in trust for his widow. The only snag is, she can only inherit when she reaches the age of fourteen.'

Sabir stared at him. 'That's it?'

Calque shrugged. 'I thought it was very funny. I laughed when the Polish man told it to me. The other one is better, though. Much better.'

'Okay, shoot.'

'There you go again with this silly expression. Why should I shoot? It simply doesn't translate into French. When you speak French, you should use the French idiom. Not an American one.'

Sabir turned down the radio, which was still blaring the local news at them. 'I would very much like to hear the second joke, Captain Calque.'

Calque nodded. 'Very well. I shall give it to you. This is even funnier than the first one.'

Sabir squeezed shut his eyes.

'Two rednecks from Alabama are approaching each other on the road. One has a sackful of chickens in his hand. The second redneck says, "If I can tell you how many chickens you have in your sack, will you give them to me?" The first redneck thinks things over. "If you can guess how many chickens are in this sack, I will give you both of them." The second redneck stares down at the sack. "Five?"'

Lamia gave a hoot from the back of the car. Even Sabir had the grace to laugh.

'You see,' said Calque. 'I told you the second joke was better. In France we tell such jokes about you Yankees.'

'Yeah, well, that doesn't surprise me in the least,' said Sabir. 'We Yankees tell such jokes against you French.

I learned dozens of them when I was in the National Guard.'

Calque pointed his finger in Sabir's direction. 'You are half French. Don't forget that, Sabir. You owe a duty to your maternal homeland.' He was beginning to look slightly nervous.

'How can I ever forget it? That's why I was the butt of the damned Frenchy jokes in the first place. However, I figure that any man who can't tell a good joke against himself doesn't deserve the claim to a sense of humour. Don't you agree?'

'Go on,' said Lamia from the back of the car. 'Tell us an anti-French joke.'

'You sure?'

'Positive.'

'Okay. How many Frenchmen does it take to screw in a light bulb?'

There was silence in the car.

'One. He holds it, and the rest of Europe simply revolves around him.'

Calque took both hands off the wheel and made a disparaging motion. 'That is not very funny at all.'

'Okay. Try this then.' Sabir took a preparatory breath. He was beginning to feel a sense of impending doom. Still, for some reason he couldn't quite figure, he felt unable to stop himself. 'How do you confuse a French soldier?'

'How?'

'You give him a rifle and ask him to fire it.'

Calque slammed the steering wheel with the flat of his hand. 'That is outrageous. Did they really tell such jokes as this against you when you were in the army?'

'I wasn't in the army. I was in the National Guard.'

'The National Guard, then. Pah.'

Sabir's jaw was beginning to freeze with the tension

of his unwanted position. 'Yes. All the time. Comes from having a foreign-sounding name. The true joke was really on them, because my father was pretty near 100 per cent pure American – it was my mother who was French.'

'Tell me another joke. One about women this time.' Lamia was sitting up straighter in the back of the car.

'It'll be about soldiers. Those are the only ones I know.'

'That's all right.'

'What do female snipers in France use as camouflage?'

More silence.

'Their armpits.'

'Their what?'

'Their armpits.' Sabir knew for certain that he'd gone too far this time.

'What does that mean?' Lamia was leaning towards him from the back of the car. 'I don't understand that joke. How can a woman use her armpits for camouflage? And anyway, we don't have female snipers in the French army. Women are not allowed to engage in combat.'

'It's a joke. It's not meant to be taken seriously. Like the movies, jokes rely on a willing suspension of disbelief.'

Calque turned towards Lamia. 'Sabir is trying to tell us that the Yankees think French women never shave their armpits.'

Lamia's mouth dropped open in horror. 'Where did you see this, Adam? Where did you see French women not shaving themselves?'

Sabir was tempted to say 'Oh boy', but didn't. 'It's not me who's saying this, Lamia. It's the joke. It's an archetype. Yanks during the war simply found that French women didn't shave.'

'How could one shave during the war? There were no razors.'

'Good point. Great point. That answers it then.'

'But that is unfair. How can you blame French women for what happened during the war, when there were shortages, and when it was impossible to shave themselves?'

'Jesus Christ, people. We're meant to be having fun here. Cracking a few jokes. Having a laugh.'

'But you are not being serious, Sabir. For a joke to be funny, it should be based on truth.'

Sabir grabbed the collar of his shirt and pulled it over his head like a cowl. 'If the Corpus comes to get us, don't bother to call me. I'm fine just as I am.'

32

—

'Are you still behind them?'

'Yes, Madame.'

'Do you know where they are going?'

'I think it is to Mexico, Madame.'

'How do you work that out?'

'We are near to Houston, in Texas. Draw a straight line between Stockbridge and Houston and it leads you to Mexico. To the Brownsville–Matamoros border crossing in particular. I believe that that is where they are going to enter. If you ask my opinion, I think the eruption of the Mexican volcano triggered this decision of Sabir's.'

'I think you are right. But that doesn't take us much further, does it? Thanks to your failure to force information out of Sabir when you were offered the chance, we have no idea what they are doing, nor why they are doing it. Have you had any trouble along the way?'

Abi flared his eyes. He had been dreading the arrival of this question ever since the start of the conversation with his mother.

'Abiger?'

'Yes, Madame.'

'Don't lie to me. I can always tell if you are lying. I have been able to do this ever since you were a little boy.'

Abi glanced across at Vau, who was resolutely concentrating on his driving, and pretending that he was not privy to the conversation emerging loud and clear through the rental's hands-free speakers.

'Yes, we have had some trouble.'

'Who caused it?'

'Aldinach. She got the wind under her tail a little.'

'I'm sorry?'

'It's what happens with mares. When they come into season. It's called "getting the wind under their tail". They charge around the paddock with their tails cocked to one side, causing trouble.'

'And this is what Aldinach did?'

'Pretty much.'

'And the outcome?'

'Fourteen people in hospital. Hells Angels, mostly.'

'Any of our people?'

'Of course not. The opposition over-faced itself. They did not possess the will to win. They did not realize who they were up against.'

'Anyone killed?'

'No.'

'So there will be no problems with the police?'

'No. I guarantee it.'

'Did you join in this fracas?'

Ah. Here was the trick question. Abi had known it

was coming, but still it turned his blood to ice. Answer wrongly, and he would be hung out to dry like a strip of biltong. 'Of course not, Madame. I followed your orders to the letter. Vau and I were watching Sabir's motel. I had given the others time off to eat and to relax. I had not anticipated Aldinach's bout of brain fever. She went into that place determined to start a fight involving everybody.'

'Have you punished her?'

'What's the point? Everything turned out well in the end. We didn't spook Sabir. The police weren't involved until afterwards, by which time we had all dispersed to different locations. No harm was done. And it allowed everybody to let off a little steam.'

'I think you need to place a tracker in Sabir's car.'

Abi mouthed a swearword. 'Is that wise, Madame? We have Sabir and Lamia and the policeman sewn up. They can't so much as whistle without one of us hearing them.'

'How much further do you have to go, Abiger?'

'I have no idea.'

'Exactly. And how long until the next "wind under the tail" moment?'

Abi swallowed. 'I can't say, Madame. It could be any time. It could be never.'

'Mexico is a country where things happen, Abiger. The police are endemically corrupt. There are drug wars going on all along the border. I don't want Sabir lost because a maniac like Aldinach gets ants in her pants.'

Abi slapped Vau on the arm to catch his attention and then mouthed 'ants in her pants' and 'maniac' and raised his eyes heavenwards. 'No, Madame. Of course not, Madame.'

'Can Vau get inside their car without triggering the alarm?'

'Vau can get inside any car. You know that, Madame. You were responsible for having him taught by the best car thief in the business. But it will be tricky. If something goes wrong, we risk stampeding them.'

The Countess sighed melodramatically. 'Then we must risk a stampede, don't you think, in view of the greater benefits involved in having a fallback position? But kindly do not tell your brothers and sisters that you have done this thing at my request. I don't want them thinking that I don't trust them. Do you understand what I am saying, Abiger?'

'Perfectly, Madame.'

'And Abiger?'

'Yes, Madame.'

'This one time I will not hold you personally responsible for what has happened.'

'Thank you, Madame. You are very kind.' Abi terminated the connection with one slow-motion finger. 'Fucking old cow.'

Vau turned towards him. 'You must not speak of Madame, our mother, that way.'

'Oh really? Well what is she then? She sits in that spider's web of hers, with that bastard Milouins and the fragrant Madame Mastigou always on hand to protect her from the real world, and she still thinks she can pull all the strings. Why doesn't she come out here if she's so eager to run everything?'

'Because she's an old woman. And because she's rich.'

Abi turned to his brother. 'Truly, Vau? Is that so? Well you could have fooled me.'

33

During your next two days on the road, you had achieved three lifts. Firstly to Minatitlan, in a brewery truck, then, after a long wait, to Agua Dulce, with a gringo, in his private car.

Agua Dulce was partially off your road, but you accepted the lift nevertheless, on the assumption that anywhere south was good and, on the whole, productive. It was better to keep moving than to remain static, with all the dangers that inactivity entailed, such as losing heart, or spending money that you could ill afford.

But the trip to Agua Dulce proved fortunate in more ways than one, because the same gringo saw you waiting on the road again the very next morning, and gave you a further lift, this time all the way to Villahermosa. The only thing you did not understand was that the gringo asked you, many times, if you had ever dug things up in your garden. Stone carvings. Pottery. Old necklaces. Obsidian knives. You tried to tell him that you did not have a garden – that you worked for your boss, the *cacique*, in his garden, and that therefore anything that you dug up legally belonged to him. That even in the *cacique*'s garden you had never dug such things up in the entirety of your life.

The gringo had seemed very disappointed when you told him this. But still he had taken you on to Villahermosa, and had offered to buy you lunch from a roadside stall, which you had refused, on account of the gringo's strange attitude. Were all gringos like this? Plunderers? Like the Spanish? You had only met two gringos in the entire course of your life, but they had not impressed you. A man should always speak directly of what was in his heart. Not come at a subject from the side. Or from on top.

From now on, you decided, you would avoid gringos, and stick to your own people. Peasants. Indios. Mestizos. People who made their living from the land, and not from thievery.

34

Vau waited until 2.30 in the morning before making his move on the Grand Cherokee.

He'd brought his bunch of skeleton keys, with a wedge and a flexible car antenna for back-up in case he couldn't get inside in the conventional way and needed to break in through a side window. Either way would leave no traces. Sabir's Cherokee was a few years old, fortunately, so didn't have the most up-to-date remote keyless entry and remote start and alarm. That made things a lot easier.

Still, it stuck in Vau's craw that he was expected to go to all the trouble of breaking into the car when it would be just as easy to attach the tracker to a protected piece of the underbody – he could have been in and out in two minutes, with no one any the wiser. Instead, here he was having to risk himself, in a well-lighted place, where anybody could decide to exit their motel room in search of the ice dispenser or a bag of potato chips from the vending machine.

He hunched down by the driver's door, with the car between him and the trio's motel room, and set to work. As he was inserting the fifth key out of a total of fourteen possible keys, the door to Sabir's room opened, and the man himself came out.

Cursing, Vau ducked down beside the Grand Cherokee and stretched himself flat on the ground. Then he eased himself underneath the chassis skirt, using his back and buttocks as leverage.

I wished this on myself, Vau muttered under his breath – bloody wished it on myself. It's not even the fucking crack of dawn yet. Please God the bastard doesn't go for an early morning spin. Those sixteen-inch whitewalls will squish me like a rotten tomato.

35

Sabir sat down on the motel walkway. He hunched forwards like a man with stomach cramp and rested his head on his knees. Would he never again manage to sleep a night straight through? The constant waking up and drifting off was draining him of his strength. And yet he feared pills and their effects – he had seen what they had done to his mother.

The temperature on the outskirts of Corpus Christi at 2.30 that morning was a balmy twenty degrees, and Sabir could clearly pick up the scent of the sea on the incoming breeze. When he straightened up he could hear the surf pounding against Padre Island, and the shriek of distant seabirds as they fought over a school of sardines.

He sat for a long time listening to the murmurings of the night, secretly hoping that Lamia would come out and join him, just as she had done two nights before. He regretted having drawn away from her when she had reached out to comfort him, and he was looking for an opportunity – any opportunity – of putting things right with her again.

If only Calque would begin snoring. Or sleepwalking. Or throwing himself around in his bed. But when Sabir had tiptoed out of their communal bedroom, the former policeman had been sleeping like a well-fed baby

As far as the trip was concerned, the three of them appeared to have settled into a comforting routine, sharing jokes and playing car games. Somewhat to Sabir's surprise, Calque was wildly competitive in anything that involved intellectual exercise, to the extent that he would even bend the rules a little when it suited him. Sabir had decided that this might have something to do with Calque's previous profession as a policeman, but he kept the thought firmly to himself. One consequence, though, was that there had been no opportunity for any private conversation with Lamia.

Sabir was just about to head back inside and try for a little sleep when the door behind him opened. Lamia edged through it, one hand held up to shade her eyes against the glare of the safety light.

Sabir did his best to mask his delight at her miraculous reappearance. 'Don't tell me. Calque has started snoring again?'

'Yes.'

'Then why are we whispering? Nothing will cut through that racket of his and wake him up.'

Lamia laughed. She had brought a blanket out with her, as before, but this time she settled herself on it, with her legs drawn up and to the side, and then folded it across her like a four-leaf-clover. She was wearing an old-fashioned flannel nightdress, and Sabir found himself marvelling anew at her unselfconsciousness. Lamia was unlike any French woman he had ever met in that respect, in that she appeared to have so convinced herself of her fundamental undesirability that, beyond making sure that she was neatly turned out, her fashion sense erred disarmingly on the side of a studied and rather grey neutrality.

'So what's new?' Sabir grinned at her, not really expecting a serious answer to his question.

Lamia shook her head. 'I haven't told Calque yet. But this afternoon, as we were driving through Houston, I am convinced that I saw my sister Dakini following us in a car.'

'You're kidding me?'

'I couldn't be sure, because she was wearing dark glasses and a baseball cap.'

'Dark glasses and a baseball cap?'

'Yes. It doesn't sound much like her, does it? I've since managed to convince myself that I was wrong. Which I probably am. But Dakini has a face that, once seen, is never forgotten.' She blushed and turned away, as though fearing that her own face might reasonably be considered to fall within that category as well.

'What do you mean?'

'Well, in addition to having very long hair – I mean really long, falling to well below her waist – Dakini also has a sort of unfortunate rictus to her features, that gives her a malevolent look, as though she is permanently angry.' Lamia hesitated, uncertain whether to go on. Then she sighed. 'Sometimes I wonder about Madame, my mother, endlessly adopting children with disastrous tics or disabilities. Why did she never have us seen to? Surgically, I mean? In Rudra's case she could have had his

222

club foot treated. And in Berith's case his harelip. I agree that Athame's near dwarfism is incurable, as is Alastor's cachexia, and Aldinach's hermaphroditism. But she could have put Asson on a diet, instead of encouraging and funding his gourmandism – I mean they now say that excess weight is not necessarily genetic, don't they?'

'Then why didn't she? Have you treated, I mean?'

Lamia let out another long sigh. 'It's obvious, isn't it? She must have wanted us this way. We must have suited her.'

Sabir shook his head despairingly. He glanced over at Lamia, but she was avoiding his eyes. 'Can't you have your face fixed now? There have been enormous advances in dermatology since you were a child. Surely there's something that can be done?'

She shook her head. 'I'm scared to. Haemangiomas like mine need treating early. The longer you leave it, the more danger there is. If they catch you as a baby, they can sometimes use liquid nitrogen on the discoloration. That is not available later, however. Because my haemangioma did not threaten a vital organ, the nuns simply left it – or so I was told – hoping that it would go away of its own accord. But it didn't, as you can see. Maybe they even thought that as God had made me this way, who were they to change it? Nowadays, to treat it, they would have to use steroids, or interferon, or a pulse-dye laser treatment. In my case, because of the sheer size of it, they might even have to operate, with all the associated risks. I might end up looking even worse than I do now.'

'You don't look bad now. In fact I think you're beautiful.'

'Thank you, Adam. But I'm too old to believe in fairytales any more. I'm twenty-seven. Not eleven.'

Sabir sensed that it was time to change the subject. 'What about the twins?'

Lamia shrugged. 'At least Madame, my mother, had the grace to have them surgically parted. Or maybe, come to think of it, that was the nuns too? Either way, I've seen the scars on their torsos. I believe they must have shared a kidney or something when they emerged from their mother. Now they merely share an attitude.'

Sabir laughed, although he didn't really find the twins in the least amusing. 'Do you love them? I mean, do you love any of them? Your mother? Or your brothers and sisters?'

Lamia appeared to consider for a moment. 'There was a time when I was close to Athame. She is the one of my sisters who suffers from dwarfism. I mean she isn't really a dwarf, she is just very small indeed. She suffers from Ellis–van Creveld Syndrome, like some of your Amish people over here. She's a polydactyl, too.'

'A what?'

'She has twelve fingers.'

'Jesus. And she uses them all?'

'As well as you or I.'

'And are you still close to her?'

'We fell out over my attitude to the Corpus. I've been steadily easing back on my commitment for some years now. None of the others suspected, because they were not close to me – but Athame understood. And she couldn't condone it. She believes the Countess, my mother, to be a sort of goddess figure. She worships her, like the Jews of the Old Testament worshipped graven images – the golden calf, or what have you. She believes the Countess to be a sort of golem. And sometimes I think she's right. My mother is not entirely human. It is perfectly feasible that some force created her out of primeval clay, and simply gave her the face and body of a normal human being. To trick people.'

'To trick people? How?'

Lamia met Sabir's eyes straight on for the first time. 'Into believing that she was like them.'

36

Vau could hear every word of their conversation from his prone position on the increasingly hostile concrete surface of the motel parking lot.

He was starting to feel the cold in his back, and imagining all sorts of scenarios, like him sneezing, or him dozing off and then sitting up and bashing his head against the Cherokee's undercarriage and having to stifle his screams. The total nightmare scenario was the one in which the pair of them decided to go off for a sex assignation in the car together – for Vau was perfectly convinced from the sound of their voices, and the intimate way in which they were talking, that there was something more going on than a mere friendship of convenience – more than merely the random companionship of fellow travellers.

Abi could make fun of Lamia's face and her near sexless way of dressing all he wanted, but Vau knew that there were men out there who found Lamia attractive. Take that oaf Philippe, for instance. The dead footman. He had been sniffing after Lamia for years, hadn't he? It was only Madame, his mother's, complete lack of interest in matters sexual that had allowed the man to continue in his job. And much good it had done him. He was now languishing below six feet of reinforced concrete at a new Catholic girls' school the Countess was subsidizing at the Couvent des Abbesses de Platilly, near Cavalaire-sur-Mer. Nothing like keeping things cosy and in the family.

Still, Vau had all but decided that there was no way he was going to try breaking into the car again after this recent little contretemps. He would simply lie through his teeth to Abi and pretend he had planted the tracker in the spare tyre well. Instead he would attach it to the underframe of the car, and hope for the best. He had identified the perfect spot whilst lying prone beneath the Cherokee's skirts. He would do the deed the minute the two lovebirds stopped babbling and went back inside again, and to hell with the consequences.

37

Abi watched his twin brother climbing back into the rental. 'You're filthy. What have you been doing all this time? Rolling around in a midden?'

'What's a midden?'

'A shit heap.'

'Then why don't you say it the first time, instead of showing off how clever you are?

'Answer my question, Vau.'

'The answer is no. I haven't been rolling around in a shit heap. If you want to know what I've been doing all this time, I'll tell you. I've been lying underneath Sabir's car, in the parking lot of the motel, listening to his cosy late-night conversation with Lamia.'

'You're kidding me? You're not serious?'

'Deadly serious. Plus she recognized Dakini earlier on today, while we were transiting Houston.'

'Christ.'

'It's all right. She's managed to convince herself that she was seeing things. Your trick with the baseball cap and the dark glasses worked a treat. It was so unlikely a disguise, that Lamia thinks she was simply imagining the vision from hell that Dakini represents, and not really seeing it.'

'She is plug ugly, isn't she?'

'That's the understatement of the year.'

Abi laughed. 'Did you plant the tracker?'

Vau shrugged. 'Of course I did. What do you think?'

'Where?'

'Where? In the tyre well of course. Where I usually plant them.'

'Which key did you use to get in?'

'Why do you want to know?'

'Because I'm not stupid, Vau. You got surprised on the job and you were forced to hide. Then you were constrained to listen to the pair of them yakking on about Dakini for half an hour. You're lying under the car, at this point, pissed off to the nines. Don't tell me it didn't occur to you to take a shortcut?'

Vau hesitated. He was briefly tempted to try and compound his felony. Then he aimed a frustrated punch at the stowaway compartment. 'Okay, Abi. Okay. You got me. As you always do. I slipped the fucking thing underneath the chassis, not in the tyre well. Between you and me there was no way in hell that I was going to break into that car with the pair of them wide awake inside their bedroom fantasizing about each other.'

'What are you talking about? Fantasizing about each other?'

'I heard Lamia's voice. She's my sister, remember. I've never heard her speaking like that to a man before.'

'Like what?'

'Like she gives a damn about what he thinks of her.'

'You're serious?'

'I'm convinced she's got the hots for Sabir.'

'I can't believe it.'

'Yes, it does stretch the imagination a little. When you think of all the millions of women with unblemished faces out there. I mean, why take second best when you don't need to? Anyway, either she's kidding herself, or Sabir must have detached retinas.'

'Seriously. Does Sabir have the hots for her?'

Vau made a face. 'Sabir hides it better, but I wouldn't be surprised.' He grinned at his brother, pleased that he was contributing something of value for once. 'Can you use that knowledge in some way, Abi?'

Abi shrugged reflectively. 'I don't know. Maybe. Maybe not. But I'm sure as hell going to give it some thought.'

38

That morning saw the trio crossing the Rio Bravo at the Puente Nuevo, and driving through into Matamoros from Brownsville, Texas. They paid their $2.25 toll, and arranged for their temporary vehicle permit from the CIITEV office. Then they headed south down Highway 101 towards San Fernando.

Abi and Vau, who had crossed by foot earlier that morning, and secured a new, Mexican registered rental for themselves, picked up the Grand Cherokee about two miles out of town. The tracker was working fine, so they were able to follow the Jeep at a distance of about three quarters of a mile, with no possibility of a surprise sighting. The nine remaining members of the Corpus had been detailed to hire themselves two people carriers, one for the men and one for the women, and to keep in touch with Abi and Vau via cell phone. They would rendezvous every night near whatever motel the trio had chosen for themselves.

Abi had decided against concealing the existence of the tracker from his brothers and sisters for the simple reason that keeping a close tail on a car you don't really need to follow is a smart way of asking for trouble. And to hell with Madame, his mother's, worries about her children feeling she didn't trust them any more. If the others didn't tell her and trigger the predictable scene, then he certainly wouldn't. And who in their right mind trusted anybody anyway?

Any further cock-ups, and Abi knew that the Countess would take him off the case. Christ, she might even give the job to Brain-of-Europe Vau – or, even worse, to the next man down the list in the seniority stakes. Mr Harelip himself. Bullshitter Berith. The world's greatest Pseudologist.

Abi knew that his best bet with the Countess always lay in seducing her into liking him face to face. Alongside Oni and Athame, he was undoubtedly her favourite. But keeping in touch with her by cell phone was a sheer disaster. The Countess hated using telephones, and was always constrained in what she said. She started in on the offensive and stayed there. And wasn't it always so much easier to cashier somebody when you didn't have to look them in the eye?

Abi decided that he would tread very carefully indeed for the next few days. When the perfect moment came to move in on Sabir, he would be ready. He wouldn't blow things twice in a row.

39

'I think it's time you told us a little more about the Corpus Maleficus.' Calque was luxuriating across the Grand Cherokee's rear bench. Sabir was driving, and Lamia was beside him on the passenger seat.

The air conditioning was working at full stretch, and Sabir could feel the deterioration in the car's power as a result. He was sticking to a steady sixty-eight miles an hour on the assumption that any contact with Mexican traffic cops this close to the border could only lead to tears. This was drug country. Everyone was corrupt in one way or another. It was simply a matter of scale.

'Why now? Why did you not ask me this before?' Lamia glanced back at Calque. It wasn't a suspicious look so much as an old-fashioned one. The sort of look that says 'You'd better not be trying to spin me a line, matey.'

Calque straightened up. The expression on his face was that of a man who suddenly means business. 'We are maybe two, or at the most, three days' driving away from where we need to be. Sabir has chosen not to share with us the key element of his revelatory quatrain – although I should have thought he would have learned to trust us both by now. It has occurred to me that if you showed good faith, Lamia, in opening up the skeletons in your family's cupboard, then the ever elusive Sabir might prove more amenable to also confiding in his friends.'

Sabir rolled his eyes. 'Artfully done, Calque. Artfully done. I can't fault you. You got a dig in at just about everybody with that little speech of yours. Hell, you must have been a policeman in a former life.'

Before Calque could respond, Lamia turned towards both men, fixing first one and then the other with her gaze. 'I don't mind you quizzing me. I trust you, even if you don't trust me. I'm here with you because I've got nowhere else to go. And because I don't want to be alone, now that my family have excommunicated me. It's as simple as that. To have you both on my side – to be able to share my fears with you – is very precious to me.'

Chalk one up for the distaff team, thought Sabir. He checked out Calque's face in the rear-view mirror. The man was as pink as a sand shrimp. Unprecedented. That was the only word for it. He had never seen Calque colour up to an even mildly roseate tinge before. The bastard had seemed impermeable to normal feelings of guilt and embarrassment.

Sabir realized that he was feeling pretty guilty, too. It was becoming ludicrously obvious that both he and Calque had been holding out on Lamia through some sort of misplaced survival instinct. Maybe now was the time to bring things out into the open a little?

Sabir cleared his throat. 'Right. Me first. Cards on the table. I'm sorry I've appeared so elusive. The verse you are all feeling hurt and resentful about goes as follows:

"In the land of the great volcano, fire
When the rock cools, the wise one, Ahau Inchal Kabah,
Shall make a hinged skull of the twentieth mask:
The thirteenth crystal will sing for the God of Blood."'

There was a stunned silence. Calque was the first to break it. 'That's it? That's the quatrain?'

Sabir nodded. 'Lock, stock, and barrel. What you see is what you get.'

'My God. It doesn't take us very far, does it?' Despite his words, Calque's eyes were fervid with speculation.

'It takes us to the Palace of the Masks at Kabáh, doesn't it?'

'Does it, Sabir? How do you read that one?'

'Well. The "of the twentieth mask" bit. That must be the Codz Poop. Or whatever your website called it, Lamia. It ties right in, don't you see? That's why I felt such a fool when you sprang the Orizaba eruption on me. Though how Nostradamus came up with this is way beyond me. Perhaps he's simply sent us all on some sort of posthumous wild goose chase halfway across the world? A final exercise of power from beyond the grave?'

'It wasn't a wild goose chase in France. Everything he said in his quatrains was true.'

'Yes. But that was in France. Nostradamus knew about France. He lived there for more than sixty years. But what the heck did he know about the New World?'

'Quite a lot I should imagine.' Calque held up a restraining hand. He was back in his element again, all thoughts of previous blunders forgotten. 'The man was born in 1503, remember, just three years before the death of Christopher Columbus. And Columbus discovered the New World in 1492. With Hernán Cortés invading Mexico twenty-seven years later, in 1519. That gave Nostradamus, who died in 1566, forty-seven years in which to find out all he wanted about the new Spanish colonies. He would no doubt have been familiar with Cortés's own *Cartas de Relacíon*, which appeared in print during the 1520s. And with the personally written account of the conquistador, Bernal Diáz de Castillo. Also Friar Bartolomé de las Casas's excoriating description of the *Destruction of the Indies*. Also Bernardino de Sahagún's *Florentine Codex*. For we know for a fact that Nostradamus both spoke and read Spanish, as well as a number of other languages, including Latin, Greek, Italian, and Franco-Provençal.'

'For pity's sake, Calque. What were you doing all those years in the police force? You're a born historian, man.'

Calque managed to look both pleased and peeved at the same time – as though he had just been surprised, in flagrante delicto, albeit with a particularly beautiful woman. 'I have indeed been doing my homework over the past few months. Those futile weeks I spent spying on Mademoiselle Lamia's family were not entirely wasted, you see. I read dozens of books both before and during that period – and everything about Nostradamus that I could find.'

'So . . .'

'So there's no reason why Nostradamus should not have shown a keen interest in the New World – the place and its riches were an object of endless fascination for the whole of literate Europe. Remember the myth of El Dorado? And remember, too, that Nostradamus came from an ancient family of assimilated Jews? Just as with the Gypsies, the forcibly ex-Jewish Nostradamus would have known exactly what kind of a threat the combined forces of Spanish Catholicism, the Inquisition, and the Auto-da-Fé posed to a country and culture that they considered pagan – and, in consequence, damned.'

'You mean he would have felt a kinship with the Maya?'

'Exactly. Just as he had previously felt a kinship with the Gypsies. To the extent that he might even have compared the wholesale destruction of Maya culture to similar Inquisitorial threats against the four levels of the *Kabbalah*. As always, therefore, with Nostradamus, he would have infibulated his quatrain with hidden codes and meanings to protect it from prying eyes – codes which could only be teased out via the use of *gematria*.'

'Jesus Christ, Calque. "Infibulated"? "*Gematria*"?'

'Infibulated means to interleave, or to lard with a knitting needle – I'm using the word in its figurative sense, needless to say, rather than in its explicit sense of sewing up the labia majora. And *gematria* is the Hebrew system of numerology.'

Sabir flared his eyes in quiet desperation. 'Are you trying to tell us that you have somehow deduced a whole series of hidden codes in the – what? – five whole minutes since you have had access to the quatrain?'

Calque threw himself back on his seat. 'No. I am sorry to disappoint you both. But I have deduced no hidden codes as yet. I am merely speculating that they might – no, change that to must – exist.'

40

It had been a bad day. Probably the worst day that you had ever suffered in your life.

At Villahermosa you had been robbed while you were sleeping in the market square. The thieves had taken the two hundred pesos that you had been keeping as a reserve in a pouch tied to your waist. But, far worse than that, they had taken the bag in which you were keeping the codex. You had been using this bag as a pillow, and the thieves' act of slipping it from underneath your head had woken you up.

You had identified the thieves and given chase. But you had not been eating well these past few days, and your strength was, in consequence, diminished. But you were still able to shout, and to summon aid from the other Indios who were sleeping in and around the square.

At first the thieves had seemed certain to escape, but, at the very last moment, two Indios entering the square after a night of heavy drinking had managed to stop them. The thieves did not have machetes, but these two Indios who had been drinking were carrying theirs.

Quickly, a crowd gathered around the thieves, and you were called upon to explain exactly what had happened.

You told about the pesos, and about your bag with the book that you were carrying for a friend.

A policeman came to join the crowd and to see what was occurring at this early hour of the morning, before the market had begun.

The thieves pretended to the policeman that they had not been doing as they had done. They were very convincing. You argued against them, but the policeman was not inclined to listen to you, as you were a stranger, coming from Veracruz. At length the policeman took the two thieves aside, and the three of them stood talking together for some time. The two thieves gave the policeman something, the policeman nodded, and the thieves hurried away. Quickly, like mist dispersing on a lake, all the Indios surrounding you also melted away.

Then the policeman came back. He was carrying the bag in which you kept the codex. 'Is this your property?'

'Yes, Señor.'

'This is a valuable property no doubt?' The policeman took out the codex and began to leaf through the folded pages.

'No. It is not valuable.'

'Then you will not mind if I confiscate it?'

You shook your head. Your heart was as ice in your chest. 'I would very much mind for it to be confiscated. This thing belongs to another. I have promised to take it to him. I have taken an oath.'

'The thieves gave me two hundred pesos. What will you give me?'

You opened your hands and turned them upwards. 'The two hundred pesos the thieves gave you belonged to me. It was the money the thieves stole from me.'

'I am sorry for this. But I can do nothing. If you want your property, you must pay a fine. That is the law.' The policeman opened the notebook he was carrying at a certain page, and pointed to the text, which you, of course, could not read.

You reached down and slipped off one of your shoes. In it, you had fifty pesos of your one hundred remaining pesos. You took out the fifty-peso note and placed it in the policeman's book.

The policeman shrugged. 'Is that all you have?'

'The thieves . . .' You also shrugged. But still, hidden inside your other shoe, was the remaining fifty-peso note. You prayed to the Virgin of Guadalupe that the policeman would not ask you to reveal what was in that shoe as well. If he did this, you would be lost.

The policeman snapped shut his book. 'Very well then.' He dropped the bag with the codex onto the ground, as if by error. 'You have paid your fine. You are free to go now.'

You quickly picked up the codex, bowed to the policeman, and turned away.

Now you knew you would certainly starve. You had just fifty pesos left to your name. And you still had to pass through Ciudad del Carmen, Champotón, and Hopelchén, before you reached your final destination at Kabáh, at the Palace of the Masks.

A friendly Indio had told you that there was a chance, if you waited for the ending of the market, that if one of the market traders had done particularly well, they might possibly agree to take you back with them in their empty truck. Many came from Ciudad del Carmen to the market in Villahermosa – almost as many as went to Campeche. If you were lucky, and had the patience to wait without complaining, you might find such a person.

In the meanwhile you knew you would be forced to loiter around the market all day, praying that you would not meet the policeman again, and that one amongst the many market traders might throw some of his rotting fruit away into the gutter. If this was the case, then you would be able to eat a little, and settle your stomach. For the fifty pesos that you had left in your shoe would doubtless be needed at Kabáh – as a bribe, maybe, in case the man at the main gate would not let you in to wait.

When you fell to thinking about this waiting, your stomach pained you even more than it had before. It was like the ache of a blow – your belly seemed to expand and contract with the pain at one and the same time. Originally, you had promised yourself eggs – in the form of *salsa de huevo* – for breakfast that morning, in a bid to keep up your strength. But now, because of the thieves, you dared not waste your remaining money on such luxuries.

Truly, this had been a bad day. Probably the worst day that you had ever suffered in your life.

41

'Despite all that you say about her, Madame, my mother, is an honourable woman.'

Sabir checked out Calque's response to Lamia's statement in the Cherokee's rear-view mirror. Calque was clutching his head as if somebody had just struck him a glancing blow on the temple with a meat mallet. Fortunately for Calque, Lamia did not appear to notice the movement.

'What's all this "Madame, my mother" bit? I've been meaning to ask you that for some time now.' It wasn't the smartest question in the world, but Sabir knew he had to do whatever was necessary to divert Lamia's attention away from Calque, who was behaving as if he wanted to trigger a riot. Where it concerned the Countess, the ex-detective's mind was unquestionably a no-through-road.

'It's a term of respect. All of us children use it. Monsieur, my father, was a very old man when we knew him – more like a grandfather than a father, really – and it seemed only right to show him respect. The usage then carried over to Madame, my mother. And we have never seen any reason to change it.'

'So you still respect her?'

'Of course. But I also disagree with her. In the strongest possible terms.'

Sabir pulled into a lay-by and switched off the engine. They were a little way short of Ciudad Madero and Tampico. The trucks and pickups on nearby Highway 80/180 buffeted the Grand Cherokee each time they passed, causing the vehicle to rock on her springs like a spavined old lady. 'I'm sorry. I can't possibly drive and concentrate on a conversation like this at the same time.' He turned to Lamia. 'Let me get this straight. You still respect the woman who had you drugged and tied up, and who would most probably have had you killed if Calque's buddy hadn't ridden in on his white charger and rescued you?'

'Madame, my mother, would never have had me killed.'

'Oh, really? Well she sicced Achor Bale, your brother, onto a bunch of entirely innocent Gypsies, two of whom

238

he killed, one of whom he as good as crippled, and the other one of whom he tried to give permanent, screaming nightmares to. And that's not to mention a security guard, his Alsatian dog, and Calque's assistant, Paul Macron, each of whom suffered lethally in the fallout.'

'Rocha thought they had information we needed.'

'Oh. So that's okay then?'

'I don't believe Madame, my mother, knew quite how out of control Rocha was. I don't believe she wanted to have anyone killed. Rocha was working to his own agenda.'

Calque chose that moment to wade back into the conversation. 'Rocha, or whatever you want to call him – I can't think of him as anything other than Achor Bale myself – was definitely not working off his own bat. He was working at your mother's instigation, and doing her bidding in everything.'

'Can you prove that?'

'Of course not. That has always been my problem. Which is why the Countess got away with her dirty little scheme. In any halfway decent society she would have gone down for at least five years as an accessory before the fact. But she was far too well connected for that, wasn't she? My Commandant actually admitted as much to my face. Which is one of the reasons why I took early retirement.'

'Perhaps you were wrong? Perhaps she was innocent all the time? Have you thought of that?'

Calque made a pfaffing sound through his nose, like an irritated horse. 'I knew it then, and I know it now – she's guilty as hell.'

Sabir turned to Lamia. He took a deep breath. One part of him felt he needed to pin Lamia down about her family – the other part felt he ought to cut her a little slack. The first part won. 'And your twin brothers? Were

239

they just out to have a friendly little conversation with me up there in Stockbridge? Just chewing the fat, so to speak? Did I misunderstand their intentions? Maybe they didn't really intend to burn down my house. Maybe they were just joshing me?'

'Possibly.'

'Oh, for God's sake, Lamia. What's got into you? Are you regretting coming with us? Would you rather go take your chances back with the Corpus?'

Lamia turned on Sabir. The unmarked side of her face had gone a deathly white. 'No, of course not. But I don't want you to demonize my family either. They really believe in what they are doing. They really believe that the de Bales have been tasked with protecting the world from the thousand-year return of the Devil. We have been doing it – not unsuccessfully – for nearly eight hundred years now.'

'Well thank Christ someone's been on the job.' Sabir's patience was wearing thin. How could an intelligent woman like Lamia act so blindly when it came to her family? He felt like reaching out and shaking her.

'Just how have you been achieving this?' This from Calque, who had taken advantage of his companions' temporary lapse of attention to light a cigarette. As he spoke, he puffed smoke busily out through the open window.

'All right. I will give you one example. During the French Wars of Religion, the Corpus, being good Catholics, targeted the Huguenots. It was a de Bale who, alongside the de Guises, persuaded King Charles IX to agree to the St Bartholomew's Day massacre. It was a Corpus member, also, who tried to assassinate Admiral Gaspard de Coligny. This was done specifically to trigger the massacre. In this way, France was spared the greater horrors that would later be visited on the German princely states.'

240

Sabir shook his head in blank incomprehension. 'So the Massacre of the Huguenots was a good thing, was it? The way I understand it, out-of-control French Catholics went on to slaughter thirty thousand innocent men, women, and children in the months following the St Bartholomew's Day massacre. It was a bloodbath, Lamia. But now you're belatedly claiming that it was actually done to guarantee peace further down the line. Have I got that right?'

'But these were Devil worshippers, Adam. Cultists. People who thought the Pope was the Antichrist. They had to die.'

'You can't be serious?'

'There are times when innocents must be killed in order to protect the majority.'

'Oh, so they were innocent?'

'Innocent in the sense of misguided. Yes.'

Sabir turned to Calque. 'You're a Catholic, too, I suppose?'

Calque gave an uncertain nod. 'Yes. But I haven't massacred anybody yet, so don't look at me like that, Sabir.'

'What do you make of what Lamia is saying?'

Calque hesitated. 'I think the whole thing is a lot more complicated than it looks.'

Sabir pretended to fall backwards on his seat. 'Oh, so now you're in agreement with Lamia? The Corpus did do the right thing after all?'

Calque shook his head. 'No. They didn't do the right thing. It's never right to massacre people, whatever you may think of their religion, or ethnicity, or point of view. But the Corpus *thought* they were doing the right thing. That's the point that Lamia is trying to make. And that's the point I realize we haven't been taking into account about her mother.'

241

'God God, Calque. If you carry on like this I may start suspecting that you have an open mind.'

'An open mind? Perish the thought. But we do need to understand what actually drives the Corpus – the better, eventually, to defeat it. In my view Lamia has just made her own situation perfectly clear. She respects her mother's viewpoint, but rejects it for herself.'

'What are you saying? That we ought to share our information with the Corpus? Bring them into the loop?' Sabir cradled his head on his hands, and gave Calque a sickly smile. 'Perhaps you could offer the Countess a friendly hug when next you are passing Cap Camarat? I'm sure she would welcome you with open arms, Captain.'

Calque shrugged. 'I'm not insane, Sabir. I remember only too well what that maniac Achor Bale was capable of. He killed my assistant, remember. A man no better than he should have been, perhaps. But a man, nonetheless, with a family, a fiancée, and a future. Achor Bale snuffed all that out without even pausing to draw breath.'

'Then what are you suggesting?'

'I'm saying that we need to understand exactly where the Corpus is coming from. What they are trying to achieve. Look, Lamia. You have to be considerably more open with us if we're to have any chance at all of combating this thing. First off, does the Corpus still have the same sort of influence it appears to have wielded when France still had a king?'

Lamia hesitated. For a moment Sabir feared that she intended to duck the question. Then she shook her head. 'No. All that ended with the Second World War.'

'The Second World War? Explain yourself.'

Lamia took a deep breath. 'Maréchal Pétain, the leader of Vichy France, was almost certainly a Corpus member. He attended both the St Cyr Military Academy

242

and the École Supérieure de Guerre in Paris, both of which were hotbeds of Corpus activity towards the end of the nineteenth century. Later, Pétain became a close friend of the Count, my father. But he and the Count disagreed bitterly on the Maréchal's policy of appeasement towards Germany. My father did not believe, for instance, that Adolf Hitler was the Second Antichrist. He thought, instead, that this particular distinction belonged to Josef Stalin. He disagreed, also, with the Vichy government's policy towards the Jews. If he hadn't been seriously injured in one of the early German bombardments, he might have been able to take all of this much further – made his influence felt behind the scenes in some way.'

'Are you serious?'

'Very. He was convinced, for instance, that France was a natural ally of Russia, and not of Germany, and that we should never have tacitly allied ourselves with the Nazis against Stalin.'

'So he was a communist?'

'No. But he was prepared to use communists for his purposes.'

'A nice distinction.'

'My father's injury put an end to France pursuing that particular line – in a way, you see, his injury paved the way for the eventual disintegration of the Corpus.' Lamia glanced back at Calque. 'A bit like the injury suffered by the Fisher King which diluted the power of the Round Table. You understand the parallels, Captain?'

Calque nodded. 'Succinctly put. I understand you very well.'

'Before that time we had been strong in the cadet schools, the military academies, and also in the civil service. Like a sort of Freemasonry, really. But the war changed all that. With Monsieur, my father, *hors de combat*, and taking into account his virulent dislike of the Hitler regime – which he privately believed to be Devil-driven – all Corpus influence collapsed. Laval and Pétain had their revenge in the end, you see. By the time my father recovered from both the physical and the psychological damage that he had received, France had changed utterly, becoming riddled with retrospective guilt and denial. The Count simply withdrew from public life in order to allow the Corpus a dignified final disintegration. It was only with the advent of Madame, my mother, thirty years later, that the Corpus was to some extent renewed.'

'In what form?'

'In the form that you see before you now. The Count only allowed the Countess to adopt their thirteen children on the strict understanding that she, under the aegis of his still influential family name, would actively attempt to reintegrate the Corpus into public life. At his instigation, she would send each of their children out into the world to begin a new strand of the Corpus's sworn duty. They would, within their ranks, incorporate all of the four great factors which determine aristocratic prestige – *l'ancienneté*, *les alliances*, *les dignités*, and *les illustrations*. They would represent ancient nobility, they would cement new alliances, they would hold high office, and they would perform great and noble actions. But none of this ever occurred. Society had changed too much. Monsieur, my father, had alienated too many right-wing establishment figures with his excoriation of Nazi Germany. We still had a certain degree of influence, but it was based upon nostalgia rather than on any real access to the corridors of power.'

'So where does that leave the Corpus now?'

'Working to a different stage of logic. What we cannot steal, we buy. And what we cannot have by right, we seize. With us, it has become a case of the law of the jungle.' Lamia raised her head defiantly. 'If you wish to defeat the Corpus, you will only do so by using the law of the jungle against them in return. Otherwise the Corpus will chew you up and spit you out like a piece of rotting meat.'

Sabir scrunched himself back into his seat, his neck against the window frame, his head against the glass, so that he could see both Calque and Lamia at the same time. 'So now we come to the million-dollar question, Lamia. The one that secures the prize. Why are your people still pursuing us? What can they conceivably hope to gain? What do they figure to get from the lost prophecies of Nostradamus?'

Lamia looked shocked. 'But it is obvious, Adam. I thought you knew this without my having to tell you? It is all about power. The need to know what the future holds. And for this they require three things.' She marked the points off on her fingers. 'They need to know the identity and whereabouts of the Third Antichrist, whom some people call the "Wilful King". They need to know the identity and whereabouts of the Second Coming. And they need to know whether 21 December 2012 marks the true end of the world, or merely the start of the predicted thousand-year return of the Devil. If it is the latter, then the Corpus will protect the Antichrist and kill the *Parousia* – in this way they will effectively delay the advent of the Devil because he will no longer feel that he is under-represented on earth. In this manner, also, they will have fulfilled their ancient task. If it is the former, they will commit collective suicide, and be translated into heaven to sit at the right hand of God the Father Almighty.'

Calque let his unlit cigarette flutter from his fingers. 'Mary, Jesus, Joseph, and all the Saints. What? Like the Rapture?'

'A little like that.'

'But the Rapture relies on the Second Coming, Lamia. It *relies* on the *Parousia*. It's not about killing Him, for pity's sake.'

'But the Pre-Wrath Rapture is, Captain. This is the moment when we are told the sun turns black and the moon turns red. An era of wars, famines, earthquakes, volcanic eruptions, and tsunamis – what the Bible calls the time of the "abomination of desolation". God's wrath will fall on the unbelievers when the sixth seal is finally opened. There will be a long period of tribulation before the Second Advent.' Lamia looked at her two companions. 'Does any of this sound familiar to you, gentlemen? Does any of this ring a bell with you?'

Sabir felt as if his brain had been run through a clothes' mangle. 'You mean the eruption of Orizaba? The earthquake in L'Aquila? Global warming? The Indian Ocean tsunami? The melting of the polar ice cap? That sort of thing?'

Lamia made a tired face. 'Yes. And all the rest of it too.'

42

Abi was acting as look-out and Vau was driving. At first glance, the tracker had appeared to be misbehaving, which meant that the twins found themselves blundering past the stationary Grand Cherokee when they were least expecting it.

'Christ. Did you see them? Did you see what they were doing? It was them, Abi, wasn't it? Did they see us?'

'Calm down, Vau. There's no damage done. They were just sitting in their car talking. Or at least so far as I could see. We were moving way too fast when we passed them. Plus we've got a fresh car. Plus we're wearing these stupid American baseball caps. They won't have made us.'

'I wish we'd planted a proper bug on them when we had the chance.'

'Oh yes? And this from the man who couldn't be bothered to break into their car when the opportunity was handed to him on a plate, but simply latched his tracker onto the fucking undercarriage in the fond hope that it wouldn't fucking jerk off when they fucking went over their first fucking speed bump?'

'Okay, Abi. Okay. You don't have to rub it in.'

'What do you think they were talking about? Maybe you've got a view on that too, Vau?'

'How do I know? What do you think?'

Abi closed his eyes. He scrubbed at his face, then let his head fall back against the built-in headrest. He motioned to Vau to pull the car over. 'Us, probably.'

'How do you figure that, Abi? They don't even know we're following them.'

'What? You think they've just relaxed down and forgotten about us, maybe? Put us out of their minds completely?'

'No, Abi. I don't think that.'

'Why ever not?'

Vau's face lit up. 'Because they're too smart. Lamia knows we'll never give up. And she'll have told them that. They'll be shit scared we'll spring out from nowhere and get them.'

Abi hunched down even further in the passenger seat in case the Cherokee overtook them again. 'You know something, Vau? I think you're right.' He nodded his head a few times, thinking. 'I think we need to rush things a little. I think we need to put the fear of God into them, and get them to make a few unforced errors. I'm fed up to my back teeth with all this pussy-footing around.'

'But Madame, our mother, told you to hang back, Abi. I heard her say so. She told you to let them lead us to wherever they are going, and not to interfere with them until she tells you to do so.'

Abi glanced across at his brother. 'Well we know that wherever they are going is in Mexico. And probably in either Veracruz or the Yucatan.'

'How do we know that, Abi?'

'Because they are taking the coastal route, dummy. If they were transiting through to Guatemala, for instance, or Honduras, or Panama, they'd go the fuck down the centre, wouldn't they? Past Mexico City.'

'I suppose so. But you don't have to swear at me all the time to get your point across.'

'You suppose right. And yes I do.' Abi yawned. He was beginning to lose interest in winding Vau up. 'So we're getting near to where we need to be. And they don't know we've got a tracker planted on them. So I say we scare the living bejasus out of them, and set them to running at double speed. Because if we carry on the way we are going, Aldinach's going to get ants in her pants again, and trigger another riot. Or that stupid bastard Oni is going to fall foul of the Mexican cops. I mean, have you seen him recently? He's taken to wearing floral shorts. The idiot stands out like a cockroach on a teacake.'

Vau slapped at the steering wheel. 'Hey, that's funny. I like that. A cockroach on a teacake.'

Abi gave Vau a pitying look. 'It's not original, Vau. I stole the idea from Raymond Chandler. Only he said "a tarantula on a slice of angel food".'

'Angel food? What's that?'

'Fairy cake.'

'Fairy cake? And Raymond who, did you say?'

'Forget it, Vau. It's really not that important.'

43

Sabir pulled off the Veracruz *cuota* road and into the village of La Antigua for lunch. The trio had approximately two days' driving left before they reached Kabáh, and Sabir figured that a treat was called for.

'What is this place?' said Lamia.

'It's where stout Cortés scuttled his ships so that his men wouldn't dare back out on him and return to Cuba.'

'Stout Cortés?' Calque stretched both hands above his head, like a man trying to reach for a light bulb. He stared down towards the river, which curled like a dirty brown ribbon towards the nearby Gulf. 'The man was a barbarian. He almost single-handedly destroyed two great empires.'

Sabir threw back his head. 'I'm not giving him a testimonial, Calque. I'm quoting Keats's "On First Looking Into Chapman's Homer".'

Calque acknowledged Sabir's point with a hitch of his shoulders. 'And how do you happen to know about this place? It's not exactly on the beaten track, is it?'

'A holiday. With my mother and father. The only one we ever took together as a family.'

'Why here?'

A dead look came into Sabir's eyes. 'I was seventeen. My mom was going through a stable period for once. Semi-sane, anyway. My dad paid for us to take a trip to Mexico because he thought it would be good for her. We came down here via Oaxaca and Monte Alban, to see the ruins at Zempoala. It was a disaster. My mom had to be airlifted back to the US under sedation. But La Antigua was the very last place we had something approaching a good time. We ate *langostinos al mojo de ajo* just up the road there, and drank *mojitos*, and my father told us all about what happened when Cortés landed here with his men. We even took a boat up to the mouth of the river, and walked around on the headland.'

'So you speak a little Spanish?'

'Not a word. How about you, Calque?'

'My Spanish is a fraction better than my English. And you know how good my English is.'

'I wondered why you let Lamia do all the talking when we checked into our posada.'

'I couldn't help noticing you didn't say much either.'

Lamia had already started down towards the restaurant. 'Well, I shall just have to do your translating for you, shan't I? It will give me a role to play. Fortunately I speak Spanish fluently. As well as Italian, English, Portuguese, German, and a little Greek. Not to mention French.'

'Show off.'

She turned around and flashed them her most captivating smile.

44

Calque and Sabir chose a table overlooking the river, while Lamia went to visit the powder room. It was the first time the two men had been alone together since they'd crossed the Mexican border two days before.

'Do you really think we can trust her, Calque? After what she said about the Corpus back there in Tampico? About still respecting the Countess?'

'If she was trying to outwit us, Sabir, do you think she would have been quite so painfully honest?'

'She might be trying a double bluff?'

'Yes, and God is an Englishman. Come on, man. One has only to look at her to see that she is a decent person. I feel privileged to be travelling with her. Just think what it would be like if there were only the two of us here. What a state we would be in by now. At least she is keeping us focused. Not to mention up-to-date with our laundry.'

'Yeah, well, it's clear that you've got an almighty crush on her, Calque. You fuss around her like an old mother hen.'

Calque straightened in his chair. 'And what about you? Haven't you noticed yourself recently? Your own behaviour?'

Sabir pretended to watch some fishermen jump-starting their boat. 'That's bullshit.'

'It's not bullshit. I know you both hold secret assignations together. I woke up one night and heard you.'

Sabir shrugged. He was still pretending to watch the fishermen. 'It's because we both can't sleep. I have nightmares, and you snore. So between us it's no wonder

Lamia needs a break now and again. If we meet outside the room, it's only by accident – not by intent.'

'I do not snore.'

'Oh, really? When did you last share a room with anybody, Calque? The early 1950s? Of course you snore. Like a steam locomotive winding up before its first big run of the day.'

Calque threw both hands out as though he was trying to snatch at a runaway loop of knitting yarn. 'I object to your example, Sabir. You are purposely exaggerating. I may snuffle a bit, but that is only when I inadvertently lie on my back. It is a common enough ailment.'

'Snuffle. Snore. Have it your own way.'

'You are still artfully avoiding my question.'

'Which is?'

'You and Lamia.'

'Are you her daddy?'

Calque bridled. 'I feel I am somewhat *in loco paternis*, yes. I inadvertently brought her into this, therefore she is my responsibility.'

'Admit it. You'd like her to be your daughter, wouldn't you?'

'See? You are changing the subject again? Perhaps you are simply too stupid to acknowledge your feelings for her?'

Sabir gave up all pretence of staring at the fishing boat. 'Who the heck are you calling stupid? And this from a man who doesn't even realize he's got an Oedipus complex.'

Calque slapped the table. 'I do not have an Oedipus complex. You've completely mixed up your Freudian terms. An Oedipus complex is when a boy competes with his father for his mother's attentions. So you are certainly wrong there. My mother paid no attention either to me or to my father, so there was nothing even to play for.

And don't tell me I have the opposite of an Oedipus complex, because that is an Electra complex, and Lamia certainly does not have that about me.'

'I'm not talking about her. And I'm not talking about your mother. I'm talking about you. Who's changing the subject now?'

'I do not deny that I still feel very damaged about the loss of my own daughter's affections. Although I'm surprised and a little disappointed that you should choose to bring the matter up again. I told you about it in confidence, in a weak moment, Sabir, and I foolishly supposed that the subject would end there. However neither do I deny that I feel a quasi-paternal interest in Lamia. It would be strange, in the circumstances, if I did not.'

Sabir snapped his fingers together. 'I've got it. I've remembered it. It's called a Lear complex. When a father has a libidinous fixation on his daughter.'

Calque's voice rose effortlessly above the hubbub surrounding them – a hubbub which was further aggravated by the restaurant's resident trio attempting their own unique version of *Besame Mucho* on matching marimbas. 'I most emphatically do not have a Lear complex, Sabir. And I would like to point out that Lamia is not, in fact, my daughter. And that therefore if I did happen to feel any sexual desire for her, it would not, in and of itself, be incestuous. Nor even inappropriate in terms of age difference. For you may not have noticed it, Sabir, but I am not quite in my dotage yet. I am still only fifty-five years old.' Calque fumbled around in his pockets for a cigarette. He found one and lit it, flicking the extinguished match through the open window beside him. 'However it is not predominantly sexual desire that I feel for Lamia, but rather admiration and liking. I also feel a curious protective urge to shield her from the attentions of younger men such as you.'

'Younger men such as me? And what are younger men such as me, when they are at home?'

'Younger men who have taken immaturity to an entirely new level. Younger men who mistake bravado for experience. Younger men who have no earthly sense of self-preservation. I remember you in France, Sabir, blundering from one disaster to the next without the faintest effort at self-control. It was an absolute miracle that you and your two Gypsy friends survived the eye-man's attentions. In a rational world, you would all three be dead by now.'

'And then you would have Lamia for yourself? Is that it?'

Calque thrust himself up from the table. Sabir did the same. One of the waiters had been just about to ask them for their drinks order, but, sensing their lack of attention to the menu, he veered towards another table like a liner changing tack mid-ocean.

'I don't believe this.' Lamia was heading towards them from the direction of the restrooms. 'Are you two arguing again? I could hear you all the way across the restaurant. Must this happen every time I go away? It is impossible. I know you like each other. Why can't you simply acknowledge it, and stop competing all the time? What were you arguing about this time?'

Calque made a sheepish face, and sat back down to finish his cigarette. Sabir shrugged, and pretended to watch the marimba trio.

'Were you arguing about me? Is that it?'

'Of course not. Why should we do that?'

Lamia sat down beside them and signalled to the elusive waiter. 'Why indeed?'

45

Abi left it until well after Veracruz to put his plan into action. The trio were approaching Lake Catemaco on the coast road when he told Dakini to dish the baseball cap and sunglasses, and make her presence felt. Athame, Nawal, and Aldinach – who had chosen to join the other de Bale women as a female for the duration – were hunched down out of sight in the well of the people carrier.

Lamia was driving the Cherokee, with Sabir asleep on the back seat. Calque was reading a book.

Lamia lurched upright. Then she poked Calque in the ribs with her elbow. 'I knew it. It *was* Dakini I saw back in Houston. I've just seen her again. With a different car this time.'

Calque threw the book aside. 'Where?'

'She was pulled over in the Pemex station getting fuel. That one. Back there.'

'Was she alone?'

'Looked like it. But it was a very big car for just one person.'

'Are you sure it was her?'

'Don't you think I know my own sister?'

'Step on the gas then. We've still got a chance of losing her. She can't leave without paying and giving the guy his tip.'

Lamia threw the Cherokee into the first serious curve she'd encountered since the service station. 'I knew we should have taken the *cuota* road out of Veracruz. There's only one way out of here. They'll simply be waiting for us at the junction at Acayucán.'

'Give me the map.'

'Sabir's got it.'

Calque stretched over to the rear seat and prodded Sabir's leg.

Sabir cracked open an eye. 'What is it? Why are you waking me up? And why is Lamia driving like a maniac?'

'We have company.'

Sabir jack-knifed into a sitting position. 'Where?'

'Back at the Pemex station. They were still tanking up. With a bit of luck, we'll have a couple of kilometres head start on them.'

'Forget it. They'll simply wait for us at Acayucán.'

'That's just what Lamia said. But I remember a smaller road on the map. A dirt road that runs through the mountains towards Jaltipan. If we get to the turn-off before they see us, we'll have a fair chance of giving them the slip. They'll never expect us to do such a stupid thing as that.'

'Stupid. Yes. You said it, Calque, not me.' Sabir blitzed a look at the map and then passed it across the seats. 'You're right about the dirt road, though. But I don't like it. It's no more than a farm track, really – they even show it as a fractured orange line on the map, and that's never a good thing.' He glanced at the empty road behind them. 'If the Corpus see us taking it, man, we'll be sitting ducks.'

'So what's the difference? We're sitting ducks already.'

46
—

'That's it. They took the dirt road, just as you expected.'

Abi clapped his hands together. 'They'll have tremendous fun going over the Cerro Santa Marta.

From sea level to 1879 metres in just under twenty kilometres. On a road that isn't paved. With drops either side you wouldn't even want to throw your grandmother over.'

'Shall we follow them?'

'What's the point? They'll pop out again in three or four hours' time in Jaltipan. Gasping for breath, probably. We can pick them up with the tracker there, no problem. That's if they don't break their necks thinking we're following them. I love doing things like this.'

'Like what?'

'Unexpected things. What the Americans call coming in from left base.'

'Like what you did with the railway inspector and his wife? Downloading the child pornography?'

'Exactly. It makes me sick coming at things straight on. There's always another way – a roundabout way – to achieve the same end.'

'Tell me another one you did, Abi.'

Abi relaxed back onto the passenger seat. 'Okay. Seeing as we unexpectedly have a few extra hours to waste.' He pretended to be thinking. In fact he'd been rehearsing the story he was going to tell Vau for the past fifteen minutes. Telling stories was the only way you could ever teach Vau anything – he was like a child that way. 'You remember that bastard de la Maigrerit de Gavillane?'

'The one who insulted Madame, our mother, over the table placement while I was in hospital with a torn meniscus?'

'Yes. Him. Because she was a widow, and because she had come without an escort to a formal dinner, he placed her below those upstarts with the Napoleonic title. The Prince and Princesse de . . .' Abi shrugged. 'They're so insignificant, I can't even remember their names.'

257

'It doesn't matter, Abi. Tell me about de Gavillane.'

'He knew exactly what he was doing, the bastard – his father, and Monsieur, our father, had fallen out during the war over the Nazi question. You know how the Count felt about Hitler. Well, the de Gavillanes were enthusiastic fellow travellers to the Third Reich. After the war they hushed it all up, of course, and made out that they were Resistance heroes, but nobody believed them. The de Gavillane name even appeared on denouncements secretly given to high-up Nazi Party members and to the Milice – all the denouncements concerned people who just happened to own land abutting the de Gavillane's country estate. By the end of the war, they had a 10,000-hectare park around their chateau. People don't forget that sort of thing.'

'What do you mean "people"?'

'I mean we weren't the only ones who wanted de Gavillane punished.'

'You mean these other people paid you?'

'Why would I need paying, Vau? I have more than enough money as it is. No. They simply made it easier for me to do what I had to do. Told me de Gavillane's habits. What clubs he belonged to. Where he hung out. I finally narrowed it down to his health club, or the Turf. But the Turf is too public. His health club was better. I watched de Gavillane without his noticing it. People have habits, you see. And de Gavillane had one particular habit that amused me no end. He hated people leaving their plastic cups of water in the sauna. Whenever he went in he would throw the water onto the stone furnace, and then dispose of the plastic cups in the bin outside. Made no end of a song and a dance about it to the staff.'

'I don't understand, Abi. Why is that interesting? Why were you amused by that?'

'Because it was a tic. And tics make people vulnerable.'

'Vulnerable? Vulnerable to what?'

'I left three full cups in there one day. Just before he came in.'

'Yes. And so?'

'I filled them with vodka, Vau. Pure vodka. Bulgarian Balkan 176 degrees proof – 88 per cent alcohol. Clear as a mountain stream. When de Gavillane threw them onto the furnace he started a fireball in the narrow space of the sauna cubicle you wouldn't believe. Fourth-degree burns. The man came out looking like a peeled tomato. Blind. No ears, lips, or eyelids. His penis stripped like a papaya. He's still in hospital more than fifty operations later. The man is so seized up with scar tissue that he can't even scratch his own arse any more. That's what I mean by coming at a thing from the side, Vau.'

'It's perfect, Abi. And no one can hold you responsible.'

'The man did it all by himself. Any evidence got burned in the great flame-up. The club talked about nothing else for weeks. A lot of people had been pissed off by de Gavillane's high-handed behaviour. Funny how someone else's bad luck cheers people up.'

'Why are you telling me this, Abi? You usually have a reason.'

Abi inclined his head. 'Well you're certainly on the button today, little brother. What I wanted to get over to you is that Madame, our mother, sometimes needs protecting from herself. She's an old lady now. She's not as with it as she used to be. If I sometimes seem to go against what she tells us, Vau, you mustn't be surprised.'

'Like in the case of de Gavillane?'

'Exactly. She knew nothing about that. But when she heard what had happened to him, she was extremely pleased. She never asked me if I did it, but we both know she knew.'

'She must have been really proud of you, Abi.' Vau took a deep breath. 'I wonder what that feels like?'

Abi punched his brother on the shoulder. 'Don't worry, Vau. You'll know soon enough.'

47

'Looks like we lost them again.' Sabir glanced down at the map. 'We've got to decide fast. Do we want to take the coast road to Villahermosa, or do we risk the *cuota*? Put some more distance between us?'

'What we do is stop this car right now and check for a tracker.'

'Oh, come on, Calque. They haven't been following us with any tracker. They just worked out which direction we were headed in, and spread out like a seine net to trap us. Lamia says that if Dakini's here, all eleven of them are probably here by now. So they've more than enough manpower to do the job. Dakini just happened to luck into seeing us at Catemaco. They probably had her patrolling the coast road while the rest of them watched the *cuota*.'

'I still think we should look for a tracker. Achor Bale used one on you and your friends during that trip you took down through France. So did we amateurs at the Police Nationale. The Corpus have doubtless all been trained in their use.' He glanced at Lamia, but she contrived to ignore his leading question.

Instead, she pulled the car over into a Pemex station, edging it around behind the shop so it wouldn't be visible from the highway. 'I need to wash and tidy up. I've just been driving for three straight hours over a cattle trail, through a mountain range, with my own family chasing after me, and I'm tired, and I'm irritable, and I probably smell. You both certainly do. If you men want to look for trackers, be my guest. But I'd appreciate it if you washed and changed into fresh clothes afterwards.' She got out of the car, grabbed her overnight bag, and disappeared into the restroom.

Sabir flapped his hand. 'Women. It's probably her time of the month.'

Calque gave him a look.

Sabir caught the look but chose to ignore it. It irritated the hell out of him when Calque grabbed the moral high ground for himself. 'Come on then, Chief Inspector. Stop all your horse-arsing around. Let's get this over and done with.'

Calque groaned, and slid out of the passenger seat. 'I'll take the rear. It'll most probably be in there. You take the front.'

'You seriously think they broke into the car and planted a tracking device? And we didn't notice or hear anything?'

Calque straightened up from a stretch. 'Didn't it ever occur to you that they allowed us to get away just a little too easily, back there in Carlisle? And that they picked us up again, two and a half thousand miles later, just a little too easily too?'

'With eleven of them potentially following us, according to Lamia's calculations? No. That wasn't the first thing that occurred to me.'

Calque threw open the back hatch and began to feel his way around. Sabir did the same in front.

After fifteen minutes, Lamia came back, holding a takeaway cup of coffee. She perched on the walkway watching them. 'Any joy?'

261

Sabir straightened up. 'There's no tracker in here. If they hid it, they hid it beneath the actual fabric of the car, and we'll never get to it like this.'

Calque shook his head. 'No. They had neither the time nor the facility to do that.'

'Then how about underneath?'

Calque made a face. 'People hide bombs underneath cars, Sabir, they don't hide trackers. It's not professional. The first major bump, the tracker would probably fly off. It's just too great a risk. No. They'd have put it inside. And I'm convinced now that they didn't do that. I think we're in the clear again. For the time being, at least.' Seeing Lamia eyeing up his shirt, Calque sniffed at his armpits, then flared his eyes, as if the smell had overwhelmed him. 'They'll be spreading out, though. Trying to edge ahead of us. All any of them has to do is look at a map, draw a few straight lines, and you can see which direction we're headed in. It might as well be lit up by a strobe.' He started to wipe his hands on his trousers and then thought better of it. 'We probably should have zigzagged on our way down, but you can't have everything. It's taken us far too much time as it is. My view is that we should drive straight through the night and try to get to Kabáh in the morning. Lamia is exhausted. I'll take the first four-hour stint, you take the second. The ones who aren't driving, try and get some sleep.'

Sabir nodded. 'We'll go and get washed up then.' He cocked a finger in Calque's direction, then picked at his own shirt with a mock sour expression on his face. 'Lamia, will you buy us some junk to eat on the way? You know the sort of thing Calque likes. The stuff that normal, everyday people snack on. Chocolates, and crisps, and soft drinks with E numbers. Shit like that.'

Calque shuddered as if someone had just wiped their clammy hand down the small of his back. He stood watching Lamia as she made her way back to the *tiendita*. Then he cocked his head at Sabir. 'Did you notice that, Sabir? She's wearing make-up. And she's put on a skirt and a fresh blouse and the closest approximation to a set of high heels I've ever seen her in. They're called kittens, if I remember rightly. I've never seen her looking so feminine.'

Sabir shrugged noncommittally. He was becoming adept at sliding out from under Calque's elaborate traps. 'Look. You were dead right to make us look for the tracker, Calque, and I was wrong. We'd have been made to look like complete fools if there was one in there. In fact you've been pretty much on the ball all the way along. I'm sorry, too, about what I said to you yesterday. All that shit about Lear complexes and daughter fixations. I don't know what got into me. I was way out of line.'

Calque gestured towards the *tiendita* with his thumb. Then he spread his hands expectantly, as if it were about to rain.

Sabir followed Calque's glance back towards the *tiendita*, a rueful expression on his face. He knew exactly where the conversation was heading. As usual, Calque had successfully set him up for the *coup de grace*. 'I know you think that Lamia's gone to all that effort just for me. But you're wrong about us. I promise you that. We don't hold out anything for each other. Lamia doesn't even allow that I exist most of the time.'

Calque sighed. 'Sometimes I think being a young man is the mental equivalent of snow blindness. How old is Lamia, Sabir?'

'She's twenty-seven. She told me so herself the other day.'

'And how old are you?'

'Thirty-four. Rising thirty-five.'

'Still young enough to be a fool. Yet old enough to know better.'

'What are you getting at, Calque?'

'You have before you a beautiful woman who does not know that she is beautiful, Sabir. She is damaged. All her life she has seen how people look at her, and she has made some deductions about it for herself. And her deductions are these. I am not a normal woman, she says to herself, nor ever can I be. I am not worthy to be desired. If a man desires me it is because he feels pity for me, and I am a proud person, and I cannot tolerate this. So I will close myself down. Deny my femininity. Work on other aspects of myself that will make me feel valued instead. I shall learn languages. Read books. Study obsessively. Develop my brain. I will take the woman part of me and I will simply kill it off. That way I won't be vulnerable. That way I can't be hurt.'

'Jesus, Calque. Where do you get all this stuff?'

Calque jabbed at Sabir with his finger. 'I have seen the way she looks at you, Sabir. You will be mindful of this one. You won't hurt her. You will consider her feelings. It is not enough just to be a man, and follow your hormones, and not bother to feel the need to think. If you don't care for her, show it. If you do care for her, show it. Or else I shall be very, very angry at you, and our friendship will be at an end.'

'We have a friendship?'

'Isn't that what Lamia said we had?'

'I guess it was.'

'Then you would be a wise man to believe her.'

48

By the time you had passed through Santa Elena the hunger was giving you hallucinations. First you saw a small animal that looked like a dog, but which wasn't a dog. It had a squared-off tail, and was grey all over. This animal watched you from the side of the road as you began walking. Then it followed you, darting in and out of the scrub at the edge of the highway. At one point you took out your machete and brandished it at the beast, but the creature lay hidden, perhaps anticipating your aggressive actions.

Then, later, you saw a snake at the side of the road. It was emerald green. As you watched, it coiled itself back and tried to thrust itself towards you. But the snake didn't move. This was such a curious thing that you edged closer to see what had happened to the snake. It was then that you saw that a vehicle had at some point driven over the snake's tail. This had become glued to the road by the blood, leaving the snake both free and not free. It could curl itself and lash out, true, and act in every other way as a snake should. But the blood had long since dried, and the snake was effectively anchored to the asphalt until another vehicle happened by and completed the job that the first vehicle had started.

This time you used your machete skilfully, as you used to do when you were cutting the pampas grass outside the *cacique*'s house. The snake assuredly felt no pain. But, nevertheless, you regretted its passing.

You had already walked on some metres from the snake's body when you realized that the creature contained meat. And that, freshly dead, it was of no use to anyone but the man who had killed it.

You took the snake with you into the underbrush, and you made a small fire, and cooked the snake over the embers, spitted onto a stick. When you ate the snake, the meat was tender and soft, like a chicken's flesh. You could feel the meat rushing through your body, overwhelming you with its protein. You stood by the side of the track down which you had taken the snake, and you vomited, your stomach spasming with the unexpected food.

You stood for a long while, holding yourself. Then you reached down and picked up the parts of the snake that you had vomited out. Carefully, with great tenderness, you cleaned these parts and ate them a second time. On this occasion you managed to keep them in, for you knew that without food inside you, very soon you would die. And then the oaths sworn by your father, and your grandfather, and your great-grandfather, would come to nothing. Later, when it was time to be judged by the Virgencita, you would be found wanting, and she would get her son to condemn you to the *purgatorio*, where you would linger in the offal of your shame.

After this thought you sat by the side of the road and you watched the cars flow past you for some little time. But eating the snake had not helped you. Neither had the vomiting. In fact you no longer had the strength even to raise your hand and ask for help. Dusk fell, and still you sat by the side of the road. You were seventeen kilometres from Kabáh, and you might as well have been seven hundred.

Once, a Maya man walked past you, carrying a rifle. You raised your head. He stared at you strangely. These Maya were a curious-looking people, you said to yourself. Small, and round of face, with backward sloping ears, curved noses, and protruding bellies. Not thin and lanky like the mestizos from Veracruz. This man even wore his hair short, like a scrubbing brush. As you watched him the man sneezed, then cleared his nose onto the ground.

'Jesus,' you said, meaning it as a blessing.

The man smiled, and pointed to his rifle. 'I am going to shoot a pheasant,' he said. 'Or failing that, an iguana.'

'An iguana?'

'Yes. They are very good to eat. Except in August and September when we cannot kill them.'

'Why? Why cannot you kill them then?'

The Maya laughed. 'Because they turn into snakes.'

'Madre de Dios.'

'And not only that,' said the Maya. 'If we kill one during this period and then we marry, our wives will be vipers.'

'It is October now. You may kill one then?'

'Yes. Yes. I will try to do that.' The Maya started away. Then he stopped. 'I have a *triciclo*. When I have killed my iguana, I shall come back this way. If you are tired, you may sit in the front and I will cycle you.'

'Why will you do that?'

'Why not? You are a tired man. You have come a long way. I can see that in your face. When I come back with firewood and an iguana you will tell me where you are going, and then you will share my meal. I live the time it takes to smoke two cigarettes further up this road. You are a foreigner here. You will be my guest.'

You dropped your head between your knees as the man walked away into the woods. So the Virgencita had indeed heard your cry. And she had answered it.

You were blessed.

267

49

It was one o'clock in the morning. The Cherokee was approaching the outskirts of Campeche. Calque was fast asleep in the back of the car after his four-hour stint at the wheel, and Lamia was curled up on the passenger seat, watching Sabir.

Sabir stretched his hand out to switch on the car radio, and then thought better of it. He fiddled a bit with the air conditioning vents, then he adjusted the rear-view mirror. The last thing he wanted was for Calque to wake up again, or to go into snoring mode.

'You're a beautiful man, do you know that?'

Sabir turned towards Lamia, a quizzical expression on his face.

'Your profile. It is very beautiful. Like Gary Cooper's. That is the actor whose name I was trying to remember. That is who you look like from the side.'

Sabir was at a loss for words. No woman had ever spoken to him in that way before.

Lamia looked out of the window. The lights from the Cuota road played across her features, alternately darkening and lightening them every fifty metres. 'I have never let a man kiss me. Did you know that also?'

Sabir gave a silent shake of the head. He didn't want to break Lamia's train of thought.

She turned to him. 'Would you like to kiss me?'

Sabir nodded.

'Then, when you wish it, I will not push you away.'

Sabir stared at her. Without even realizing he was doing it, he let the car slow down to a crawl.

He stretched out his right hand. Lamia snuggled herself towards him and rested her head on his shoulder. He kissed her hair, and squeezed her tightly against him. He was speechless. Quite incapable of uttering a word. His chest felt as if it were about to burst apart.

He drove like that for some time, with Lamia curled against him. He was aware that she was watching him. Aware that her eyes were playing over his face.

'How did you know?' he said at last.

She shook her head.

'I wouldn't have said anything. You knew that too?'

She nodded. Then she tensed inside the circle of his arm. 'My face. It doesn't disgust you?'

'I like your face.'

'You know what I mean.'

He raised his hand to touch her, but she shied away from him.

'You promised you wouldn't push me away.'

Lamia gave a deep sigh. Then she nodded, and let him touch her. Let him cup her face with his hand.

'I'm going to stop the car and kiss you.'

Lamia glanced behind her. 'And Calque?'

'Fuck Calque.'

Calque was watching them from the shadows in the back of the car, a half-smile on his face.

50
—

'I think you need to tell us about the names, Lamia.'

It was three o'clock in the morning and they were thirty

miles from Kabáh, at the Hopelchén intersection. Sabir was still driving, and Calque had chosen that moment to pretend to wake up.

Lamia glanced back at him. Her pupils seemed unnaturally large in the car's interior gloom. There were no street lights any more, and for some time now they had been cutting through a seemingly endless section of wood and scrub, interspersed with the occasional plantation of blue agave and maize, and the odd slash-and-burn clearing intended for assarting or swidden farming.

'What names do you mean?'

'I'm talking about the names given to your brothers and sisters. There's something odd there. Dakini, for instance? What sort of a name is that?'

In the last few hours Sabir had become so hyper aware of everything that concerned Lamia that now he even fancied he picked up a momentary hesitation he might not have noticed otherwise – a sort of physical stutter, as though, walking along an otherwise smooth pavement, she had inadvertently caught the toe of her shoe on a protruding paving stone.

Lamia tried to conceal her hesitation behind a sudden play of turning down the interior visor, opening the courtesy mirror, and then checking her hair and face. Seemingly satisfied, she snapped the mirror back into place. 'The name is Tibetan. It means "she who traverses the sky". Also a "sky dancer" or "sky walker". A *dakini* appears to a magician during his rituals. She carries a cup of menstrual blood in one hand, and a curved knife in the other. She wears a garland of human skulls, and against her shoulder, a trident. She has long wild hair and an angry face. When my mother first saw Dakini's face, she called her this. Dakinis dance on top of corpses, to show that they hold power over ignorance and vainglory.'

Sabir shot her a look. 'You can't be serious?'

'Madame, my mother, is always perfectly serious in everything she does, Adam.'

'Then the other names. What are they?'

'A *nawal* is a Central American witch who can transform herself into whatever animal she chooses. She can be either male or female. Nobody can harm her, because whatever is aimed against her rebounds on the perpetrator. She can use her powers for either good or evil, depending on her whim. According to the Nahuatl, all of us are given familiar animals at birth. Certain *nawal*s or *nagual* choose at this time to transform themselves into jaguars or vampire bats. Then they can suck the blood from innocent victims at night, while they are asleep. The Jakaltek Maya believe that a *nawal* will punish any of their number who transgresses from their society and marry mestizos. That is a person of mixed blood. Not pure Indio.'

'Your mother certainly has a way with her. You can believe that.'

'Oni, my youngest brother, who is both a giant and an albino, is named after a Japanese demon, with claws, and wild hair, and of an enormous size. These demons have horns growing out of their heads. Their skin is always an odd colour. Red. Blue. In my brother's case, an unnatural white. An *oni* has strength beyond strength and cannot be beaten. He is like a ghost. In European folklore, he would be likened to a troll.'

'And the others?'

'Asson is named after a sacred voodoo rattle. This rattle would be used by the Hougan priests and the Mambo priestesses during a vodoun ceremony. It will be decorated with beads and the bones of snakes. Alastor, his brother in real life, is named after the Chief Executioner of Hades. He is the avenger of evil deeds – Zeus sometimes used him as an amanuensis. He can be

271

the personification of a curse, similar, in some forms, to Nemesis. His name can also mean a scoundrel.'

'Neat. Great names. Must be nice to be saddled with that all one's life.'

'My brother/sister Aldinach is a true hermaphrodite – Aldinach was originally an Egyptian demon who caused violent tempests, earthquakes, and natural catastrophes. He always appeared in the shape of a woman when he did these things. He was a ship-sinker, too.'

'Well, they had to blame somebody.'

Lamia refused to be bated. She could see the men's embarrassment at what she was telling them, and the manner in which she was telling it, but she was not about to let them off the hook now. 'My brother Rudra was named after an Indian demon god. This god used arrows to spread disease. He could also summon up storms and natural disasters. His name can be translated to mean the "roarer", or the "howler", or the "wild one", or simply the "terrible". Rudra can also mean the "red one" – Nostradamus uses this nomenclature in some of his quatrains, if you remember. It was the equivalent for him of the Devil, or maybe of one of the Antichrists. Rudra might reasonably be viewed as a storm god by people who did not understand his true function.'

'Which was?'

'To cleanse things.'

'Christ. Any more?'

'Berith was an evil duke in the annals of demonology. He wears red clothing and has a golden crown on his head. He is the alchemist's demon, because it is said that he can turn any metal into gold. He is also a notorious liar. Athame, the favourite sister I told you about, is named after the sword, or dagger, usually with a black or obsidian handle, used by priests and priestesses. The blade has a

272

double-edge – both a positive and a negative if you like. There are also symbols on the knife. Curiously, though, the athame was not used for cutting but for channelling energy. Such a knife is mentioned in the *Key of Solomon*. My sister Athame is a dwarf. She is a good person. The blunt knife is a good description of her.'

'And the twins? One hardly dares ask.'

'Vaulderie, the youngest twin, and now Viscount de Bale after Rocha's death, is named after the word the French Inquisition used to describe the act of forming a satanic pact. Such a person could take to the air and go wherever he wished, thanks to the use of a flying ointment. Anyone found guilty of *vaulderie* would be tortured, and then burned at the stake. Vau's elder brother, Abiger, now Count de Bale, is named after the most senior of all the demons of hell – the Grand Duke of Hades himself. He is always depicted as a handsome and mighty knight, master of many armies, with sixty of the infernal regions under his command. He carries with him a lance, a standard, and a sceptre. He can read the future, and is wise in the ways of war. Other warriors come to him for help in mastering their men.'

'Why was your eldest brother, Rocha, not named in this way? Rocha means nothing as far as I am aware. A rock, maybe. That would be appropriate, mind you.'

'Rocha was already a young man when he was adopted by Madame, my mother. It was thought inappropriate to rename him.'

'So he renamed himself. Achor Bale.'

'That is simply the use of a mirror image. It is common in certain quarters. We all have two sides to ourselves. Rocha decided that his dominant side was not as Count Rocha de Bale, but as Achor Bale. It was his choice. He is dead now, so it no longer matters.'

'And your name, Lamia? Where does that come from?'

Lamia closed her eyes, as if what she was about to say had caused her much suffering in its time. 'I, too, was older when I was adopted. In fact I am the oldest surviving child of my parents. My younger brothers are simply senior to me according to Salic law. As far as my name is concerned, Lamia was the daughter of Poseidon and the mistress of Zeus, I think. One of his many mistresses.' She opened her eyes and laughed, although the laugh seemed to hold more regret than actual mirth. 'That is her only significance. I think maybe Zeus accorded her the gift of prophecy as a down payment for her services to him in bed. That is all I know. She is an unimportant figure in the scheme of things.'

Calque looked at her strangely – then he shook his head, as if trying to rid himself of the presence of an intrusive fly. 'The site at Kabáh won't be open until eight o'clock this morning at the earliest. We might as well get as close as we can and then pull over down a track. Get a little sleep in the car. Anyone have any better suggestions?'

Lamia and Sabir glanced at each other. Then they both shook their heads.

Calque threw himself back onto his seat. 'Like Sabir always persists in saying, in that curious American way of his – I'll take that as a yes, then, shall I?'

51

You had not expected the Maya man with the rifle to come back. Maybe, you thought, his pursuit of the pheasants had taken him far away – too far, perhaps, to consider returning? Or else his iguana had proved more elusive than expected? Maybe he had found no firewood? Your head sank lower on your chest.

Soon, you knew, you would simply curl up on the spot and fall asleep. The road between where you were and Villahermosa had been particularly difficult to accomplish. First you had been lucky. A market trader, his truck empty, had agreed for you to go in the back. Later, as was his right, he had taken on others. By the end of the journey, you were hanging out over the road, scared that you would fall off and burst your head on the highway. But somehow you had held on, your fingers turning into claws.

Then you had waited many hours for your next lift. But this man had taken you all the way to Campeche in his air-conditioned white car. The air had been so cold in the car that you had started to shiver. You would even have asked him to let you out if you had not been so sure that, after him, no more cars would stop for you. This man was a miracle in himself. A rich man. From Sinaloa. A man of substance.

At first you had been scared you would dirty his car, but later he told you that his father, too, had been a campesino, and that this was why he always offered lifts to those who needed them.

Campeche had been endless. You had walked and walked. After much time you had signalled a *colectivo* bus.

You knew this was unwise, since you only had fifty pesos left to your name, but otherwise you knew you would collapse, and they would take you to the Cruz Roja, and you would lose your belongings, if not your soul.

When you looked up again from your thoughts, the Maya man was watching you. When he knew he had your attention he held up two iguanas. Two.

'You see? You have brought me luck. Climb onto the front of my *triciclo*. I shall take you home. Can you cook?'

You shook your head. Your mother still cooked for you, and, in consequence, you had never learned how, as it would have been insulting to her.

'No problem. I can cook. Can you make a fire at least?'
You nodded.

'Bring yourself, then. We can make a space for you in here, by the firewood.'

52

Both Calque and Sabir were too wound up to sleep. Lamia had no such reservations. She drifted off right away, curled up on the back seat, like she always did, with her ankles drawn up beneath her, and her arms cradling her shoulders. But this time she was using Sabir's jacket as a pillow.

The two men finally gave up the uneven struggle of the front seats. Without even discussing the issue, they both went outside to watch the sunrise.

'You know what I love best in this world, Calque?'

Calque snorted in a lungful of fresh air. 'No. But I suspect that you are going to tell me.'

Sabir closed his eyes ecstatically. 'The way girls' bottoms stick out when they walk.'

Calque pinched the bridge of his nose with his forefingers, as if he had acquired a sudden headache. '*Putain.* But you've got it bad.'

'So you *were* awake, huh? I thought you might have been. Being a police officer and all that. Trained to spy on people.'

Calque shrugged. 'What did you want me to do? Pipe up and spoil your moment? There are things called Chinese walls, you know. You must have known I was awake because I wasn't snoring for once. At least according to your theory.'

'No. You did right. And I thank you for it. You called it, but I was too dumb to listen. If Lamia hadn't taken the initiative, I'd probably be sitting in some bar in twenty years' time, wallowing in regret.'

'What? Like me, you mean?'

'I didn't say that.'

'But you thought it.'

'Haven't you ever thought of remarrying, Calque? Starting another family? As you made so clear to me the other day, you're not too old to begin again. Have another kid. You'll only be seventy-five or thereabouts when she waltzes off with a serial-killing truck driver.'

'Thank you. That's very encouraging. I'll definitely consider your proposition. Any particular woman in mind? Lamia, excepted, of course.'

'Of course. Give me a little time to think about it. I'll come up with something.'

'Ah, what joys and sudden enhancements to confidence the unexpected possession of a woman can bring. You've changed, Sabir. Within the space of twelve hours you've become a human being again.' Calque's attention began to wander. 'But not an American, eh? This woman you are proposing for me? You wouldn't suggest that, would you?'

'No. Never that. I'm not a sadist. You being a Frenchman and all.'

'Thank you.'

Sabir snapped his fingers together. 'How about a Mexican woman? Mexican women value men. They know how to treat them properly. Not slice off their balls and serve them back with a topping of vanilla sauce.'

Calque looked at Sabir, his face aghast. 'Now you may really be on to something. Apart from the testicular analogy, that is.' He appeared to be lost in thought for a moment or two, as if he were pondering some great, but as yet little-known, truth. 'You do realize, Sabir, that no woman in the history of this earth knows what she really wants? She only knows when she gets it.'

Sabir was preparing to respond to Calque's *aperçu* when Lamia emerged from the back seat of the Cherokee, stretching.

'What are you two talking about? You woke me up.' She looked suspiciously at both men, weighing up their mood. 'At least you're not arguing again.'

Calque put on his most innocent smile. 'We were talking about women.'

Lamia flushed.

'Not specific women, you understand. Just women in general. Except in one particular respect.'

'And what respect is that?'

'Sabir tells me he particularly likes how your bottom sticks out when you walk.'

Sabir aimed a pretend cuff at the back of Calque's head. 'Damn it, Calque. What are you trying to do to me?'

'Did you really say that, Adam?'

278

'He really did.' Calque was grinning from ear to ear.

'And you like that? That part of me? How it moves?'

Sabir hesitated, sensing a trap. Then he threw caution to the winds. 'I love it.' He glanced up at her, gauging her reaction.

'I like your saying it, then.'

'You do?'

'Yes. No one ever talked to me like that before. I like it.' She turned back to the car, amused by their open-mouthed response to her statement. 'Are you both coming? We could stop off for some breakfast before Kabáh opens.'

'No. We'll just sit here and watch you, thanks.'

Lamia reached down and picked up a stick, which she brandished at them. 'I don't like it that much.'

'Okay. Okay. We'll go first. That suit you?'

'No. I'll go first. I think I've just decided I enjoy being admired.'

53

Acan Teul had been spending the entirety of every day at Kabáh since the news about the eruption of the Pico de Orizaba volcano had reached the Halach Uinic.

There had been many occasions during that period when he had been tempted to bunk off and visit his girlfriend at her juice shack six kilometres down the road, but each time he felt tempted by the anticipation of the joy she would no doubt show at his presence, he allowed his thoughts to wander back to what exactly the Halach Uinic might do to him if he was caught abandoning his post, and he thought better of it. There were always the evenings to look forward to, when the Kabáh site was shut.

The problem was that Acan didn't really know what he was looking for. The Halach Uinic – who was the most important Maya priest in the whole of the Yucatan, or so people told him – had not exactly bombarded him with information.

'We are expecting something to happen at Kabáh following the eruption. This has been predicted. But we do not yet know what it will be. You were once a guide at Kabáh, were you not, Acan? You will stay there during the day, therefore. If anything strange happens, you will use the security guard's cell phone, and you will call me. Your brother Naum will keep watch during the night. After the first two weeks, you will both be allowed time off.'

'Two weeks?'

'You will be paid from the fund. More than you could earn from labouring. Isn't it better to laze around drinking Coca Cola than to break stones for a cheating boss?'

As always, the Halach Uinic had put his finger straight on the meat of the matter.

'I shall do as you say.'

'Anything. Anything strange. And you will call me?'

'I will.'

Now, eight days in, Acan was sitting under the shade of a carob tree, fantasizing about his girlfriend and wishing he was sitting in her fruit booth pinching her bottom. He loved the way she shrieked at him when he surprised her in this way. Sometimes she would even hit him with her towel, which afforded him great pleasure.

Just as he was beginning to doze off in the early morning sun, Acan's attention was caught by a stranger

– a mestizo, it looked like – arriving on his cousin Tepeu's *triciclo*.

How did Tepeu, who spent his entire time hunting, ever get to know a mestizo? And, even more unlikely, give him a lift on his *triciclo*? Acan stumbled to his feet and shaded his eyes. Tepeu and the mestizo were negotiating with the man at the gate. Voices were briefly raised, and then Tepeu handed over a dead iguana, and the gatekeeper waved the mestizo through.

Acan watched as the mestizo walked towards the Palace of the Masks. The man stood for some time staring at the multitude of carved masks that adorned the wall, and then he shook his head, as if something puzzled him. After a moment's further hesitation he turned around and walked down towards Acan. At first, Acan thought the man was going to talk to him, but then the mestizo chose a neighbouring carob tree, about twenty metres to Acan's right, and sat down beneath its shade. Then he lay down, using his bag as a pillow, and prepared himself to sleep.

Acan glanced over at the gatekeeper's lodge, but his cousin had already cycled away. Acan shrugged. What did it all have to do with him anyway? A mestizo turning up at Kabáh, although rare, was not an event in itself. And the man was now clearly asleep.

Acan allowed himself to collapse back onto the ground again. He took a languid sip of his Coca Cola, and then set himself back to thinking about his girlfriend, Rosillo, and what he might do to her, come Saturday night, if he could only persuade her to drink just a little of his *aguardiente* stash.

54

Acan awoke from his doze at a little after ten o'clock in the morning. Gringos were coming – he could hear the confident boom of their voices from a hundred metres away.

The arrival of gringos was not, in and of itself, strange, as Acan knew that most of the small trickle of people who ever bothered to visit Kabáh were gringos of one sort or another. Most visitors to the Yucatan, however, chose the more famous tourist destinations of Chichén Itzá and Uxmal instead, leaving Kabáh to wallow in its peaceful backwater isolation.

These gringos had a US registered car, though – Acan had very good eyes, and he could make out the number plate in the scant parking lot that serviced the site. And this was strange in itself. It meant that the gringos had driven many thousands of kilometres to reach here. Unless, of course, they lived in the country for part of the year, as some gringos did, and merely drove their car down for convenience sake.

Acan shook his head. He glanced over to his right. The mestizo was also interested in the gringos. As Acan watched, the mestizo took the bag that he had been using as a pillow, and hid it behind the trunk of the carob tree, as though he feared that the gringos might steal it. And that was also a strange thing. Why should the mestizo fear that the gringos might steal what he had? Surely, it would be the other way around? Mestizos were terrible thieves, or so his father had warned him when he became interested in a mestizo girl, one time.

'Maya marry Maya,' said his father. 'If Maya marry half-Spanish thieves, they lose their souls and the *nawal* gets them.'

Acan had soon lost interest in the mestizo girl anyway, the first time he saw Rosillo working in her juice booth. Now *she* was a little piece of paradise, that girl. And Maya, too. His father wouldn't dare call *her* a thief.

Acan decided to take a closer look at the gringos. He got up, stretched, and sidled over to where they were standing, admiring the Palace of the Masks.

'Do you guys need a guide? I'm an expert on this place. I can tell you everything. If you pay me in US dollars and not pesos, I can tell you even more.'

The younger man laughed, and turned towards the woman, inviting her opinion. It was then that Acan saw the woman properly for the first time. He felt himself go cold, and his neck and arms prick up in goose-bumps.

One side of her face was covered in a veil of blood.

Acan grabbed hold of his shoulders for comfort, forcing his thumbs between the index and middle fingers of his hands – this phallic gesture, of the thumb as penis and the fingers as the vagina, had been taught to him by his mother as a talisman against curses.

Acan was briefly tempted to cross himself too, but then he remembered what the Halach Uinic always said about old Christian habits, and how they diluted true belief – true openness of mind. God was God. Hunab Ku was Hunab Ku. Itzam Na was Itzam Na. God was Hunab Ku. Itzam Na was God. God was both Hunab Ku and Itzam Na. In other words God was the same God for everyone. He did not belong to one religion more than any other. You did not own Him simply by giving Him a name.

The woman was looking at him strangely, and Acan realized that he was still gripping his shoulders like a young girl trying to protect her breasts from public gaze. He dropped his hands and attempted to smile.

The woman sensed his fear, however. Sensed that his throat had dried up. That he could barely swallow. This much he knew. Please God his talismanic gesture of the thumb between the two fingers had worked, for he also knew from his mother that this movement represented the dried-out and impotent penis being restored to life by the moistness of the vagina. In this way only could the evil eye be counteracted by the natural scheme of the earth.

Acan shivered, and turned to the older man of the group. Perhaps he would make a decision for them all? Acan wanted to be back underneath his tree. He wanted to drink half a litre of Coca Cola, very quickly, and very cold. Then he wanted to go and find Rosillo and tell her all about the gringa with the bloodied face. Maybe he would even get Rosillo to pass a raw egg over him, then crack it into a bowl of water and examine it. In this way would the *mal de ojo* be absorbed into the egg. Later, Acan would cover the bowl with straw and sleep with it underneath his pillow.

The older gringo cleared his throat. He tried a few words in Spanish, and then shook his head when he realized that Acan could not understand him. The old gringo's English, too, was very poor indeed, but at least one could make out his basic meaning.

'Five dollars, then? And you take us around the site and explicate everything to us?'

'Sure, *papi*. Sure. I do that. Only you give me what you want at the end. What you think I deserve. Maybe less than five dollars. Maybe more. Okay?'

The older man laughed. 'Okay.'

Acan could see out of the corner of his eye that the younger man had his arm around the woman and was talking softly to her. He didn't dare turn back and look at them directly. He couldn't trust himself.

He pointed up at the great facade of masks confronting them. 'Here you see the Codz Poop. Also known as the Palace of the Masks. It is dedicated to Chaac, the rain god of the Maya. It is he who splits the clouds with his lightning axe, and fills the cenotes throughout the dry season.' Acan's voice had taken on the sing-song automated note of the professional guide.

'Do you know how many masks there are? Or at least were?'

Acan searched his memory – it was a long time indeed since he had guided anybody in this spot. 'Before the destruction there were 942 masks. Or so they say. You can see where the second line of masks would have been. Now there are only 500 left. The number 942 held a special significance for the Maya.'

'What significance? I've never heard anything about the number 942.' This was the younger gringo. The man holding the woman with the bloodied face. 'We know 365 was a key number for the Maya, being the number of days in their solar year. Also 260, being the approximate span of parturition. But 942? It doesn't make any sense.'

Acan felt raw and on the defensive after his unexpected reaction to the gringa's *mal de ojo*. Why was this young gringo pushing him so hard? What did he want? Was he still angry about Acan's reaction to his woman? 'We no longer know. The secret has been lost with the destruction of nearly all our painted books.'

'The codices, you mean?'

'That word I do not know. But of all the books, only three, and the fragment of a fourth, are left intact. It is the greatest sorrow of the Maya people. These books contained our history. And the Spanish priests destroyed them.'

The older man with the strange accent was frowning at him. 'Bishop Diego de Landa. July 1562. He tortured

285

and killed all the Maya Chilans and notables. Then he destroyed five thousand cult objects and twenty-seven books. Thus the Black Legend. *La Leyenda Negra*.'

Acan looked away. 'I know of no such Black Legend, Señor. All I know is that the Spanish priests tortured and killed any person they believed to have gone back to the old ways of thinking. And the Monsignor Bishop did not destroy twenty-seven books, Señor. He destroyed ninety-nine times twenty-seven books. The Halach Uinic has told me so, and he knows about such things. Later, the Catholic Church explained to us that the Monsignor Bishop was really being charitable when he destroyed the history of our people. He was trying to protect us from ourselves.'

Acan had no idea why he was describing all this to the gringos. Had he gone crazy? When he had been a guide here, five years before, he had never gone into things with such detail. But the stories of the Halach Uinic were fresh in his head, and the sight of the woman had unsettled him. At this rate the gringos would tip him one dollar, not five, and kick his ass into the bargain.

'That is terrible.'

The woman had spoken for the first time. Acan could feel her gaze piercing through the back of his neck.

'*Asi es la vida*. My grandfather always said that to have the Spanish as friends was far worse than to have them as enemies.' Acan shrugged, but he couldn't quite bring himself to laugh. Part of him knew that he was attempting to play down something that, if he ever truly acknowledged it, would probably overwhelm him.

The younger man came up and touched him on the shoulder. Acan jumped, as if he had been hissed at by a snake. Then he realized that it was not the woman, but the man, who had touched him. And the man did not have the evil eye.

'Let me get this right. You did say there were originally 942 masks on the Palace wall?'

'That is what I have heard, yes. That is what the Halach Uinic has told me.'

'The Halach Uinic? Who is this person you keep mentioning?'

'He is the highest priest of all the Maya. He understands many things.'

'And you know this man?'

'Of course. Everybody knows him.'

The younger man turned to his companions and said something to them in a low voice. Acan could not completely make out what he was saying, but it had something to do with the number 942, and certain prophecies, and also the Halach Uinic.

Acan decided that, apart from the woman's face, these gringos were unimportant. They were just as all the other gringos – hungry for knowledge that they would soon forget. He decided that he would wring as much money in tips as he could possibly get from them, and then go and share a cigarette with the mestizo, and find out what relationship the man had to his cousin Tepeu.

Now that was a real mystery.

55
—

Sabir sat on an upended barrel in the little shack that the Kabáh gatekeeper had set up as an outlet for his soft-drink concession. He was still upset about the Maya guide's response to Lamia's face. He had never experienced anything quite like it. The man had taken one look at Lamia and then reacted as though he had seen a ghost. He had seemed truly terrified.

Sabir decided unilaterally that now Lamia and he were – how would one term it? – dating? – an item? – he would try to persuade her to go to Massachusetts General Hospital's dermatology department in Boston once all this was over. He had a friend there, a senior consultant. He hadn't seen the guy in years, but friendships were all about need, weren't they? He'd call this person at home and seek his opinion about Lamia's condition. Rekindle the friendship a little.

He knew he'd have to tread carefully around Lamia – she was hypersensitive about her face for obvious reasons – but he couldn't imagine her objecting that strongly to his interference. All he'd have to do was to make sure she didn't think he was doing the thing just for himself – that some unconscious part of him found her face distasteful, perhaps, and wanted it changed to suit him. If she ever thought that, he'd be sunk.

Lamia and Calque ducked in under the shade of the plastic awning just as Sabir was perfecting his game plan. Sabir wondered what they'd found to talk about out there in the heat. Maybe Calque was doing his Big Daddy bit again and had been reassuring Lamia about her face and the guide's weird reaction to it. Maybe he ought to consult Calque about his idea for the dermatology clinic? Calque could be a know-it-all asshole when he wanted to be, but he was also oddly wise in the ways of women.

Sabir ruefully acknowledged that for a man of his mid-thirties age range, he was wildly out of practice in terms of female psychology. Still. When he looked at Lamia and thought of her in his arms, his heart took a pleasant little turn around his chest – he hadn't felt like that for years, and he found it a very satisfying emotion indeed.

Calque sipped from his can of Sprite, his eyes playing over Sabir's face. 'Give us the quatrain again.'

'Do you want me to write it down for you?'

'No. Write nothing down. The Corpus might catch up with us again. I'm sure they'd be more than happy to have everything presented to them on a plate.'

'Okay. It goes like this:

> *"In the land of the great volcano, fire*
> *When the rock cools, the wise one, Ahau Inchal Kabah,*
> *Shall make a hinged skull of the twentieth mask:*
> *The thirteenth crystal will sing for the God of Blood."'*

Calque shrugged. 'Well? What do you make of it? We've looked at the Temple of the Masks. By a sheer fluke we've established that there were originally 942 masks, just as there were 942 Nostradamian quatrains. My view is that this number linkage is just a ridiculous coincidence, and not worth wasting time on. Do you agree?'

'Personally? No.' Sabir glanced across at Lamia. He sensed that she did not have her entire concentration focused on the subject at hand.

He reached across the table and took her fingers in his. He kissed them, and then pressed them to his cheek. He saw the sudden change in her expression caused by his unexpected movement – she seemed to sway back into view again, as if returning from a faraway place.

Frankly, he was astonished at his own audacity. What deep wells had that come from? He had always considered himself inept with women, and here he was working from a part of himself that he had never hitherto known existed.

'What do you mean, no?' said Calque. 'You think there's some link between an obscure site in the Yucatan and a sixteenth-century French scryer?'

'But, Calque. We already know there's some link. You've heard the quatrain. It's categorical. Nostradamus wasn't making all that up about "Ahau", "Inchal", and "Kabah". He even got the spellings right, give or take an acute accent – except when he was purposefully obfuscating, as with Inchal. Almost as if someone was looking over his shoulder when he was writing the verse and making sure he didn't blow it. And remember this. The manuscript had been hidden for more than four hundred years in a waxed and sealed bamboo tube secreted in the base of a statue of Sainte Sara when we found it. Impossible to tamper with. Impossible even to know it was there without Nostradamus's say-so. So yes. I think we need to take every possible connection between Nostradamus and this place seriously.'

'So what's our next move?'

Sabir shrugged. 'I'd have thought that was obvious. We come back tonight, when it's dark, and we lever out the twentieth mask in the wall with the help of a couple of tyre irons. What else can we do in the circumstances?'

56

'They've come to a place called Kabáh, Madame. It's an insignificant site, well off the beaten track. This morning we watched them as they made a tour of the site. They seemed to pay particular attention to the Temple of the Masks.'

'Were they alone? Or did they meet somebody?'

'They were alone. Apart from a local guide who ran up and bothered them, and whom they subsequently employed.'

'Have you talked to him?'

Abi hesitated, aware that danger loomed. 'No. I didn't think it necessary. It was obvious the man was employed by the site. He was lying there sleeping before Sabir and his little gang arrived.'

'Maybe he was waiting for them?'

'Madame, no. I really think not.'

'Speak to him anyway. Do you understand me, Abiger?'

'Yes, Madame.'

'Where have our trio gone?'

'To a motel. Twenty kilometres down the road. But I have something else to tell you, Madame. Something of key interest, I believe.'

'And what is that, Abiger?'

Abi cleared his throat. He didn't know quite how the Countess was going to take this next piece of information. Still. He knew he had to give it up, or else one of the girls – Athame, maybe, who had always been close to Lamia – would simply get in there ahead of him and queer his pitch.

'All the way down, the three of them have been sharing a room. Through fear, probably, of us breaking in on them'

'Get to the point, Abiger.'

'Now Calque, the policeman, has taken a room on his own.'

'And Lamia?'

'She is with the American.'

57

Lamia stood at the very centre of the small motel room and waited as Sabir got the fan going. The fan made a chopping sound, and then settled into a wheezing rhythm, thanks to its worn-out ball bearings.

She glanced at the twin beds. The late morning heat was already lurching in through the windows. She could feel the moisture gathering in the small of her back, then trickling down the gap between her underwear and the base of her spine.

'Do you want to move on from this fly tip?' Sabir was pacing the bounds of the room as though he was trying to memorize it. 'The drive from Ticul to Mérida would only take an hour or so. We could get ourselves an air-conditioned room in a modern hotel. You might be more comfortable.'

'I don't want to drive any more.'

'Okay.' Sabir stopped his pacing. 'Are you hungry?'

'It's too hot to eat.' She turned her face up to the fan. 'Can you make this go any faster?'

'I hardly dare. Let's see though.' He tripped the mechanism. 'Christ. I think it's going to take off.'

She laughed, and eased her dress away from her skin so that the air could circulate and cool her.

Sabir checked inside the bathroom. 'There's a tiled shower you could fit the entire Pats Football Team in. And we've got clean towels and soap. Things aren't as bad as I thought. Shall I order some cool drinks?'

'That would be nice, Adam. But who are the Pats? And why would they want to come into our bathroom?'

Sabir closed his eyes. 'You really don't want to know.

Pretend that I never said it.' He opened his eyes and flared them at the ceiling. 'Okay. Maybe you do. They're the New England Patriots. They play American football.' He knew he was talking too much, but he couldn't stop himself. He moved over to the telephone, shaking his head at his own stupidity. He raised the handset to his ear, then let it fall back into place. 'Doesn't work. I'll have to go downstairs and put in the order personally. What do you want?'

'Something sweet. A 7UP, maybe.'

'Sure you don't want a beer?'

Lamia cocked her head to one side and watched him. 'A beer. That would be nice.'

'Sol? Corona? Dos Equis? Negra Modelo? Pacifico?'

'You choose, Adam.'

He hesitated, then headed for the door. As he passed her he stopped. He seemed about to say something, but then he just reached out and touched her arm. He retrieved his wallet from his discarded jacket. 'I'll be back soon, okay?'

'I'm going to take a shower. Without the Pats.'

He nodded absent-mindedly, not even picking up her attempt at a joke. 'Sure you want beer?'

'Yes.'

'I'll get some potato chips, too. And maybe some peanuts.'

She turned to him. 'Adam. It's all right. I came to this room of my own volition. I'm not regretting it. I'm not going to run away if you leave me alone for two minutes.'

Sabir took a deep breath. He reached for the door. Then he turned back and strode across the floor to where she was standing.

Lamia leaned forwards and rested her head against his collar bone.

Sabir encircled her with his arms and squeezed her against him. 'I love you. I want to tell you this now.

Before anything else happens.' He swallowed, but his throat didn't seem to be functioning to quite its usual standard. 'I've never said this to a woman before. I've never felt remotely like this.' He buried his face in the valley between her neck and shoulder, breathing her in.

'I love you too. I wanted to tell you in the car, early this morning, but I thought you might not like me that way. That you might just be drawn to me in the normal way, because we had been travelling together. You still might be.' She looked up at him, a fleeting uncertainty on her face. 'I would understand that. You can make love to me, if you want, and then decide how you feel. You can tell me afterwards.'

'I'm telling you now.'

'Adam. You don't have to go down for the beers, you know. Or the potato chips. Or the peanuts.'

'I know. I'm not going. I don't know what I was thinking of.' He led her slowly to the bed. They stood facing each other. Everything was all right again with the world. Sabir felt like a man on a plane watching a shed-load of passengers streaming expulsively out through the main exit after an inordinately long and claustrophobic delay on the tarmac. 'I liked it when you put on that dress yesterday. And the make-up. And the high heels.'

'Why? What's so different about a dress, and make-up, and high heels?' She was teasing him.

He laughed. 'You know very well why. Because they're feminine. Because they draw attention to parts of your body that particularly please me.'

'Parts of my body? Like what?'

Sabir hesitated, gauging her mood. Then he turned her around, so that her back was to him. He liked the way she was letting him toy with her.

He drew in a quick breath, like a surgeon faced with a particularly delicate stitching job. 'The nape of your neck, for instance.' He cupped her neck, enjoying the heft of her hair on the back of his hands. 'And your shoulders. And your upper arms.' He touched each element in turn.

'What other parts of my body please you?' She had a smile in her voice.

'Hmm. Let me think. Your elbows. Your forearms.' He touched each named part, taking pleasure in the feel of her weight against him – keenly aware, too, of the bed just below them, but in no hurry to urge her there.

'What else? What else makes a woman different from a man?'

Sabir gave it a moment or two's thought. 'A man has no hips to speak of.' He ran his hands down Lamia's flanks. 'But you do. I like how your hips flare out from the narrowness of your waist. Like this.' He touched the indentation on each side. 'Like a violin. I like how a dress accentuates that.' He reached around her and let his fingers travel lightly down her upper thighs, then up again in a more forceful sweep from the back of her knee to her buttocks. 'This is an area I particularly value.'

'Oh really?' Lamia's breath caught as she uttered the words.

He went down on one knee behind her. 'And then your calves.' He allowed his fingers to trace the outline of her leg. 'And those shoes you wore. With the high heels. I like the way they show off your ankles.'

'My ankles?'

'Yes. These.' He reached down and encircled each one in turn with his hands. 'But there's more.'

'More?'

He turned her around so that her belly was parallel to his face. 'This is your belly. When you wear a skirt, it shows the little bump you have down there – the woman's bump, just above your pudenda. I like that. It's suggestive.'

'Bump? Pudenda? Adam, really. You sound like a biology professor.' She hesitated, stopping well short of what she had meant to say – desperate not to change his mood. 'Suggestive of what?'

'Of other things.' He smiled, and rested his head against her stomach. He could feel the warmth of her against his cheek. Catch the scent of her – a mixture of clean clothes, perfume, and her own special scent, which he had first recognized in the brief instant he had carried her in his arms while they were escaping from their motel in Carlisle.

Lamia's fingers wandered idly through his hair. 'You like women, don't you?'

'Yes.'

'But you are wary of them?'

He nodded.

'Why?'

Sabir closed his eyes. He didn't want to talk any more. Didn't want to spoil the moment. But something forced him on. Some recognition that if he didn't explain exactly how he felt, he would be cheating Lamia of something she had earned by right – his formal acknowledgment of a grace she had accorded him that no other woman had ever come close to providing. 'Because of my mother. I watched her destroy herself, and take my father down with her. It hurt me every second of my life until she killed herself. Then it hurt more after that.'

'Does it still hurt?'

'Not when I'm holding you.'

'Like now?'

'Like now. I can't think of anything but you.'

Lamia crossed her arms below her upper thighs and drew her dress slowly over her hips – over the swell of her breasts – around her shoulders. Then she uncrossed her arms as the dress rode over her head, freeing itself from the temporary prison of her hair. She let the dress float gently down onto the bed beside her.

Sabir stood up. They were still touching along the entire length of their bodies. He undid Lamia's brassiere and let it fall onto her discarded dress.

She sat down on the bed. Then she allowed herself to fall backwards, like a rag doll. She looked up at him expectantly, laughter in her eyes.

He reached down and drew her panties over her hips – she had to wriggle a little to help him.

Then she was lying naked in front of him. Not covering herself. Confident about her beauty. Wanting him to admire her.

He consumed her with his gaze, and Lamia accepted it as nothing more than her due. Without taking his eyes off her, Sabir discarded his own clothes. Lamia's eyes travelled quickly over his body as he undressed himself, and then up again to his face.

Sabir slid onto the bed alongside her.

They lay, facing each other, feeling the beat of the fan against their skin.

It was a long time indeed before Sabir bent forward to kiss her.

58

Oni de Bale slapped at the mosquito which was hovering just above his right eye. He flopped backwards against the tree and lathered some more 'Scoot' on himself. He wondered if the others were being eaten alive too?

They each had separate cars again now – Abi had taken advantage of Sabir and Lamia's sex interlude that morning to send them all into Mérida, to the nearest Avis drop-off point.

Now that was a strange thing. Never would he have dreamed of Lamia and Sabir getting it on together. Especially with Madame, his mother's, virginity hangup. What was that junk from the Bible she always used to quote at them in an effort to get them – well, particularly Aldinach, let's be honest – to behave themselves?

These are they which were not defiled with women; for they are virgins. These are they which follow the Lamb whithersoever he goeth . . .And in their mouth was found no guile: for they are without fault before the throne of God.

Of course in Aldinach's case the target was both men and women – whichever was the opposite of whatever sex he had chosen to be that day. Convenient, that, when you came to think of it. It doubled the possible catchment area. Mind you, Aldinach wasn't gay. Oni had to give the little nymphomaniac her due. She only worked on polar opposites. Never own sex. It was a sort of morality, when you came to think about it.

Anyway, much good Madame, his mother's, virginity imprecations had done them. Rocha had fallen for her line, though, and look what had happened to him. But he was the only one, apart from Lamia – the rest of them rutted like rabbits whenever they could. And now here was Lamia obviously deciding that enough was enough, aged twenty-seven, and reeling old Sabir into her bed. Frankly, he couldn't blame her. With a face like hers you needed all the luck you could get in the jiggy jiggy stakes.

Oni knew all about it. The size he was, most females ran a mile, scared that he would squash them. All right, he wasn't a disgusting fat pig like Asson, whom he had once seen consuming four pitchers of Ben & Jerry's Cherry Garcia ice cream at a single sitting, but he was upwards of seven feet tall, and most women reached just about as far as his navel. As a result, Oni had taken to hiring professionals, who weren't put off by the – what did Aldinach call it? – outsize aspects of his persona.

Now Abi had ordered them all into the forest to watch the site at Kabáh, and here was Oni, with his extra-large body surface – wasn't it the Cathars who said that human skin connected us to the Devil? – serving as dish of the day to a particularly virulent variety of mosquito. Fuck it. Fuck it all to hell.

He reattached his night-vision goggles and focused them on Sabir's back. The guy was busy counting the masks on the facade of the temple. Each time he came to one he liked, he fetched a sheet of paper out of his backpack and taped it over the mask. He'd covered five sections in this way already – only the single remaining upper section still to go. The paper shone up in the moonlight very well indeed – Oni had to allow the bastard that much.

Oni now reckoned, by dint of careful counting, that Sabir was choosing the twentieth mask in each separate mask section. Must be some significance to that, wouldn't you say? He punched his cell phone and passed on the information to Abi.

Sabir had snuck in to the Kabáh site not half an hour before, just as Abi had said he would, wearing a rucksack and carrying two tyre irons. The policeman had snuck in beside him. Lamia wasn't with them. Probably recovering from her orgy, out in the car. Oni grinned. Bet she was sore. She'd probably be walking splay-legged for days. Serve the bitch right for leaving it so long to get started.

That footman who got himself squished – Philippe, yes, that had been his name – he'd been dogging her for ages.

But Lamia had brushed him off like a cobweb. And now he was dead, propping up the walls of a girls' school in Cavalaire-sur-Mer. Did people still have sex in hell? Oni shrugged. Only one way to find out. On second thoughts, though, maybe he'd leave that little task to Philippe.

Oni swung around and focused his night goggles back on the Indian. Yes, the man was still hiding behind the tree, watching Sabir's every move. Next, Abi swung his goggles over to the courtyard on the left of the Temple of the Masks. Yup. The night watchman was still lurking in a doorway there. The guy was whispering into his cell phone like he was making love to it.

It seemed pretty much impossible that Sabir and the policeman weren't aware that they were being watched by at least three separate parties, but then Oni had to accept that they didn't have the advantages he had – his night-vision goggles turned the whole of the scene in front of him into a sort of pallid, moonlit playground, where everything took on the surreal shape of one of Salvador Dali's dream landscapes.

Oni could hardly wait to find out what would happen when whoever the night watchman was calling – cops? museum archivists? eco-warriors? – would come piling in through the front gates like the 7th Cavalry in a John Ford movie. The expression on Sabir's face would be worth the price of entry alone.

Oni whispered once again into his own cell phone, bringing Abi up to date, and ending up with, 'What do you want me to do?'

'Stay where you are. Watch. And wait. Don't – I repeat don't – interfere.'

Oni grunted, and slapped at another damned mosquito. Easier said than done. He squirted out another palm full of 'Scoot' and plastered it all over his face. 'Fucking buzzers!'

59

You watched the two gringos with a sinking sensation in your heart. What were they doing? Why were they here in the middle of the night? The younger gringo was counting the masks in each section, and then taping sheets of paper over the ones he chose. A strange procedure, surely? And no doubt illegal. Otherwise why would they come here at dead of night rather than during the daytime, when their activities would have been open to the public gaze?

You recognized them both from earlier on in the day. Only now the woman that had been with them, the one with the blood-soaked face, the one the guide had thought had the *mal de ojo* – yes, you had noticed him making the phallic gesture with his hands to ensure that the *mal de ojo* did not turn into the more dangerous *ojo pasado* – this woman had gone away. Maybe, being a woman, she did not approve of what these men were doing?

Earlier that evening, Tepeu had tried to persuade you to travel home with him on his *triciclo*. Tepeu was an estimable man. A man to honour. You had told him that you needed to stay here, near to the temple, and he had not questioned your motives, or tried to dissuade you. Instead he had arranged for a blanket for you, and also that you would be brought some iguana stew from the wife of the gatekeeper.

This woman and the gatekeeper lived in a hut about half a kilometre from the site. At eight o'clock Tepeu had cycled over and he and you had eaten the stew together, and shared a litre bottle of beer. You had told Tepeu that you could not repay him, but he had brushed your protestations aside like a man who flaps his hand at a hornet.

Now the gringos were here, and you did not know what to do. Did they intend to steal, as all gringos did? And why would they steal the masks? What could they hope to do with them? Sell them? Impossible, surely. The authorities would discover them, and then they would face prison.

As you watched, the younger gringo retrieved an implement from his rucksack and started to lever at the first of the stones. The older man took a similar implement and began to work at the stone from the other side.

You stood up behind your tree to get a better view of what they were doing. It was nearly full moon, and the two men were bathed in the reflected light off the white face of the temple.

What should you do? Speak to them? Run off and fetch Tepeu? Or the gatekeeper? Yes, maybe that would be the correct thing to do in the circumstances. The man lived only half a kilometre away, and you knew where his hut was situated, thanks to Tepeu's description.

For some reason, however, you did nothing, and simply watched the gringos as they levered and struggled with the masks.

60
—

'Do you think we're crazy doing this? I mean, we're standing here in a foreign country, at night, on a protected archaeological site, destroying one of their ancient monuments. If they catch us at it, they'll toss us into prison and throw away the key.' Sabir's face had taken on a livid tinge in the moonlight – he did, indeed, look half mad.

'We're putting the stones back, Sabir. Nobody will know the difference.'

Calque and Sabir were onto the third of the marked masks. Each time they succeeded in levering one of the stone masks partially out of its sconce, one of them would hold the torch while the other felt around in the space behind the mask, pretending not to be worried about scorpions, biting spiders, and snakes.

'Maybe Mexico doesn't have scorpions?'

'Of course they do. They're strictly nocturnal creatures, though. And they only get angry when disturbed.'

'Thank you, Calque. Thank you very much indeed.' Sabir was feeling around behind one of the sconces with his hand. 'They're not deadly, are they?'

'Just the Centruroides. The rest are okay.'

Sabir snatched his hand out of the hole. 'Nothing there.' He shivered, as if someone had just walked over his grave. 'Where the heck do you come up with this sort of information, Calque? Do you just gen up for the fun of it? Or is it a nervous tic?'

'Yes to both.'

'You're doing the next hole, then.' Sabir's cell phone buzzed. He slapped at his pocket as if he thought there might be a scorpion lurking in there too. 'Yeah?' He listened. Then he nodded. 'Okay. Thanks. We're fine here. No luck yet. Three to go. Then we can all go back home and have a holiday. The Caribbean, preferably. I've already got the double-hammock and the rum punches lined up. And there are no scorpions over there to leap out at you.' Sabir pocketed the cell phone and turned to Calque. 'Lamia says the roads in each direction are clear. She'll continue to run interference for us until we call her in.'

'The Caribbean is full of scorpions. You really are an ignorant man, Sabir.'

Sabir pointed at him. 'Okay then, how's this for ignorant? The Maya write from left to right, just like us. Except that everything's in pairs with them. Glyph blocks, and suchlike. You told me that yourself, didn't you?'

Calque gave a cautious nod.

'What if we miss out the next section and just start at the far corner, which we probably should have done in the first place? Not waste our time here pussyfooting around on the right. In fact, why don't we treat this whole temple wall as if it's the stone equivalent of a written parchment?'

'Why not just toss a coin?' Calque sighed. 'If your theory is right, Sabir, we have been wasting our time looking behind the wrong stones. We have been counting the twentieth mask from the right in each of these sections. If we had followed Maya practice, we ought to have counted the twentieth stone from the left. And started from the top. Is this what you are saying?'

'My point exactly. Only I'm a stupid idiot who doesn't know there are scorpions all over the Caribbean.'

'It was a joke, Sabir. If a man is really secure in his intelligence, he doesn't need to lash out whenever anyone teases him.'

Sabir was only slightly mollified. 'Okay. I'm sorry.'

'I'm sorry too. And I'm even sorrier that your theory, much as it pains me to admit it, seems a good one. Let's go straight to the twentieth mask from the left.'

'What forfeit will you pay me if I'm right?'

Calque sighed. His face took on the expression of a

cartoon dog being forced to placate an over-bumptious puppy. 'I'll speak up for you with Lamia whenever she asks me about you. Which she does, incidentally, nearly all the time. How would that be? Previously I've always tried to drop you in it on account of my sexual jealousy. But from now on I'll praise you to the skies. Will that satisfy you?'

'It's a deal.'

'Of course, if we don't find whatever it is we're looking for, I will still consider myself free to undermine you at every opportunity.'

Sabir shook his head. 'Thank God you're French and not Belgian, Calque. Otherwise I might have a real problem with your sense of humour.'

61

—

'Your turn to stick your hand in, Calque. Are there any particular bequests you wish to make? I'll see to it that your posthumous instructions are carried out to the letter.'

Calque ignored him. He felt around in the first of their new series of holes. Then he closed his eyes. 'There's something in here. Something smooth. And cold.'

'You're kidding me?'

'No. I can feel it quite clearly. It's got teeth. And a nose. I can even feel the indentations of the eyes.'

'Jesus Christ. What is it? I'll kill you if you're bullshitting me.'

'I'm not bullshitting.' Calque withdrew his hand from the hole. 'We're going to have to take the whole sconce out. There's no way I can lever this thing through the size of hole I have here.'

Sabir stuck his hand into the hole and felt around. 'You're right. But we can't risk taking the whole mask out of its niche. It'll be too heavy. We'll never get it back inside again.'

'Then we'll just have to leave it here on the ground. Maybe they'll think it fell out due to condensation?'

'Yes. That's likely. Good call, Calque. I can just see the curator now. "Hey, guys! We just lost another of these 1,200-year-old masks. Bastard thing must have fallen out due to condensation."'

Both men stepped back and stared at the sconce.

'We'll just have to tug like hell and then get out of the way. Thing'll probably lose its nose when it hits the ground. That'll really buff up our grave robber credentials. One thing I can tell you, Calque. When we get hold of whatever it is that's tucked in behind this mask, I'm not sticking around.'

'Neither am I. Come on. Let's do it.'

The two men levered with their tyre irons until the mask was teetering at the very edge of its sconce.

'It's going to tip. Watch your feet.' Sabir pulled at the mask, and then stepped quickly back as the entire structure overset towards him.

The mask hit the ground and bounced.

'Christ. It's still going.' The two men turned around to watch the mask pounding its way down the steps behind them, stone-chips skittering in every direction.

Only then did they see the eight Maya standing in the moonlit courtyard. Each man held a rifle in his hands. Lamia was standing beside one of the Maya. Her mouth was bound with a cloth.

Sabir glanced at Calque. He spoke out of the corner of his mouth. 'Any more funny jokes to share?'

Calque sucked at his teeth. 'Not offhand.' He gave a sudden Burt Lancaster grin. 'No. Wait. Maybe these gunmen aren't interested in us after all? Maybe they're on a night training exercise for the Mexican army?'

'Yeah. Right on, Calque. That's a good one. Glad I fucking asked.'

62

Tepeu watched the two gringos with a horrified sort of fascination. They were smiling. It seemed impossible, but it was true. Here they were, facing eight armed men, seconds after being caught by the Halach Uinic in the very act of plundering the holy temple, and they were smiling. Had they no idea what might happen to them? Had they no idea of the severity of what they had been doing?

The younger man sat down at the top of the stone steps and put his head in his hands. The older man stood beside him, staring down at the Halach Uinic.

The Halach Uinic stepped forwards and indicated that the band should be taken from the woman's face.

It had been Tepeu who had captured her. He felt very proud indeed of this fact. He had turned his *triciclo* over in the middle of the road and had lain beside it, as if he had been involved in an accident.

For one brief instant he had thought that the woman had not seen him and was about to run him over. But at the very last moment she had stopped and climbed out of the car – it later transpired that she had been talking on her telephone at the time.

Tepeu had then stood up and covered her with his rifle. His cousin Acan had warned him about the *mal de ojo*, but Tepeu only saw that this woman had a defect from birth on her face. This he had seen before, in Mérida, on a man in the market. It was certainly no *mal de ojo*, but something to be regretted instead. How would it be to spend your entire lifetime being looked on and pitied by everyone who passed? And the woman was beautiful, too, apart from her blemish – at least for a gringa. Acan, as always, was dramatizing the situation out of all proportion to its significance. Still. The man was little better than a *guero*. Endlessly chasing after girls, and dollars, and the main chance. Tepeu was fond of his cousin Acan, but he did not respect his way of life.

Now he looked furtively around for a sign of his new friend, the mestizo from Veracruz. He had to be here. Wisely, though, he was hiding. Tepeu liked this man. It was not his fault that he was of mixed blood. But he was an honest man. And modest. This shone out of him.

When Tepeu had first come across the mestizo, he had immediately realized that the man was close to starvation. At first he had not known how to play the situation. It was not customary among the Maya to invade a stranger's privacy unless specifically requested to do so. Tepeu had decided to leave the outcome up to God. He had told the man that he was going hunting, but that when he came back he would take the man with him to his home. In this way face had been saved by both parties.

If the man did not wish Tepeu to feed him, he would go away. If he was too weak to go away, Tepeu would find him again, and take him under his wing. Tepeu had always taken people under his wing. This was his nature. The first animal that had crossed the invisible circle his mother had marked around his birthing bed had been a hen. From that moment on, Tepeu had had no choice in the matter.

Now the Halach Uinic was walking up the steps towards the two men. The woman was accompanying him, as well as Acan, and his brother, Naum. Tepeu hurried up to join them. From there, he would get a better view of the surrounding forest. If he saw the mestizo, he might be able to signal him away. Indicate to him in some manner not to become involved.

The older of the two gringos was speaking to the Halach Uinic in broken English. Pointing backwards to the hole where the mask had been ripped out. Making a shape with his hands.

The Halach Uinic flapped his fingers, and this older gringo now started up the remaining steps ahead of him. The whole party, Tepeu included, followed the gringo until they stopped near the opening.

The older gringo then stepped forwards and thrust his hand into the hole he and the younger gringo had made.

Tepeu could feel his breath catch at the back of his throat.

Something was about to occur.

Would the gringo bring out a weapon of some sort? And why was the Halach Uinic humouring him? Tepeu had not fully understood the English the gringo had used. Perhaps the older man had begged for his life, and the Halach Uinic had agreed to spare him if he thrust his hand back into the rain god's mouth?

The older gringo pulled an object out of the hole. This object was pale and round, and appeared to capture the light of the moon within its circumference.

The gringo held it up so that the Halach Uinic could see it.

The Halach Uinic dropped to his knees. Acan and Naum dropped to their knees. Tepeu, without quite knowing why, did the same. Behind him, the three remaining men who had accompanied them prostrated themselves on the ground.

It was at this exact moment that Tepeu's friend, the mestizo, chose to appear from behind the shelter of his carob tree.

Tepeu froze into place, halfway between kneeling and stretching himself out. There was a sudden noise in his head like the hissing of a thousand snakes. Through this noise Tepeu could hear the mestizo's voice echoing off the walls of the buildings.

'What you are holding,' the mestizo said, 'is pictured. Here. In this book I have. This book that I must now give to you. See? I have it here in my hands. I have brought this book all the way from Veracruz, but it is too heavy a burden for me to carry alone any more. My father, and my grandfather, and my great-grandfather protected this book for you before I did. Now that the great volcano of Orizaba has burst into flame, the time has come for the book to return to its own people. This is what I have been told to tell you. That we have done as we promised.'

63

—

'You're not going to believe this, Abi.'

Abi stared at his cell phone. 'What am I not going to believe? Wait. Don't tell me. There's been a *crime passionel*. Calque has murdered Sabir through thwarted love for our sister.' He shook his head, half convinced by his own casuistry. 'All joking aside, Sabir must be blind.

Or maybe Lamia's just hot as hell in bed, and they've both gone pussy crazy?'

'No. No. It's nothing like that, Abi. It's not that at all.' Oni was so excited that he failed to pick up the customary sarcasm in Abi's voice, or even to notice the new wave of mosquito attacks that were being unleashed against him. 'You've still got all the roads out of here covered, haven't you, Abi?'

'Oni, get to the point.'

'The point. Yes. *Putain*. The point.' Oni was sweating even worse now – the perspiration was streaming off him in runnels, diluting the 'Scoot' until it was only fractionally better than useless. 'You should have been here, Abi. It was like an Indiana Jones movie. Picture this. Sabir and Calque are standing out there in the moonlight, levering away at one of the temple masks, and trying to grab at something that is tucked away behind it. Then the mask they are levering at topples out of its niche and clatters down the temple steps like that bouncing bomb that flattened the dam in that stupid war movie the *Rosbifs* have.'

'That's two movies in one sentence, Oni. I can only take so many movies.'

'Okay. Okay. No more movies.' Oni slapped at a rogue mosquito that had broken away from the flotilla encircling him. 'So then Sabir and Calque turn around like the idiots they are and stare at the mask as if it's going to stop bouncing and magically swoop back inside its hole again. And that's when eight Mayan guys appear out of nowhere, with our sister in tow, and cover them with rifles.'

'What did they find, Oni? Calque and Sabir?'

'What? But I was telling you about the armed men.'

'Forget about the armed men, Oni. I already know about the armed men. You may find this impossible to believe, but you're not the only fucking fish in the fucking sea. Now tell me what they found.'

'Who's telling this story, Abi? You or me? I was just building up to the punchline.'

Abi glared at his cell phone as if he intended to sink his teeth into the keyboard and chew it up. 'Then you'd better get to the fucking punchline, Oni, or I'll fucking flatten you just like that fucking dam you were fucking wittering on about.'

'Yes, you and what man's army? And you shouldn't swear so much, Abi. Madame, our mother, says it's a sign of a lack of imagination.'

Abi consciously reined himself in. It was either that, or swear out a contract on his brother. What was the point in working himself up over nothing? He knew what Oni was like. Had always known. He sometimes forgot that the idiot was only eighteen years old.

He had actually received reports of the coming of the armed men some little time before. For some reason the news had not surprised him. You don't single-mindedly follow three people day after day without the expectation of some sort of violent payback. And here it was, beckoning to him like one of Homer's sirens.

Abi had immediately ordered the others to stand by, and to follow when and where possible. Now all he needed was to get a little sense out of his humungous fool of a brother, and he would have the situation nicely back under control again. 'I'm sorry, Oni. Continue in your very own time. I'm entirely at your disposal, as always.'

'There's no need to be sarcastic. I know I get a little carried away sometimes. But this was special, Abi. Listen.'

'I am listening.'

'When the mask had finished bouncing, there was a sort of powwow, with everyone putting in their centime's worth. Lots of hand-waving and rifle-shaking. Then a decision must have been made, because Calque turns around and leads everybody back up to the face of the temple. Then he stands there like a stage magician – like George Sanders as Svengali in that movie with . . .'

'Oni . . .!'

' . . .until he shoves his hand up inside the hole left by the mask and comes out with a . . .' Oni stopped. He was grinning at his cell phone like a chimpanzee.

'With a what? For pity's sake, Oni, tell me what he came out with.'

'A crystal skull, bro. A crystal fucking skull. Can you believe it?' Oni shook his head at the cell phone, as though it might somehow jerk into life and be able to discern his thought processes. 'It was more than a foot tall. With a jaw on hinges like a real skull. And something black for its eyes. Emeralds probably. Or maybe jade. I couldn't make it out. Well the assholes with the guns take one look at this thing and drop to their knees like they've just seen the Pope. And what do Sabir and Calque do? Do they leg it? Do they leg it hell. Instead of sprinting back to their car, they stand there like they're expecting to be given a gold medal at the Olympics for their trouble. Like they expect a pat on the back rather than the bullet in the head they'll probably get when these bozos with the rifles come to their senses again.'

'What happened then, Oni?'

'Wait for it. It gets better. Much better. What happens then is that this guy I've been watching for the past three hours – the guy hiding behind the carob tree I told you about, Abi – this guy comes breezing out from his hiding place waving a book. "It's all written down in here," he shouts. "I can't carry this thing about with me any longer. The volcano has spoken." Or some shit like that. My Spanish isn't too good.' Oni was really getting into

313

the swing of things now. 'Well the gunmen nearly pissed themselves, I can tell you. They were lurching around, not sure who to cover, who to shoot, or whether they should throw themselves on their knees again and start worshipping Calque and Sabir as gods.'

'How did it all end?'

'Three of the gunmen got together and manhandled the busted mask back into its hole. Then they tidied up all the stone chips and made the whole place shipshape again, just like nobody had ever been there. Then the boss man gathers everybody up, they have another powwow – believe me, these guys are good at powwows – and then they head off to wherever they need to get to in three separate cars, including Sabir's Grand Cherokee.' Oni searched wildly for a suitable flourish with which to end his story. 'Now there's nobody left here but us chickens. And a few bloodthirsty fucking mosquitoes feeding on us. Can I come home now, Abi?'

64

'I recognize you. You're the guide, aren't you? The one who told us about the 942 masks?' Sabir was driving the Grand Cherokee. Acan was seated beside him, with Calque and Lamia taking up the back seats. 'So you were out there watching us all the time? How come? Were you expecting us? But that's impossible.' Sabir turned his head sharply. 'You're not with the Corpus are you?'

Acan was still nervously watching the woman. Hoping she wouldn't stare directly at him. Give him the evil eye.

314

He was clutching his rifle between his legs, so he wasn't able to make the appropriate countermovement to diffuse the curse. 'The Corpus? What is that?'

'Forget it. It's not important.' Sabir glanced at Lamia in the rear-view mirror. 'Look. Do you have to keep staring at my girlfriend that way? You may not realize it, but it's damned off-putting. What is it with you people? Isn't kidnapping us enough?'

Acan blew out noisily between his lips. Now that the subject was out in the open, he felt better. 'She has the evil eye.'

'The what?'

Calque leaned forwards. 'He thinks Lamia has the evil eye. On account of her face. That if she stares at him he will be cursed.'

'Oh, for pity's sake . . .'

'This is serious, Sabir. You need to explain it to him.'

Lamia reached forwards between them. 'I will explain it to him. I speak his language. It is my face that is frightening him, not yours.'

Calque dropped back into his seat. Sabir turned his concentration back to the road. Both men were acutely embarrassed. The placation and the bringing to understanding of this young Maya man had become far more important than any half-baked ideas of getting themselves out of the spot they were in.

Lamia hunched towards Acan. She spoke softly to him in Spanish. He began a reluctant nodding of the head. At one point Lamia took Acan's hand and held it to the side of her face. Acan snatched it away and crossed himself. Lamia watched him, sadness mingled with her desire to make him understand. Then, unexpectedly, Acan stretched out his hand one further time. This time Lamia did not attempt to influence what Acan could or couldn't do.

Acan's fingers were trembling. He had quite forgotten about his rifle.

Sabir instinctively sensed that he was in the perfect position to wrest the rifle away from Acan and take control of the situation again. True, he was top-and-tailed by two other vehicles, each with a number of armed men inside them, but he could see a side-turning looming half a mile further up the road. All he needed to do was to time his move to coincide with the arrival of the slip road.

Only then no crystal skull. No book. No answers. Sabir hesitated for a moment, his skin crawling with a sudden inner certainty which whispered 'and no more Lamia, either'. She would never forgive him for abusing her tacitly given word.

So Sabir did nothing. For the very first time since his mother's suicide, he realized that he was putting the welfare and happiness of another person before his own. The thought was a novel one. Was he really beginning to emerge from nearly ten years of emotional lock-down? He glanced possessively at Lamia in the rear-view mirror.

Acan reached out and touched Lamia's face. Something changed in his eyes as he made the movement. The fear went out of them. He nodded, as if something had been successfully explained to him – some secret to which he had always wished to be privy.

He turned back to the front. 'It is all right now. I am very sorry.' Then he began to cry.

Sabir stared hard at Lamia, and then at Calque. 'What brought that on?'

Lamia shook her head. 'It was nothing. I reminded him about the mark of Cain. I said that God had given me this mark because I had come of an evil cradling. And that I took the mark as a sign to me that I must turn my back on the evil represented by my family and stand on my own two feet. Like Herman Hesse's *Demian*.'

316

'Which he'd read, of course?'

'Don't laugh, Adam. I explained to him that the god Abraxas concatenates all that is good and evil in this earth, and that we each have to destroy a world if we wish to be reborn. I quoted to him from Hesse's book. The original goes "*Der Vogel kämpft sich aus dem Ei. Das Ei ist die Welt. Wer geboren werden will, muß eine Welt zerstören. Der Vogel fliegt zu Gott. Der Gott heißt Abraxas.*" I translated it for him like this: "The bird fights his way out of the egg. The egg is the world. He who wishes to be born must destroy a world. The bird flies to God. The God is called Abraxas."'

'Lamia, he's crying, for Christ's sake.'

'My image of the egg. It meant to something to him. Over here they use the egg to rid themselves of evil thoughts. I think he understands about me now. He no longer thinks I have the evil eye.'

Sabir glanced furtively across at Acan. Then back at Lamia. He could feel Calque's eyes burning into the back of his head.

Sabir felt uninformed and inadequate. Unworthy of Lamia's love. What was he doing here? What right did he have to interfere in all these people's lives? To act as some sort of unholy catalyst, uniting forces that he little understood, in ways over which he had even less control?

'I'm sorry I made that crack about the Hesse book. I don't understand my own motives sometimes. I felt possessive of you, and didn't like the fact that you weren't involving me in what you said to . . .' He hesitated, really acknowledging the man beside him for the very first time. 'What is your name?'

'My name is Acan.'

'This is Lamia. Lamia de Bale. Back there is Calque. Joris Calque. And my name is Sabir. Adam Sabir.'

Acan smiled through his tears. 'My name is Acan Teul. I am Maya. From the village of Actuncóyotl. My father is called Anthonasio – Tonno for short. And my mother is called Ixtab.'

Lamia smiled gratefully at Sabir. Then she turned back to Acan. 'Ixtab. That is a beautiful name.'

'Yes. She is named after the Rope Woman. Our goddess of suicide. In Yucatec Maya, suicide can be a positive thing. It can be an honourable way to end one's life. Ixtab is the goddess who accompanies the person who has killed themselves to paradise, making sure that they are welcomed there, and given the respect that is their due.'

Sabir turned on him, his face instantly suspicious again. 'Suicide? Why are you talking about suicide all of a sudden?'

Calque laid a restraining hand on Sabir's shoulder. All of their nerves were on edge, and Sabir's most of all. Calque knew that Sabir hadn't been sleeping. During the past few days the man had been becoming more and more wound up – just as he'd been in the aftermath of his tangle with Achor Bale. It was as though Sabir lacked three or four of the normal protective outer layers of skin that ordinary people possess by default.

At first Calque had made the not unreasonable assumption that Sabir's newly fledged relationship with Lamia might even serve to calm him down a little. But, paradoxically, the love affair appeared to have had the exact opposite effect, turning Sabir into an even more hyper version of himself. Calque decided that he and Lamia would have to tread very carefully indeed if Sabir was not to crack up on them. He measured his words carefully, therefore, like a schoolmaster addressing a room full of freshmen.

'He means that the goddess Ixtab acts as a psychopomp, Sabir. A spirit guide. Escorting the newly deceased to the afterlife. Shamans can also fulfil this role, I understand. It's a quite innocent pastime.'

'Yes. Yes.' Acan looked grateful for Calque's intervention. 'This is what my mother does. My mother is *iyoma*.'

'*Iyoma*?'

'A female shaman. A midwife, really. It is she who tells, when a child is born, if he will become a shaman or not. Whether he is born with a separate soul, like a true shaman, and will give his mother much pain in the birthing. This can be a very bad thing for the mother. Sometimes the *iyoma* will not even tell the mother and father about their child for this reason, but only reveal what she has learned later on.'

'Why was your mother called after the goddess of suicide?' Sabir was still staring at Acan as if the young Maya was personally responsible for his mother's death.

In his own heightened emotional state, Acan picked up on Sabir's anxiety and didn't feel threatened by it. He waved one hand in a downwards movement, as if calming a child, using the back of his other hand to brush away his remaining tears.

'The old *iyoma* we had in the village at that time recognized my mother as a shaman at birth. She knew instinctively that my mother was connected by her umbilical cord to the goddess Ixtab. Without telling my father and mother, she went to the old people and suggested the name to them. In our village we respect our elders. We do what they ask of us. So my mother was named Ixtab. She has guided many people into the afterlife – and brought many others into this world as earth fruits. She is a very wise woman.' Acan nodded, as if what he was saying was self-evident. 'You will meet her, Adam. We are going to Ek Balam. Very near to my village. My mother will be there, waiting for you.'

Acan looked strangely at Sabir. For suddenly, without any warning, Sabir, too, began to cry.

65

The Halach Uinic had never known the like before. Who had dictated the events of the past few hours? Hunab Ku? Itzam Na? The maize god? The god who had no name? And what was their meaning?

Why, for instance, had foreigners been needed to find the thirteenth crystal mask – the mask without which the twelve other ritual masks would not sing? And why had it needed another foreigner – a man from Veracruz, of all places – to bring the Maya this incredible gift of a fourth complete codex, to stand alongside the Dresden, the Madrid, and the Paris codices, all of which had been stolen from the Maya by descendants of the conquistadors? The Halach Uinic realized that he was being told something – that voices were being carried to him on the wind, and that he urgently needed to listen to them.

The Halach Uinic turned to the mestizo who had brought him the book. His face in no way revealed the tenor of his inner thoughts. 'We cannot take this book from you. It has been in your family's possession for many generations. It belongs to you, and not to us. It would be wrong of me not to tell you what value this book has. If you were to take it out of the country – to the United States, for instance, or to England – the gringos would make of you a very rich man. You could buy cars, and houses, and make love to a different woman every day.

You could travel on aeroplanes through the sky, and see things that most of us know nothing about. You must not give us this book, therefore. It is yours. You must do with it as you will.'

As the Halach Uinic said these words, he felt a pain in his lower back, as if a kidney stone had formed there and was struggling to get out. He knew that by saying the words he risked losing the greatest gift his people had ever received. Yet he also knew that he had to say them – and mean them – or the gift would be worthless.

The mestizo was looking ahead of himself, out of the car window. He seemed to be concentrating on the vehicle in front of them – the vehicle that was carrying the gringos.

He half-turned towards the Halach Uinic. 'And the skull? The gringos found that, not you. Will you offer that back to them as well?'

The Halach Uinic felt the weight of fate descend upon him like the lid of a coffin. How was it possible that this campesino could see things with such clarity? Pose him such questions? The man must have been chosen by God. There was no other possible answer.

Before the Halach Uinic could address himself to the question, the mestizo turned to look at him face on for the very first time. 'You are the High Priest, are you not? The one they call the Halach Uinic?'

'So they tell me. I am not entirely in agreement with them on this subject, however.'

'The other priests . . .'

'The Chilans and the Ah Kin?'

'They will do as you say?'

'No. They will do as their spirit tells them.'

'But still. They listen to you?'

'I am a mouthpiece. Yes. That is so. This much they accept.'

'Then will you offer the gringos back the skull?'

The Halach Uinic closed his eyes. This was the thirteenth skull they were talking about. The skull of power. He had heard tales about this skull for the entire length of his life. Of where it might be hidden. Of the secrets to which it might provide the key. Some thought that it might even hold the answer to what would happen after the time of the Great Change – the date of 21 December 2012 that marked the end of the Maya Long Count calendar.

The Halach Uinic knew that only with this skull in place, and with suitable offerings, would the twelve other ritual skulls agree to sing and tell the Chilans of what might come to pass in the future – of what might come to pass when all was said and done.

You are being a *nicanic*, the Halach Uinic said to himself – a simpleton. The others priests would do well to tie you up now and throw you into the X'Canche cenote – let you drown upside down as a sacrifice to the gods.

'I will offer the gringos back the skull. Just as I have offered you back the book that you brought us. Will that satisfy you?'

'Yes. And when will you do this? Now?'

'As soon as we reach Ek Balam. I will order the site closed for the day. We will mount the great pyramid together. I will make you both the offer there. In front of the Ahau Kan Mai, the Chilans, the Ah Kin, and the shamans, all of whom I will request to assemble.'

You nodded. What had caused you to make this stipulation? Why had you spoken in this way to the great man? Had you turned mad? In your entire life, you had never spoken back to one in authority. You had surely entered a realm of being beyond even your wildest dreams.

Your stomach gave a sudden lurch, and you found yourself picturing your hut, and the figure of your mother waiting for you in the doorway at the end of the day. You wished to be back in Veracruz, returning from your day's work, tired but content. You wanted your mother to scrub your back and face with a damp cloth. To tease you about not yet finding a wife to do these things for you. A daughter-in-law to help her in the kitchen and about the hut. To give her grandchildren.

You closed your eyes and you thought of all the money the Halach Uinic had said would be yours if you sold the book to the gringos. Surely the Halach Uinic could copy the book? This way you could take the money with a clear conscience. Wasn't this what he had been suggesting?

Then you could build a larger house for yourself and your mother. Find a wife to marry, who would honour your mother and make her life a little easier. You might buy a small *chayotal*. Grow squash and coffee beans. Even run a few cows.

You knew the Halach Uinic was watching you. He had a strange expression on his face. As if he understood the thoughts that were passing through your mind, and was refusing to judge you for them.

66
—

Alastor de Bale watched the Mexican with what passed for interest. In truth, it had been many years since Alastor had taken an interest in anybody but himself.

He had the wasting disease, cachexia – in Alastor's case it wasn't caused by cancer or Aids or any of the other usual suspects, but came about thanks to metabolic acidosis, as a result, his doctors told him, of decreased protein synthesis twinned with increased protein catabolism caused by five or six generations of inbreeding.

Alastor had no idea what any of this meant, nor was he interested enough in his condition to find out. He knew that the cachexia would do for him in maybe two to three years tops, and all that concerned him now was to procure himself a regular adrenalin rush – this was the only thing that cut through the inevitable lethargy, fatigue, and weakness bought about by his condition. And if he read the signs right, the bumptious Mexican he was looking at was definitely going to come up trumps on that score.

'I can get you anything you want, man. If you can pay, that is. US dollars. Small denominations only. Nothing over a twenty. I get you Uzi. Even Mini-Uzi. I got a Model 12 Beretta. I got a Heckler & Koch MP5K. I even get you a Stoner M63. Still in its wrappers. Never used. Guy who ordered it got himself whacked on the way to pick it up.'

'Handguns?'

'Anything you want, man. Anything you want. I got Makarov. I got PSM. I got CZ.'

'I don't want anything Eastern bloc.'

'Okay. Okay. I got a Glock 18. I got a Walther P4. I got a Star 30M. I maybe even got a MAB P15.'

'I don't want a MAB P15.'

'Anything you say, man. I get you anything you say.'

'You got a Beretta 92SB?'

'What? US military model?'

'With the extended hammer pin. Yes.'

'I get you that too.'

It was at this exact moment that Alastor knew that he was about to be taken for a ride. Manna from heaven was all very well, but, like walking on water, you had to believe in it in the first place. 'We need eleven guns in total. Get me everything we talked about bar the big Uzi. And no Eastern bloc crap, remember?'

'No. No. I'm not stupid. The customer always king in my book.'

'How much?'

The Mexican almost drooled. 'Ten thousand bucks.'

'Go fuck yourself.'

'Eh, man. I don't want to do that. I get girls for that. All sorts. You want girls too? I get you anything you want. Green. Black. Red. White. Pussy on the slant. Pussy straight up. You call it.'

'I'll give you five thousand bucks.'

'Now you got to be kidding me, man. You know how hard it is to get these things into the country?'

'About as hard as trafficking those girls you told me about. I know all about the tunnels you guys have got below Agua Prieta.'

'Lower your voice, man. Are you crazy?' The Mexican didn't seem too bothered by Alastor's comments though – his eyes were still flashing dollar signs. 'Okay. Nine thousand. But that's my final offer. The Federales are cracking down on illegal guns. We got serious trouble here now. We got extra expenses.'

'Six thousand.'

'No. No. Man. That's impossible.'

Alastor was enjoying the Mexican's discomfiture. The guy was having to decide just how amenable he could appear to be in order to reel in his prey. Too amenable, and the minnow would run. Not amenable enough, and the same thing happened – Alastor would simply put two fingers up and go someplace else. It would take fine judgement.

So Alastor sat watching the Mexican. Waiting. He had learned that waiting nearly always produced results.

'You need to eat something, man. You real thin. Too thin.'

'Six thousand.'

'Is impossible. But I tell you what. We forget the Stoner, and I can do it for seven thousand straight.'

'Okay.'

'Okay?'

'I didn't want the Stoner anyway. Too big. Too loud. Too easy to fucking trace.'

'I thought the same, man, I thought the same.' The Mexican was sweating now. The thought of the seven thousand dollars was eating into him like nitric acid. Maybe he could have driven the gringo up to eight?

'Where do I pick up the material?'

The Mexican glanced around the cantina. It was an all-male watering hole, as good as empty now in the early afternoon, with most of its denizens either taking their siestas or pretending to work. 'You coming alone?'

'Yeah. I got a car. Easy to move the stuff into the back.'

'You ever done this before?'

'No.' Alastor smiled. The stress lines in his face looked like glacial grooves. 'This is all new to me.'

The Mexican grinned. He already knew he had a real sucker here. This proved it once and for all. No one admitted to inexperience in his world. In his world everybody had done everything a thousand times over. 'We meet this evening. Six o'clock. There's a cave complex near Valladolid. They call it the Gruta de Balancanché. We meet in the car park there. You can't miss it, man. It's only a few kilometres south of Chichén Itzá.' He frowned at Alastor. 'You remember now. Nothing bigger than twenty-dollar bills?'

'Seven thousand. That's what we agreed?'

The Mexican almost gave himself away then. He almost laughed. This gringo was priceless. One felt tempted to pick him up in one hand and twirl him about one's head like a lasso. 'Yeah. Seven thousand. You get the best ordnance in the whole of Mexico, I promise. I tell you this. You've come to the right place.'

'I know that, my friend. I know that very well.'

67

Lamia settled herself on the ground. She curled her legs beneath her and off to one side just like the Maya women she saw scattered about the compound, all of whom were either weaving, pounding maize, cooking, or endlessly patting tortillas into shape – and pretending not to watch the gringos, and, in particular, the gringa with the damaged cheek.

Lamia flashed a look at Sabir. There was a hunted expression on her face he had never seen there before.

'What do you think they are going to do with us?'

Sabir squatted down beside her, his eyes fixed on the two guards standing at the edge of the clearing, their rifles at the ready. 'Between you and me, they can do anything they want. Nobody knows we're here. Nobody gives a damn about us. They could kill us and bury us somewhere in this endless scrubland and no one would be any the wiser. Then all they'd have to do would be to strip down the Grand Cherokee and ship it over to Guatemala. We changed our dollars into pesos on the US side of the border, Lamia, and we paid cash all the way down for everything we bought, including gas, food, and accommodation. It seemed like a heck of a good idea at the time. As a result there's no official record of us anywhere beyond Brownsville.'

'I don't think they'll do what you suggest. Acan is a nice boy. He's not a killer.'

'I don't think so either.'

Lamia let out a heavy sigh. She was clearly grateful that Sabir was agreeing with her. 'What have they done with Calque?'

'They've got him over the other side of the clearing. He's probably eating something. Or perhaps the priests are putting on his skin like a cloak and eating *him*? Christ, maybe I got it all wrong, and we're next for the pot after all?'

Lamia threw a handful of dirt at him. She laughed in delight when he lost his balance trying to dodge it, and went sprawling.

Sabir stood up and made a great play out of shaking out his shirt. 'I guess I deserved that. I never realized you were such a dangerous and impulsive woman.' He grinned and resettled himself at the squat, pleased that he had triggered her change of mood.

'Do you have any idea where we are?'

'Yes, oddly enough, I do. On the way here I saw a sign that said Ek Balam. And there's a pyramid over there. Can you see it? Just peeking through the trees. So it seems we're at or near the site, which, if I remember correctly, is situated a few miles north of the main Cancun turnpike, just up from Valladolid. Frankly, they don't seem too worried about us knowing where we are.'

'That might mean that they don't need to bother themselves with what we know because they're going to kill us anyway. Maybe you were right in the first place?'

'Yeah. And maybe the cup's half empty, and never half

full. No, Lamia. I think we've set them a problem that they're going to have to work out for themselves. You saw how they responded to the crystal skull? And now they've got this man with the book to deal with too. That's quite enough for one day. I'm convinced these guys are bona fide Maya, and that they genuinely thought we were grave robbers or something, and simply stepped in to protect their holy sites. I'm trusting that Calque can straighten them out on that angle. He's good at that sort of thing.'

'And my brothers and sisters?'

Sabir threw back his head as though he'd been slapped. 'Let's hope that they did indeed lose us back there near Jaltipan.'

'Have you any reason to suppose that they didn't?'

'No. None whatsoever. But I wouldn't like to imagine how far they'd go to get their hands on the skull and the book. The minute you bring firearms into an equation, like these Maya have, all rational judgement flies out the window. People behave like animals. I'm not so dumb that I don't realize that if it came to a fight between these people and the Corpus, the Corpus would win hands down. That the way you read it?'

Lamia nodded. Here eyes were like dark wells within the paler framework of her face.

68

—

It was late afternoon by the time the Halach Uinic had succeeded in assembling all the people he would need for the ceremony of the tearing of the flesh. For this was what he now felt was necessary if the decision he had come to that morning in the car was to be acted upon.

After private prayer and a lengthy internal debate, the Halach Uinic had decided that he must offer himself up as a sacrifice to propitiate the gods, and through them, the composite, alchemical God that was Hunab Ku – the one monotheistic God who encapsulated and concatenated both Quetzalcoatl and Kukulcan.

The Halach Uinic didn't intend to sacrifice himself in any purely physical sense, needless to say. That sort of thing was well past its sell-by date. The Spanish colonizers had been right to ban human sacrifices – there was a time and a place for everything, and in the early twenty-first century, unnecessary death, even if followed by inevitable rebirth, was notably inappropriate.

No, the sacrifice the Halach Uinic intended to make was a harder one than simply the giving up of one's own life. The offering back of the book and the crystal skull to those who had found them needed to be paid for. And he, as chief representative of all the other priests, was the one who needed to do the paying.

He glanced across at the main temple. Everything was ready. The priests and the shamans were in place. The steps up to the top of the pyramid had been decorated with water lilies, *pitaya* flowers, and fronds from the *corozo* palm. Ritual objects and offerings of all sorts had been arrayed up the steps, including cigars, orchids, chocolate, sugar candy, *aguardiente*, burning bowls of *sacpom* tree resin, and many candles. Prayers had been chanted and fires had been lit. The lilies were correctly placed facing in towards the fires, showing a symbolical willingness to face the flames. The Calendar of the Days had been formally counted out by one of the priests, and white *copal* incense from the north of Mexico was being burnt as a nod to wider confraternity. Crosses had been drawn in honey on each of the steps leading to the top of the pyramid, reflecting the *chaacoob* – the four directions of the compass – each direction with its colour laid out in spices within the circle. East was red, north was white, west was black, and south was yellow.

The shamans and the *iyoma* – collectively known as the *ajcuna*, or spirit lawyers – each carrying their own personal bag of ritual objects, were arrayed, every one at a different level, up the entire length of the steps. Some of them wore elaborate spondylus shell necklaces and headdresses of quetzal, ibis, flamingo, and parrot feathers. Each person was dressed differently, for there was a hidden language of clothes amongst the Maya, and those able to speak that language could learn many things – about age, rank, status within the community, and even the level of psychic awareness of which that person was deemed capable – simply by what a man or a woman had chosen to wear that day.

The Halach Uinic recognized Acan's mother, Ixtab, standing halfway up the steps leading to the top of the great pyramid. Of all the *iyoma* he had known in his lifetime, Ixtab was the most perceptive. He was pleased that she had put aside her usual duties and had hearkened to his call. He wanted her to see the gringos. Wanted her opinion.

He closed his eyes and concentrated for a few moments, hoping that amidst all the excitement and anticipation of the ceremony, his usual channels of communication with her might still be open. For the Halach Uinic and Ixtab met regularly inside their dreams. The connection between them might be an unspoken one, but the Halach Uinic knew beyond any doubt that his *nawal* had chosen Ixtab to be his shadow guide. That it was she who had been detailed to guard him from the mistakes vainglory –

and the inevitable vanity of men – might otherwise cause him to make. She was his protector and his conscience. His spirit doctor and his companion in the web of life.

The Halach Uinic looked up. Ixtab was staring down at him, her face pale beneath her headdress. In a covert gesture, the Halach Uinic raised his hands and opened them upwards, as if forces greater than himself were at work around him. Ixtab, in an equally covert gesture, turned her palms towards the ground, and gestured downwards, as if she were kneading dough. Male upwards and airborne, female downwards and grounded.

The Halach Uinic understood what she was telling him. Few people knew that this little-known site at Ek Balam was the true spiritual centre of Maya belief. A place to which Maya priests had come for countless generations, sure in the knowledge that a resident guardian would always be on hand to welcome them into the site via the ritual stone archway that still guarded its entrance – known privately as the Temple of the Praying Hands. The resident guardian would then wash the visiting priest's knees, feet, and hands, before allocating the priest a place in one of the few still unburied stone cubicles. The visiting priest would then use the stone cubicle to re-energize himself and reconnect himself to nature.

For most enlightened Maya, Chichén Itzá, Tulum, Palenque, and many of the other great sites of the former Maya hierarchy were simply sad reminders of lost greatness. They had nothing further to offer. Whatever energy they had left was hidden so far underground that it could only be reached via extreme and thorough ritual. At Ek Balam, however, the energy still brimmed from the ground like a fountain.

In addition, Ek Balam, or the Black Jaguar, was the only site left in the whole of Mexico, Guatemala, and Belize that still incorporated all three of the essential elements and energy centres – the sky, the earth, and the underworld. The downward movement of Ixtab's hands, echoing and counterpointing that of the Halach Uinic, had been a recognition of this fact, therefore – a reminder to the Halach Uinic that he must submit, and trust, and not attempt to dominate.

The Halach Uinic acknowledged Ixtab's warning with a downward inclination of the head. Then he signalled to Acan, Naum, and Tepeu that they must bring forward the three gringos and the mestizo from Veracruz.

The Halach Uinic could sense the intense interest aroused by the appearance of the strangers. He allowed the collective emotion of the crowd to leach deep into his body until he could feel each individual's response as if it were his own.

Only when he felt full to the brim – only when he felt as if he were carrying the entire wishes and the hopes of the crowd within himself – did he start up the stone steps.

69

Sabir felt at peace. He didn't fully understand why this should be so, but neither did he feel any particular desire to investigate his newfound condition. He was content simply to bask in the unfamiliar harmony, and allow the long-awaited healing process to begin.

After half an hour or so of near total detachment, something snapped Sabir out of his reverie. He began to monitor the preparations being made by the Halach Uinic with more than the usual amount of interest. At first he couldn't understand what had triggered this intense curiosity, but then he realized that the High Priest was communicating in some quasi-telepathic way with a middle-aged woman standing halfway up the stone steps of the pyramid. It was this that had caught his attention.

Sabir was at a loss to understand how he had achieved this insight, but he could definitely sense the energy passing between them. It resembled the sudden flapping of a curtain in the wind, or the unexpected tightening of a sail out at sea in the run-up to a squall. The impression was so overwhelming that Sabir was instantly overcome by the conviction that he could intervene between the two of them if he so desired, transforming their duologue into something approaching a round table discussion – but that it would probably be considered the height of rudeness were he to do so.

He glanced at Calque to his left, and then at Lamia to his right. Both were deeply involved in watching the preparations for the ceremony.

Had he gone stark staring mad? It was obvious that his companions hadn't the remotest idea of what was going on his head – and neither were they picking up anything of a similar sort themselves. Instead, they were watching the preparations going on around them with the natural interest of the outsider.

Had his never-ending litany of sleepless nights caught up with him at last? Was he hallucinating? Sabir shook himself like a dog and concentrated all his attention on the scene around him. Best drag yourself back to reality, man. No more airy-fairy nonsense. You'll be dreaming of pixies next.

The first thing Sabir noticed following his reality check was that the Maya en masse were even smaller than he had imagined them to be – much smaller than a similar random grouping of Westerners, or even Latins, would have been. Both men and women had round faces and wide cheekbones – they smiled a lot, and were quick to mirth. Most of the women standing in the group nearby were squat, square, and useful looking, with a low centre of gravity. Some had an almost Asiatic cast to their features. The older women were stocky, with solid bellies and protruding bottoms, although some of the younger women were very beautiful, with an almost sinister cast to their features – they had curved noses, almond eyes, dark, fine hair, and expressive, sensual mouths. Their colour varied from a light macadamia to a darker chocolate. Few of the women were heavy-breasted, with the young girls in particular seeming to retain their flat chests well into adolescence. Most of the women Sabir could see wore their hair long, while some of the men cut theirs *en brosse*.

Sabir also noticed that the Maya strolled rather than strode – in fact they almost bundled along, blowing their noses onto the ground whenever they felt like it. Ponytails were popular amongst the women, with the hair pulled tightly back from the forehead. The older women wore white shifts, with floral borders, visible petticoats, and occasional *rebozos*, worn across the shoulders like a shawl. The younger women wore wheel earrings – Sabir noticed that both the men and the women's ears aimed backwards, just as in the sculptures.

'Come on, Sabir. Snap out of it. We're on the move.'

'What?'

Calque was staring at Sabir as if the American had taken leave of his senses. 'The ceremony. The one they've been preparing for two hours right in front of your face. All that clattering and banging. Don't tell me you missed it?' He turned to Lamia. 'Do you think an alien life-form has taken over our friend here?'

'Yes.'

'I think so too.' Calque turned back to Sabir. 'Oh, Alien. Return our friend to us. You have taken all his secrets. You know that he is simply an empty vessel with nothing inside. Be satisfied with that. We earthlings are no threat to you.'

'Yeah. Very funny. I love a good joke. Maybe you could become a stand-up comedian when you get back to France, Calque? You could call yourself "*Flic-Flaque*". Otherwise known as the "Wet Policeman".'

Calque stared incredulously at Lamia. 'My God. He really *is* an alien. That was a halfway good French pun he managed there.'

Acan, Naum, and Tepeu were approaching from the direction of the pyramid. It was this that had triggered Calque's wake-up call to Sabir. None of the three were carrying rifles, and they had changed from their usual work clothes into simple white shifts.

Acan split off and came towards Sabir. Naum had clearly been detailed to mind Calque, while Tepeu walked up to Lamia and invited her and the mestizo to accompany him.

Sabir was still feeling awkward following his unintentional detachment from his companions. Even Lamia was staring at him as if he had recently undergone some disastrously botched plastic surgery. He decided to try and patch up their fractured bond with a little forced bonhomie. Plastering an artificial grin on his face, he said, 'Everything's sweetness and light, now. Do you see? They've even ditched their rifles.'

Calque shook his head in mild despair. 'Sabir, you probably haven't noticed, but there are maybe a thousand Maya surrounding us at this very moment. Who the heck needs rifles?'

70

Alastor de Bale sat in his car in the parking lot of the Balancanché caves. It was six o'clock in the evening. He had been there since four o'clock. At five o'clock all the staff had packed up and left. Only the elderly carwash man had stayed behind, hoping for one final commission. Alastor had given him one hundred pesos and told him to get lost.

The man had hung around on the periphery of the lot for a further ten minutes until Alastor had made a throat-cutting motion at him. Then he had fled. The carwash man had never been given one hundred pesos for doing nothing before, and he had been hanging around to make sure that the skeletal gringo was actually real, and not simply the fiend Paqok, come out at night to feast on hapless men and women after tricking them into a false sense of security.

Alastor glanced back at the entrance to the parking lot. The gun-running Mexican wasn't dumb. There was only one road into the space, and that was hemmed in on both sides by forest and impenetrable scrubland. Behind him were the caves – sealed tight now that the tourists had gone home. And there was no caretaker. What would be the point? There was nothing here to steal.

Rudra and Oni had taken up their positions half an hour before, following Alastor's all clear, at which time Berith and Asson had also taken their places in the Hyundai's trunk. It was stiflingly hot in there, but the two men were used to waiting – they simply switched their brains on to autopilot and their lungs to shallow yogic breathing. The time passed quickly. It always did when action was in the offing.

At exactly 6.15 a white Suzuki 4WD nosed its way down the Balancanché track. It paused at the entrance to the parking lot while the driver looked around. Then it engaged in a jerky three-point turn until it was entirely blocking off the parking lot's only exit, with its nose facing back in the direction of the main road.

Alastor smiled.

Three men got out of the 4WD. The Mexican he had met in the cantina was flanked by two other Mexicans, both carrying Mini-Uzis. The first Mexican was holding what looked like a Glock 18 in the hands-down position.

Now Alastor was full-on grinning. Three guns down – eight to go.

He got out of the car with his hands held high. 'You guys going to shoot me?'

'Not if you give us the money.'

'You got the guns we talked about?'

'We got these. Will that do?' The men were walking slowly towards Alastor. The two men flanking the first Mexican were looking around themselves just like they'd seen it done in the movies.

'That's three. I asked for eleven.'

'Eh, man. That's too bad. I must have forgot the rest.'

Alastor hunched his shoulders. 'Well okay then. Three is better than nothing, I suppose. But we'll have to renegotiate the price.'

'What will we have to do?' The first Mexican raised his Glock to the firing position. He was ten yards away now.

'Ah, shit. I see your point. Maybe we'll just stick by our original agreement.'

'Yeah. We do that. Where you got the money?'

'In the trunk. You want me to open it?'

'No. We open it. You stand to one side.'

'Okay. Here's the key. You press the middle one. The

one with the open trunk drawn on it. The money's in a cardboard box.'

'What do think I am? Stupid?'

'How do you mean?' For one awkward moment Alastor thought the Mexican had changed his mind about opening the trunk.

'You think I don't know which button to press on an automatic key?'

'Hell, man. No. I didn't think that. I only wanted to make it easy for you.' Now that the Mexicans were within three or four feet of him, Alastor could smell the liquor on their breaths. Maybe they'd needed to pump themselves up for the job of killing him? Give themselves Dutch courage? Either way, the alcohol would slow down their reaction times.

The men with the Mini-Uzis were flanking Alastor now, while the first Mexican was moving forward to deal with the car.

Alastor let the fighting batons slide gently down inside his sleeves, one into each hand. Then he crossed both hands in front of him, as if he had been handcuffed, or as if he were protecting his balls from a free kick at soccer. He could feel the adrenalin piping into his veins. Two at once. Christ. Could he do it? Could he pull it off?

The first Mexican tripped the trunk. As the hatch rose, Berith and Asson rose with it. Oni and Rudra reared up from their dugout positions on either side of the car, their groundsheets, and the sand which had been covering them, erupting into the air like the aftermath of a grenade attack.

Alastor threw his arms wide, the fighting batons at full extension. He felt the satisfying crunch of teeth and bone.

He looked back. Both men were flat out on the ground. In front of him, the first Mexican, not knowing which way to look, had succumbed, first to a blow behind the knee from Rudra's baton, followed by a second, straight-arm jab in the sternum from Asson. He was choking and gulping for breath.

Alastor motioned for Oni and Rudra to pick up the Mini-Uzis. 'Check out the car. Also back on the main road. They may have back-up.'

The two men jogged off in the direction of the highway.

'You.' Alastor pointed at the first Mexican. 'Are you left- or right-handed?'

The man was still struggling to regain his breath. He shook his head, unable to string two words together.

'Okay. You held the Glock in your right hand. I'll assume that one's the master. Berith, cut off this guy's right hand. Just below the elbow will do.'

The Mexican began to scream.

Berith pulled a machete from the trunk of the car. 'I've been sharpening this bastard thing all afternoon and I still can't get a good edge on it. Why can't they sell these things pre-sharpened? It wouldn't take much, you know.'

'What are you trying to say?'

'What I'm trying to say is that I'm not sure I can make the cut in one. I might have to chop a few times. Three maybe. Otherwise I won't make it through the bone. I'm sorry, friend.' He said this to the Mexican. 'But you can see my problem, can't you?'

The Mexican, with one of his legs still dead from the baton blow, was trying to lever himself underneath the car.

Asson grabbed both his legs and yanked him out. Then he strolled over to one of the fallen men who was struggling to get to his feet and smashed in the back of his head with a backhand blow of his baton. He checked on the other man. 'You killed this one clean, Ali. Heck of a shot. Did you really get them both at once? Or did you one-two them? Be honest now.'

'Left and right. Just like a brace of pheasants. They should have a social club for people like me. Dinners once a year. Designer blazers with crossed batons on the pocket. Two witnesses needed or you don't get in. They've got one like that in London I hear – only it's for left and rights at woodcock. I'm going to suggest they expand their remit.'

'What do you want from me?' The Mexican was quieter now. Now that the two freaks – the fat one and the thin one – were talking amongst themselves, he was starting to think that maybe he could save his arm.

'We'll ask you after the amputation. Berith. Go to it.'

'No. No. No. I tell you where everything is.'

'What? You mean the rest of our order?'

'Yeah. Yeah. We were going to fulfil it. We only wanted to check you hadn't come armed.'

'What? You mean armed like you three guys?' Alastor pretended to think. 'How were we going to come armed? We came to you to buy weapons, not to discharge them, you moron. Cut off his arm, Berith.'

The Mexican thrust both his hands under his armpits like a child having a tantrum. 'No. Listen to me. We got a warehouse. Just one guy guarding it. No alarms. I take you there.'

'You're not taking us anywhere. You're going to be bleeding to death.'

'It's only ten kilometres from here. At Xbolom. You take the turning from Chandok. There's a sign saying *Agave Azul – El futuro de Yucatan*. You turn off down there. The barn is two hundred metres on the right. Corrugated iron with a *Juano* palm roof.'

'You're sure of this? If you're lying, I take both your hands off.'

'No. No. I'm not lying. You go there and check it out. Take anything you want.'

Alastor picked up the Glock and shot the Mexican in the head. 'Don't worry. We will.'

71

'This place is perfect.' Abi looked around himself. The warehouse stood by itself down a country track, surrounded by a field of blue agave. Rifle, shotgun, pistol and ammunition cases were stacked haphazardly throughout the building. 'Nobody will hear anything that goes on here. When we get hold of our three little piggies, we can take our own sweet time with them. What have you done with the stiffs?'

'They're in the car.'

'And the watchman?'

'He's outside. He's got a broken jaw, but he can still talk.'

'Get him in here.'

Oni brought the watchman in. The man was bleeding from his mouth.

'You got a cenote around here? You must get your water from somewhere. And it surely isn't the national grid.'

The man ducked his head like he couldn't believe what he'd been asked.

'Hit him, Oni.'

Oni raised his hand, but the man slithered out of his grasp and tried to make a run for it.

Abi raised the Glock and shot the man's leg out from underneath him. 'Oni. Go outside and ask Berith if he heard that shot.'

'Okay.'

Abi waited. The watchman was writhing around on the floor of the warehouse. A viscous pool of deep-crimson blood was oozing from his leg.

Oni came back. 'No. You can't hear anything out there.'

'Good.' Abi shot the man in his other leg. 'Now look here, my friend. It's obvious you're not going anywhere in a hurry with both your legs smashed. I'm going to shoot you in the arm next. Then in the stomach. Each time you don't answer a question, I'm going to shoot you someplace else. You understand my Spanish?'

The watchman nodded. His face was pale and his eyes were fluttering. It was clear that he was going into shock.

'The cenote. Where is it?'

The watchman indicated with his head. 'North. Through the woods. About six hundred metres.'

'Who else knows about it?'

'Nobody comes here, if that's what you mean.' The man could hardly get the words out through his broken jaw. 'Nobody dares. Bad people own this place.'

'Yeah. And now they're dead.'

The watchman shook his head. 'No. There are more. They come to get you. You people will die.'

'How many more?'

The man hesitated.

Abi raised the Glock.

'Six. Maybe eight. I'm not sure.'

'Where are they now?'

The man sighed. It was as if he knew that he was coming to the end of his life. 'You going to kill me?'

'Where are they now?'

'Up at the US border. They got a big consignment of weapons coming in. They away for maybe six days. Pepito was just working something on the side when he

343

made the deal with you guys. The boss left us here to watch this place. Pepito shouldn't have left me alone here. But he said he'd pay me a hundred dollars if I watched the warehouse for an hour or two.' The watchman was losing consciousness. His voice was fading away. 'You going to kill me?'

'Break his neck, Oni.'

'Break his neck? Why should I break his neck? It's hard to break somebody's neck. Why don't you just shoot him?'

'Because I need you to keep in practice. That's why. Okay?'

Oni smiled. 'Okay.'

The watchman closed his eyes. He was pleased now that he'd lied to the gringo. Pleased that he hadn't told him the truth about the boss, and the consignment, and how many people the boss had, and the number of days they would be away.

When Oni broke his neck it was almost a relief.

72

Abi stared down at the cenote. You got to it through a thick stand of pampas grass. The sinkhole was maybe sixty feet wide, and situated fifty feet straight down, with sheer walls on all sides. It was shaped like a cylinder. Trees grew up from the vase of the cenote, and trailed their fronds in it, but none of them reached anywhere near the lip. Around midday the pool would probably be bathed in sunlight, but now, nearer to eight o'clock in the evening, it looked like the entrance to hell.

A pipe had been let down one side, feeding a series of pumps that took water to the warehouse. Aside from the pipe, there was no way up or down to the cenote. What went in stayed in.

'Strip the four stiffs and burn their clothes. Then put the stiffs in the Suzuki. Crack the windows about fifteen centimetres – enough to let the water in, but not enough to let anything leak out. Then drive it here and dump it in the cenote. Try not to disturb the grass too much.'

'But the stiffs will spoil the water, Abi.'

'We'll drink bottled water while we're here, Vau. We won't be staying long enough to require baths.'

'Okay. You're the boss.' Vau hesitated. 'Are you going to bring Sabir, Lamia, and Calque out here to the warehouse?'

'Yes. We'll sweat everything out of them soon enough. Sabir will crack the moment we start in on Lamia. That's what true love does to you, Vau. Makes you vulnerable. Some people admire that about it. I think it stinks.'

Abi watched Vau negotiating his way through the pampas grass and back to the warehouse via the track alongside the agave field. He shook his head. Things couldn't have fallen any better really. They'd lucked into the perfect base. They had more weapons than the CRS and the Foreign Legion combined. And they had the aquatic equivalent of a batch incinerator to get rid of any inconvenient cadavers that turned up as a result of collateral damage.

'Collateral damage'. How it rolled off the tongue. Abi loved American euphemisms. When he was really bored, he would make up new ones, like 'inadvertent blood donors' and 'residual throw-downs'. But 'collateral damage' was still the best. He'd never come near matching that one.

Now all Abi needed to make his happiness complete was Madame, his mother's, okay to go in and snatch Lamia, Calque, and Sabir and whatever else he could get his hands on, including the mestizo's book and the crystal skull. Which, given the Countess's recent form, would be easier said than done.

Abi called up Athame's cell phone. He knew that her position might be compromised if she answered the phone at the wrong moment, so he let the phone ring twice only, and then hung up. She would feel the vibration through her clothes and know that he wanted to speak to her.

He sat on the lip of the cenote and stared down into the pool, waiting.

When his cell phone finally rang, it took him a moment to respond. Dusk had fallen. The forest all around him was alive with the furtive movement of animals.

'Can you talk?'

'It's fine. There's so much noise coming from over by the temple that I could bellow like a bull and they wouldn't hear me.'

Abi smiled. The thought of the dwarf-like Athame bellowing like a bull tickled his sense of the absurd. 'What's happening?'

'They're holding some kind of ceremony.'

'Can you make out what it's about?'

'I can't get close enough. You could try Aldinach for that. She's up in a tree, over on the other side of the site. She might have a better view. I don't know where Dakini and Nawal are hiding. It was a brilliant idea of yours to use us girls. If we get caught, they'll just think we're a bunch of New Age gringas trying to cop a view of the ceremony.'

'What do you figure is happening?'

'You want my guess?'

'Yes.'

'I think they're discussing what to do with the skull and the book. They've got my sister and her two boyfriends up there with them on top of the pyramid. Maybe when they've made up their minds they'll cut their hearts out and offer them up to the jaguar god? Then someone could dress up in their skins and go cavorting about the sanctuary like in the good old days. That would save us all a lot of trouble.'

'Who's running the show?'

'The High Priest. If we can keep tabs on him, we'll know where to find the book and the skull.'

'Stay where you are. I'm coming over to join you with Vau, Asson, Alastor, and Rudra. I'm leaving Oni and Berith here to watch the warehouse.'

'What warehouse?'

'I'll tell you later. But we've got all the weapons we need. You can take your pick. Glock. Beretta. Heckler and Koch. Star. Walther. Smith & Wesson.'

'I'll take the Walther.'

'Nice choice. It's a P4. I'll bring it to you personally.'

'Then what?'

'I'm about to find out. I'm about to call our mother.'

73

Sabir followed the Halach Uinic up the pyramid steps. He knew that every eye in the house was fixed upon him and his party. The crowd, for the most part, had fallen silent, but an underlying murmur remained, like that made by a distant swarm of bees.

Dusk was only gradually falling, but the brightness thrown out by the candles, the bonfires, and the burning bowls of incense exaggerated its effect. The higher Sabir rose on the pyramid, the easier it became to discern the endless blanket of forest stretching in every direction around him. It was like a great murky ocean, with the pyramid as a fragile island of light at its epicentre.

The wind picked at his clothes as he made his way up the endless stone steps. He turned his head briefly towards the west, relishing the cooler air. Was this why the ancient Maya had built themselves pyramids and not long houses? An understandable desire to compensate for the fearful heat of the Yucatan summers? The whole thing was probably as simple and as straightforward as that. All the rituals and the contrivances must have come later. Like the chaser to a glass of beer.

Sabir smiled to himself, pleased at his capacity for lateral thought. After all, there was not a single mountain in the whole of the peninsula, nor a single volcano, nor a single hill worthy of the name. Surely the Maya would have had a race memory of travelling through the alpine lands of the northern Americas before they settled? Maybe they wanted to recreate the details of their journey in stone? Or perhaps they simply wanted to match the gods? Or was it subtler than that? Was it flattery they were after?

Sabir had reached the halfway stage in his ascent of the steps. Some instinct made him glance to his left. He realized that he was exactly parallel with the woman whom he sensed had been telepathically communicating with the Halach Uinic. He took a step towards her.

Acan put out a hand to stay him. 'Adam,' he whispered. 'That is Ixtab. My mother. I told you of her. But we will see her later. You must come with me now. You cannot wait here. The Chilans are coming up behind us. They will be very angry if you disrupt the ceremony.'

Sabir shrugged off Acan's hand. He broke clear of the ascending line of priests and made his way to where Ixtab was standing. He was frowning, as if someone had set him an unexpected puzzle. He was half aware that the Halach Uinic and his party had stopped their progress and were watching him, but he didn't care. All of a sudden he knew exactly what he had to do.

He held out both his hands to Ixtab.

Ixtab smiled and took them. She nodded her head a number of times, as if something she had hitherto only suspected had now been proved true. 'Welcome, Shaman. I have been expecting you.'

A fearsome energy seemed to be transferring itself from her hands into his.

'Shaman?' The energy flowing between Sabir and Ixtab's hands now seemed to be stemming directly from him.

'Why are you surprised? You have been fighting it for many years. Were you not told?'

Sabir closed his eyes. 'A Gypsy *curandero* in the south of France. He told me. Earlier this year. In a way he even saved my life.'

'There. I knew it. He was your messenger. He sent you here to us. If you had been born here, amongst us, it would have been I who would have told you.' She stared at him for a long moment. 'Your mother, too. She was a shaman.'

Sabir looked up sharply. 'What are you talking about? My mother killed herself. She was disturbed in her mind.'

Ixtab shook her head. 'No. She went unrecognized. She lived amongst people who did not understand her true function. She consumed herself. This can happen. You must not do the same.'

Acan had fallen in behind them. He was frowning. Things weren't going quite as planned.

Sabir shook his head, as if by so doing he could physically discourage unwanted thoughts. 'That's not possible.'

'But you know it to be true.'

Sabir allowed his eyes to play over Ixtab's face. There was no room for doubt. What this woman said, she believed. And he believed it too. 'I had no idea. She was too damaged by the time I was old enough to understand.'

'She did not know it herself. You are not to blame. Your father loved her too much. She was swayed by that. She should never have married. Shamans should remain single. They are wedded to the truth.'

'But you? You are married. You have a son.'

'Two sons. And three daughters. But I am not a shaman. I am an *iyoma*. My duty is simply to recognize those whom the gods have marked out, and to guide those who are lost.'

'Would you have guided my mother?'

'If she had come to me. Only then. But I cannot search people out. This is beyond my power. Beyond anybody's power but Hunab Ku's.' Ixtab glanced up at the Halach Uinic. She nodded. He nodded back.

Sabir turned to face the Halach Uinic. The Halach Uinic held out a hand and beckoned Sabir and Ixtab to follow him. Sabir turned to Lamia. She was staring at him with a quizzical expression on her face. He gestured to her, but she shook her head, and fell back in line behind Calque and the mestizo from Veracruz.

Sabir felt a sudden coldness overwhelm him. The feeling was so powerful that it was as if he had been touched by the shadow of his own death.

He turned to Ixtab. She was mentally urging him to climb the rest of the steps. This fact was so clear in Sabir's head that it didn't even occur to him to question it. He began dutifully to ascend. He had no idea what was happening to him, nor why he was behaving in the odd way that he was. Who was this woman? And why did he feel so connected to her? Why, moreover, had Lamia refused to accompany them? And what was the significance of the invisible triangle that now seemed to exist between him, Ixtab, and the Halach Uinic?

Instantly, in his head, three images appeared, just as they would have done in a dream. Together, they made perfect sense of everything he had been asking.

In them the Halach Uinic was the sky, Ixtab was the earth, and he, Sabir, represented the underworld.

74

'We're to do nothing.'

'What do you mean?'

'Exactly what I said. Madame, our mother, says we are to do nothing. We are to watch and wait.'

Vau, Asson, Alastor, and Rudra were sitting in the car with Abi. They had each stripped, oiled, and tested their chosen weapons. Rudra had found some old wine corks at the warehouse, and had seared the ends to produce a quantity of charcoal substitute. Each of the brothers had camouflaged his face, hands, and forearms, so that no pale skin showed outside the borders of their clothes.

Alastor was still fired up from his activities at the Balancanché caves. He sensed that his brothers were experiencing the same physical lift. This is what they were trained for. This is what they lived for. There was little sense in doing anything else. 'But we've been watching and waiting for more than a week.'

'Exactly. Now we must do more of the same.'

The brothers looked at each other.

Abi was driving, so he couldn't immediately identify the focus of their attention. But he knew just what they were all thinking. And he knew that this was the moment, if any, to engineer an invisible coup against Madame, his mother's, leadership. 'You all happy with that? At least you'll get to go to the party. Asson, have you got the girls' guns?'

'A Walther P4 for Athame, Berettas for Dakini and Nawal, and the Heckler and Koch for Aldinach. I've got that right, haven't I? I'm not missing anything? Like why do we need weapons at all if all the fuck we are doing is fucking watching a fucking ceremony?'

'You're right, Asson. And you argue your point so eloquently. We'd better leave them in the car then.' Abi was enjoying winding them up.

'The hell with that.' It was Alastor. The starved planes of his face were drastically exaggerated by the black stripes of his camouflage. 'I'm not letting this work of art out of my hands. I felt naked all through the US and most of Mexico without a pistol. Now I've got this Glock I'm going to keep it. Seventeen rounds of 9mm Parabellum – muzzle velocity 375mps – effective range 100 feet. And it's all mine to do with as I please. God Himself couldn't separate me from this piece.'

'And this from the man who got a straight left and right of Mexicans with two hidden fighting sticks?' Asson was grinning. 'Alastor might not look like much, but he packs a mean backhand.' Asson's grin faded away. 'Abi, are you serious? She really wants us to hold off? But what have we been doing all this past week? Pissing in the wind?'

'Is your face wet?'

'Fucking streaming.'

'Then you just answered your own question.'

They fell silent for a while on the approach to Ek Balam. They could see the pyramid glowing in the distance. It looked like a Christmas cake with a thousand candles planted on it.

'I'm going to leave the car down this track. We'll walk in from here.'

'What's the point?'

'The point is that we're going to wait until the crowd disperses and everyone goes off to beddy-byes. Then we'll strike. Athame says that the Maya aren't carrying their rifles any more. My guess is that Sabir and company have inveigled their way into the High Priest's good graces, and that they're no longer considered prisoners. So we snatch the three of them, together with the book and the skull for good measure, and get out of here. No killing. No noise. We don't want the Mexican police on our tail. Those boys don't joke around when it comes to firearms. They'll kill you as soon as look at you.'

Vau turned to his brother. 'But Madame, our mother, told you to hold off.'

'What Madame, our mother, doesn't know won't hurt her. Are we all agreed on that?'

There was silence in the car.

'Listen. We get this done and then we present her with a *fait accompli*. She's not here on the ground. She hasn't got the necessary facts to make an informed decision. Plus she doesn't know about the warehouse.'

'Why not?'

'Because I'm not going to talk about it on an open phone line, am I? Do I look like a moron? The fewer people who know about it the better. By the time we're finished up here there'll be seven bodies down in that cenote. And I want them to stay there. Forever. When the guys who think they own the place come back from picking up their consignment in six days' time, I don't want them sniffing around the cenote. It's got to look normal. Untouched. Because we're going to be dumping most of the remaining ordnance down there too.'

'Why, Abi?'

'Because we want the big boss to think that dear old Pepito and his three cronies took off with all his junk. Instead, he'll be brushing his teeth and showering in a mixture of corpse water and rust for the next ten years.'

'Won't he phone up from wherever he's going? When he doesn't get an answer, he'll send someone down to check the place out.'

'He's up at the US border, for Christ's sake. And he's not going to phone in the middle of the night to check if his watchmen are still on duty – that's what they're paid for. Do you think he *expects* his warehouse to be invaded by a bunch of Frenchmen? By the time he gets someone on a plane, maybe tomorrow afternoon, maybe later, we'll be long gone. Anyway, I've told Oni and Berith to set up the Stoner and that piece of shit AAT we found in crossfire positions to cover the approach road. Anything comes up from there unannounced, we can blow it into a hundred thousand pieces. Does that answer your question?'

'Sort of.'

'Is "sort of" enough to grow your balls back?'

'You mean are we going to follow your orders and not Madame, our mother's?'

'Bingo.'

Alastor glanced around at his brothers. 'I don't know about you, but it felt good killing those guys this evening. It felt like we were finally getting somewhere. I don't want to lose that rush. Right now, I've got it. But if we sit around for the next seven days just watching people and getting eaten alive by fucking mosquitoes, I'm going into town to rob me a bank just for the kicks.'

Rudra glanced at Abi. 'And you say we've only got a small window of opportunity to use the warehouse?'

'According to what the watchman said, six days. But we can cut that down to twenty-four hours after the big boss phones up tomorrow and deduces that his own people have probably run off with his investment.'

'Then I say we go with Abi. If we all stick together, we can square it with Madame, our mother, later.'

Abi reached back and punched him on the shoulder. 'That's my boy. To infinity and fucking beyond.'

75

Sabir stood at the very top of the pyramid and looked out over the Yucatan. It was nearly dark now, but just enough residual light was left in the evening sky to suggest the immensity of the landscape stretching away below him.

'What do you see?' The Halach Uinic was standing beside him.

'See? I see forest. And then more forest.'

'No. Nearer home. Across the way there.' The Halach Uinic was pointing towards a second pyramid, four hundred metres across the tree-dotted plain in front of them. He moved his hand in an elegant arc to encompass the even smaller pyramids surrounding it.

Sabir shook his head, as if some extraneous thought were intruding on his attention. When he spoke, his tone was matter-of-fact. 'I see a family.'

The Halach Uinic took a pace backwards. 'You see what?'

'I see a family. We're standing on the father pyramid. He probably represents the sun. And across there is the mother pyramid. She's probably the moon.'

'Why do you call her the mother?'

'Look. You can see she's a woman by the way your ancestors built her. There are two buildings high up either side of her flank. Those are her breasts. Then further down, between where her legs would be, you can see a slit. That is her vagina. And on her left. The two matching pyramids. Those are her twins. The smaller pyramids are her other children. They all stand in the shadow of their father, who overlooks them. Christ, they've even got eyes.' He turned to the Halach Uinic. 'It's all there. One has only to look.'

The Halach Uinic had gone pale. 'Where did you hear this?'

'Hear it? Where should I have heard it? I never even knew this place existed beyond seeing it depicted on a map. It's obvious, though. Anybody can see it.'

'Obvious to you, maybe. But in my entire life, no one has mentioned this to me before. Ever. It appears in no book. It is written up in no scholarly papers. The site is not spoken of in this way even by the priests.'

'Well I'm probably wrong then. But you asked me what I saw. And I see that clearly. The buildings seem alive to me. As if they're breathing, almost.'

Ixtab, who had been standing behind the two men and listening to their conversation, moved forwards. She gestured to the Halach Uinic, and then placed one hand on her heart. 'You must tell him.'

The Halach Uinic turned towards her.

'He is the one. You must tell him.'

'You are sure?'

'Aren't you?'
'Yes.'
'Then speak.'

76

'I have a story to tell.'

The Halach Uinic was standing just in front of you, at the very pinnacle of the great pyramid. As he spoke, his voice was snatched up by the pyramid's acoustics and transported over the waiting crowd.

Earlier, while the Halach Uinic had been occupied with one of the gringos, Tepeu had touched your arm to gain your attention. When you had approached him with your ear he had whispered many things to you about the pyramid and about the Halach Uinic. He had told you, for instance, that the pyramid had been built as a mouthpiece for the priests, and that the priests had been selected, from birth, to be mouthpieces to the gods. That the Halach Uinic was both their temporal leader – the so-called 'true man' – and also their spiritual leader – the Ah Kin Mai, or 'highest one of the sun'. For one person to hold both of these titles was unprecedented, said Tepeu. It was a measure of the severity of the coming times. Everything must be concentrated into one vessel.

You had no idea what Tepeu was talking about, but you did not tell him this. You did not wish to abuse his faith in you. So you nodded at everything he said, and encouraged his speaking.

Then, unexpectedly, the Halach Uinic motioned to you to approach him. You moved towards him without hesitation. But as you walked, you were already asking yourself questions.

What were you really doing here, standing high above the crowd as if you were someone of importance? You were only a campesino, with no land, no money, no education, and no knowledge of anything beyond the tending of a vegetable plot and the harvesting of a field of chayotes. What worm had entered into you to cause you to question the Halach Uinic while you were travelling together in the car? If you had not insisted that if you were to be offered back the book, the gringos should also be offered back the crystal skull, then none of this would have happened. There would have been no gathering. There would have been no ceremony. You would have been free to return to Veracruz and to your mother – if you had been able to make it back, of course, without food, or money, or transport, and with no real understanding of the geography of your own country.

Now the Halach Uinic was speaking out in Spanish, and not in Maya. This was a good thing. You had tried to understand Maya when Tepeu had demonstrated it for you, but you had failed entirely. Not a single word had made itself clear to your understanding. You looked back over your shoulder and you saw the woman with the damaged face translating for the two other gringos, and this was good also, because the gringos, too, needed to understand what it was the Halach Uinic was offering them. They needed to be free, as you were, to either agree to, or to refuse, the Halach Uinic's offer. This much was plain to you.

Next, the Halach Uinic was holding up your book. He began to tell the story of your family's guardianship of the book over many generations. He told how one of his priests, who had been trained to read the language of the ancient Maya, had read the book, and that it contained a story that everyone needed to hear. But that the priest could only recount this story with your permission. For the book was yours, he said, not theirs. You had been chosen to guard it, and not a Maya. Just as the gods had chosen a gringo to discover the thirteenth crystal skull.

These choices made by the gods constituted a message, the Halach Uinic continued – a message with two tongues to it. The first tongue told that the Maya were in no way special. They had not been selected over others. They took no precedence in any hierarchy. They were not 'chosen people'. Like a priest, their function was simply to be the mouthpiece for whatever the gods, and through them, the one god, Hunab Ku, had to tell the world.

The second tongue referred to the end of what the Halach Uinic called the 'Long Count', which he described as the end of the last great 52-year cycle of the serpent wisdom – the final 'sheaf of years'. This, he said, was the only time when the first day of the 365-year calendar and the first day of the 260-year calendar intersected during the 52 years of the Calendar Round. It marked the end of the Fifth Great Cycle. The end of the Fifth Sun.

Your head was beginning to spin at this stage. Why was the Halach Uinic concentrating on these things? What did they mean?

Next he told how the beginning of the first of the Five Great Cycles had begun with the birth of Venus, on 4 Ahua 8 Cumku. At this point he turned towards the gringos and explained that in their calendar – which he called the Gregorian – Venus's birth date fell on 11 August 3114 BC. The Fifth Great Cycle was due to end on 21 December 2012, not with the death of Venus, but with the possible destruction of the earth. This was not the first time the earth had faced such a crisis, he added. For during the preceding 5126-year period, the world

359

had been created five times, and had been destroyed on four separate occasions.

The Halach Uinic now told a story to further illustrate his meaning – just as the priest at your church in Coscohuatepec did when he spoke of the parables of Jesus Christ. The story went as follows:

When the Halach Uinic was still a young man and unsure of his destiny, he had travelled to Palenque to sit at the feet of the great Lacandon shaman and elder, the *t'o'ohil* Chan K'in. At this time Chan K'in was already more than a hundred years old, and he had seen many things. The Halach Uinic had spoken to Chan K'in of the coming of the Great Change – of his fears, and of his lack of understanding about the event.

At first, Chan K'in, chewing on a large cigar as was his habit, had replied only in the negative. 'The land is weary and must be destroyed before Hachäkyum, the Creator, can revitalize it. The quetzal bird no longer flies. Men cut down the forests and no longer respect nature. The god Mensabak no longer speaks to me.'

The Halach Uinic, being only a young man at the time, had refused to accept this negativity as Chan K'in's last word, and he had pressed the old one for further details.

After some hesitation, Chan K'in had gone on to tell the Halach Uinic that if this coming event were approached in the right way – through the ritual of atonement, perhaps – the Great Change might not be as bad as he had at first made out, but might instead give birth to a new Great Cycle of Time. If it was approached in the wrong way, however – through anger and greed – this would foretell the world's final destruction. Such an event would affect all people throughout the world, and not just the Maya. This fact, Chan K'in had said, must be taken into account.

The Halach Uinic now drew himself up and addressed the assembly in a louder voice than normal. 'It is for this reason that I intend to step down from my position as both Halach Uinic and Ah Kin Mai to make way for someone better qualified to pass on the word of Hunab Ku. A non-Maya, perhaps. Someone more competent to speak beyond our borders. This is my decision.'

77

There was a hiss from the crowd, as of a vast expulsion of breath.

The Halach Uinic turned his back on his people and made as if he would hide himself amongst the other priests. But the priests pushed forward and gathered themselves around him. No word was said, but the Halach Uinic was left with no option but to return to his place at the head of the assembly. He lowered his head and nodded, as if a burden had been placed on his shoulders, and a tumpline attached to his forehead with which to carry it.

Without pausing for thought, you chose this exact moment to walk to the very forefront of the pyramid. You stood beside the Halach Uinic and you looked out over the crowd.

These Maya were not your people, but you felt a kinship with them. Guarding their book had given you this feeling. As if the book, which you were unable to read, nevertheless held within it the distilled spirit of the people you saw below you.

'The Halach Uinic says that this book is mine. And that I may do with it as I please. That it is worth great sums of money to the gringos in the north, and that I will be a rich man when I sell it. I understand why he is doing this – why he is offering me this choice. But what the Halach Uinic says about the ownership of the book is not true. This book is not mine to give. For it is already yours.' You drew yourself up, scared in case you had angered the priests. Scared that you had pushed yourself forward without merit.

The Halach Uinic opened one hand to you in a sign of encouragement. Then he moved the hand out in an arc to encompass the people below him.

You nodded. The Halach Uinic's intentions were clear. He wished you to address his people.

'Now I, too, must tell you a story.' Your ears were hurting with the tension of your position. You had never in your life spoken to so many people at one time. In fact you had never spoken to more than a gathering of four. 'Many, many years ago, one of your people was escaping from bad happenings here. What happenings, I do not know.' You hesitated, unsure how to continue.

The Halach Uinic stepped forward to help you. 'It was during the time of the Caste War between the Maya and the Yucatecos. This war occurred between 1847 and 1901. The Chilan protecting this book was the *ak k'u hun* – the "guardian of the sacred books". He was caught up in the uprising at Valladolid, followed by the great revolt of the Maya people in the spring of 1848 and its aftermath. He writes all this on the back leaf of the book. Here. You can see.'

The Halach Uinic was excited – you could see the tension in his face. He was clearly moved, also, by the confidence the other priests had placed in him. He had been prepared to sacrifice his own position in order to give you the freedom to act as you saw fit. For this reason you realized that it was up to you to continue with the story, even though it was a difficult thing to do. Up to you to convince everybody here that the book was, indeed, rightly theirs – rightly what the Halach Uinic claimed it to be.

'This Chilan was pursued by those who wished to steal the precious book in his charge. He fled as far as Veracruz. His enemies caught up with him there, and wounded him – wounded him so badly that he knew that he would soon die. He found my ancestor working in a clearing. With his last strength, he approached him. The father of my father's father saw what the Chilan's enemies had done to him and he felt sorry for this man, and hid him in his hut. He risked his life for this man. He was a good Catholic. He knew the parable of the Good Samaritan. When the Chilan was on the very verge of death, with no hope of survival, he told my ancestor of this book. Of its importance to the Maya. He asked my ancestor if he would swear an oath to guard this book until such time as our great volcano, the Pico de Orizaba, would choose to come alive again. Then he or his successors must then take this book to a special place and give it to those who were there. My ancestor did not wish to do this. He could not read. He did not know what the book might contain. It might have been evil. It might have contained magic. But the Chilan called upon him to honour the wishes of a dying man. This my grandfather had to do, according to the custom of my people. And the Chilan seemed a good man. Upon hearing my father swear the oath, the Chilan pricked himself with a thorn on the tongue, then on his cheek, his lower lip, and his ear. He wrote things in his own blood, both on the blank pages of the book, and on a separate leaf he had about his person. This leaf was a map.' You held it up. 'And this map took me to you. So you see, I have no right to the book. It is truly

363

yours. Now that my task is done, you must let me return home to my mother and to my work. I have been away for far too long.'

78

'Well stone me – we've got ourselves an honest-to-God ragged trousered philanthropist.'

Abi was tucked into the lee of one of the more extreme of the ruined buildings. It was situated outside the main Ek Balam tourist zone, on a raised tump, thick with ancient scatterings. Athame was standing beside him. The Glock was tucked into the back of Abi's trousers, disguised by the Guayabera shirt that he had bought for exactly that purpose in Veracruz. Athame was carrying her Walther P4 in the backpack she wore at all times. Given her diminutive size, the backpack made her look like Dopey, from Walt Disney's *Snow White*.

'I don't think you should do this.'

'Do what?'

'Go against Madame, our mother's, wishes.'

'What she doesn't know won't hurt her, Athame. And I don't intend to blunder into that crowd over there, six-shooters blazing. I've got a more subtle approach in mind.'

'She could simply cut us all loose. Without a penny to our names.'

'So what? We can always steal. We've spent the past fifteen years being trained in every damned knavery known to man. And for what? To baby-sit the man who killed our brother? And the policeman who harried him to death? Calque and Sabir aren't leaving Mexico alive, I can tell you that much. And if I have to do them myself, I will.'

'And Lamia?'

'I know you've always had a soft spot for her, Athame, but she's in with Sabir now. She's given herself to him. And she's not the sort of woman who goes off half-cocked, if you'll forgive my pun. She burned her bridges back at the chateau, and as far as I'm concerned that puts her out of the running for Barbie Doll of the Year Award. If I get my hands on her I'm going to use her to wring whatever I can out of Sabir. And when I'm through with her, she dies. Straight into the cenote with the rest of them. Christ, she'll have six men all to herself down there.'

'You're sick, Abi. You know that?'

'Are you going to stand in my way when it comes to it?'

Athame shook her head. 'No. She burned her bridges, as you said. But I won't let you abuse her. You can use her, fine. Threaten Sabir all you want. But I won't see her hurt more than necessary. We were sisters once, remember.'

'Does she remember that, do you think? Does she think as kindly of you as you do of her? I doubt it somehow.'

Up on the pyramid, the Halach Uinic was making way for one of the other priests.

'Looks like we're about to get the straight guff from the mestizo's book. This, I want to hear. Think what that damned thing's worth, Athame. One of only four remaining Maya codices. And with an attribution, to boot.'

'What do you mean, an attribution?'

'The mestizo's got a mother, hasn't he? And she knows all about the book his family have been guarding for hundreds of years. We get hold of the thing and we can work on him through her. *Cherchez la femme*. Isn't that what the English tell us we French say all the time? They're right, of course. Achilles's problem wasn't with his heel. It was with Briseis. If he hadn't fallen in love with her and lost the plot, he would have survived the Trojan campaign and probably lived to a wise old age. Instead he let that bastard Paris skewer him in the foot. The same thing is going to happen to Sabir. Only his foot will be the last one of his body parts I'll focus on.'

'Listen, Abi. The priest is starting to read from the book.'

'I can't wait. I love bedtime stories.'

79

The Chilan bowed first towards his master, the Halach Uinich, and then towards his audience. He raised the codex briefly to his forehead, and then kissed it. Carefully, even tenderly, he opened the manuscript and began to read.

'I, Akbal Coatl – which the Spaniards would translate as "night serpent" – Chilan and *ak k'u hun* – which is priest and chief guardian of the sacred books – write this on the evening of the twelfth day of July in the year of our Lord 1562, which is the worst day the world has ever known. I write this to bear witness against Friar Diego de Landa, because such must be done. I write this in the last remaining of the Maya holy books, using the backs of the holy leaves, and for this blasphemy may Kukulcan, who is the true God, forgive me.

'For three months now Friar de Landa has travelled throughout our country, a few days behind his soldiers, enforcing the orders of the Franciscan monks. As Provincial of the Franciscan order in the Yucatan, Friar de Landa has the full backing of the Judge of the High Court of Guatemala and the Confines, Tomás Lopéz. It must be added here that Judge Lopéz is also a friar of the Franciscan order, and that Judge Lopéz has directed, in this capacity, that any and all Maya towns still remaining outside the Franciscan remit be turned over instantly into Franciscan hands.

'In addition, Judge Lopéz has given Friar de Landa full Imperial authority, using the Papal Bull *exponi nobis* as his justification, in respect of what is called "the regimentation of daily and social life". Judge Lopéz also stipulates that any violations of the Friar's rights in this matter, and all infringements by the native Indians in misguided support of their previous rights, "be punished as by the Inquisition". Here is the full text of the Ordinances of the Royal Audience of the Confines, promulgated by Judge Lopéz in 1552:

"Coming from the Royal Audiencia in Guatemala, at the request of the Friars in Yucatan, and decreed for the conduct and treatment of the Indians.

In exercise of the power of our Emperor, vested in me, I command you, the caciques, chief men and people, as follows:

No cacique shall be absent from his town, save for the temporal or spiritual good, or as called by the padres, for over 50 days, on pain of loss of office.

The Indians must not live off in the forests, but come into the towns together, in good strong houses, under pain of whipping or prison.

To avoid difficulties in doctrination, no Indian shall change from one town to another without permission of the local Spanish authorities.

Since many of the chiefs and older men, in the respect they hold by their ancient descent, call the people into secret meetings to teach their old rites and draw them from the Christian doctrine, in their weakness of understanding, all such actions and meetings are prohibited.

The caciques shall not hold gatherings, nor go about at night, after the bells are sounded for the souls in purgatory.

Every cacique or chief of a town shall carry in mind the list of all the people. Every man of the common people absenting himself from his town for over 30 or 40 days, save in public service or with the padres, even with permission from his cacique, shall be punished by 100 blows and 100 days in prison.

Every town, within two years, must have a good church, and one only, to which all may come. Nor may any cacique build any other church than the one, under pain of 100 blows.

Every town shall have schools where the Indians shall be taught the necessity of baptism, without which no one can enjoy God. The schools shall be built by the town, and the caciques shall compel them thereto, in the form and manner required by the padres, and at places designated by them.

On the days for doctrination, one shall go through the towns, bearing a cross and cloth, to call all people together, where all shall gather in order, those of each town by themselves.

If any one, after having heard the holy word and left his false doctrines, shall return to these, he shall be imprisoned to await the due punishment to be ordered by the Royal Audiencia.

No Indian shall undertake by himself to preach the holy word save by express license of the religious fathers.

No baptized person shall possess idols, sacrifice any animals, draw blood by piercing their ears or noses, nor perform any rite, nor burn incense thereto, or fast in worship of their false idols.

No Indian baptized, shall return to be baptized a second time.

Many Indians having been told that their children will die if baptized, I command that all children be brought for baptism.

Matrimony being in great respect among the Indians, I ordain that no one shall have more than one wife, and that an adulterer shall receive 100 blows, and other punishments if he does not amend.

No cacique shall have to do with a female slave.

No one shall be so daring as to marry secretly.

No one shall marry twice, on penalty of branding with a hot iron in a figure 4 on the forehead.

No purchase gifts shall be made to the woman's parents, nor shall the youth be required by them, as by their old customs, to remain and serve in their father-in-law's house for two or three years.

No one shall give a heathen name to his children.

All people must bend the knee before the sacrament, recite the prayers fixed when the Ave is rung, and reverence the cross and images.

Every one, man or woman, must go to the church both morning and evening, and say an Ave and Paternoster with all reverence.

At meals all shall say grace before and after, and on retiring at night cross themselves and recite the prayers the fathers will teach them.

No one shall cast grains of corn for divination, nor tell dreams, nor wear any marks or ornaments of their heathendom, nor tattoo themselves.

So lacking in charity and care even for their wives or husbands, or family, are the Indians, that I command that all shall care for them when sick, etc.

Where much sickness comes to a town, it shall be reported, and the fathers shall have those at hand for instruction in holy dying.

All inheritances shall be properly cared for.

There shall be no holding in slavery, and all so held shall be set free. But allow to the caciques, principal men or other powerful Indians to hire people for their service, all of whom shall be reported to the padres and taken to them for doctrination.

The custom of banquets to large numbers is so common, and so destructive of Christianity, that I order that no general banquets be given by any one save at marriages or like fiestas, but then no more than a dozen people may be invited.

No dances shall be held except in daytime.

God gave us time for work, and time for his service; whereby I order the keeping of all church fiestas, as and in the manner fixed by the religious fathers.

All preparation of their ancient drinks is prohibited, and the caciques, principal men, and even the encomenderos are ordered within two months to gather and burn all utensils or cups used therein, on penalty of 20 pesos fine if they allow more to be made.

Towns must be in the Spanish fashion, have guest-houses, one for Spaniards and another for Indians. Also marketplaces to avoid all travelling about to sell or buy. Nor shall any merchant, Indian, Mexican, mestizo or negro, be lodged in any private house.

Proper weights and measures shall be provided within two months, on penalty of 20 pesos gold.

I command the raising of cattle to be introduced among the Indians.

The chief tribute of the country being cotton mantles, I order that teaching for this be given.

I order that all women wear long skirts and over them their huipiles; and that all men wear shirts and go shod, at least with sandals.

Since the Indians are always wandering the woods to hunt, I order that all bows and arrows are to be burned. But each cacique shall hold two or three dozen bows, with arrows, for special occasions, or necessity as against tigers.

Good roads from town to town shall be kept in order.

No negro, slave or mestizo shall enter any village save with his master, and then stay more than a day and night."

'All this I know and can transmit to you because I am Friar de Landa's private secretary, charged with translation, notation, and documentation of the rights of the Church – in this capacity I work alongside the Friar's official notary, Francisco de Orozco, as his trusted lieutenant. Why then, you ask, am I bearing witness to de Landa's perfidy by writing in the last of the Maya holy books when, to all intents and purposes, I am an integral part of his retinue, an honorary member of the Franciscan order, and de Landa's personal representative amongst the Maya? This I will now explain to you.

'When I was a young child it was decided that, as second son of the noble household of the Ah Maxam, I should be trained in the duties of royal scribe, so that I could arrange royal ceremonies, oversee royal marriages, keep the genealogical lists, and record any tributes and offerings paid by client states. As *ah ts'ib* – "he of the writing" – I was an honoured and valued member of the royal household.

'When the Franciscans came and took over our city, my father and the few remaining of our priests decided that I must become as one with the Spaniards – take on their customs, learn their language, study Latin, acknowledge their ascendancy – so that one at least amongst us could understand the full implications of the horror that was clearly about to fall upon our people. This I agreed to do.

'To that end I studied hard, making myself useful to the friars in any and all capacities, until I attained a position as high as it was possible for one of Maya ancestry to go. Thanks to this I was able also, and via subterfuge, to warn my people of impending problems, destroy offending documentation, and influence Friar de Landa, to the extent that I was able, in the hope that, as one interested in our culture and history, he would ride upon the backs of our people without the use of his spurs.

'This situation continued until three months ago. Some years before this time, thinking that Friar de Landa was a more tolerant man than he was, Nachi Cocom, last great ruler of the Cocom lineage, and imagining himself to be Friar de Landa's friend, had shown the Friar the secret library of Maya writings, which included 2673 books and codices, 5000 sacred images and idols – including those to Kan u Uayeyub and Bolon Dzacab used during the Year-Bearing Ceremonies – and 13 large altar stones we know as *kanal acantum*. These, together with 22 smaller stones, and 127 vases and funerary urns containing the bones of priests, noblemen, and kings, made up the complete historical record of our people from the beginnings of the first Great World Age.

'Cocom showed Friar de Landa these things on the understanding that they were no longer used, but merely kept as part of Maya historical record, and that he trusted that he could rely on Friar de Landa, as his friend and as a man of God, to honour the trust he was putting in him. Friar de Landa at first appeared to accede to this stipulation, leading Nachi Cocom to tell Friar de Landa about our belief in Los Aluxes. This belief states that a certain number of enlightened beings have been left behind by the gods to guard the magnetic spiritual places and objects of the earth, and that it is only via the intercession of these spiritual guardians that the destiny of the world may be secured. Cocom foolishly believed that Friar de Landa, with all his stated interest in Maya culture, was one such person.

'When Nachi Cocom died, Friar de Landa repaid Cocom's trust by seizing the library and all its contents, and by posthumously accusing the Chief of idolatry, digging up his body from its grave, burning its remains, and scattering his ashes across the fields. You must know that for a Maya king and spiritual leader, the manner of his death and burial is of the utmost importance. To die well is considered a blessing amongst our people. Maize would have been placed in Cocom's mouth, and jade and stone beads would have been added as currency to pay for his spirit's journey through the underworld. His corpse would have been wrapped in cotton, and both his body and his grave would have been covered in cinnabar, as red is considered by us to be both the colour of death and of rebirth.

'By digging up Nachi Cocom's body, Friar de Landa thought to deprive Cocom's soul of eternal rest, and by seizing the library he thought to manifest his and his Church's dominance over our traditional spiritual leaders.

'Then, more recently, Friar de Landa received further information from the traitor Antonio Gaspar Xiu [the former Chi Xiu], descendant of Tutul Xiu, great chief of the Xiu clan, traditional enemies of the Cocoms, about the continuing power of the Maya religion. Thanks to this information, and to the privileged knowledge he had of our holy books, Friar de Landa convinced himself that those who had allowed themselves to be baptized by the Franciscan order were secretly continuing in the faith of their forefathers. I attempted to explain to him that what was in fact occurring was a natural thing – an inevitable misunderstanding occasioned by Friar de Landa's transformation of the great Maya pyramid at Izamál into the Catholic Church of San Antonio. I told him that my people were bewildered by the mass of contradictory messages they were receiving.

'"Then we must un-confuse them," said the Friar.'

80

'So Friar Diego de Landa, scourge and nemesis of the Maya, was born. But the Friar was careful not to take on too much responsibility for the outrages he was about to perpetrate, as he did not wish to alienate his masters in Rome. Instead he sent the army on ahead of him. Then he followed along, some days behind, to sweep up the army's leavings. He took me along as aide, secretary, and translator, so I am able to bear witness to what happened next.

'In the town of Cupul, the army decided to burn the headman and his advisors alive. To achieve this, they crucified them, and placed braziers beneath their feet. Then they lit the braziers and forced the townspeople to watch the scene. Those they did not burn, they hanged.

'Later, the Spaniards moved against the Yobain, in the town of Chels. In this town they took all the leading men and placed them in the stocks, and beat them. Then they placed the men, still in the stocks, inside a house, which they then burned down. This was a different system to that which they had used in Cupul.

'Next, they moved the women and children out of the village. Feeling that they had not sufficiently made their point to the outlying villages, the Captain of the Spaniards then took the women and ordered them strung up to the branches of a great tree, with their children hanging beneath them like fruit. This, I believe, was done to undermine Maya belief in the Great World Tree, which to us supports all life. This particular Maya tree, we were to observe, supported only death.

'In the next town, Verey, and feeling that some of the women were too beautiful and that they might therefore inflame the soldiers to unholy acts, the Captain of the Spaniards ordered that their breasts be cut off, and that they should then be hung in full view of the whole village to prove to our people that the Spaniards were indifferent to our women. These women, too, died.

'The Friar and his retinue, of which I formed a part, arrived in these towns two to three days after the soldiers had passed. The people, fearing reprisals, had not dared to cut down the bodies, which stank and putrefied in the midsummer heat. The Friar, wishing to be seen to act in a kindly fashion after the outrages of the soldiers, allowed the townspeople to cut down the victims of his purge – their bodies, however, could not be buried, but must be burnt, and, like Nachi Cocom's, be scattered over the fields. This the Friar ordered.

'Next, our retinue moved to the provinces of Cochuah and Chetumal. Here our people, hearing of what the Spanish had done to their brothers and sisters, rose up against them. But without proper weapons, fighting dogs, and horses, they were powerless. Those who were captured had their noses, and their hands, and their arms, and their legs, and in the case of the women, their breasts, and in the case of the men, their genitals, carved off. Then all were taken, alive or dead, to the cenote from out of which the people drew their water, and, with gourds tied to their feet or what remained of their trunks, they were thrown into the deep waters. Children who could not walk as fast as their mothers were speared. This we heard from the survivors, of whom there were few, as most had been taken into the Spaniards' service as slaves.

'The Friar declared himself outraged at what had occurred. He conducted formal ceremonies over the dead, and blessed the survivors. I joined in with these ceremonies, and made much of the wisdom of the Friar's doings, as my duty was to remain always at his side and to represent our people – for such was the quality of the oath that I had undertaken before the assembled Chilans. An oath that forced me into seeming what I was not. An oath which forced me into observing and annotating the horrors which I saw perpetrated against those of the same blood as myself – those who worshipped the same gods – those who stemmed from the very same clay.

'This I tell you, in advance, so that you may better understand why I am desecrating the last of our holy books with my writing. For now I am going to recount what happened today, at Maní, under the Friar's direct supervision, and which makes all that we had previously seen appear as the dalliance of un-parented children.'

81

Sabir was focusing all of his attention on Lamia's translation of the Chilan's words. At one point he reached forward and took her hand in his, either to offer or to receive comfort, he was not entirely sure. She allowed her hand to rest in his for a moment, and then she withdrew it, as if she were unable to countenance such a two-way split in her concentration.

Calque stood beside them, his head turned away, to all intents and purposes as if he were refusing to listen to de Landa's story. But Sabir knew him well enough by now. He could tell by the way Calque stood – by the stiffness in his back and by the sideways tilt of his head – that he was concentrating on every word that Lamia was translating for him.

The Chilan paused in his reading. He was dripping with sweat. His voice was growing increasingly hoarse. His hands shook where they held the book, and he seemed unable to meet anyone's eyes. It was as if the horror of what he was reading formed a direct part of his own experience, and was not merely a story, written by another, which he was recounting to a partially illiterate audience.

Acan's mother, Ixtab, hurried to his side. She unpinned her rebozo and mopped the Chilan's brow and face. He nodded to her in grateful acknowledgment, but he was unable to summon up a smile. The Halach Uinic stood off to one side, his face in his hands. There was neither a mutter nor a murmur from the vast audience below them.

The Chilan gave a profound sigh, and addressed himself once again to the book in front of him.

82

'The Auto da Fé began today, the twelfth day of July 1562, in the early morning. What occurred was a fulfilment of the first part of the prophecy of the Cycle of the Nine Hells, the first 52-year cycle of which began with the arrival of the Franciscans in the Yucatan in 1544 under Luis de Villalpando, and the final cycle of which will be due to end in the year 2012, marking 9 by 52 years, being 468 in total, between the start of the cycle and its eventual end.

'At the break of dawn, Friar de Landa ordered the great square at Maní to be cleared of people. Then he ordered his prisoners, the so-called *indios rebeldes*, to be brought in from their place of incarceration, where they had been constrained to fast for eight hours, as a legally imposed prelude to their torture. Amongst these prisoners were all the remaining great nobles and their families – the Pat, the Xiu, the Canuls, the Chikin-Chels, the Cocoms, the Cupuls, the Hocaba-Humúns, the Cochua, and many others. Their names had been given in by their children, whom the Franciscans had seized from their families, indoctrinated, and forced to submit to the Christian catechism. Thus it was that the children unwittingly became the executioners of their own parents.

'I, Akbal Coatl, the "night serpent", whom the Spaniards call Salvador Emmanuel, had not been privy to the kidnap of these people, and thus I was horrified to see that many of the remaining members of my family were amongst their number. At first I was minded to join them. To throw myself into their midst and die with my people. But the man I knew to be the Halach Uinic – the High Priest and leader of all the Maya, whose identity we had kept secret even from the friars – made a sign to me that I should not reveal myself to the Spaniards by word or by gesture. He also made the sign of the written scroll to me, indicating that what I saw must be written down. I believe now that he had been told, or had seen prophesied, what was about to occur.

'Bowing to my fate, I forced myself to attend to Friar de Landa's demands on me, which included the formal noting of the names and descriptions of all the people present, their place in our hierarchy, and the crimes, mainly of idolatry, that were to be laid at their feet.

'Then the questioning began. First, Friar de Landa made it clear to those who admitted to their crimes and repented of their sins that even they would not escape punishment. Instead, they would be forced to stand in full public view, with an idol held in one hand and a candle in the other, and with ropes strung about their necks. In addition, they were to wear the high, cone-shaped hat of shame, known as the *coroza*, and the penitential robes, known as the *sambenito*, undergo a full mass and a sermon, have their heads shaved, and then suffer whipping, with a prescribed number of strokes, to be conducted in the public stocks.

'Despite these warnings, many amongst the number of those present chose this course of action, having heard stories of – or perhaps merely suspecting – what lay in store for those of an unrepentant, or even entirely innocent, demeanour.

'The penitential were then led away to suffer their punishment. The remainder were formed into lines.

'Now the torture and mutilation of our people began in earnest. The first chiefs were brought forward and fastened to the hoist, which the Spanish know as the *garrucha*. This caused them to have their arms pulled back behind them and then to be lifted into the air and dropped, repeatedly, all the while submitting to questions from the friars. When the questioning did not bear fruit, Friar de Landa, claiming to act under the aegis of the Consulta da Fé, ordered that the chiefs have heavy weights of stone attached to their feet, the better to dislocate their members. Time was allowed to elapse between the repeated drops, the further to enhance the pain of those suffering them, and in order to ordain them to "tell the truth for the love of God". During this period of false release, the Miserere was to be sung by all those not undergoing the question. Should this method be seen to fail, the offending chief was to be first whipped, and then splashed on the face, body, and back with hot wax.

'The women were given special dispensation by order of Friar de Landa, and only tortured by the garrotte, which involved being placed on a seat, and then having sharp cords, known as *cordeles*, two on each arm and two on each leg, tightened by means of a short lever. If either of these tortures failed, then the water torture was to be used, in which the victim was to be placed on a trestle, known as the *escalera*, or *potro*. Following this, a *bostero*, or iron prong, would be fitted inside the mouth, after which a strip of linen, known by the Spaniards as the *toca*, would be forced into the throat in order to guide the flow of water from the *jarra*. Depending on the number of quarts consumed, the body of the tortured person would distend, forcing the flesh against the seven garrottes with which they had been fastened. Few resisted this technique, and many "spontaneous recantations" were achieved.

'During the course of the day, many people were brought to torture. Some repented. Many died. Many had their limbs torn from their muscle beds. One great chief, whose name I will not here recount as he is connected to me by family, and from whom I had received especial kindnesses as a child, was accused of conducting a human sacrifice. He had the garrotte placed around his head and tightened by seven turns, which cause his eyes to pop out of their sockets. After this he was allowed to live by order of Friar de Landa, as a warning to his people.

'By late afternoon the square at Maní was thick with carrion and with clotted blood, despite the many sweepings and cleansings ordered by Friar de Landa. At this point the sun was briefly eaten, as in a *chibil*, or eclipse. Some of the unwilling spectators that Friar de Landa now ordered to enter the square whispered amongst themselves that the *xulab* ants had swarmed across the sky to protect the sun, ashamed that he should see such horrors occurring in his realm.

'At this time, the moon, our grandmother, also appeared in the sky, which came as no surprise to those of us acquainted with the Tun-Uc, or moon calendar, as the moon always accompanies great disasters and violent deceit. The moon goddess Tlacolteotl had clearly heard that members of her own priesthood, the Nahau Pech, were being tortured, and she had arrived to oversee and monitor their deaths. This was as it should be, for the Nahau Pech knew, as did we all, that the unpredictable moon was considered by many of our people to be representative of the Spanish ascendancy, and of the final end of the old order. In this way the sun and the moon had always been in conflict one with the other, and now it was clear that the moon had finally won.

'Darkness was in the ascendant.

'We understood that there would be no further harmony between our Father the sun and Our Lady the moon until the Cycle of the Nine Hells had been completed.'

83

＿

'When Friar de Landa felt that enough torturing had been done, and that he had sufficiently re-established the Church's authority over its errant flock, he called me to him. He asked me if there were still men who could read the ancient scripts that he now held within his grasp. And that if there were such men, that I should immediately bring them to him.

'I admit now that I feared for my own safety.

'I turned towards the square and pointed to the dead men littered across its wastes. "All these could read the ancient scripts. And also the chief whose eyes you started out of his head with your garrotte. They are now dead, and he is blind. So the books are blind too. None are left to call them out."

'Friar de Landa stared at me for some little time. I felt then that he was delving into my soul like One Death and Seven Death, the Lords of Xibalba, in the Place of Fear – that his eyes were piercing through me to the five levels of creation that made me up.

'This is when the terrible fear came upon me that our understanding of the five levels of creation would be lost forever were I, too, to be killed. Which Chilan would be left to teach our children the knowledge of the first level of stone and fire that makes up their bones, their heart, and their gall? Who could tell them of the second level of plants, flowers, and trees, that makes up their flesh? Of the third level of waters, lakes, and rivers that makes up their blood, their nerves, and the liquid essences of their body? Who could describe to them the fourth level of wind and animals that encompasses their breath and their vision? Who would be left to tell them of the fifth and final level that makes of them "earth fruits"? That makes of them human beings, similar in essence even to Friar de Landa?

'"And you?" he said to me. "Can you read these books and write this script? I conjure you, upon your Christian oath, to speak truly."

'Then came upon me the spirit of the Lak'ech. The spirit of our Maya code of honour. The Halach Uinic had called upon me to mould myself, *pari passu*, with the Spanish. To defend our people from my place of concealment. To this end there was a saying amongst us: "I am another yourself." Before this day, I had attempted to put this into practice. To understand Friar de Landa – to place myself in his shadow and understand his doings to the extent that I was able. The time for understanding had now passed.

'"On my Christian oath, I cannot."

'"And the thirteenth crystal skull? The so-called 'singing skull'? The skull that the most credulous amongst your people think activates the twelve skulls stolen from Nachi Cocom's secret library? My soldiers and my friars have searched everywhere, and put many people to the question, and still they have not found even one of the thirteen. I know these skulls exist, for I have seen them. Who has them now?"

'I pointed to the greatest of the dead chiefs. "He does. He was the guardian of the skulls."

'Friar de Landa smiled, and his smile was terrible. "Shall I put you to the question, too, Salvador, my son?" Here he used the name the Spaniards had given me. My so-called baptized name. The name by which I was known to all but the dead.

'"I am your loyal servant, and a loyal servant of the Church. I will answer all of your questions, however they are posed to me."

'Now the friar laughed. How he laughed. He clapped his hands together and he danced a dance, his skirts swinging in the dust. He shouted to his soldiers, his voice like the song of the macaw. "Bring me their books. Bring me their idols. Bring me their altar stones."

'The Spanish soldiers drove our people who were their slaves before them, staggering under the weight of our patrimony. Now the sacred books that Nachi Cocom had shown to Friar de Landa were laid out like strips of maize across the square. As were the sacred objects. As were the sacred altar stones. Stakes and shafts of wood were piled across them, then brushwood was placed on top of these. Incense was interleaved inside the branches, and crosses made from withies were planted on the periphery of the pile. Soon, the skeleton of a great bonfire was revealed, twenty feet high, and one hundred feet around in its circumference, and designed in the form of a volcano.

'Night was falling. I, Akbal Coatl, the "night serpent", whom the Spaniards call Salvador Emmanuel, had never feared the night. Now I feared it.

'Our people stood in lines around the unlit bonfire. Some vomited. Others took out knives and slit their own throats.

'I stood next to my master, Friar de Landa. I raised my pen and wrote as he dictated. The friars had provided me with a lectern for my convenience. They also brought me water to drink, from the very same source they had used to fill the mouths of their victims. I brushed it away. My throat was parched. My eyes were streaming. I could scarcely see the vellum on which I wrote for tears.

'A soldier brought the Friar a burning branch, swathed in cotton and liquor. The flames from the branch played over the Friar's face.

'I thought of our code, the Lak'ech. I thought of our saying, "I am another yourself." I knew then that this friar was no part of me, or of anything that I represented or believed in. I was glad that the thirteenth crystal skull had been given into my possession. Glad that I knew the location of the greatest of our sacred books. For through me, the future of the Maya might be secured. Through me, our customs and beliefs would not be lost when the skull and the book were once again reunited at the end of the period known as the Cycle of Nine Hells.

'For was I not Chilan and *ak k'u hun* – priest and chief guardian of the sacred books? Was I not the friend and devoted servant of the friars? Party to their confidence, and privileged witness to their outrages? Was I not destined to travel back to Spain with Friar de Landa and visit the monasteries and libraries of our order when the time for an accounting came? Had I not sacrificed myself sufficiently to placate the gods?

'Friar de Landa turned to me. He pointed to the skeleton of the mighty bonfire. He made the sign of the cross over me and he smiled. "Here." He handed me the burning branch. "You light it."'

84

'No more. It is enough. The road of words must end here.'

The Halach Uinic's voice echoed out over the assembly. The light from the guttering candles reflected back off his face, which was drained of all colour, like a corpse's.

The Chilan who had been reading the codex handed the book to the Halach Uinic. The Halach Uinic held it at a distance, as if he was scared that it would burst into flames and consume him. Freed from his burden, the Chilan stumbled and nearly fell to the ground. Some of the younger priests hurried forwards and helped him away.

The Halach Uinic closed his eyes. 'Bring the thirteenth crystal skull.'

A sigh passed over the crowd.

Acan stepped forward. He unwrapped the crystal skull and offered it to the Halach Uinic.

'Give it to the shaman.'

Acan hesitated. It was clear that he did not know to which shaman the Halach Uinic was referring.

Ixtab gently took the skull from her son's hands. She passed it to Sabir. Her movements were so forceful that Sabir had no choice but to accept the skull.

'Why are you giving it to me? I'm no shaman.' Sabir tried to pass it back, but Ixtab shook her head.

Sabir looked wildly around him. 'Look. We came here with no idea of finding anything like this. No idea at all.' He looked entreatingly at Calque and Lamia, as though they might be persuaded to intercede for him in some way. 'I don't understand what is going on.' His words trailed off irresolutely.

The Halach Uinic lowered his voice so that only those nearest him could hear it. 'Of course you were sent here to find this. There is more written in this book than was read out by the Chilan. Much more. There are urgent questions I must ask you. Questions to which you may not consciously know the answer. A secret which is not a secret. But for this we need a *touj*.'

'A what?'

'Later. Later I will explain everything to you.' The Halach Uinic turned back to his people. He stood waiting, the codex held high in his left hand.

Sabir's eyes opened wide. It dawned on him that the entire assembly, including the Halach Uinic, was patiently waiting for him to act.

He looked around himself in ill-disguised panic. Here he was, after a week spent trying to outrun and outwit the eleven brothers and sisters of a man he had inadvertently – or as far as the Corpus Maleficus was concerned, very much advertently – killed. And all he could think of to do was to stand on top of a pyramid in the Yucatan, with a thousand strangers drinking in his every move, and wave a crystal skull over his head. Was that some kind of dumb, or was it not?

No sooner had this absurd thought flashed through Sabir's mind than an extraordinary sense of well-being began to flow through his body, as if he briefly added up to more than the actual sum of his parts. He glanced at Ixtab, certain that the support he felt was coming from her.

She smiled at him and nodded.

All at once Sabir knew exactly what to do. He walked towards the Halach Uinic, holding up the crystal skull so that the crowd below could see it. He bowed before the Halach Uinic and then stretched the crystal skull out before him, as though he were about to throw it down the steps of the pyramid. Then he motioned to Lamia with his head.

She hesitated, and then stepped towards him.

'I want you to translate for me. My Spanish is too rough. It will mean calling out to all these people in your loudest voice. Do you think you can do it?'

Lamia hesitated once again. Then she inclined her head

He mouthed the words 'I love you' to her.

She held his gaze with hers and mouthed the words back to him.

'Tell them that a great man, who died almost four years to the day after the events they have been hearing about, showed us, more than four centuries later, and seemingly from beyond the grave, where to find the skull.'

Lamia frowned. But then her face cleared in sudden understanding, and she began to translate his words.

'That this great man intended the skull as a gift to the Maya people. A gift of something they had once possessed and must now possess again.' He paused, waiting for Lamia to translate his words. 'That we from across the sea ask them to accept this gift in the same spirit as our friend from Veracruz has offered them the return of their sacred book.' Sabir glanced around, searching for inspiration. The fresh words came to him in a sudden rush, as though they had been banked up behind the others, just waiting to pour out. 'That we foreigners are proud to have been the unwitting guardians of the location of your treasures – the only two objects saved from Friar de Landa's annihilation. That we offer them back to you with the greatest respect, and in only partial restitution for the evils done to your people in the name of our Christian Church.'

Sabir knew that these were not his own words he was speaking, but the words that Ixtab and the Halach Uinic desired him to speak, channelled through his lips. The hidden, super-rational part of him still resisted the possibility that one could be fed words via other people's thoughts.

The Halach Uinic accepted Sabir's offer of the skull. He held the skull and the book high above the assembly for a moment, before handing them to the attendant priests. 'The book will be copied and translated. What it contains will be available to all as soon as the work has been completed.' He waited for the murmuring of the crowd to die away. 'The skull can only be reunited with the remaining twelve skulls on the final day of the Cycle of Nine Hells, which falls on 21 December 2012. Only then may we learn what the thirteen skulls have to say to us. Is this acceptable to you all? Will you permit me to represent you in this matter? If not, I will step down and make way for another.'

A great crashing and banging began from below. Sabir squinted into the gloom. He shook his head in wonder. The Maya women had brought their cooking implements with them in preparation for the forthcoming feast, and now they clashed their saucepans over their heads while their menfolk twirled their machetes, smashing them one into the other as in a sabre dance.

Sabir sat down on the top step of the pyramid and put his head in his hands. He felt drained. Unwitting. Incapable of action. Lamia crouched beside him and rested her head against his.

'You did the right thing. What you said was beautiful. How did you grasp so perfectly what was needed?'

Sabir leaned across and kissed her tenderly on the mouth. Then he tilted back his head, looked at her speculatively, and kissed her again. 'If I told you, you'd never believe me.'

85

Abi held the cell phone tightly to his ear. He protected his other ear from the racket with his free hand. With all the din going on around him, now seemed as good a time as any to get his telephoning done. 'All well at the warehouse? No unwelcome visitors?'

'It's quiet as the grave here. I've told Berith to get some sleep while he can.' Oni cocked his head. 'What's all that banging I can hear?'

'Sabir's been playing the crowd. And our sister's been translating for him. Went down a storm. Like something out of *King Solomon's Mines*.'

'What mines?'

Abi shrugged. Pointless explaining. You could take a horse to water, but you couldn't make it drink. 'Athame's gone to see if she can find out where they are taking the skull and the book. In these happy egalitarian days, nobody dares object to a female even smaller than themselves, so if she's unlucky enough to be seen there's a fair chance that nobody will dare pay any attention to her. The rest of us are in hiding and have the camp encircled. When the main body of the Maya have fed themselves, and either gone to bed or drifted off home, we'll pounce. We'll fix it so they'll think Sabir and Calque changed their minds and ran off with their holy relics. Greedy gringos, out for the main chance – that sort of thing. Playing to the archetype, Monsieur, our father, would have called it. Should create one hell of a stink, and keep us nicely in the clear. We don't want trouble at Cancun airport when we leave the country. There's no telling with these people.'

'Wish I was with you.'

'No you don't. It's boring as hell out here. This could take hours yet. I'm beginning to wish we'd thought to bring some sandwiches.'

'I've got sandwiches here. *Chorizo*. *Lomo*. Cheese. Chicken. *Aguacate* . . .'

'Fuck off, Oni.'

86

—

The Halach Uinic motioned to Calque, Sabir, and Lamia that they should enter the sweat lodge ahead of him. 'This is the *touj* I was telling you about. What they call a *temazcal* in other parts of Mexico. Please wear no metal or other ornaments about your person. Any such possessions will be taken out and looked after for you while the ceremony is under way.'

Ixtab stood at his side, as did the Chilan who had read from the codex. The mestizo from Veracruz stood a little behind them, looking apprehensive. The evening's events had clearly told on each of them, just as they also appeared to have done on Sabir, for he stood there, staring at the sweat lodge, shaking his head like a horse tormented by flies.

The Halach Uinic glanced at Ixtab, and then made a small inclination of the head towards Lamia.

Ixtab approached Lamia and lowered her voice. 'Señorita, forgive me, please, but I have to ask you this. Are you menstruating? For it is not allowed to enter the *touj* when that is occurring. It is not good for the womb, you see.'

'I am not.'

The Halach Uinic nodded and cleared his throat. 'This place will allow us to talk freely amongst ourselves. No one can hear us in here. I have prepared four substances. Firstly, peyote, from the Huicholes, which we call *aguacolla*. Secondly *k'aizalah okax*, which is known to your people as *psilocybe cubensis* or the "magic" mushroom, and to our people as the "lost judgement" mushroom. Also seeds from the *quiebracajete*, which you would call "morning glory", which we shall mix with *balché*, our sacred drink that the Spaniards forbade us to make. And finally venom from the cane toad, *bufo marinus*, which we shall mix with tobacco made from the water lily, *nymphaea ampla*. Some amongst us also use *vuelveteloco, datura*, for spiritual purposes, but Ixtab tells me that this is not suitable for use by Westerners. She has heard of gringos going mad under its influence. These substances will allow us to see clearly, and for our bodies and souls to unify, as they should, and allow the life force to come through. Ixtab will search inside each of you, and decide which of the preparations is in tune with your nature, for they may not be mixed. Are you willing to experience this?'

'I'm not going in there.' Sabir's head was still now, but his face was deathly pale. 'I'm claustrophobic, you see. Nothing you say or do is going to make me go in there.'

'But . . .'

'I don't mean that I just don't like small spaces. I mean that I'm *seriously* claustrophobic. Shrieking the house down claustrophobic. Drooling and gibbering and pleading to be let out claustrophobic. Grovelling and mewling and scratching my fingernails to the quick claustrophobic. Bashing my head against the wall claustrophobic. Do you get the picture? Have I made myself clear?'

There was a short, awed silence.

'I've heard about these places before. They seal you inside with a bunch of red-hot volcanic stones. Then they ratchet up the temperature to 180 degrees. You can't see anything. You're in pitch darkness. Sort of like hell, but without the River of Fire.' Sabir gave an involuntary spasm. 'I can't do it. Drugs or no drugs.' He shook his head. 'Can't do it? What am I talking about? I won't do it.'

The Halach Uinic placed his hand on Sabir's arm. 'Ixtab has warned me of your fears. She has prepared you a bowl of *chocah*, which is principally made of chocolate, which we call *xocolatl*, and peppers, and honey, and tobacco juice. This will calm you before you enter.'

'How the hell did Ixtab know I was claustrophobic? Who told her?' Sabir glared at Calque and Lamia.

Both of them shook their heads.

Sabir's voice trailed off after his initial diatribe. He was getting used to Ixtab's uncanny insights into his psyche. 'You don't understand the half of it. Six months ago I had a crazy experience. It was like being buried in one's grave, but with all one's everyday faculties still intact. I died, in a manner of speaking, and then came back to life again.' He glanced at Lamia, hoping she'd forgive him for rekindling memories of her brother's death, and also for his tacit accusation that she had betrayed the secrets of his claustrophobia to Ixtab. 'It echoed a similar experience I'd had as a child, in the trunk of someone's car. But not in a way I ever want to relive. I can't go in there, I tell you. I don't see why I should do it.'

The Halach Uinic held up both his hands. 'We are not going to force you, Mr Sabir. Please stay outside the *touj* if you so wish. It will be a tragedy for us, however, as I believe you have a further gift to pass on to us. A secret gift which Akbal Coatl says in his writings that you received via the prophet Nostradamus.'

Sabir's eyes opened wide. 'I don't fucking believe this.' He took a step backwards. 'Calque. Did you tell them about Nostradamus?'

Calque shook his head. He looked as mystified as Sabir. 'I never mentioned Nostradamus to them. Nor your claustrophobia, come to that. What would have been the point? And I don't know about any secret gifts, either. And particularly not in your case, Sabir.'

Sabir turned back to the Halach Uinic. 'Are you seriously trying to tell me that Akbal whatever-his-name-is mentioned me in his writings? And linked me to Nostradamus? You've got to be kidding.'

'Not by name, no. Of course he did not. Our brother wasn't a prophet – he was a scribe. He merely said that a messenger, guided by the writings that he and Nostradamus had devised between them, would come, following the eruption of the great volcano of Orizaba, to restore the thirteenth crystal skull to its rightful owners. Just as he wrote that a guardian – an elected *ak k'u hun* – an elected keeper of the sacred books – would return the sacred codex to us at the appropriate time. Here is the guardian.' He pointed to the mestizo. 'And here are you. You are both clearly members of Los Aluxes. You remember what Akbal Coatl said about them? That the Aluxes are enlightened beings who have been left behind by the gods to guard the magnetic spiritual places and objects of the earth, and that it is only via the intercession of these spiritual guardians that the destiny of the world may be secured? Do you remember this?' The Halach Uinic couldn't disguise his satisfaction at the outcome of proceedings. He pointed first to Sabir, and then the mestizo. 'You and he.'

'You don't even know this guy's name, for Christ's sake. And if you do know it, you never bother to use it.' Sabir waved at the mestizo, forgetting, for a moment, that he had never got around to finding out the man's name either. 'And yet here you are, busy trying to convince me that his coming was in some sense preordained. What is it with you people? It doesn't make any sense.'

The Halach Uinic looked first at the Chilan, and then at Ixtab, as though in search of some much needed moral support. He seemed unaware that not everybody was privy to the minutiae of Maya religious custom. 'But we don't need to know his name, you see. For us he will always be the "guardian". Just as a shaman loses his name and inherits a different one when he is dreamed of by a third party – for it is only then that he can begin to heal. When the "guardian" brought us the book, we recognized immediately who he was. Both Ixtab and I had dreamed of his arrival on the night following the eruption of the Pico de Orizaba. It had long been written that a revelation would be made to us in Kabáh. But I was scared to believe in the reality of my dream.' He held his hands up, palms to the fore, in a gesture acknowledging his guilt. 'Ixtab persuaded me of the dream's truth, however, when she recounted all its details back to me without my having told her anything about it. It was then that I decided to station a man both day and night at Kabáh. And it was for this reason alone that we came so swiftly when you and your companion discovered the crystal skull. To find the "guardian" there as well reinforced for us the truth of the dream. This was why we were able to hold the ceremony so quickly. We had long prepared for it, you see.'

'I am the "guardian"?' The mestizo stepped forwards in response to Ixtab's simultaneous translation of the Halach Uinic's words. 'This is what you call me?'

The Halach Uinic turned towards him. 'You are the "guardian", yes. You will be forever known amongst our people also as the "bringer of the book". Whatever you need, you will have from us. A collection has already been made for you. Each has given according to his capacity. Tepeu has told us that you have no wife. That your mother is lonely in her hut. This is not acceptable to us. If you had sold the book, as was your right, you would have had untold sums of money in your possession from the gringos. But you chose not to do so. We cannot replace or match this money, as would have been just. But we can offer you enough to enable you to build another hut next to your mother's – for you to afford a wife – for her to provide grandchildren to comfort your mother's old age. This we can do for you. This you must accept.'

'I cannot accept.'

'You must accept. Or we must return the book.'

The mestizo stared at the Halach Uinic. Then he turned to Ixtab. Then he turned to the Chilan who had read out the words from the book. All were waiting for his response. All were urging him with their eyes not to let the Halach Uinic down. Not to reject his offer.

The mestizo nodded. 'I accept. My mother will be happy with me. She has despaired in the past of my bachelorhood. There is a young widow. Her name is Lorena. She lives in Miatlisco, which is the next village to ours. If I were to build her a house, she would come to live with me and be my wife. This she has told me. I have explained to her that I cannot do this. I have told her to search for another man. A man more suited to her needs.'

'Now you can do it.'

'Yes. Yes. Now I can do it. Now I can build her a house.'

87
—

Athame de Bale watched the group outside the sweathouse. When she cupped her hands behind her ears, she could make out about one word in every three of what they were saying. She clearly heard the words 'Nostradamus', prefaced by 'secret', and then 'gift' – all hidden amongst a pile of other dross.

She could feel her stomach churning in triumph. What was said to the mestizo didn't interest her. She was only interested in Sabir. Would he have the balls to enter the sweathouse or would he not? Dare she make that assumption? Either way, she would only have the briefest window of opportunity to do what she needed to do.

For the time being the group seemed totally preoccupied with soft-flannelling the mestizo and persuading Sabir that he would really – no really, despite his hysterical protestations to the contrary – benefit from the sweat-lodge experience.

Athame offered up a silent prayer. If only the Maya woman with the spondylus necklace would move to another spot, she would have a free run of it. Lamia and the ex-policeman both had their backs to her, as did the Halach Uinic and the priest who had done the reading. Sabir was too wound up inside his own problems to notice anybody else, and the mestizo was pissing himself with joy at the thought of getting married, and wasn't looking anywhere but at the big chief.

As if to order, Sabir abruptly twisted on his heel and began to stalk off back towards the pyramid. The Maya woman with the necklace made a 'cool it' sign to the Halach Uinic and hurried after him. For a moment, everyone was busy watching Sabir's antics and not the sweat lodge.

Athame sprinted across the open patch of land between her hiding place and the sweathouse. Without daring to look behind her, she ducked down and slipped through the doorway. The narrow opening was no problem for one of her diminutive size, and she was soon comfortably out of sight of the assembly.

The lodge was in total darkness. Athame slipped a torch out of the side pocket of her backpack and cracked it on, shielding most of the glow with her free hand. She looked wildly around for a hiding place, still unsure whether anyone had caught a hint of movement out of the corner of their eye. A ring of small boulders had been constructed in the centre of the sweathouse in preparation for the coming of the heated stones. It was surrounded by a dozen or so fabric-covered cushions. The sweathouse was built like an igloo, with an internal circumference of maybe thirty feet, and a gap of perhaps seven feet between the circle of cushions and the retaining wall.

Snatching two of the cushions from out of the circle, she wriggled into the farthest corner of the lodge and adjusted the cushions so that they covered the entirety of her four-foot ten-inch frame. She could feel the hard edges of the Walther P4 digging into her ribs through her backpack. Perhaps it was a message?

She reached behind herself and freed the Walther. At eight and a half inches in length, it was a very big gun for a very small woman. A P5 Compact would have been eminently more suitable. But Athame was happy with what she had, even though her tiny six-fingered hands could scarcely span the butt. Two-handed, she could handle it perfectly well.

She cocked the pistol and unhitched the safety. Then she switched off her torch, cradled the weapon against her chest, and settled down to wait.

88

Ixtab caught up with Sabir just as he was beginning to wind down from his snit. He was leaning against a tree, sucking in great lungfuls of night air, and staring at the distant pyramids as if he suspected that they might have something of great wisdom to impart to him.

Thirty or so volunteers were handing buckets up to each other on the main, father pyramid. First they hosed down the steps. Then they swept them clear of all their ceremonial detritus, in preparation, or so Sabir supposed, for next morning's grand reopening to the tourist trade.

Ixtab came to a halt behind him. Sabir knew that she was there, but he refused to acknowledge her.

'We have been waiting many years for your arrival. You know that.'

'Bullshit.'

'Still. You know it to be true.'

Sabir inflated his cheeks and then blew out through them, like a child. 'If you've come here to try and persuade me to go inside that fucking cabin of yours, you're wasting your time.'

'Drink this anyway. I made it for you. It will calm you down.'

'You've laced it with one of the Halach Uinic's concoctions, I suppose?'

Ixtab hardly registered the insult. 'No. I would never do that. Everything in it is natural. There are no hallucinogens. The whole point of the Halach Uinic's preparations is that people must take them voluntarily, in the correct frame of mind, and towards a spiritual end. They are not toys for gringos to play with. And you are in no frame of mind to take anything at the present time.'

Sabir accepted the gourd with a grudging inclination of the head. He hesitated a little, and then drank deeply from it, surprising himself with the sudden extent of his thirst. He felt churlish, and ungrateful, and angry, and small, all at the same time. 'Thank you. I meant no offence, you understand that?'

She nodded. 'We should have prepared you. Explained the purpose of the ceremony beforehand. But the Halach Uinic has the second sight. He is very advanced in these things. It was his instinct that we should continue right

400

away. He senses something evil approaching. According to him, there is a deadline we must fulfil, or all will be lost. I have never known him to be wrong in these things.'

'And you? Are you ever wrong?'

Ixtab touched her heart. 'I was wrong about you. I thought you would welcome the ceremony. I didn't see the fear in you. The justified fear. That is unforgivable.'

Sabir nodded, more moved than he cared to admit by her obvious concern. 'I don't want to be a shaman. I don't know any secrets. I've just met the woman of my life. All I want to do now is to take her back home with me and see if I can shuck off twenty years of thinking I'm an introvert – of thinking I'm some sort of a recluse – of thinking I don't amount to anything.'

Ixtab said nothing. She just looked at him.

Sabir found her silence awkward, just as he was meant to. He hastened to fill it. 'This has all become a massive red herring, you understand? If I'm honest, I came into it strictly for the cash. I wanted to be the guy that published Nostradamus's lost prophecies. I wanted all the celebrity crap that would have come with it. If things had panned out the way they were meant to, I'd have appeared in a raft of documentaries. Done a few signings. Maybe even sold a movie option. Made a wad of cash, in other words. Instead, it got ugly. My Gypsy friends and I were unlucky enough to become entangled with Lamia's crazy mother and her family of Devil-fearing freaks – without realizing it, I fell personally foul of the super freak, Achor Bale. It got so I was swimming way out of my depth. Last May I was nearly killed. This past week we've been running just ahead of the whirlwind again, and I'm tired of it. I just want to go home.' He could feel Ixtab's *chocah* drink calming him. Paradoxically, though, it was also making him more garrulous than he had intended to be.

'And Lamia? How is she taking this? She seems uncomfortable.'

Sabir shrugged. 'She doesn't know what to think. She doesn't know what to do. She's like the rest of us. We're taking each day as it comes.'

'Are you sure?'

Sabir nodded his head in slow motion. He felt drowsy and relaxed. A sudden wave of self-confidence surged through him, surprising him with its vehemence. 'Sure I'm sure. I know her. She's hurting. So she's withdrawn inside herself. She let me take her virginity today – after holding off for twenty-seven years – and that will have destabilized her too. The whole thing's scarcely surprising.' He stopped dead, stunned at his capacity for indiscretion. Stunned at what his mouth was saying. 'I don't know why I just told you that.' He shook his head incredulously. 'I didn't mean to when I started out.' He looked suspiciously down at the empty gourd, and then handed it back to Ixtab.

She shook her head in reaffirmation that the drink didn't contain anything untoward.

Now that he'd let the cat out of the bag in such a spectacularly tactless manner, Sabir reckoned that he might as well call the beast by its true name. 'All her life Lamia's never let a man come near her because of her feelings about her face. You realize that, don't you? But she let me. And then all of a sudden I start to go crazy. No wonder she's feeling a little vulnerable.'

'Don't you think you owe it to her to put all this to bed?'

Sabir laughed at Ixtab's inadvertent use of the American idiom. 'Is that some kind of a Freudian slip? Or are you getting around to trying to persuade me to go inside your damned *touj* again?'

Ixtab ignored his false levity. 'You're carrying something inside you, Adam. A secret. Something you don't know what to do with.' Ixtab fixed him with her gaze. 'This is a burden to you. This is why you do not sleep. Not the other thing. Not the claustrophobia. Not the memories.'

'How do you know I don't sleep?'

Ixtab sighed. 'Must I explain?'

Sabir shook his head. 'No. I suppose not. I sort of know.'

'Only sort of?'

'I know.'

'Then you have mastered the first step. Now you need to pass on to the second step.'

'Oh? And what's that?'

'To find out what you *don't* know.'

Sabir burst out laughing. 'Oh that's cute. That's very cute. That's right on the button, that is.'

'Cute? What is cute?'

Sabir sighed. 'Forget it.' He gave a wry smile. He was slowly beginning to feel like a man again – the sort of man a woman like Lamia might conceivably have fallen in love with. He looked at Ixtab. He trusted her – there was no doubt about that. It was a deep instinct with him. This was a woman who would always choose the right path. Always guide you in the direction you needed to go. 'I don't know what was in that damned concoction of yours, but if you ever wanted to sell it on the open market, you'd make a fortune. I can hardly believe I'm saying this, but I'm about ready to take a shot at your sweat-bath. If I don't do it now, I'll never do it.'

'Are you sure?'

'Of course I'm not sure. That's why I reserve the right to make a second break for it anytime before I physically step inside the lodge. But this time around, you don't follow me? Is that a deal?'

Ixtab returned his smile. 'This time, if you run, I will not follow you. But you will not run, Adam. And later, you will sleep.'

89

The Halach Uinic shook his head. '*Datura*? No. This is impossible. I may take it – or you, Ixtab – because we understand the extent of its toxicity, and know, too, how it has been grown, and the weather conditions that accompanied its growth. But for a gringo it is dangerous. The side effects can be extremely unpleasant and long-lasting.'

Ixtab shook her head. 'None of the others will do. We three must take it together. We need to communicate on the other side. We need to summon up the Vision Serpent.'

Sabir looked bewildered. The effects of the *chocah* were slowly wearing off.

The Halach Uinic turned to Calque and Lamia. 'Here. Chew this peyote. Chew it for a long time. If you swallow it too quickly you will be very sick. Do not worry about the bitter taste – this is normal.'

'Why should we take this?'

'Because it facilitates transcendence. It will allow us to unify. To go on a collective journey. Ixtab has looked into your hearts. She feels that this particular substance is suitable for you both. Later on in the ceremony, you shall have another piece. The Chilan will drink from the cane toad mixture – this he has always done, so he is used to its effect.

The guardian, because he is only part Indian, will drink the pounded seeds of *quiebracajete*, from the morning glory flower, which we shall mix with *balché*. He has told us he is accustomed to drinking *pulque* on market days in Veracruz – this will have no bad consequences for him, therefore.'

'Why are you people taking something different from us?'

The Halach Uinic shook his head. 'I cannot tell you because I do not know.' He gestured towards Ixtab. 'Ixtab is the midwife of our journey. We are in good hands. She has guided many people through the underworld. If any one requests it, she will give them syrup of *ipecac*, from the *ipecacuanha* plant, and they will vomit out anything that is left inside their stomach.'

'Great. Excellent. We shall all become bulimics. This has been one of my ambitions for many years.' Calque shook his head, as if he was standing amongst a group of madmen. He hitched his chin at Sabir. 'Are you absolutely sure you want to go through with this?'

'What do you think, Calque? Of course I'm not sure. But if I think about it any longer I'll do another bunk. So here goes.' Sabir glanced quickly at Lamia. Then he held his hand out to the Halach Uinic.

The Halach Uinic placed fifteen seeds in the palm of Sabir's hand.

'This is it?'

'More would be dangerous. And unnecessary. When gringo kids take more, they end up schizophrenic. Their pupils enlarge for days, and they suffer from photophobia. Some become amnesiac. They are fools. They are simply concerned with gratification and not with knowledge.'

'And this won't happen to us?'

'No. Not if you chew the seeds well. Not if you ask the right questions.'

Sabir poured the seeds into his mouth. The Halach Uinic did the same. So did Ixtab. Sabir saw that the guardian was drinking his mixture, as was the Chilan.

Calque shrugged and popped the peyote into his mouth. He began to masticate the pulp, a disgusted expression on his face, as if he were being forced to swallow a tablespoonful of castor oil.

Lamia was the last to make up her mind. She turned and looked into the darkness surrounding them for a very long time. Then, with a shudder, she placed the peyote on her tongue.

90

At first Sabir felt very little. It was almost as if the *datura* wasn't working. Perhaps they'd given him a bunch of sunflower seeds to chew on by mistake? Every now and then he found himself stretching his hand out as if he were reaching for a cigarette. But he had never smoked. This fact struck him as strange.

The Halach Uinic's voice droned on. He and the Chilan had been praying for over an hour now, and the sound had become like a sort of sonic wallpaper behind which Sabir could dimly make out the presence of other people. But the room was entirely dark – not a sliver of light entered from anywhere. Even the stones heating the air were dark – Sabir had assumed, for some obscure reason, that they would glow like household coal.

Thanks to the heat from the stones he was now sweating uncontrollably. He began to picture himself as a cold bottle of beer on a midsummer's day. The thought of the beer made him want to salivate, but he found that he couldn't produce any spit at all. He thought about asking for a glass of water and then decided against it. The idea of the seven of them sitting packed together around the stones and still not being able to see each other struck him as ludicrous in the extreme.

Every now and then there was a mild clattering and banging – the susurration of things being shifted and of liquid being poured. Sabir reckoned that this represented the sound of the Halach Uinic, Ixtab, and the Chilan arranging their offerings in the dark. Each had brought with them various vessels filled with deer blood, *sacpom* resin, and certain other accoutrements, while Ixtab, as usual, had been carrying her shamanic bag of tricks.

Sabir began to muse on what was secretly hidden inside Ixtab's bag. A powder compact? A lipstick? A cell phone? He began to giggle at the thought of Ixtab as some sort of super-urban Maya princess. The idea was so absurd that he felt an overwhelming urge to communicate it to the assembly at large so that everyone else could appreciate it too. But for some reason he found himself unable to speak.

Slowly, Sabir began to realize the full enormity of what was happening to him. He no longer felt remotely claustrophobic. In fact he had not felt claustrophobic since entering the sweat lodge. This fact struck him as so absurdly unlikely that he began to search around inside his head in a vain effort to reclaim the comfortably ingrained emotions of fear he had now so palpably lost track of. But try as he might, he couldn't reconnect with them. Was it someone else who had been claustrophobic, then, and not him?

He felt around with his fingers, anxious to know who was sitting beside him. The process was a difficult one, however, as he did not wish to invade anyone else's privacy. By a process of elimination, he decided that the Halach Uinic was sitting directly opposite him, with the Chilan on the Halach Uinic's left, and Ixtab on his right – the sounds of praying were coming from over there, and they were site specific. This left the guardian, Lamia, and Calque as his potential next-door neighbours.

Sabir lowered his nose and began sniffing. For some reason he felt that he ought to be able to tell who was sitting next to him simply by their smell. This seemed entirely reasonable, to his way of thinking, and he was surprised that more people didn't use the procedure in the ordinary run of their lives. He had a sudden clear vision of approaching people on the street and sniffing at them. Of discovering their secrets that way. Whether they were menopausal, on heat, full of testosterone, angry, in love, etc., etc. Someone or something had come up with this theory before, but he couldn't remember who or when.

'It was dogs!' he screamed, surprising himself with the sound of his own voice.

The Halach Uinic and the Chilan stopped their chanting.

'I knew it. Dogs go around sniffing.' Sabir raised one hand to his face in yet another cigarette-smoking movement. He swept the hand out in an arc, like an over exuberant actor, then stopped abruptly when he felt some resistance. But the resistance wasn't physical. He was only inferring it. 'It's you, isn't it?' He had forgotten to use the person's name, but he suspected it was Calque.

'Yes, it's me.'

'I knew it. I nearly hit you.'

'You were a long way off. You were nowhere near me.'

'Oh yes?' Sabir allowed himself to flop backwards. He lay, looking up at where the roof was supposed to be – but it might as well have been the floor for all the evidence it gave of its existence. 'Can anyone tell me why I'm here?'

The Chilan and the Halach Uinic began their chanting again.

Sabir decided that he would go to sleep.

91
—

Athame had been lying without moving for close on three hours. During the whole of that time, the Halach Uinic and the Chilan had only stopped their chanting once, when someone – she supposed Sabir – had shouted out something about dogs.

She had taken to working on one part of her body at a time. Small movements. Flexions and tensions. Tiny spasms of the muscles designed to keep the blood flowing around her body and to protect her from cramp. She wondered how much longer she would have to suffer this torment for the sake of – well what? Nobody had said anything worth missing supper for so far.

At one point her cell phone began to vibrate. Fortunately for her, the bass-baritone droning emanating from the Chilan and the Halach Uinic, with the occasional contralto interjection from the witchdoctor woman, more than compensated for its sound, and Athame was able to dampen it with her hand until it switched itself off. She had arranged with Abi that he only let any of his calls run for two rings – if she didn't answer, it meant that she was otherwise engaged. This foresight had now saved her from the embarrassment of premature discovery –

a discovery which would have forced her to act in a manner directly contrary to Madame, her mother's, wishes. Athame was sufficiently level-headed to realize that in those circumstances Abi would gleefully have fed her to the dogs, transferring all responsibility for his own maverick actions onto her head.

Once, when the chanting became especially raucous, Athame achieved a partial change of position, turning from facing the wall to facing outwards. What were these people thinking of? Why were they all sitting in a pitch-dark space chanting nonsense? She began to regret her super-smart, on-the-hoof idea of sneaking inside. Now, given the impossible situation she had contrived for herself, she knew that she would have to see the thing through until the bitter end.

She silently prayed that Abi might somehow be able to deduce what had happened to her, and detail one of the others for skull and codex duty.

92

The temporary camp had gone quiet. People were either curled up on the ground or sleeping in hammocks they had strung up between the trees. Some had attempted to build bivouacs out of palm fronds and plastic sheeting, but most seemed content to lie out beneath the stars.

Abi had the entire area covered. With Oni and Berith back at the warehouse, he still had Vau, Rudra, Aldinach, Alastor, Athame, Asson, Dakini and Nawal to police the temporary camp. Each was in contact with him via their cell phone, and each was covering one particular section of the camp.

Thanks to Aldinach – who was in fully female distaff mode at the moment for reasons best known to himself – he knew to an inch where the skull and the codex were. Thanks also to Aldinach's intuitive genius in policing areas he was not directly responsible for, he also knew that Athame was hidden somewhere inside the sweat lodge, cosying up to all the major players.

He had cursed Athame's impetuosity at first – what had she been thinking of, putting herself in imminent danger of detection? But once he'd calmed down and began to think rationally about the whole thing, he started to feel better. He'd tried her once on the phone, moments before Aldinach had told him where she was hiding, and if that degree of buzzing hadn't give her away to the sky pilots, he reckoned nothing else would.

Madame, his mother, had also telephoned earlier. Sensing that the whole affair was now entering its final phase, she had recently taken to calling him every hour on the hour. Abi felt a deep sense of satisfaction, therefore, that he had been in a position to tell her pretty much the entire truth about their situation. They were doing exactly what she had asked them, after all – monitoring events with no direct intervention. No one, bar Athame, had made anything like a proactive move. No one was going against her wishes. Yet.

Abi knew that the Countess was disturbingly adept at discerning lies. He had stuck to the strict letter of the truth, therefore, in a desperate effort to stave off the evil day. He wanted to be able to report total success to her: the securing of the Maya codex and the thirteenth crystal skull; the identity and geographical location of the Second Coming and of the Third Antichrist; and the gruesomely drawn-out murder of Adam Sabir, for which he had already earmarked Aldinach and her deliriously transformational scalpel – then, and only then, might he expect to be forgiven. The deaths of Joris Calque and Lamia would simply add an extra layer of icing to the celebratory cake.

He looked at the time on his cell phone – 2.30 in the morning. He'd better get on with it. People woke up early here, and he reckoned some might be moving by as soon as four o'clock, if they needed to get to distant places of work.

He began the necessary round of telephone calls.

93

The snake was approaching him again. The same snake he had seen whilst imprisoned in the cesspit below the Maset de la Marais safe house waiting for Achor Bale's return.

This time the snake slithered past him. He could feel the roughness of its skin kissing his.

Sabir tried to turn his head to follow the snake's progress, but he was unable to move. It was then that he realized that his skull was being held in a vice.

He corrected his eye-line and stared to his front. He instantly knew what he was looking at. It was the exact same scene described by Akbal Coatl, the chief guardian of the sacred books, in Maní, in the run-up to the burning of the Maya relics.

Sabir tried to shout. To break through the reality he now found himself in, and back to the reality he felt he should be inhabiting. But his words were eaten – no sound came out of his mouth.

He remembered then that time was a spiral. Wasn't that what both the Maya and Nostradamus believed? That at any given moment, granted the right conditions, you could encounter time past, or even time future, in time present? The poet, T.S.Eliot, had taken the idea and run with it in the 'Burnt Norton' section of his *Four Quartets*:

> *Time present and time past*
> *Are both perhaps present in time future,*
> *And time future contained in time past.*
> *If all time is eternally present*
> *All time is unredeemable.*

The words repeated and repeated themselves in your brain.

You were clearly going crazy. A Spanish soldier was approaching you. He held a *garrotte* in his hands.

The soldier turned towards a friar dressed in the dark-brown habit of a Franciscan Minorite. Friar de Landa. It couldn't be anybody else. The man's face was smooth and blameless – the face of someone who knows that whatever they do, whatever outrage they choose to commit, is, by godly implication, the right thing. Beside him a man you also recognized was busy scribbling onto a vellum sheet, supported on a lectern. You knew this man well – he was a member of your family. For a moment you resented him. What was he doing, hobnobbing with the Spaniards? He should be out here, with you, suffering for his beliefs.

Then you remembered. He had taken an oath. You had administered it yourself. In this oath he had undertaken to protect two sacred items – the last remaining copy of the sacred codex, designed by the priests as the final back-up to the library revealed to Friar de Landa by the terminal folly of Nachi Cocom – and the thirteenth crystal skull, the so-called 'singing skull', without which the twelve remaining skulls of wisdom might not speak. To fulfil his task, Akbal Coatl had agreed to placate – even to become one with – the Spaniards. This he was clearly doing to the best of his ability.

The Spanish soldier wired the *garrotte* in place over your forehead. The snake was close behind you too. He was whispering in your ear.

You knew now that the snake was the Vision Serpent. The Serpent who only appeared to those whose eyes were no longer sufficiently acute to view the reality about to encompass them.

The first turn of the *garrotte* was made. You shrieked in pain. You could feel the blood starting from your forehead.

The Vision Serpent whispered the first of the seven secrets to you.

Then came the second turn. Your eyes clouded. Your ears began to hum with the pressure of the *cordeles*. Four turns. That was the maximum you had ever heard inflicted. You would be able to withstand that much. You were a strong man. You would be scarred, yes. Badly scarred. But you would live.

The Vision Serpent whispered the second of the seven secrets to you.

When they turned the garrotte for the fifth time, you no longer knew or cared what they were asking you to say. You could feel the *cordeles* knotting against the bones of your skull. Blood clouded your vision. Pain was your only reality. You could feel the teeth breaking off in your mouth as you ground your jaws together in a vain attempt to loosen the pressure.

The Vision Serpent whispered the fifth of the seven secrets to you.

With the seventh turn, your eyes burst out of their sockets and fell onto your cheeks. This you could see. For you were seeing through the eyes of the Vision Serpent. You were dead and you were alive at the same time. Your skull was cracking under the pressure of the *garrotte*. Your brain was compressed inside the *cordeles*, which were binding it as in a vice.

You were dead. No man could survive seven turns of the *garrotte*.

The Vision Serpent whispered the seventh of the seven secrets to you.

'He is still alive, sir. Shall we tighten the *garrotte* another turn so that his skull breaks in two?'

'No. Let him live. As a lesson to the other chiefs.'

At first, when they untied the *garrotte*, it was found impossible to free it from your skull. The *cordeles* had ground so far inwards that they and your skull had become one.

You were dead. You felt nothing.

You could see the soldiers still, but only via the eyes of the Vision Serpent. One soldier cut the membranes that supported what remained of your out-spurted eyes. Another cut the *cordeles* and ripped them from your forehead, just as you would rip a congealed bandage from an infected wound.

You were lifted. You saw this clearly. Lifted by four men and a woman. Your head lolled backwards. You could see the blood rushing from your wounds.

You were dead. No man could survive what you had endured.

Then the pain came. And with it the final whispers of the Vision Serpent. The final sighting of yourself through the Vision Serpent's eyes.

94

Sabir opened his eyes. He was blind. He closed them again.

It had all been true then. They had taken his eyes. He felt consumed by the darkness. He screamed.

Hands took hold of his body. He was carried out of the *touj* and into the open air.

Sabir threw his forearms across his face. It was dark. All was darkness. He could not bear to acknowledge his blindness.

Ixtab leaned forwards and rested her hands on his. 'Try to open your eyes again,' she said. 'You will see. You are not blind. Trust me.'

'No. No. I can't.'

'Open your eyes.'

Sabir was placed gently on the ground. He could smell the odour of the dust. Smell the bodies of those around him. He could identify each by their smell.

'Where is Lamia? I need her.'

'Open your eyes, Adam.'

Sabir opened his eyes. It was still dark, but he was just able to make out the faces of those immediately surrounding him in the first suggestion of pre-dawn.

It was then that he knew that he was not blind. That he had merely been having a mimetic vision. Hacking sobs racked his body. In a sudden cognitive rush he remembered taking the *datura*. He remembered the ceremony. He remembered going to sleep. When he had recovered sufficiently to speak, he made a grab for Ixtab's arm. 'What did I do? What did I say?'

'You told us many things.'

'Did I tell you the seven secrets?'

'The seven secrets?'

'Yes. The seven secrets the Vision Serpent told me.'

There was a heavy silence. Sabir could almost smell the excitement emanating from his companions.

'No. What are those secrets?'

Sabir sat up. 'What did I tell you?'

Calque moved in closer. He crouched down beside Sabir. 'You told us that the Third Antichrist was already living amongst us. That you knew his name and his condition, but that no one else must be allowed to know it. That if they did, the Corpus Maleficus would seize it from them in an effort to support the Antichrist and delay the return of the Devil.'

'Christ Jesus. That's it? That's what I told you?'

'Yes. You quoted Revelations to us too: "And when the thousand years are expired, Satan shall be loosed out of his prison; And shall go out to deceive the nations which are in the four quarters of the earth, Gog and Magog, to gather them together to battle: the number of whom *is* as the sand of the sea."'

'Yes. Yes. It's what Achor Bale said to me when he had me imprisoned in the cesspit. "AND AFTER THAT HE MUST BE LOOSED A LITTLE SEASON." The maniac thought he was still protecting us all from the Devil, just like his de Bale ancestors had done for the kings of France.'

The Halach Uinic motioned to Ixtab. She crouched forwards and spoke to Sabir. 'We do not understand this. How can the de Bales imagine they are protecting us all from a Devil they themselves seem busy conjuring up?'

Calque laid a hand on Sabir's shoulder to stop him from responding. 'Let me answer this. I've become something of an expert on the subject in recent months. The Devil-Antichrist question is a tricky one. In a nutshell, the Corpus believes that only by *placating* the Devil – that is, by supporting

417

his earthly representative, the Third Antichrist (the first two Antichrists being Napoleon and Hitler, according to Nostradamus) – can the Devil be *seduced* into allowing the earth to follow its own devices. To run its own shop. Once the Devil himself is tempted to intervene – once he loses patience, in other words, with the machinations of his henchmen – we are doomed to Armageddon.'

Ixtab shook her head. 'How can this be? Is there no way to stop it? Or does the Corpus think this is all preordained too?'

'To the de Bales' way of thinking, the only palpable threat to the Third Antichrist is via the Second Coming. Because the Antichrist is the evil mirror image of Christ – Christ's dark shadow – the *antimimon pneuma* – the counterfeit spirit, or what have you, only a true representation of Christ – ergo the Son of God – ergo the *Parousia* – ergo the Second Coming – can possibly hope to overcome him. The Corpus Maleficus can't afford to let that happen, because then they would have failed in their sworn duty. The crazy thing is that they think *they* are the goodies. That whatever they need to do to keep the Devil at bay is justified, within the greater scheme of things. That is their gage. The rest is irrelevant to them. The Devil is God's evil brother – the Antichrist bears the exact same relationship to Christ. The one, in both cases, presupposes the existence of the other. The Antichrist is therefore Christ's dark shadow or mirror image, and can only be overcome by his opposite number. And vice versa. You see? It's simple, really.'

Ixtab shook her head. She glanced at the Halach Uinic. He met her gaze, then let his eyes fall to the ground.

Sabir made a grab for Ixtab's hand. 'What else did I say?'

'You also spoke of your blood sister, Yola Samana. You told us that she had been made pregnant by her husband, Alexi Dufontaine, on a beach on the island of Corsica. But that her coming child was no normal child, but the one predicted by Nostradamus in his lost prophecies – the prophecies that you had read and then burned in order to keep them out of the hands of Achor Bale and the Corpus Maleficus. That this child was indeed the *Parousia*, which some call the Second Coming. That because of his background, and the cursed nomadic tribe from which he sprang, the child would grow up to be a representative of all faiths, both religious and secular – of all people, not simply the Christians – of all races, not simply the Aryan and the Semitic. That his birth was designed by God to bring the peoples of the world together, and not to separate them, just as Revelations had foretold. "In the midst of the street of it, and on either side of the river, *was there* the tree of life, which bare twelve *manner of* fruits, *and* yielded her fruit every month: and the leaves of the tree *were* for the healing of the nations."'

'Oh, God. I told you all that? But I swore not to tell.'

'To whom did you swear?'

Sabir shook his head uncertainly. 'I don't know. I can't remember. To myself, I suppose. Whoever I swore it to, in my delirium, is irrelevant. I owe Yola my protection. She is my blood sister. There are vows I have taken in front of her tribe. The more people who know of this thing, the more danger she stands in.'

The Halach Uinic smiled. 'All is well then. No one here will abuse your trust. You told us because you had to pass on the message. The Vision Serpent made you do so. The cult of the Second Coming shall start here. When the time is ripe we will proclaim his name. And that will be on 21 December 2012. At the very end of the Cycle of the Nine Hells.'

'Then you'll be signing the child's death warrant. I shouldn't have spoken. You were wrong to give me the *datura*. I have betrayed my blood sister.'

'No, Adam. You told us because your unconscious mind sensed that you must share the secret you had stumbled on. That it would only be believed if it emerged under such circumstances. Such a secret is too much of a burden for any one man to carry.'

Sabir shook his head. 'Wrong. I told you because I thought I was the chief whose eyes the Spaniards started out of his head with the *garrotte* – that I was about to die, in other words, and carry my secret to the grave with me. I dreamed that I was in the clearing with Friar de Landa. That I saw Akbal Coatl writing his record. That I saw the broken bodies of those the Friar had already tortured. When I was blinded, the Vision Serpent briefly lent me his eyes so that I could bear witness to what had occurred.' Sabir ground the heels of his hands into his eye sockets. 'It's all nonsense, of course. I wasn't there. The drug was simply working on me. I was on a fucking trip, that's all. And my unconscious mind grabbed hold of the first thing that suggested itself to me, which just happened to be the de Landa story. Under different circumstances it could just as easily have latched onto the storyline of a book I'd just been reading. Or a movie. Or something that had happened to me earlier that day in the street.'

'You were that chief. You did see the Vision Serpent.' The Halach Uinic was bending forwards at the waist. He was urging Sabir to believe him with his eyes.

'Bullshit. How can that be possible?'

'Because we were with you, Adam. All of us. We witnessed what happened to you. Ixtab was one of the ones who carried you from the square. As was I. As was the guardian, and the Chilan, and Calque. We all carried you out of there. We were chosen to share your vision. It was a communal one. As an acknowledged midwife, Ixtab was even told by the Franciscans to tend to your wounds so that you would not die. So that your torment could serve as an example to the other chiefs.'

Sabir looked uncertainly at the Halach Uinic. Then he gave a bitter laugh. 'This is all madness. You all carried me out here, now, this minute. Not out of the square at Maní four hundred and fifty years ago. I don't believe a word of it. Where was Lamia in all of this? I need to speak to her. I need to ask her something.'

The Halach Uinic stood up. He looked around himself in the darkness. 'This is impossible, I am afraid. For Lamia has gone.'

95

Calque shrugged. 'She was definitely here a few minutes ago. I saw her. We were in that place for more than four hours. It's my guess that she's gone to pay a visit to the bushes – and fast. That's not something you particularly want to communicate to everybody when they're carrying your boyfriend out in a dead faint.'

Sabir grimaced. 'I'm tired. I don't want to talk about this any more. Is it all right if we leave it to the morning? I'm going back to our lean-to. Lamia will be waiting for me there. I'm sure of it.'

'You know how to find it?'

'Yes. It's starting to get light. Look.' Sabir pointed to a vague luminescence in the eastern sky. 'We're right next to the tallest tree in the place. It's virtually impossible to miss it.'

'I'm coming with you.' Calque stepped quickly to Sabir's side.

'What for? To hold my hand? To make sure I don't get lost in the dark?'

'I want to make sure that Lamia's all right. That was an uncomfortable experience to witness back there. You were screaming, Sabir. Like they were really squeezing out your eyes.'

'They were.'

'But you just told us it was bullshit. Get your story right, man.'

In the dim light of the pre-dawn Sabir could just make out that Calque had his head cocked to one side, as if he were talking to someone with a particularly low IQ. This was a specialty of Calque's. Something he'd clearly perfected over thirty years of questioning obstreperous – and often none-too-bright – suspects.

Sabir bitterly resented being on the receiving end of that particular look. Especially now, when he was feeling more than a little fragile. 'Well maybe I was wrong. I can still feel pain there, for Christ's sake. Like someone slammed a car door on my head. Then pulled it back and slammed it again for good measure.'

Calque sighed. 'That happened years ago, Sabir. It's been obvious to me for a long time. There has to be some rational explanation for the way you behave.'

The Halach Uinic raised his hand placatingly. He was keen to put as much distance between himself and the smart-talking ex-policeman as possible. 'We all need some sleep. We'll see you both in the morning. At breakfast. Much will have clarified itself by then, I am sure. And Ixtab will be able to explain the rest to you. How the *datura* works. Collective visions. Things like that.'

'Well I'm glad somebody will be able to.' Sabir's head was about to burst. He felt desperately thirsty. He wanted to skulk off and drink a gallon of cold water, take three Advil, and then escape into Lamia's arms. It was with considerable relief that he watched the silhouettes of the four figures disappearing into the murk.

As soon as they were safely gone, Calque grabbed Sabir by the shoulder and started hurrying him in the opposite direction.

'What the heck's the matter, Calque? Why are we in such a rush? You're behaving mighty strangely all of a sudden.'

Calque hustled him towards the great tree. 'Listen. I'm probably about to make the biggest mistake of my life. But just bear with me, Sabir. If you've ever felt one iota of friendship for me, then now is your chance to prove it.'

96
—

Lamia wasn't waiting for them at the lean-to.

Sabir grabbed his head in both his hands in an effort to ward off his migraine. 'She's lost. It's still dark as hell out there. And everyone's asleep. There's nobody to ask for directions. She'll not have wanted to disturb anybody.'

'That's nonsense and you know it.'

'I don't know it. What are you trying to tell me, Calque? What's this great call you intend to make on our friendship? You're not going to tell me that Lamia has somehow moved from being your blue-eyed girl to being one of the enemy again?'

'That's exactly what I'm telling you. Where are your car keys?'

Sabir slapped his pockets. Then he looked blank. 'They were in here.'

'But she needed them for something, no?'

Sabir nodded slowly. 'Yes. She wanted a change of clothing before the ceremony. Access to her toothbrush. That sort of thing. That still doesn't put her back in the Corpus camp. Come on, man. What are you thinking? That after all they did to her she's still loyal to them?'

'But what did they do to her?'

'You tell me. You're the one that found her. You're the one that brought her along on this trip. You're the one that tipped me the wink that she was attracted to me. Christ, Calque. You're the best friend she has in the world. You're going to feel like a total asshole when she comes skipping back in from wherever she's managed to lose herself. I'll do you a real favour, though. Give you a real proof of our friendship. I won't tell her what you suspected.'

Calque stared out at the gradually lightening sky. 'They tied her up, put her on a table, and gave her a tranquillizer. That's all they did to her.'

'That would be enough for most people.'

'There's something else.'

'What's that?'

'Her name.'

'Her name?'

'She lied to us about her name.'

'Oh, for Christ's sake.'

'She told us that Lamia was the daughter of Poseidon and the mistress of Zeus. That that was her only significance. That Zeus accorded Lamia the gift of prophecy as a down payment for her services to him in bed. That she was unimportant in the general scheme of things.'

'So?'

'So I thought about it. And then I thought about it some more. It niggled at me. All the other adoptive names – except for our old friend Achor Bale, aka Rocha de Bale, who was adopted at far too late an age for a name change – which in the case of a teenager like him would have had to have been referred to a *juge des affaires familiales* anyway . . .'

'Calque, for crying out loud. You're not on the police force any longer. You're not making out a case for the prosecuting judge.'

'The examining magistrate, please.'

Sabir slapped his forehead in frustration, and then instantly regretted it. 'What about the names? Tell me.'

Calque sighed. 'All the names of the Countess's adoptive children are specific to some sort of demon or other. To one of the Devil's henchmen, maybe, or to some other freak out of hell. Lamia explained all that to us. It's categorical. Another of the Countess's endearing little tics. So why should Lamia be any different?'

'Why indeed?' Sabir was beginning to look rather sick.

'So when you were both up in your room doing whatever you were doing in that motel at Ticul, I phoned an old friend of mine in France. Got him to consult Lemprière's *Classical Dictionary*. And one or two other books he happened to have to hand.'

'Don't tell me? Lamia was the Devil's handmaiden, code name 666? Or maybe the Countess gave her the name of some famous female serial killer? The Countess Báthory, maybe?'

'Nothing like that. The Countess Báthory's given name was Erzsébet – Elizabeth to you.'

'Come on, Calque. Don't keep me in suspense. This is Lamia we're talking about. The woman I happen to be in love with.'

'That's why I'm finding it so hard.'

'Then make a superhuman effort and get over it.' Sabir's face looked livid and tormented in the fractional light of the early dawn. He looked as though he wanted to tear Calque apart with his bare hands.

Calque cleared his throat. 'Lamia was indeed Zeus's mistress. But she wasn't unimportant. Far from it. In fact Zeus's wife, Hera, became so jealous of Lamia's sway over her husband that she killed all Lamia's children and deformed her.'

'Deformed her? How?'

'She turned her into half woman, half serpent. She became a child-murdering demon. Her name means "gullet" in Ancient Greek. She'd kill other people's children in revenge for her own, and then suck their blood and eat them. Zeus tried to placate her by offering her the gift of prophecy. He even gave her the ability to pluck out her own eyes, the better to see into the future – a little like your Vision Serpent, no? Horace writes about her in his *Ars Poetica*: "*Neu pranse Lamiae vivum puerum extrabat alvo.*"'

'Go on. Translate it for me. You're dying to. My everyday Latin's a little rusty.'

'"Shall Lamia in our sight her sons devour, and give them back alive the self-same hour?" Forgive my English accent. That's Alexander Pope's translation. The best, really.'

'There's more. I can smell it on you. Don't tell me you're not enjoying this?'

'I'm not enjoying it, Sabir. It's making me sick to my stomach.'

Sabir looked up quickly. The expression on his face underwent a brief transformation, as if a searchlight had shone across it. 'I'm sorry, Calque. I must be feeling a little rattled. That was unfair. I know how fond you are of her. Go on. Tell me the rest. I promise not to murder the messenger.'

Calque shrugged, but he was clearly touched by Sabir's change of heart. 'Some authorities even link her with Lilith, the first wife of Adam, believing they were one and the same person. Jerome, in the fifth-century Vulgate – Isaiah 34:14 to be precise – even translates Lilith as Lamia. His version of Lamia conceived a brood of monsters with Adam, and then later transmogrified into the sort of fairy-tale nasty that nurses and nannies used to threaten their charges with.'

'My name is also Adam, Calque. The same as Lilith's husband. You may not have noticed that.'

'I noticed it. As, I believe, did she. She seduced you on purpose, man. Because she'd been told to. In Apuleius's time, they used Lamia as a name for seductresses and harlots. John Keats said "Her throat was serpent, but the words she spake/Came, as through bubbling honey, for Love's sake . . ."'

'All right. Enough now. I can see why that poor bastard Macron found you so intensely irritating.' Sabir was hiding it well, but the nausea in his stomach was rapidly overtaking the pain in his head. 'I think I'm about to be sick.' He pushed Calque away, and then doubled up, retching.

When Sabir finally straightened up again, he realized that Calque had been joined by two new figures – one on either side of him. The first, an almost dwarf-like figure, was holding a very large pistol straight out ahead of her. Despite the fact that her hands could scarcely encompass the grip, the pistol was rock steady.

The second person, also a woman, but this time of normal height, had her head cocked to one side, as though she was secretly rather amused by Sabir's temporary affliction. 'Is this them?'

The smaller woman nodded. 'It's them.'

'They don't look like much. I say we kill them now and have done with it. We've got most of what we need already.'

'Do you want to wake up the whole camp?'

'I could slit their throats with my scalpel. No one would hear that. The foot drumming would be lost amidst all the snoring.'

Sabir was still dry-retching after his major evacuation of two minutes before. He pinched his nose between two of his fingers and snorted the final remnants of his stomach contents on to the ground. Then he looked up and shook his head fatalistically. 'Are you two who I think you are? No. Don't answer that.' He reached inside his pocket. 'How the heck did you find us again?'

'Keep your hands out where we can see them.'

'I only want my handkerchief.'

'A bit of vomit never hurt anybody.'

Sabir took his handkerchief out anyway. 'Then shoot, why don't you?' A part of him didn't care any more whether they killed him or not. He walked over to the water bucket he and Lamia had shared and began to rinse his face. Aldinach accompanied him, her pistol held casually at hip level.

Sabir's oddball mixture of acute oversensitivity and irrational bravado never ceased to amaze Calque. Sensing that the tall woman was getting ready to pistol-whip his friend, Calque raised his voice in an effort to deflect her attention. 'They are who you think they are, Sabir. I've seen them before. At the Countess's house. The smaller one is Athame. The taller one is . . .' He hesitated, praying he'd got his timing right.

Aldinach stopped what she was about to do and turned towards Calque. 'Aldinach. I am Aldinach. The hermaphrodite. You remember? Half man, half woman. But today I am only a woman.' Aldinach did a sarcastic little pirouette to show off her figure.

'Where is Lamia? Have you taken her?'

'Ah. Our elusive elder sister. Do you know where she is, Athame?'

'She bolted. I think at the end, that she suspected my presence in the *touj*. I had only a split second to decide on my priorities. So I chose these two.'

'Good choice.'

'You were inside the *touj*? That's impossible.' Sabir sank to his knees beside the bucket. He could still feel the cramping effects of the *datura* at work on his stomach. 'We would have heard you.'

'All of you were as high as kites in there. You were busy screaming that your eyes were being torn out, and the other idiots were chanting like a bunch of Hare Krishnas. None of you would have heard a siren in a snowstorm. Later on, after you all left, I even crept to the entrance and listened to your absurd post-mortem discussion.'

Sabir doubled up with another intestinal cramp.

'Interesting about the identity of the Second Coming. I think a visit to Samois – for that's where my brother Rocha told us your Yola Samana lives – will soon be in order. Shame you didn't follow through with information about the Third Antichrist. It'll make things harder for you. My brother Abi is still very unhappy about Rocha's death. When he finds that you've been holding out on us . . .' Athame stopped. 'What do you think, Aldinach?'

'I think both you boys will be gratified to know that we've reached a consensus. We've decided not to kill you for the time being.' Aldinach waved her pistol at the two men. 'Avanti. And don't make a sound going through the camp. If you wake anybody up, we'll kill them.'

97

Abi watched the four figures approach with a half-smile on his face.

Everything had gone far more smoothly than he had expected. Vau, Rudra, and Alastor had secured the codex and the thirteenth crystal skull with no difficulty whatsoever. The priests, and the three Maya who the Halach Uinic had clearly detailed for guard duty, had all been fast asleep, with the two objects wrapped in calico situated plumb in the centre of their sleepover. Like presents left by Father Christmas.

Now both Sabir and Calque, looking very much the worse for wear, were shambling towards him, flanked by Athame and Aldinach.

Abi chucked his chin at Aldinach. 'Where's Lamia? You didn't kill her, did you?'

Athame approached him and began to whisper in his ear. Abi hunched down, nodding.

'Right. I want you and Aldinach to take the fastest car we have. There's only one possible direction she can have gone in, and that's back towards the Cancun toll road. If she's got any sense at all she'll be heading out of the country. Fast. If you push it, you should be able to pick up her transponder signal after maybe fifteen or twenty miles. This whole country is as flat as a damned graveyard.'

'But I thought you wanted me to question Sabir?' Aldinach looked crestfallen, like a child who has unexpectedly been deprived of her fair share of the birthday cake.

'We can manage all that. You and Athame are by far the best shadowers amongst us. I want you to follow Lamia wherever she is going. If she leaves the country, go with her. If you lose her, go straight to the Gypsy camp at Samois. My guess is that you'll encounter her again there. There's something more to this than meets the eye. But first things first. Calque and Sabir are going to come on a little trip with us. Put them both in the trunk of the Hyundai.'

'So you did have a tracker in our car?' Calque muscled his way a little nearer to Abi. By temperament he was unwilling to engage any further than was strictly necessary with those he thought of as the enemy, but, this time at least, his curiosity had got the better of him. 'Where did you put it? We turned that vehicle inside out. I'm willing to guarantee that there was nothing concealed inside it.'

'My brother Vau here is an electronic genius. You hear that Vau? I'm giving you a compliment.' He turned to Calque. 'He stuck it underneath the chassis.'

'Underneath the chassis?' Calque looked crestfallen. 'But that's the best way to ensure it gets knocked off over the first speed bump. Or in heavy rain. Or going through a field. We travelled thousands of miles in that vehicle. You people just struck lucky, that's all.'

Abi laughed. 'I said Vau was an electronic genius. I never said he was smart.'

Still shaking his head, Calque allowed himself to be manhandled into the narrow trunk. Sabir was unceremoniously tipped in beside him.

'What? No conniptions, Mr Sabir? Rocha told my mother that you were terminally claustrophobic. That he'd seen you locked inside a wood box at the camp in Samois, and that you were half raving when they took you out of it. I understand that a similar event occurred around the time you murdered him. In a cesspit, wasn't it?' Abi's words were lightly inflected, but his eyes were dead.

'I'm not claustrophobic any more. Something happened in the *touj*. You can lock me in here as long as you want. I won't care.' Sabir put as much conviction as he could into the words. The truth was that he was scared witless they'd lock him up in an even tighter space than before. Give him the water treatment, maybe.

'Oh, never fear. We'll think of something else for you. We have time to spare for all of that.' Abi slammed down the Hyundai lid.

98

Abi stepped out of the Hyundai sixty metres short of the warehouse. He programmed Oni's number into his cell phone. Then he raised both hands above his head. The dawn was well up now, and visibility was improving by the minute. After ten seconds he cut the connection with a movement of his thumb.

He knew all about Oni's itchy trigger finger. And he also knew that two heavy-duty machine guns – the Stoner M63 and the notoriously unreliable AAT – were covering the approach road. He didn't want Oni and Berith to think the Mexican owners of the arms dump had returned early from their border run, and commence firing. And neither did he want to walk into a trap.

The cell phone cheeped. Abi put it to his ear. 'Can you see us?'

'I've got you.'

'Any trouble?'

'Nah.'

'We'll come in then.'

'Yeah. Come on in. You're a tempting target out there. I nearly let loose on you just for the hell of it.'

Abi got back in the car and signalled to Alastor behind him. The convoy moved forwards. 'We'll go straight to the warehouse and get this over and done with. We don't want to stay here any longer than we need to.'

'You think the Mexicans are on their way back?'

'Wouldn't you be?'

Abi backed the Hyundai up to the warehouse and got out. He slung the rucksack containing the codex and the crystal skull over his shoulder. 'Get the two of them out of the trunk. Be as rough as you like. They're both for the cenote, whatever happens. Doesn't matter what shape they're in. Nobody will ever find them. I doubt the guys that own this place are sub-aqua enthusiasts.'

Rudra and Asson manhandled Sabir and Calque out of the trunk of the car.

'Vau. You and Alastor take over from Oni and Berith at the machine guns. They'll be jaded and resentful by now. I'll let them loose on our prisoners in compensation. Give them a little entertainment to take their minds off things.'

'Okay. But do you really think we might have trouble?'

'Unlikely for another few hours. Unless they've got access to a helicopter, that is. The guys that own this joint might not even have called in yet. Why should they? Who in their right minds would attack an arsenal? But at some point they will. And then they're going to be very, very angry. Nobody likes cuckoos in their nest.'

Abi joined the others inside the warehouse. He dumped the rucksack unceremoniously onto a nearby counter, as if its contents meant nothing to him at all. 'It's a shame we don't have Lamia – that could have been really amusing. I love a quorum. We'd soon have

433

found out whether Mr Sabir is the gentleman he likes to think he is.' He stood for a while, weighing up his two prisoners. 'String the policeman up first. Strappado style. Arms stretched behind his back. I don't care if you dislocate the hell out of him. We'll see if Mr Sabir enjoys watching his friends whimpering in pain.'

Oni was beckoning to him from the corner of the warehouse. 'Abi, have you got a minute?'

'Can't you see I'm busy?'

'Seriously. I think you ought to come over here and take a look at this.' Oni was pointing to a trapdoor, now only partially covered by some of the packing cases they'd plundered earlier. 'I noticed this an hour or so ago when I came in for coffee. Didn't have time to check it out then, because there were only the two of us here. Don't you think we ought to take a look? Might be something of interest down there.'

Abi glanced over at Calque. Rudra had just finished roping him to one of the packing hoists. Sabir was seated between Calque's legs – his arms were tied behind his back at the wrist and the bicep.

Asson grinned when he saw the direction of Abi's gaze. 'This way the policeman can piss on Sabir's head when the pain gets too bad.'

'Hold off a moment. I want to check what's beneath this trapdoor first. You can boil me a kettle while you're waiting. And scissor off the policeman's shirt. We haven't got time for any finesse. We'll see if Mr Sabir likes eating parboiled copper.'

Oni pushed the packing cases aside. He wrenched at the trapdoor. It groaned a little, but didn't give. 'Hand me the Mini-Uzi. Now stand away, all of you, unless you want your teeth blown out.'

Abi clapped his hands over his ears. He had an inordinate fear of losing his hearing.

Oni let rip with the Uzi. Chunks of wood and metal shavings sprayed off the trapdoor. Oni tentatively kicked at it with the heel of his shoe. 'Once more.' This time the 9mm Parabellum slugs knocked a hole the size of a man's head in the woodwork. 'Okay. We're through.'

Abi let his hands flutter down from his face. He watched as Oni manhandled what remained of the trapdoor onto the warehouse floor. 'Go on down. I'll follow you.' He stepped brusquely across to the workbench and helped himself to a Maglite.

'Jesus and Mary!'

Abi hurried after Oni. 'What is it? What have you found?'

'Come down here and take a look at this.' Oni had located a light switch. The whole of the newly-revealed cellar area was now bathed in strip-lighting.

Abi ducked down the trapdoor staircase. He straightened up and then tossed the unused Maglite onto a nearby table. 'Holy shit.'

Thirty industrial-sized vats took up a full third of the available cellar space. Another third was taken up by a forty-foot long by ten-foot wide pile of shrink-wrapped plastic bricks – some were packed in shiny green polythene, some in white, some in blue. The remaining third of the floor-space was taken up by an armour-plated Hummer H1 Alpha and a massive display case containing a series of gold-plated sub-machine guns, diamond- and emerald-encrusted pistols, and about a thousand platinum-jacketed slugs. Some of the pistols had images of the Virgin Mary tooled into their grips, while others had fake Versace logos.

'This is no arms dump, Abi. This is a crystal meth factory.' Oni was crouched down over one of the polythene-covered bricks – he had his knife out and was tasting the powder. 'This is first-grade pure ice.' He shivered as if someone had just walked over his grave. 'Must be a ton and a half of the stuff here. Worth maybe five million dollars out on the streets.' He stood up. 'The narco-bling is probably worth an extra half mill on top. And how the hell did they get that Hummer down here? Must have a jump switch linking this place to the surface. Must have.' He began checking around, like a child searching for Easter eggs. 'Yeah. Here. Look.' He hit the switch. A section of the roof began to fan open – a separate, driveable section unravelled itself like the outstretched palm of a hand and came to rest with its rubber shock absorbers onto the concrete surface of the floor. Daylight streamed in from outside. 'Now that's cool. That's really cool.' Oni was caressing the built-in servo-control mechanism as if it were a woman. 'This is better than a thousand-dollar whore, Abi. We can truck this stuff out in the Hummer and stash it wherever we want. We've hit pay dirt at last.'

Abi shook his head. 'No we haven't. The watchman you killed lied to us. The bastard must have known all about this. His bosses weren't ever up at the border on any fucking arms deal – they were preparing for a major methamphetamine shipment. Look at this.' He pointed to a gold plaque screwed into the wall – the mountings were decorated with diamonds. 'Listen to what it says. "It is better to die fighting head on, than on your knees and humiliated; it is better to be a living dog than a dead lion. We don't kill for money. We don't kill women. We don't kill children. We don't kill innocent people, only those that deserve to die. Know that this is divine justice." Look. They've even made up their own personalized copy of the Bible, with extra pages tipped in – and I don't like the look of the leather it's bound in.'

'What? You don't think it's made of human skin?'

'It could be pig, but I'm not betting on it. The bastards

who made it are probably waking up just about now after a night out on the tiles in Cancun. One failed call to our friend Pepito and they'll be over here like a pack of ravening wolves. We get out of here, Oni. And we get out now.'

'What? And leave all this?'

'You can take a brick for your own personal use. How about that? But the rest stays put. What do you want to do? Rot your teeth out?'

99

The heavy machine guns opened up just as Abi reached the top of the stairs. He shook his head in mute acknowledgment of the instantly transformed status quo.

Asson straightened up from his perusal of the packing hoist's block-and-tackle system. He had Calque's arms stretched out behind him, and had already begun winching him partway up.

'Leave the bastard hanging, Asson. We've got trouble. There's enough crystal meth down those stairs to launch a spaceship. Berith. Rudra. Oni. You three go with Asson and arm yourselves. Dakini. Nawal. This is going to get very messy indeed. If you want to light out, then light out now. Crawl through the agave if you have to. Go straight to the airport any which way you can. Take the codex and the skull with you. Don't wait for us and don't look back. Nobody will think the worse of you for it. We'll stay in touch by cell phone.'

'We'll stay and fight with you. You'll need the extra guns.'

Abi stared at his sisters. Then he nodded. 'Okay then. We'll sort out the rest of this shit later. You'll all need grenades and sub-machine guns and pump-action shotguns. Pistols won't come into this. If they get that close to us we're dead anyway. When we leave the building we charge straight at them, giving them everything we've got. Vau and Alastor will cover us with the heavy machine guns. If we get into a siege situation, we're done for. They can call up reinforcements anytime they want and swamp us. So we have to sort them now. Before they know how few people they're really facing.'

100

As soon as the Corpus made their sortie from the warehouse, Sabir crawled directly underneath Calque so that the Frenchman could rest his feet on his shoulders.

'Christ Jesus! I couldn't have held that position much longer. My shoulders were about to dislocate.'

'Well you're going to have to hold it again. I intend to go and get you that chair. Then we're going to have to cut ourselves free. I have a funny feeling that any minute now this place is going to be riddled with incoming fire.'

'You're not going to leave me hanging here again, Sabir?'

'I've got no choice if we want to get out of here. Now tense your muscles. Keep your arms in as close to your back as possible. If you loosen them your shoulders are going to pop out of their sockets like a stick puppet.'

'*Oh putain!*'

Sabir eased himself away from Calque. He needed to get up on his feet. He rocked onto his knees and then surged forwards, like a sprinter at the start of a race. At the third stride he missed his footing and fell headlong. He was unable to protect himself because his hands and arms were securely tied. At the very the last moment he twisted his head to the right, so that only his cheek and ear slammed into the concrete. It still felt as though he had been blindsided by a steam iron.

'Get the chair, you damned fool. My arms are going.'

Sabir rolled over and over towards the chair. He shunted it hard, using both his legs like a scythe. The chair came to a stop just in front of Calque's swinging body.

'Quickly, damn you.'

Sabir rolled back the way he had come. He kicked the chair the last few feet.

Calque fished at it with one foot, and then pulled it towards him. He tottered for a moment, as if he was about to fall sideways, and then he somehow managed to regain his balance. 'Oh God. Oh God. I think my right shoulder is out of its socket.'

Sabir rolled over onto his knees. This time around he gathered himself for a moment or two before trying to rise to his feet. He stood up, rocking in place like an emergent jack-in-the-box.

'I can't hold this position for very long.' Calque was shouting in an effort to be heard over the gunfire.

The barrage from outside had redoubled in energy. Stray bullets began to thump into the warehouse. The ones that found their way in through the windows zipped and twanged through the warehouse's interior space.

Sabir went in search of a knife. He tried the kitchen area first. A stray bullet smashed through the window in front of his head, showering him with glass.

He turned his back to the chest of drawers and began feeling around behind him. Third drawer down, he struck lucky. He got his hands on a serrated bread knife with a fair edge to it. He hurried over to Calque.

'Here. Hold this between your knees.'

'Cut me free, you imbecile.'

'I can't with my back to you. I can't reach up that far. Do as I say.'

Calque scissored his knees together around the hasp of the knife.

'Hold it tight now.'

'What do you think I'm doing? I wish I'd pissed on your head while I had the chance.'

'Watch your language or I'll leave you hanging.'

'Yes, you'd do that, Sabir. That would be just like you.' There was an edge of raw humour in Calque's voice.

Sabir worked his wrists against the bread knife. The knife popped out from between Calque's knees and clattered to the floor.

'I don't believe this.' Sabir dropped to his knees and felt around behind his back for the fallen knife.

'I just felt a bullet tug at my shirt.'

'Then hold the knife tighter. Imagine you've got diarrhoea and you're trying to hold it in. If you tense your arse cheeks, your knees tense too.'

'Very funny. I've got a dislocated shoulder, you bastard. You try and tense your arse cheeks with a dislocated shoulder.'

Sabir ignored him and replaced the knife between Calque's knees. He began to saw away at his bonds for a second time. 'I'll shove this damned thing up your arse if you let it fall again. Do you hear me, Calque?'

'I hear you. If we ever get out of this, Sabir, remind me never to turn my back on you.'

Both of the men began to laugh.

'Damn!'

'What is it, Sabir?'

'I think I've jut been hit by a bullet.'

'Where?'

'I can't tell. My middle, somewhere. It felt like someone just rabbit punched me.'

'It was probably spent. Rabbits don't punch that hard.'

'Thanks. That's very comforting.' Sabir had his hands free now. His biceps were still bound, but he was able to bend one hand outwards, like a claw. 'I need to stand on your chair. Otherwise I can't reach you.'

'No. I can't take that again. I can't take the weight on my arm.'

'I'm going to do it anyway. It's our only chance. I can feel something wet down the front of my pants. We may not have that long.'

'You probably pissed yourself. Aaaahhhh!'

Sabir eased the chair out with his knee and positioned it behind Calque. He heaved himself up, balancing first on one leg, then on both. He twisted to one side and then stretched his forearm out to its full extent and began to cut.

101

Abi knew they were in trouble as soon as they emerged from the building.

Almost immediately, Berith jerked backwards and fell. The rest of them began to zigzag, firing as they ran.

The two heavy machine guns were still laying down covering fire. Then one of the machine guns abruptly stopped.

Abi could put two and two together as well as anyone. 'They've got snipers. Disperse. Get under cover. We haven't got a chance out here in the open. Get out wherever you can. Every man for himself.' He grabbed Dakini with his free arm and dragged her towards the field of blue agave. He saw Rudra doing the same thing with Nawal.

Asson appeared to lose his footing, catch himself, and then trip again, spread-eagling himself flat on the ground. He lay there for a moment as if he was winded, and then his head exploded in a frenzy of blood, brains and bone matter.

Primary shot and follow-up – the bastards had semi-automatics.

Abi realized the snipers must be up in the trees overlooking the warehouse. Maybe they'd even placed deer platforms up there for just such an eventuality? He cursed himself for not having taken more pains reconnoitring the place. He'd simply assumed it was exactly what it looked like, and left it there. Now he and his siblings were paying for his slapdash ways.

'We'll make for the cenote. That'll be outside their line of fire. We can regroup there.'

The second heavy machine gun stopped firing.

Abi was beginning to get a very bad feeling indeed.

102

Sabir placed his right foot in Calque's left armpit, and grabbed the Frenchman by the wrist. 'Are you sure you're up for this?'

'Of course I'm . . .'

Sabir jerked Calque's arm towards him before he could finish his sentence.

Calque's face went white. Then he let out a series of expletives under his breath. He was holding his left bicep with his right hand, tight to his side.

'Did I do it?'

Calque exhaled. 'You did it.'

Both men were lying pretty much flat on the ground in an effort to avoid any more ricochets.

'Let me see your stomach.'

Sabir raised his shirt.

'Spent bullet. I though as much. You're lucky. If that had hit you in the face you could have auditioned for Victor Hugo's *The Man Who Laughs*.' Calque glanced across the room. 'There's some tequila. We need to rinse your stomach with it. Then we need to get out of here.'

'We're never going to get out of that front door.'

'Then we go down. To the crystal meth laboratory they were talking about. We can hide in one of the vats if we need to. We can get out later. When things have quieted down.'

Calque crawled over to the counter and made a grab for the tequila bottle with his good arm. The firing had died down a little outside, and there was now only the occasional shot. 'How are you feeling, Sabir?'

'As you said. It was only a rabbit. But he must have been a big one. Someone's got it in for my stomach, what with the *datura* and the odd bullet. Do you think it's still in there?'

'It never was in there, you fool. The ricochet just messed you up a little.' Calque pushed Sabir back and raised his shirt. 'You're not going to enjoy this.'

'I suppose this is revenge for your arm?'

'You suppose right.' Calque upended the bottle.

'Oh Jesus. Jesus.'

Calque took a swig from the bottle and then handed it to Sabir.

Sabir took a long pull, and then shook his head. 'Come on. We can't lie here forever. Someone will come back and find us. I don't know who I dread more. The Corpus or the drug traffickers.'

Calque stood up. 'If we get hit now, it's fate.'

'Wait. Look. They left the rucksack with the codex and the crystal skull behind them. I'm taking it.'

'Okay. Why not? We might as well die rich.'

103

Abi knew they were near the cenote. But how near, he couldn't tell. Dakini was a yard or two behind him. Also flat on the ground. Twenty yards away he could see Nawal and Rudra. He'd lost sight of Oni maybe two minutes before. He was probably dead too. The guy was so huge he'd have made an obvious target for the snipers.

'We're going to have to make a stand of it. If we keep the cenote behind us, it means they can't get around and backshoot us. They'll have to come in from the front. You all still got your weapons?'

The others nodded.

'Okay. Let's run for it.'

He stood up and took Dakini's hand again. She'd never been a particular favourite of his, but now he felt a sudden protective urge towards her. It must be hard to be so damned ugly that people crossed the street to avoid meeting your eye.

They ran as fast as they could. For some reason the shooting had fallen away behind them. Then, as Abi ran, it redoubled in violence, but not, oddly enough, in their direction. Was Oni making a break for it? Were Vau and Alastor still alive?

Abi didn't care. He needed the cenote. When they got there they could plan their next move.

He glanced back over his shoulder. Nawal and Rudra were making ground. So he'd have four guns.

Not a lot. But it would have to be enough.

104

Sabir had to help Calque down the trapdoor steps. Calque's left arm hung uselessly at his side, and he was forced to descend the steps sideways, like a crab.

When they reached the bottom, Calque let out a soft whistle. 'I think we've just found our way out of here.'

With its 130-inch wheelbase, the armour-plated Hummer H1 Alpha looked like some low-crouching animal, waiting to pounce on its prey.

'Look at this, man. Gold-plated sub-machine guns. And how about these pistols. What sort of people gild their pistols?'

'You'd be better off looking for the Hummer keys. The firing's died down. Someone's going to be coming in here soon. And this will be the first place they make for.' Calque was staring at the bricks of crystal meth. 'Have you ever seen anything like it? You're looking at ten thousand ruined lives.'

'The keys, Calque.'

Both men began to search feverishly through the collected paraphernalia in the display cases. Sabir's military reservist training was beginning to come back to him. He selected two Heckler & Koch MP5Ks, because he knew how to use them, and also two of the gold-plated Smith & Wesson 469s. One had an engraving of the Mexican eagle figured into its grip, and the other an engraving of a Rottweiler.

'I've got them.' Calque snatched a set of keys off a communal hook set into the end of the display cabinet.

'Try them.'

Calque aimed the keys at the Hummer. There was an answering click-click. 'We're in business, Sabir. I hate to restate the obvious, but you'd better drive.'

Sabir threw the guns and the rucksack containing the skull and the codex onto the back seat. Then he helped Calque into his seat, and belted him in.

'Wait. Let me out again.'

'Are you crazy? We haven't got much time left.'

'Let me out, I say.'

Sabir unbuckled Calque from his seat and helped him from the vehicle.

'Find me something flammable.'

'For Christ's sake. You don't mean to burn this place down?'

'I'm a policeman, Sabir. Have been all my life. I can't let this filth get out onto the streets. If you don't want to help me, leave. But I've got to do it. I've just got to.'

Sabir sighed long-sufferingly. 'You're right. I should have thought of it myself, of course. But I was too busy thinking about my own skin and yours to give much of a damn about ten thousand complete strangers.'

Both men began ferreting through the detritus surrounding the industrial vats.

Then Calque straightened up. 'I saw hand grenades, didn't I?'

'Gold-plated ones. Yeah. They're probably fakes. You can't persuade me that anyone in their right mind gold-plates a live hand grenade. But we should be able to tell if they're real by the weight.'

'Worth a try, then. Crystal meth produces a highly flammable vapour. The slightest spark can ignite it. Chuck a grenade into one of those vats and the whole place would go up.'

'The death grip. How opposite. Yes. With us in it.'

'We'd have eight seconds. Isn't that right? Particularly if you back the Hummer right up to the vats, Sabir.'

'Five seconds, not eight. Just how long ago did you do your military service, Calque? The Franco-Prussian war? You like to live dangerously, don't you?'

'You're the one to talk. Shall we do it?'

'You take one vat and I'll do a second. But I won't have time to strap you back in. You'll have to take your chances leaning out of the window. If you fall out, I leave you. Okay?'

'Who did they torture, Sabir? You or me?'

'You, I'm glad to say.'

'Did you leave me then?'

'Stupidly, no.'

'Then you're not going to leave me now.'

447

Sabir backed the Hummer up to the nearest of the industrial vats.

Both men removed the safety pins from their grenades, keeping their fingers tight down on the spoons.

'You on the death grip, Calque?'

'The death grip. How apposite. Yes. I'm ready.'

'I'll call it. Okay? To a count of three.'

'Okay.'

Calque was half-in half-out of the Hummer's front window. He had a six-foot throw to the nearest vat. Sabir's throw was about eight foot. The Hummer's engine was throbbing quietly beneath them.

'One. Two. Three. Fire in the hole!'

Both men threw their grenades.

Sabir launched himself back onto the front seat, grabbing Calque by the shirt as he did so.

He engaged the Hummer's automatic gearshift and aimed it up the ramp.

Then he began to pray.

105

Emiliano Graciano Mateos-Corrientes stood down his snipers. He had the entire eighteen-hectare warehouse site ringed with his men. No one could escape. The ones that had run, shooting, from the warehouse, were all being herded towards the cenote – that was the obvious place for them to go. The rest were dead.

It was still somehow inconceivable to Emiliano that a bunch of gringos should come all the way down to the Yucatan simply to take over his crystal meth factory. Were they insane? Didn't they know he had fifty foot-soldiers under his command, all armed with the latest weapons? That he had snipers equipped with the most up-to-date 'light fifty' Barrett M107 rifles, complete with Leupold 4.5 x 14 Mark-iv scopes and AN/PVS-10 day/night optics? And that these snipers knew how to shoot the nipples off a three-year-old?

Crazy. Crazy.

He spoke briefly into his walkie-talkie.

What annoyed him the most was that the gringos had managed to time their incursion exactly right. Normally, there would have been a minimum of fifteen men guarding the factory. But someone – that fucker Pepito, probably – must have tipped the gringos off that with the consignment now ready, Emiliano was treating his foot-soldiers to the best whores and liquor his brothel in Mérida could provide. It was the Day of the Dead, man. His men expected to let their hair down once in a while. And he had the local police and most of the local politicians in his pocket. What did he have to fear? A bunch of gringos invading his territory? Jesus.

The Hummer burst out from the basement area of Emiliano's warehouse and up the escape ramp. The Hummer appeared to hesitate, and then made straight for his command vehicle. Emiliano could see two men in the front seats.

His mouth fell open.

As he watched, he heard two explosions deep in the bowels of his warehouse. Then there was a brief silence. It was followed by the equivalent of a vast intake of breath, as the meth vats caught fire. Then the warehouse literally burst from its moorings, its corrugated iron roof rising on a crest of over-heated air. When the roof was about thirty feet up, it flipped over onto its side, as if a sudden gust of wind had caught it.

Emiliano instinctively ducked down beside his Toyota Roraima. As he did so he noticed the rear of the approaching Hummer rising on a tide of hot air, and then smashing down again.

The Hummer was coming straight for his Toyota.

He threw himself to one side, shrieking.

The Hummer clipped his foot as it passed, pulverizing the bone, and twisting the foot three times around on the remaining skin and gristle. Emiliano hit the ground and rolled himself into a ball. He knew something terrible had happened to him, but not quite what.

When he tried to stand up, his leg collapsed beneath him, and he caught his first glimpse of the disaster that had been his foot.

He began shrieking in earnest, now, and calling for his mother.

106

Abi, Dakini, Nawal, and Rudra lay fanned out in the gravel at the cenote's edge, listening for any pursuit. Their guns covered a 180-degree radius, with the cenote behind them forming the remainder of the circle.

'Did you see what happened to Oni?'

'No. He just disappeared. I think he went in the opposite direction to us.'

'That figures.'

They all laughed. Their faces were streaked with dust

and sweat, and Rudra had Berith's blood all over him.

'I'm going to take a look around the corner of the cenote. See if there's any way out. Come running if I whistle.'

Abi got to his feet and began a hunched zigzag run towards the far corner of the cenote. There was a burst of machine gun fire, and he threw himself down flat. Then he wriggled back into cover.

'Thought so. They've got us surrounded. They can't bring their guns to bear on our backs, thanks to the cliff face, so they'll have to come at us from the front.'

'Is there any way out down there?'

Abi crawled to the edge of the cenote and looked down. 'No. No caves. No walkway. Nothing. It just goes straight down like a chimney. But at least we won't go thirsty. I hope to heck they don't bring in mortars. I wouldn't put anything past these guys.'

'How many do you think there are?'

'Too many.'

There was an explosion from over by the warehouse. The corrugated iron roof flashed briefly in its slow-motion trajectory over the trees, and then flipped over onto its side and vanished.

'What the heck was that?'

'Five million dollars' worth of crystal meth going up in smoke. Not to mention half a million dollars' worth of narco-bling. If they were angry before, think what they're feeling now.'

Rudra began to laugh. 'Are you telling me they succeeded in blowing up their own factory? What was that you said about mortars?'

Abi shook his head. 'It wasn't mortars. We left Sabir and Calque inside, didn't we?'

'Yeah, but they'd never have freed themselves in time. They'll have gone up with the building.'

'Are you sure?'

Rudra thought about it a little. 'No. You're right. I didn't tie that bastard Sabir's legs up, did I? Didn't think I needed to. What a fool. I should have hamstrung him while I had the chance. I thought we had all the time in the world.'

'All water under the bridge now.'

'What do you think is going to happen to us, Abi?' It was Dakini.

'We're going to die. That's what's going to happen to us. How, is up to us.' Abi turned over onto his back and eased his cell phone out of his pocket – then he began to crawl. 'If you see anybody, shoot. I'm going to see if I can raise the dead. Then I'm going to talk to Alastor and Athame. Then I'm going to talk to Madame, our mother. Any of you girls needs a powder break, this may be the moment to take it.'

107
___

'So what do we do now, Sabir?'

'We assume they're going to follow us and we keep on moving. We're not exactly inconspicuous in this beast. I feel like the Terminator.'

'The who?'

'Forget it, Calque.'

'And keep on moving where?'

'First off, to Ek Balam. I want to deliver the skull and the codex back to the Halach Uinic. Tell him what's gone down. I don't want him and Ixtab thinking that we lied to them. They must be going spare back there.'

'Such wonderfully descriptive language. No wonder you're a writer. And then what?'

'We drive to the airport.'

'To the airport? Without our passports? Mexican Customs will laugh in our faces. And then they will probably arrest us. Plus, you may not have noticed it, but I haven't got a shirt on.'

'We can soon rectify that when we get back to Ek Balam.'

'But what about the passports? They're in the Grand Cherokee. And Lamia took that. And she's got the two harpies from hell on her trail. How much chance do you think we have of ever catching up with her again?'

'I don't give a damn about Lamia and the harpies. But I do have to protect Yola.'

'Then telephone her, why don't you? Warn her to get away from Samois. Tell her and Alexi to go to a location you all know about and wait for us there. That we'll meet them later.'

'They don't have a telephone. They live in a caravan.'

Calque threw his hands up into the air – it was his usual way of expressing despair. Then he grabbed his left bicep and screwed up his face in agony. He began to keen gently to himself.

Sabir glanced quickly away to prevent himself from laughing.

Calque regained his poise after a moment or two and began ferreting about in the Hummer's nooks and crannies for a cigarette. 'What are you trying to tell me? That Gypsies who live in caravans don't use cell phones?'

'Not these Gypsies, anyway. And I seem to remember that you aren't that keen on cell phones yourself.'

Calque let out a cry of triumph. He speared a cigarette out of a crumpled pack and fixed it in his mouth. 'That's beside the point. It's the height of irresponsibility for Yola not to be contactable. You're her blood brother, Sabir – or whatever the hell it was you told me they nominated you. You knew the risks. Why didn't you insist?'

Sabir's expression darkened. He lit Calque's cigarette with a gold Dunhill lighter he'd found sliding about on the dashboard. 'Don't you think I know that? Don't you think I curse myself for my stupidity every damned minute of the day? Don't you think I'm feeling sick to my soul with every mile that Lamia gains on us? I fell in love with her, man. I was even thinking about asking her to marry me.' Sabir glowered at the sudden build-up of traffic ahead of them, as if the cars and their drivers were in some way responsible for his predicament. 'This may come as a surprise to you, Calque, but people like me don't fall in love that often. In fact, pathetic as this may sound, I can't honestly remember ever falling in love before. This was a major first for me. I'd pretty much reckoned I was immune. Steamrollering my way downhill towards a lonely middle age. That sort of malarkey. How right I was.'

Calque shook his head. His eyes were troubled. 'I'm sorry, Sabir. I know how you felt about Lamia. I didn't mean to make a joke of it. I hold myself personally responsible for bringing her into your life.'

'Ah, forget it. It wasn't your fault, Calque. I'm grateful to you, actually. I've felt alive again these past few weeks – which makes a welcome change from the stumbling zombie I was before.' He looked up from his driving. 'But can't you do anything for Yola and Alexi? Surely you've still got connections in the Police Nationale? Can't you get someone to go out to Samois and warn them?'

Calque flicked his cigarette awkwardly out of the window. 'You must be joking. What would I tell them? They'd think I'd contracted post-retirement syndrome. That I'd started to go out of my head. "Someone's out to get the Second Coming, comrades. You must intervene before it happens. It's a bunch of Gypsies you have to save. Only they never use cell phones. The woman's pregnant, just like the Virgin Mary. Except this time around it wasn't the Holy Ghost who impregnated her, it was her husband." "Oh, where are you speaking from, Captain Calque? Pierrefeu? Belleville? Broadmoor? Or some other insane asylum we don't know about?" "I'm out in Mexico, actually. Blowing up crystal meth factories. I'll be with you shortly."'

'I see your point.'

'How refreshing.' Calque reached back with his good hand and fetched the rucksack over onto his lap. He fished out the Mayan codex and began to leaf through its bark-paper pages.

'Staring at that isn't going to help us.'

'Indirectly, it might.'

'How do you figure that?'

'Because something's still bothering me, Sabir. I don't see how the Chilan and the Halach Uinic connected this man, Akbal Coatl, with Nostradamus. It's simply too much of a stretch.'

'That's the least of our worries.'

'No. It's important. There are still too many unanswered questions for my liking. I don't believe in magic, Sabir. There must be a logical connection.'

'Ah. Logic. That's the old Calque speaking.'

Calque fell silent for a while.

Sabir was silent too. After about five minutes of thinly disguised tension he began unconsciously drumming on the steering wheel. Every now and then he would jerk his head forwards as if responding to an abrupt change in his internal rhythm. He cast a speculative glance at Calque. 'Don't tell me you can read Maya glyphs? And Old Spanish?'

Calque shook his head without looking up. 'No. But I can read Latin. And the last part of this book is written in demotic.'

'Demotic? I thought that was Greek?'

Calque gave a long sigh and continued with his reading.

Sabir nodded sagely. He gave it another ten minutes. 'What does it say?'

Calque glanced up. He flared his eyes. 'I'll tell you if you promise to stop that damned drumming and light me another cigarette.'

'Okay. Okay.' Sabir raised both his hands off the wheel.

'You can still drive. I don't object to that.'

'Come on. What does it say, Calque?'

Calque waited for Sabir to light his cigarette. He took a long drag and allowed the smoke to drift out through his nostrils. 'It says that when Friar de Landa was called back to Spain in 1563 to answer for his crimes before the Inquisition, Akbal Coatl – or Salvador Emmanuel as he was known to the Spanish – did indeed accompany him.'

'Jesus. Talk about swimming with the sharks.'

'Akbal Coatl then went on to assist the Friar in his writing of the *Relación de las Cosas de Yucatán*, which was published three years later as part of a successful effort to disarm the critics of de Landa's scorched-earth policy.' Calque shook his head. 'Incredible. On the surface it makes no sense at all. Can you imagine how assisting de Landa to wriggle out from underneath the Inquisition must have felt to Akbal Coatl? After what de Landa had done to his people and their artefacts? And after what de Landa had made him do?'

'So why did he do it?'

'Because otherwise the history of the Maya people would have died with him.'

'Are you serious?'

'Deadly serious. The fact still remains that Bishop de Landa's book is the single most important document regarding Maya customs and practices we have left. It formed the backbone to the decoding of the Maya glyphs, Sabir. Even today, anthropologists and historians are forced to rely on it, in the absence of anything else.'

'So de Landa created a gap in the market by burning all the Maya codices? And then he filled it with his own book? That's cute.'

'Which Akbal Coatl probably co-wrote, and which de Landa then claimed as his own work.'

'You're fishing, Calque. You can't prove that.'

'You're right. Whoever really wrote it is irrelevant. The key words are "three years later", Sabir. The book was finished "three years" after Akbal Coatl and Friar de Landa arrived in Spain. Don't you see what that means?'

'Not offhand. No.'

'Nostradamus only died in 1566. It means that Akbal Coatl would have had three years, between 1563 and 1566, in which to hear about, and maybe even meet, the seer.'

'What? Are you trying to tell me that the Franciscans let Akbal Coatl travel wherever he liked? Gave him *carte blanche* to journey through Europe? That's one heck of a stretch.'

'No it's not. He was Friar de Landa's private secretary, man. He stayed in Europe with de Landa until 1572, when de Landa returned to the Yucatan as the province's first bishop, taking Akbal Coatl back with him. The man was de Landa's major apologist amongst the disenfranchised Maya. His amanuensis, almost. One of the key elements in de Landa's fight-back from the ignominy of his former position. During the three-year writing and researching of de Landa's book, Coatl would have been sent from monastery to monastery, and from abbey to abbey, to conduct research on de Landa's part, and to garner testimonials from his contemporaries to back up de Landa's claims in the ecclesiastical court.'

'Are you making all this up, Calque? How can you be so sure?'

'Because it's all here, Sabir, in black and white.' Calque tapped the book with the heel of his hand. 'There's a complete list of Akbal Coatl's journeys around Spain and southern France during the ten or so years he spent in Europe. With dates and locations. Look. Listen to this. In May 1566 – that's two months before Nostradamus's death, Sabir – Salvador Emmanuel, aka Akbal Coatl, travelled down from Avignon to the Franciscan seminary at Salon-de-Provence.'

'You're kidding.'

'Are you beginning to get the picture?'

'Look, Calque. I know for a fact that Nostradamus was buried in the Franciscan Chapel at Salon. He was tight in with the Franciscans by that time. He would have thought of it as an insurance policy against the Inquisition for his wife and children. That much I remember from the book I wrote. It was only later, during the French Revolution, that they dug him up and re-interred him in the Collégiale St-Laurent.'

'Well that makes even more sense then, doesn't it? The two men simply must have met. Nostradamus's reputation as a prophet was Europe-wide by that time. He was at the very height of his fame. Even the French Royal Family stopped off at Salon to visit him. For all practical purposes he was a member of the Establishment.'

'So you think they hatched this whole thing up together? A member of the Establishment, deep in with the Franciscans, and a Maya renegade? Sorry to play Devil's Advocate, Calque, but somebody has to.'

'I think Akbal Coatl asked Nostradamus for help as one member of an endangered species – the Maya – to another member of an endangered species – the Jews. This would have appealed to Nostradamus, whose sympathies were always with the underdog. I'm guessing that Nostradamus then told Akbal Coatl that he'd just had a vision of another member of an endangered species – the Gypsies – one day becoming the mother of the Second Coming. And, hey presto, the dates he'd been given might very well tie in with the Maya dates surrounding the ending of the Cycle of the Nine Hells.'

'Go on, Calque. Your capacity for lateral thought is enthralling.'

'So my guess is that the two of them would have pooled their knowledge. Wouldn't you? And that after Akbal Coatl left, Nostradamus would have taken the precautions we already know he took in protecting his 58 so-called 'lost prophecies'. Which weren't lost at all, needless to say – they were merely very well hidden. Then Akbal Coatl decides to fulfil his part of the bargain by backing the whole thing up in his secret book. Only two hundred years later the War of the Castes comes along, and the book is lost. But both of them – Akbal Coatl and Nostradamus – have factored in a failsafe mechanism.'

'The eruption of the Pico de Orizaba.'

'And two potential catalysts . . .'

'Me and the guardian.'

'Yes. You – or whoever else lucked onto the prophecies' trail – and the guardian. It's incredible, isn't it? But it makes the most perfect sense. Prophet meets protector of the sacred books. The possibilities are limitless. But, as you say, Sabir, in our present situation they take us nowhere. Talking about possibilities, though, is anyone following us yet?'

'Not so far as I can see.'

'I thought so. They have other things on their mind, no doubt.'

'What do you mean "no doubt"?'

'I think you hit their Big Boss.'

'What are you talking about, Calque? What Big Boss? And why haven't you mentioned this before?'

'I had more important things on my mind.'

'I didn't hit anybody.'

'Yes you did. When you nearly rammed the Toyota. Back there at the warehouse. Didn't you feel a crunch?'

'I missed the Toyota by a mile, Calque. I'm not that bad a driver.'

'Yes. But you hit a very large Mexican holding a walkie-talkie. He had a shiny suit on. The sort of suit only drug lords dare to wear – and believe me, Sabir, I know what I'm talking about. You smashed this man's foot. Surely you saw him?'

'I was too busy trying to get us out of there in one piece. And anyway, this thing has a snout the size of a condor's. Of course I didn't see him.'

'Well I think that's why we're not being followed. I think you inadvertently took out the enemy's commander-in-chief. I was going to tell you at the time, but then I got caught up in Akbal Coatl's book.' Calque steadied his left arm as they went over a speed bump. 'It might afford us just enough of an edge to stay in the clear.'

'I destroyed this man's foot, you say?'

Calque nodded, still grimacing from the pain in his arm. 'I love people like you, Sabir. You plough through life leaving a trail of wrecked bodies behind you. Only you never notice them. It must be a sublime knack to have. I only wish I could emulate it.'

'What about your associate, Macron? Have you forgotten about him so quickly? And who brought me back into this? It was you. And who brought Lamia into

460

this? You again. Calque, sometimes when I listen to you bullshitting away at me, I get this curious image coming into my brain.'

'Oh? And what image is that?'

'Of the pot calling the kettle black.'

108

The intravenous morphine was beginning to work. Emiliano Graciano Mateos-Corrientes lay across the rear seat of the Toyota Roraima, and watched as his personal physician bandaged his foot.

'You've got a compound fracture. Every hour you don't get to hospital makes you that much more likely to lose your foot. If you're lucky, only septicaemia will set in. If you're unlucky, gangrene will follow. There's filth in there. And bits of sock. And dust you picked up from the track. And polluted bone fragments.'

'Hand me that pistol.'

One of his lieutenants handed his pistol over to Emiliano.

Emiliano pointed it at the doctor. 'If I lose my foot, you lose your life. Do you get me? I have business here first. Before the hospital. You will accompany me.'

'But the police. They will see the smoke of the fire and they will come.'

'The police will not come. It has been explained to them and to the fire brigade that we are simply burning scrubland.'

'But it's the wrong time of year for the *milpa* slash and burn.'

'It's never the wrong time of year for the *milpa* slash and burn. Do you understand me, doctor?'

'I understand you.'

'Now get into the car. We are going to a baptism.'

109

'What did Madame, our mother, say?'

Abi shook his head.

'What is it, Abi?'

Abi sat up on his haunches and stared at his feet.

'What's wrong?'

'What's wrong? We've been played for suckers, that's what's wrong.'

'What do you mean?'

'She used us. That saint, our mother, used us as expendable camouflage.'

There was a shocked silence. Then Nawal shook her head. 'I don't believe you.'

Abi eased himself onto his side. He crawled closer to Rudra, Nawal and Dakini. 'Listen to me. First off, Lamia – our so-called "wayward sister". Well it turns out she wasn't so wayward after all. She was on the same side as us right from the start.'

'No.' Nawal shook her head. 'That's just not possible. I know Lamia. She might have passed back information to our mother, but she wouldn't have given herself to that man Sabir on anyone's say-so but her own. She was far too *pudique*. Far too conscious of her face.' She avoided meeting Dakini's tortured gaze – both she and Dakini had a great deal to cope with in that department themselves. 'And anyway, she would have confided in Athame. Those two were like this.' Nawal made a knot out of her hands.

'It's true, nonetheless. I've just had it from the horse's mouth. Madame, my ever loyal mother, thought that by coming clean she might provide me with a titbit of comfort at my moment of death.'

'You're not going to die, Abi. None of us is going to die.'

Abi laughed. 'The whole thing was an elaborate honey-trap to sucker Sabir into giving out the names she wanted. The Countess set it up so that Calque and Sabir would reckon they'd saved Lamia from a fate worse than death. It's a trick as old as the hills. They fell for it. And I fell for it, too. Hook, line, and sinker.'

'It can't be true. Our mother would have told us.'

'And give the game away? No. She wanted us outraged, angry, and alert. And she got what she wanted, as she always does. Lamia is heading back to France to kill the pregnant Gypsy. And we're the sacrificial lambs that helped get her there.'

'You must tell Aldinach and Athame immediately.'

'No I mustn't. After Madame made us destroy all our personal cell phones and replace them with pay-as-you-go, I made damned sure that I never gave out Aldinach and Athame's numbers to anyone. Just like I didn't give out yours. I didn't want people calling up at potentially sensitive times for a cosy fireside chat. So if those two don't decide to call our mother – and I somehow suspect they won't – that's it. She'll have no way of warning them off from killing Lamia. And they're just about to board a charter flight to London. So they'll have their cell phones switched off anyway while they're in the air.'

'To London?'

'First flight they could get. Lamia got out on a marginally earlier flight via Madrid. They found out that

463

much, at least. So the three of them should all arrive in Paris at just about the same time. There are only so many connecting flights available. All Aldinach and Athame have to do is wait. They'll probably catch Lamia straight out of Arrivals. They might even kill her right there in the concourse. Aldinach can sting like a bee with that scalpel of his. He's twenty metres gone before the person even knows they've been stabbed.'

The others shook their heads uncertainly.

Abi grinned. 'Look around you. We're probably surrounded by fifty invisible men, intent upon our deaths. And whose fault is that? Lamia's, Sabir's, and our mother's. In the absence of a *deus ex machina* reaching down and plucking us up into the sky, we're doomed.' Abi gave a resigned shrug. 'We can't touch our mother, but we can touch Lamia. And through her, Sabir. What have we got to lose?'

110

'There's my Cherokee.'

'I figured as much.' Calque glanced around the roof lot of Cancun International Airport's long-term parking. 'We're going to have to break into it, you realize that? And they've probably got banks of CCTV cameras here.'

'No we aren't.' Sabir felt in his pocket. 'I have the spare keys. I remembered them back at Ek Balam after we handed back the skull and the codex. While Ixtab was busy strapping up your arm and measuring you for a new shirt. They were in my overnight bag.' He dangled the keys in front of Calque's face as if they were cherries.

Calque rolled his eyes. 'Let's dump this white elephant of a Hummer then. We're going to have to scrub it clean of fingerprints. I don't want the maniacs we stole it from, and whose crystal meth laboratory we blew up, coming after us in France. I wouldn't put it past them to have a cosy in with Interpol.'

Sabir nodded. He tucked the Hummer away in a remote corner of the parking lot. With Calque's left arm out of action, it was Sabir who ended up valeting the cab.

When they were finished, Calque grinned. 'When we get back home you can pay someone to come and pick up the Cherokee for you and store it somewhere. That way no one will associate it with the Hummer. You simply mail them your keys, the parking ticket, a false name and address, and some cash. Then, in a month or two, you can come back here and pick it up, with no one any the wiser.'

'You've got to be kidding.'

'I am kidding.' Calque sighed. 'I think maybe neither one of us should ever set foot in Mexico again. In a few months' time, when you haven't reclaimed the car, the storage people will simply auction it off. That's the way these things play.'

'I liked that car. It held happy memories.' The expression on Sabir's face didn't match his words.

'Get over it, Sabir. She's not worth it. She played us both for fools.'

'I still don't understand how she could have pretended to that extent. She was a virgin, man. I'm certain of it. Not some Mata Hari type, used to seduction. Not some courtesan. And her face. How could the Countess be sure I would go for her? It stretches the bounds of credulity.'

Calque shook his head. 'Because the Countess understands men and what drives them. She made a study of us without our knowledge. She realized that you were a bleeding heart from the word go. And that I suffer from absent daughter syndrome. Then she launched her perfectly primed cruise missile at us.'

'Lamia told me she loved me. You can't fake that.'

'Oh yes you can. My ex-wife did it for years.' Calque leaned inside the Cherokee and felt around in the lockbox. 'We're in business, my boy. Both passports are still here.'

'So. And that's another thing. Why would Lamia leave us our passports? Her passport was in with them. All she needed to do was dump the two of ours in the nearest garbage can.'

'Why would she bother to do that, Sabir? She knew Abiger de Bale would kill us as certainly as night follows day. Leaving the passports would just facilitate the work of the Mexican police when they found our abandoned vehicle. That way they would have known for sure we hadn't left the country.'

Sabir slammed the Cherokee door and clicked the automatic lock. The expression on his face was bleak. 'Come on, Calque. Let's go and find ourselves a damned flight out of here.'

111

It started with the stun grenades. Emiliano's foot soldiers had brought up bullet-proof riot shields, and they were launching the grenades from behind them.

Abi, Rudra, Nawal and Dakini laid down as much blanket fire as they could, but it was clearly ineffective. Their ammunition was running out. The grenades were getting nearer by the minute.

Then Emiliano's men started in with the tear gas.

Dakini was the first one to jump into the cenote.

Snot and tears were streaming down Abi, Nawal, and Rudra's faces.

Nawal was the next to go. She felt semi-hysterical. She couldn't breathe. All she could think about was how the feel of cool water on her eyes would be.

Rudra watched both of the women leap into the pool. He dragged himself to the edge of the basin. It was a fifty-foot drop. The girls had both survived it. He could see them bobbing around in the centre of the pool, violently rinsing their faces.

He glanced back at Abi, shrugged, and then eased himself over the side. He dangled for a moment and then let himself fall. The feel of the water was an exquisite blessing. He let himself sink as deep as he was able, before scissoring his legs and making for the surface.

Abi plunged in beside him.

Both men scrubbed at their faces, desperate to see again. Desperate to get their weapons clear of the water before they became useless.

Fifty feet above them, Emiliano's foot soldiers were carrying their boss out of the Toyota on an improvised bier. The morphine had already started to give him hallucinations.

Emiliano grabbed his physician's arm. 'Give me more.'

'I can't give you any more. It would be too dangerous. Intravenous morphine is an unstable drug. There is only so much the body can take. You will already be hallucinating. Later, you will be constipated also.'

'To hell with the constipation. And I can stomach the hallucinations. Give me more morphine. I'm in pain, I tell you. My foot is burning up.' Emiliano screwed up his face, as if he were trying to clear his head through the drug-induced mist. 'But not so much that I become unconscious.

Do you understand what I am saying?'

'I can't give you any more, I tell you. It might prove fatal.'

Emiliano pulled a pistol out from underneath his blanket and shot the doctor. A single bullet, direct to the head. The doctor crumpled next to the bier like an empty suit of clothes. 'Fatal? That's what I call fatal, *pendejo*. Kick him into the cenote one of you.'

Emiliano's men were gathered in a ragged line just shy of the lip of the cenote. One of the men nudged the doctor's body with the toe of his boot until it toppled over the side. He made very sure that he was not outlined against the sky while he was doing it.

'Now pick up that syringe.'

'Yes, Jefe.'

'Do you see this vein in my arm?'

'Yes, Jefe.'

'Inject the morphine into it.'

The man aimed the syringe at Emiliano's vein.

'Squeeze out a bit first, man. You don't want air in there. When you think you've found the vein, draw a little back to check if there's blood. Then shoot me up.'

The man was sweating uncontrollably by this time. He dabbed at his forehead with his sleeve. He found the vein, drew up a little blood, then forced the plunger home.

Emiliano sighed. He laid down his pistol and pressed his finger firmly onto the spot. 'You got the other bodies?'

'Yes, Jefe.'

'Throw them in there too. The good doctor deserves some company.'

The bodies of Vau, Alastor, Berith and Asson were dragged to the lip of the cenote and kicked in.

'Anyone else still to come?'

'None of our own. You were the only one of us injured, Jefe. And none of their people escaped, bar the two in the Hummer.'

'We'll deal with them later. They won't be able to get out of the country without their passports. We can pick them up anywhere. They have to eat. They have to sleep. They have to take a shit.' Emiliano raised his chin in the direction of the cenote. The pupils of his eyes were enlarged out of all proportion to their original size. 'Constipation? That damn fool doctor. I told him to give me some more morphine. You heard me. Don't people obey orders around here any more?'

'Yes, Jefe.'

'The Hummer. It's got a Snooper on board, hasn't it? So when it next sends a text, we can fix its position by satellite?'

'Yes, Jefe.'

'Okay. Now you and your men go and explain the situation to the floaters. With sound effects.'

'Yes, Jefe.'

Half a dozen of Emiliano's men spread themselves out just shy of the cenote lip. Then they stepped forward in unison and began spraying the walls and surface of the cenote with bullets. After about a minute, they stopped.

Abi, Rudra, Dakini, and Nawal were still floating in the water. They hadn't been hit, just as Emiliano had intended, but they were confused and disorientated.

'Now explain to the floaters that they have to let their weapons and their cell phones sink. In full view of us up here. If they don't, we'll bombard them with hand grenades. It'll be like a butcher's shop down there. If they're not killed, they'll be permanently deafened by the concussion.' Emiliano snatched at something in front of his face. Then again. His cheeks were numb from the new hit of morphine. Mosquitoes were beginning to seem like hornets to him.

One of his men called down the instructions. Then there was a pause. 'They've done it. They're just floating there.'

'Now tell them not to go near the edge of the cenote. Not to try and climb up the sides. That if they do so, my snipers will kill them.'

'It's impossible to climb up the sides, Jefe.'

'Say what I told you to say.'

The man did as he was instructed.

'Now carry me to the edge. And bring me a chair.' Emiliano held out his arms and two of his men lifted him to the very lip of the cenote. Two other men brought him a fold-up director's chair. One of the men held the full weight of Emiliano's shattered foot in a loop made from another man's shirt.

Emiliano sat down. His foot was settled with fastidious care in front of him. After a brief lacuna, in which he stared across the cenote pit as if his eye had been caught by an unknown variety of flower, he leaned forwards and looked down at the pool below. He made a sweeping gesture with his hand.

'You see. You've got all your friends down there with you now.' He counted with his fingers. 'One. Two. Three. Four. Five. Six. Seven. Eight.' He snatched at the air again. 'Eight Little Gringos who've destroyed five million dollars' worth of my product. The question is, are you going to be able to repay me in some way? Right the wrong you have done me? With interest, of course. Two million dollars. And also two million dollars for my foot, let's not forget that. We'll call it an even ten for the sake of argument. Can you manage this? If so, I will winch one of you out of the pool to arrange it. If you can't, you will all stay in there until you drown. The pump hose has already been drawn up. And there is no other way out of the cenote. The walls are sheer. We've done this before, you know. It takes between two and three days, as a rule of thumb, for the will to live finally to evaporate. Give or take a day or two. And depending on sex, of course. Women float for longer, usually, having more natural buoyancy.' He lashed out at another mosquito.

Some of Emiliano's men were beginning to look a little concerned. But none of them wished to emulate the doctor.

'I'm going to the hospital now. Call out, if you want to take me up on my offer. Otherwise there will be ten guards stationed here at all times. If you try and swim for the walls, they will shoot you. If you try and use the floating bodies as buoyancy aids, they will shoot you. Do you get my drift?' Emiliano threw up one hand in an imperial gesture. 'Drift. Did you get that? A pun. A very good pun indeed, in the circumstances.'

112

Oni had been wounded twice early on in the fire fight. Once through the groin, and once through the right buttock as he turned to follow Abi's party towards the cenote.

It was for this reason that he had repeated the trick he had used at the Balancanché caves. It was more difficult when you were wounded and when you had no one to help you, of course. But Oni knew without a doubt that he would die if he didn't achieve it.

So he crawled in amongst the agaves and dug himself a trench with the stock of his pump-action shotgun. Then he sank into it, levering the earth out of the way with his hands. When he was satisfied, he pulled the earth back in on top of himself. It didn't need a heavy covering. He wasn't about to move anytime soon. Fortunately, the earth in the agave plantation had been burned and turned over recently. It was as soft as thistledown. More or less.

He lay facing upwards, with the shotgun tight to his side. His hip area was numb, and growing more so by the minute. He had left himself a small air-hole through which to breathe. He only hoped that nobody would actually tread on him. He didn't think he could maintain silence under those circumstances.

He lay there for so long that he started to go to sleep. His whole body closed down on itself like the quiet time at the end of his hatha yoga class. Oni managed to get his breathing so well under control, that, by the end, he was only taking about three breaths a minute. His yoga teacher would have been proud of him.

He heard the explosion at the warehouse. Then his cell phone vibrated. He ignored that for obvious reasons. Then he heard the stun-grenade attacks on the cenote. He knew exactly what was happening. He didn't need them to draw him a picture. The nine of them had bitten off more than they could chew. It was as simple as that.

After a further quarter of an hour, Oni stood up and brushed himself off. There was another flurry of gunfire from over by the cenote. Using his shotgun as a crutch, he limped past the burnt-out remnants of the warehouse and over to where he knew the Stoner had been positioned. It was still there. But Vau had gone. There was blood on the Stoner and sprinkled over the surrounding dirt. He'd liked Vau. He hadn't been the brightest button in the bag, but then Oni knew that he was no Einstein either.

Oni looked around for his stash of spare magazines. There were two drum belt containers left. He unclipped the existing magazine and replaced it with one of the drum belts. He put the other drum belt inside his shirt – 300 rounds – 150 rounds apiece. It wasn't a lot, in the circumstances.

He thought for a moment, and then picked up the used drum belt he'd discarded earlier and tapped it against his arm. Maybe another 50 rounds. Better than nothing. He put that inside his shirt too.

He began to limp in the direction of the cenote.

113

Pretty soon Oni could hear someone shouting. It was a man sitting in a director's chair at the very lip of the cenote. Oni shook his head in disbelief.

The man and about thirty other men were all clustered in a bunch and staring into the pool. His remaining brothers and sisters must be down there. It seemed obvious to him.

He raised the Stoner and hitched it under his arm. Oni was nearly seven feet tall. The three-and-a-half-foot long Stoner looked like a child's toy in his hands.

The man in the director's chair raised one of his hands triumphantly.

Oni began to shoot.

The first drum was exhausted in a little under twenty seconds. He replaced it with the second drum. He got through that in under fifteen seconds. Then he felt around inside his shirt for the half-used drum.

Most everybody was dead. The lip of the cenote had crumbled away where they'd all been clustered together. Shooting them had been a little like playing one of those arcade games he'd been fixated on as a child. The one where the cowboys keep coming at you and your only chance of beating them is to keep on shooting.

He burped the Stoner at a moving man. Then at another. Not much left in the drum now.

He walked to the edge of the cenote and looked down. The water was littered with bodies. Some were still thrashing around. Others were just floating, face down.

'Abi? Are you down there?'

'I'm here.'

'Who else is alive?'

'Rudra, Nawal, and Dakini.'

'Oh, I'm glad. I thought I'd lost you all.'

'Can we come up?'

'Yes. You can come up now. I'll throw down the hosepipe for you. Everybody left up here is dead.'

Oni hurled the Stoner to one side and limped across to where the pump hose was neatly furled at the very lip of the cenote.

There was a noise behind him. He turned, just a few feet short of the hose.

Emiliano was on his knees. The morphine had temporarily numbed him to the Stoner bullets that had ripped through his body.

As Oni watched, Emiliano snatched at a mosquito that was hovering in front of his face.

Then Emiliano raised his pistol and shot Oni in the head.

Oni toppled over the lip of the cenote. There was a pause. Then a mighty splash.

Emiliano smiled. He glanced down into the cenote. Abi, Rudra, Dakini and Nawal were floating fifty feet below him, watching. There was no way out for them now.

Emiliano looked down at his wounds. There was no way out for him either. He touched the pistol barrel to the roof of his mouth and pulled the trigger.

PART THREE

1

Lamia de Bale was feeling the weight of the world on her shoulders. It was as if the futility of everyone else's life was accruing to – and therefore being encapsulated by – her own. In deciding to leave Sabir without speaking to him, and without any attempt at an explanation, she was aware that she had closed an opened door. Now, three miles above the Atlantic Ocean, she felt the loss of its possibilities without fully understanding why.

She waited until half an hour into the Iberia flight before getting out of her first-class seat. She had chosen the premium seat to ensure that she both entered and exited the plane after all the other passengers had cleared the terminal – airlines, she knew, made exceptions for their first-class passengers, and catered to their whims. It also gave her access to business class and economy class, without giving either of those two areas access to her.

She had lied back in France when she had told Calque that Madame, her mother, had confiscated her money and her credit cards, and that only at the last minute had she had the providential foresight to conceal her passport inside her underwear. In point of fact she had hidden her passport, credit cards, and cash money in a traveller's pouch looped onto the back of her belt and neatly flipped over to lie flush along the inside edge of her slacks – a loose blouse had completed the picture, and had served to protect her from the customary stares men give to young women's bottoms. Even young women with catastrophic birthmarks.

She had then, at the first possible opportunity, cached the credit cards beneath the base of her powder compact, and rolled her folding money inside a number of Kotex Super Plus tampon tubes, which she had then re-wrapped and re-glued so that they looked fresh from the shop. If either Sabir or Calque had gone through her things, they certainly hadn't found either one of her secret stashes. Men had an in-built reluctance to sniff around women's private knick-knacks – it was as if they didn't want to know what artifices and grimy little realities lay behind the surface appearance they valued so much.

And Lamia, of course, knew all about surface appearances. She had spent her life trying to avoid acknowledging the effect of hers on others. It was hard being a woman with a damaged face. People responded to you in one of two ways. They either showed their repulsion by avoiding you – or they overcompensated for something they were relieved not to be suffering from themselves, and sickened you with their pity.

Madame, her mother, had tried to sweeten the pill a little – financial security counted for a lot when you felt vulnerable in other areas. And Lamia was physically better off, when push came to shove, than all three of her sisters, and at least four of her brothers. So she was in the upper quadrant of the population as regards financial security, and the middle quadrant as regards disabilities. But until she had met Calque, and then, later, Sabir, she had found it impossible to respond to men without suspecting them of hypocrisy – they pretended to want the whole of you, when in reality they only wanted the hormonally charged areas they were hardwired to seek out.

The truth of the matter was that Lamia had secretly craved being sought after and pursued – just like any normal, unmarked, woman – but her face and attitude had either put men off or obviated their interest in her altogether. Lamia shrugged at herself in the powder-room vanity mirror – well you couldn't have it both ways.

Joris Calque had genuinely seemed to see beyond the surface of her face, however, and Adam Sabir had astonished her with his capacity for blinkered sensuality. She was convinced that Sabir truly believed he loved her, and a part of her sincerely loved him. But she was her mother's daughter, and she had entered into the arrangement to leave all sides in ignorance of where she truly stood – and by that she meant both Laurel and Hardy (aka Sabir and Calque) and the Corpus – with her eyes wide open. The fact that she felt sympathy, affection, and even love for the two men she had always intended to betray, was beside the point. She had a duty to perform, and perform it she would.

She eased herself through into the business-class section and began a steady perusal of all the passengers. Whenever she reached one of the lavatories she waited until it was vacated before continuing with her search of the plane. It took her a full thirty minutes to convince herself that none of her brothers and sisters were anywhere on board – if they had been, she would have escaped back to the first-class section and relied on the stewards to do the rest.

She had been made aware, of course, by Madame, her mother, that the Grand Cherokee might at some point be seeded with a tracker, and so she was labouring under no delusions as regards Abi's eventual ability to pinpoint her whereabouts at the airport. Her only advantage over both him and Sabir had lain in the speed with which she had made her decision to depart from the *touj*. Madame, her mother, wanted her to remain a free agent, and a free agent she would remain.

She returned to her seat and adjusted it to the flattest possible position. She needed to sleep. The past ten days had taken their toll on her, and she felt physically as well as mentally wrung out. She closed her eyes.

She was immediately met by the image of Sabir pushing her gently down onto the bed back at the Ticul motel. Of the feel of his hands on her body. Of the gently invasive pressure as he had first made love to her. Of her response to his lovemaking, at first tentatively, and then willingly, enthusiastically, ecstatically.

She shook her head in a violent effort to clear it of the unwanted images, but still they remained, like the fragments of another life.

2
—

Lamia arrived at Madrid Airport in good time for her connecting flight to Paris. She ignored the transit lounge, however, and after purchasing some clothes, a carry-on bag, and a few essential items at the airport shop, she descended to the taxi rank and told her driver to take her to Madrid's Atocha railway station.

Whilst on the plane she had used Iberia's in-flight internet service to book herself a Gran Clas private cabin on the Elipsos Francisco de Goya 'Talgo Night' Trenhotel, leaving from Madrid at 6.15, and due to arrive in Paris's Austerlitz train station at 8.27 the following morning. She was the only one of her brothers and sisters who knew the location and identity of the Second Coming, and she was certain that if she could only evade both them and the French border police – in the unlikely event that Calque had managed to milk some of his old connections for a favour – then she would be home clear. Explanations would come later.

She knew that the 'Talgo Night' train made a short stop at Blois, in the Loire Valley, before reaching its final destination in Paris, so she had decided to alight there and bribe a taxi driver to take her straight to Samois. What was it? A hundred kilometres door-to-door? She'd be at the camp in time for breakfast.

She had flirted briefly with the idea of using a public telephone box to call her mother and tell her that everything was still on track, but she had just as quickly discarded the idea. The logic behind all her past actions had been that only Milouins, Madame Mastigou, and Madame, her mother, would ever be privy to her hidden agenda. There were numerous other outside-the-loop servants scattered throughout the Domaine de Seyème household capable of listening in to a conversation, and who was to say that the French police, given their notoriously cavalier attitude towards personal privacy, weren't still bugging the house in unconscious mimicry of Joris Calque?

No, blanket secrecy and telephone silence were the only way in which Abi, Vau, and the others could ever have been tricked into keeping all their concentration on Sabir and Calque – and for this they truly needed to believe in Lamia's role as a fellow traveller in the enemy camp.

Sabir and Calque had had to be won over in the same way. The pair had been justifiably suspicious of Lamia from the very start. Only via the most rigorous self-discipline had it been possible for Lamia to manoeuvre herself into a strong enough position to build up a sufficient reservoir of knowledge about Sabir to be certain of getting the information she wanted – and when she got it, of being able to use it with impunity.

Lamia allowed herself to relax in the comfort of her 'Talgo Night' stateroom. It was nice being able to pamper herself again. She'd order an early supper to be brought directly to her suite, and then she'd take two sleeping pills and attempt to sleep a clear eight hours without ever once thinking about Sabir. She could count on the steward to wake her up well before Blois with her breakfast.

She had never killed anyone before in her life – far less a pregnant woman and her unborn child. That prospect, although a necessary one, still caused her some distress. But she was confident that she'd get over it.

3
–

Yola Dufontaine had spent most of the previous day fighting off a relentless migraine. She had no idea what had triggered it, but it had been accompanied by repeated images of her honorary blood brother, Damo Sabir, wedged inside the cesspit at the Maset de la Marais, just as she had found him, five months before, when she and Sergeant Spola had broken in to rescue him.

In her waking dream, Sabir had once again been dying from the distilled snake venom he had secreted in his mouth to kill Achor Bale with. But this time around, Yola was unable to force him to vomit by drenching him with mustard powder and salt water, just as she had done in real life. Instead, she knew for a certainty that he was going to die. But the curious thing was that in this new, fanciful version of events, it wasn't Sabir who was taking his leave of her, but rather she of him.

When she told her husband, Alexi, about the migraine and the waking nightmare he had said, quite simply, 'You are three months pregnant, *luludji*. The morning sickness has stopped. Maybe hallucinations is the next thing you women get? Nothing can possibly surprise me about pregnancy any more.'

Yola hadn't known exactly what she had wanted Alexi to say, but it hadn't been that. Now she wished that she could get back in touch with Sabir and reassure herself that all was well with him. He and the *curandero* were the only two people on earth who knew her secret – not even Alexi was privy to it, for reasons that still eluded her, but which were probably related to her fears about his occasional proclivity for binge drinking, and the tearaway tongue that ensued. If Alexi even once blabbed in the camp about her being the mother of the Second Coming, the cat would really hit the skylight, showering them all with broken glass. Best not.

The *curandero* was, as always, on the road to somewhere, and therefore impossible to contact – he would either turn up or he wouldn't. Sabir, on the other hand, lived a more static life.

Now, still unable to sleep, Yola rummaged around inside her and Alexi's caravan until she found where she'd hidden the piece of paper Sabir had scribbled his telephone number on. Then, well before dawn, she started down through the woods for Samois and the nearest public telephone booth. Sabir had explained to her that New England was many hours behind France in terms of time, and she wanted to try to catch him before he went to bed.

4

Athame and Aldinach had waited at Paris's Orly Airport from 16.10 in the afternoon until an hour after the final Iberia flight of the evening arrived in from Madrid at 22.35. In this way they missed both Lamia's entry into France, via the 'Talgo Night' train and the Franco-Spanish border, and also that of Calque and Sabir, who had secured themselves last-minute seats on Aero Mexico's Cancun to Roissy/Charles de Gaulle flight, which touched down at 23.10 the same evening, but at a different airport altogether.

When they were convinced that Lamia wasn't going to make a belated exit from the arrivals lounge, the pair tried and failed to contact Abi's cell phone number for the fifteenth time that day. They then debated for a moment or two about whether to call Madame, their mother, for news, but their upbringing had been so strict, and their sense of hierarchy, in consequence, so acute, that they decided to leave things well enough alone for a further twenty-four hours. They had their orders from Abi. They knew what they must do. Lamia must simply have decided to fly the coop once and for all. And the temporary breakdown in telecommunications must be because Abi and the rest of the Corpus, having milked Calque and Sabir of whatever secrets they had left to give, were already on their way back to France, and therefore temporarily off air.

The pair then hired themselves a rental car from Avis and drove the eighty kilometres separating Roissy from Samois, arriving in Samois village square at a little after two o'clock in the morning. Then, exhausted from their journey and the fruitless wait at the airport, and dead certain that they weren't going to find either a hotel room or the Gypsy camp at that unholy time of the night, they settled down to sleep in their car.

5

—

Calque and Sabir had also hired themselves a car. But they had one major advantage over the others – they already knew the location of the Gypsy camp. Furthermore, they were acting on the assumption that Lamia must already be well ahead of them, which provided them with an extra vested interest in hastening to their destination.

Sabir drove like a demon through the outskirts of Paris. At one uncertain moment, when it wasn't immediately obvious which side of a concrete bifurcation barrier Sabir intended to make for, Calque had rammed both his feet down onto the floor like Fred Flintstone.

'For God's sake, man, it won't solve anything if we get pulled over by the police. Or if we engineer ourselves a head-on collision with a wall. We're either in time or we're not. It's two in the morning. The night duty *pandores* have nothing better to do than to pick up speeding idiots like you. It's either that, or pursue real criminals, with all the bureaucracy that that entails. You are doing 200 kilometres an hour in a 130-kilometre-an-hour speed district, Sabir. They'll throw the book at you and toss away the key with it. You'll be lucky if they don't box-flatten the car and charge you for the haulage.'

'You sound just like a policeman.'

'I am a policeman.'

Sabir had a clear picture in his head of Yola pregnant. The thought of her dying, after all they had been through together, was the stuff of nightmares. She had undoubtedly saved his life back at the Maset de la Marais, just as he had saved hers down at the river, when Achor Bale had tossed her into the ice-cold water like a used rag-doll. She, Alexi, and he belonged to each other. The blood tie that he had inadvertently entered into with Yola's late brother, Babel Samana, was only a small part of it. He felt responsible for her and for the unborn child to whom he would be serving as *kirvo* – the Gypsy version of an adoptive godfather. It would be up to him to both christen and baptize the child, and also to support him with money and with mentoring whenever necessary. It would be a lifelong commitment.

Sabir had been looking forward to all this more than he cared to admit. He had no children of his own, and now that his burgeoning relationship with Lamia had been cut off at the neck, he suspected that he never would have. It was becoming painfully obvious that he wasn't cut out for the world of conventional relationships.

'What time is it?'

Sabir gave a small jump. He peered down at the car's clock. 'It's 2.15.'

'Are you intending to head straight to the caravan?'

'Yes. Do you have you a better plan?'

'No. But I dearly wish we had a weapon of some sort. That hermaphrodite one. Aldinach. He struck me as particularly sinister. He was all set to skewer you back at Ek Balam.'

'He wouldn't have stopped with me, Calque. He had you in his sights too.'

'Yes. But somehow knowing you were for it first was very comforting to me.'

485

Sabir burst out laughing. He let up a little on the accelerator.

This had been Calque's plan all along, and he let out a small sigh of gratification. Dying in a car accident on the Paris *périphérique* had never been one of his ambitions. 'I still can't believe that Lamia intends to harm Yola and her child. We can't have misread her to that extent.'

'Maybe not. Maybe we simply misunderstood her motives right from the start, and piled error onto error? My father always told me that one isn't the sum of one's past actions.'

'But we haven't misunderstood the other two. They mean Yola harm, and we have to stop them.'

'Whatever it takes?'

'Whatever it takes.'

6

Lamia had been counting on the presence of the taxi driver to help convince Yola of her bona fides – if a total stranger asks you to accompany them in a taxi, it is marginally less threatening than if they appear, out of the blue, and try to inveigle you into their own vehicle. Fifty kilometres short of Samois, however, she changed her mind and ordered the taxi driver to take her to the car rental section at Orly Airport. It simply wouldn't do for Yola and her to be connected in any way at all in the mind of a third party.

She rented herself an inconspicuous Peugeot, and then drove the remaining forty kilometres to Samois, arriving in the village at a little after 7.30 in the morning. She intended to ask for directions to the encampment at the bakery – which was inevitably the first shop open in a village, and the font of all gossip – but almost immediately she saw a young Gypsy woman single-mindedly picking her way through the early morning shoppers to the public telephone booth.

Lamia parked her car in the village square. She got out and stretched. Then she wandered, as if unintentionally, towards the booth.

The Gypsy woman was having difficulty coordinating the dialling of a number she had written on a piece of paper, the use of her phone card, and the control of the handset.

Lamia pretended that she was waiting for the booth to be free. 'Can I help you? I could hold the piece of paper and call out the number for you while you dial.'

The Gypsy woman looked Lamia over. Lamia forced herself not to look down, in return, at the woman's stomach. It was too early yet for much to show, so a glance in the wrong direction would give her away before she even had a chance to establish herself as a potential friend. And maybe her hunch was wrong? Maybe this woman was not Yola, but another person entirely? At least, then, she would be able to find out the location of the camp.

Yola took in Lamia's birthmark and the non-assertive clothes. She had seen her pulling up in the Peugeot, and knew that she was alone. A well-meaning *payo*, then – they turned up all the time. Some even wanted to become Gypsies themselves, and live the so-called romantic life. What a joke.

Yola nodded, although without smiling. 'Yes. Please do this.'

Lamia studied the sheet of paper. It was a 001 number. France to the United States. She decided to take a calculated gamble, even though she had no idea whose the number really was. If the woman wasn't who she thought she was, then nothing would be lost. 'But this is Adam Sabir's number, isn't it?' She hesitated, as if unsure of her ground. 'You must be Yola, then? Yola Samana?'

'I am Yola Dufontaine.'

'Oh yes. Of course. You're married now. To Alexi. Adam told me.'

Yola frowned. It was early in the morning. In a small village miles from anywhere. It was impossible that she could have been followed – she had only made the decision to walk down to the phone booth at the very last moment. What did this woman with the marred face want from her? Why was she here? 'You know Adam?'

'I'm his girlfriend.'

Yola blushed. It was a rare thing for her, but the strawberry birthmark on the woman's face was so categorical – so impossible to miss – that it was almost as if it spoke to you of its own accord. The birthmark was telling her that, yes, you thought I could not attract the attention of a man. Summon up his desire. Seduce him. But you were wrong.

'His girlfriend?'

'Yes. We've just been in Mexico together. I came back yesterday. I came out here especially to find you. So it's incredibly lucky we've run into each other. I can tell you now that you won't find Adam at home. He's still in Mexico with Joris Calque. They are trying to arrange for temporary passports, after their own passports were stolen. But the only place to get such things is in Mexico City, at the American and French Consulates. And the two of them are stuck in Cancun. I still had my passport, so Adam asked me to come out here and find you. I was just on my way up to your camp. But I wanted to buy some croissants first. To bring as a present.'

'As a present?'

'Yes. In the absence of flowers. I have been driving all night.'

'Flowers?' Yola was feeling nonplussed. Who was this strange woman who appeared to know so much about her? And what extraordinary stroke of chance had brought her here, just as Yola was preparing to contact Sabir for the first time in three months? 'Why did Damo tell you to contact me?'

'Oh. Damo. That's your Gypsy name for him, isn't it? He told me about it.'

'Are you really his girlfriend?' Yola was staring at Lamia as if she might be able to sense if the other woman was lying simply through some antediluvian, beyond rational, female instinct.

'How can I prove it to you?' Lamia smiled to hide her uneasiness. Yola's eyes were stripping her bare. No Frenchwoman would ever have looked at her with such a frank and unremitting gaze. She realized that she would have to dig deep in order to come up with something capable, in and of itself, of breaking through the reserve that one race sometimes feels in the presence of another – that one woman can sometimes feel in the presence of another, when both, without being previously acquainted, are nonetheless intimately connected through their mutual love of a third party. 'I've got it. This will sound silly, I know. But have you ever seen Adam without his clothes on? I don't mean in the obvious way, of course. I know you two were never involved like that. But casually. Like a brother.'

Yola shrugged. But her eyes held Lamia's in a level gaze. Woman to woman. 'Yes. I have seen him. On a number of occasions. Both sick and well. Once, even, when I was going to castrate him. When I thought he had killed my brother.'

Lamia's breath caught in her throat. 'He never told me about that.'

'He wouldn't have done. It is something we both have forgotten.' Yola cocked her head to one side. 'Why have you asked me this?'

'Because you would know about his scar.'

'Go on.'

'I, too, know about it. For obvious reasons.'

'Where is the scar?'

'There are two. One is the main scar. The other is a drainage scar. From when he lost a kidney in his late twenties thanks to a congenital malformation. The drainage scar is below the main scar. Both are very beautiful.'

Yola laughed. 'You finds his scars beautiful? Damo really must have closed your eyes.'

'He finds my face beautiful.'

Yola gave a slow nod. The expression on her face began to transform itself from one of wariness into one of acceptance. 'Your face is beautiful. In our tribe, if a person has a mark on their face or body, we say that they have been touched by *O Del*'s own hand. That it is a mark of His especial favour.'

'*O Del?*'

'It is our name for God.'

'Do you really say that?'

'I promise you.'

'It is nice to hear such a thing.'

Both women stood looking at each other. Still measuring each other up. Yola was the first to break the silence. 'Why does Damo want you to speak to me?'

'Can we talk in a less public place? I can drive you somewhere.'

'No. We must talk here.'

Lamia glanced around. The longer she remained in the

public arena, the more likely someone was to remember her – she was not, after all, inconspicuous. She decided that she must get her point across as swiftly as possible – get Yola out of there and into an isolated location without further ado. She had bought herself a lock-knife back at Madrid airport, in a hardware store situated just outside the main departure gates – rather surreally, for an airport shop, the place specialized in locally sourced Toledo steel.

Milouins had shown her exactly where and how to strike when she, and Madame, her mother, had been preparing their plans. The way he had explained it, it would only take one blow. Both child and mother would be dead in seconds, with very little pain. All she'd have to do would be to curl Yola's hand about the haft of the knife, and then leave the mess for the police to sort out. Suicide as a result of pre-natal depression? Internecine Gypsy feuds? There was fertile ground for potential obfuscation.

'The Corpus Maleficus are after you. We encountered them in Mexico. Through a terrible piece of bad luck, they learned who you are and who you are carrying.' Lamia motioned with one hand towards Yola's stomach. 'Adam sent me out here to warn you. To get you away from the camp and to a safe place. He will be over here himself in maybe two days, when he gets the passports sorted.'

All the colour drained from Yola's face. 'What did you say? About who I am carrying?'

'Listen to me, Yola. During a hallucinatory experience in a *touj*, deep in the Yucatan, Adam inadvertently let slip that you were to be the mother of the Second Coming. He was half crazy with *datura* at the time. And we had been the subject of a number of extreme experiences in the run-up to the séance, so he wasn't in his right mind to start with. The drug just made it worse. We thought we were finally amongst friends. That all the people present would be instrumental in welcoming the birth of your child. In promulgating the good news. But a member of the Corpus Maleficus was also in the room. He heard Adam's words. Now he is coming over here to kill you. I am just ahead of him. I need to take you to a safe place where we can wait for Adam and Calque. You do believe me, don't you?'

'I believe that you are Damo's lover. I can see it in your eyes. Women can't lie about such things. Emotions like that go deeper with us than they do with men.'

Lamia could sense the blood flushing into her face. She tilted her head a little to one side, in an old habit she had of protecting herself when she felt particularly threatened. 'Yes. They do.' Lamia could sense that this was her moment. If she blew this chance, she would be forced to act prematurely, and in a public place. It would be a disaster. It would mean exiling herself for life from everything she knew and cared for – but it would be a sacrifice Madame, her mother, would expect her to make. 'Will you come with me? We can go back to the camp if you want. Fetch whatever you need. We would only need to be away for a few days.'

'Can't Captain Calque and his people protect me?'

'He is no longer a policeman. He retired, Yola. A little while after you met him. He is helping Sabir now. But on a strictly private level. They are both working together on this. We travelled in a group through Mexico. Captain Calque is a good man.'

Yola nodded. 'Yes. He is. For a *payo* he is a good man. He let me collect my brother's hair from the morgue so we could bury him within the allotted time.'

'Yes. He told me that.'

Yola straightened up. Early comers to the bakery were already eyeing both women with suspicion. One was a

Gypsy, and one was freak. Yola felt an unexpected degree of kinship with Lamia. She understood only too well from her own experience why the other woman might not want to remain in the full public gaze. 'Okay. I go with you. If Damo says I should trust you, I will trust you. He would never do anything against my interests. But first we go to my caravan. We collect Alexi. He goes with us.'

'Of course.'

Yola hitched her shoulders. 'Maybe I should call this number anyway?'

'There's no one there. I promise. You can call it if you want to.'

'And Damo? Does he not have a phone he carries?'

'It was stolen. Along with his passport, his money, and his credit cards. And Calque never uses a cell phone anyway. He's a technophobe.'

'A what?'

'He hates modern technology. He works entirely from his mind.'

'Yes. Yes he does. That is what Damo told me. That is what I have seen for myself. Come. Let us go to your car. I don't need to call the number.'

The two women headed for Lamia's Peugeot. On a whim, Lamia darted into the bakery and bought a large bag of croissants and three baguettes. She was counting on them to provide her with a further level of camouflage. How could anyone think that a young woman loaded down with bread and croissants could possibly be a threat?

It was this five-minute delay, however, that dictated the way future events would pan out. For Athame, catching the fragrance of freshly baked bread wafting towards her from the bakery, blithely stuck her head above the door frame of the car she and Aldinach were sleeping in, and wound down her window.

7

The clutch on Sabir and Calque's hire car burnt out just north of Melun.

'I don't believe it. I don't fucking believe it.' Sabir hammered on the steering wheel. 'Fucking rentals. Fucking assholes. Why don't they fucking service their fucking cars?'

Calque stared at him. 'Have you finished, Sabir? There is nobody here but me to hear you. And I'm all for swearing alongside the next man, but at 2.30 in the morning, it can be a little hard on the nerves. And you've been riding this car like it's a Formula 1 Ferrari. Not an imported hatchback that has been used by a hundred people already. And all of them with markedly different gear-changing techniques.'

Sabir collapsed back into his seat. 'What do we do now?'

Calque pondered for a moment or two. 'We find a telephone. We phone the rental company. They send a trailer out here with a new car on it. They winch the old car up on the trailer. Then we continue on our way.'

'But what about Lamia? And the other two maniacs?'

'We can do nothing about that, Sabir. Yola has no phone. It is in the lap of the gods.'

'Did we pass an emergency telephone recently?'

'No.'

'So what do we do? Flag down a passing car?'

'No one will stop for us at this time in the morning. We are on the outskirts of Paris, surrounded by *bidonvilles*. Are you crazy, man?'

'All right. You stay in the car in case the police want to know what we are doing parked here. I will go walkabout.'

'Okay.'

Sabir got out of the car. He started up the hard shoulder.

'Sabir?'

'What now?'

'You'd better take the number of the rental agency with you.'

8

It took Sabir thirty-five minutes to find a telephone, and it took the rental agency a further two and a half hours to respond to their call and send out a fresh car. In the interim, both men stretched themselves out on their seats and snatched forty winks. For once in his life, Calque didn't snore.

The trailer was with them at a little after six o'clock in the morning. The actual process of changing cars was a simple one, achieved in a little under ten minutes. Sabir reined himself in with the driver of the tow truck. Calque had warned him that the man was not personally responsible for their plight, nor for the rental company's understandable slowness in responding to an early morning call.

Sabir stood by the tow truck, kicking at the tyres. He was cold. He had on only a thin jacket from Mexico, and it wasn't suitable for an early November morning in northern France. Calque looked cold too. Sabir thought about offering him his jacket, and then rejected the idea. He knew what Calque's response would be.

They were on the road again by 6.30. Both men could feel the events of the past few days beginning to tell on them. There was silence in the car until they reached the outskirts of Samois.

'Let's hope we're still in time.'

'We'll be in time, Sabir.'

'I'm glad you're such an optimist.'

Sabir drove straight for the Gypsy encampment. He missed the turning first time around and had to backtrack a little. But he made it on the second pass, and bumped the car up the rutted track, trying to avoid the worst of the potholes and the puddles. He didn't want to have call the rental agency out a second time.

People were already moving in the camp. Breakfast was being prepared. Sabir had a sudden flash back to the previous May, when he had made a similar journey, at a similar time, although on foot.

The children were the first to notice Sabir's car nosing its way up the track. They came running towards it, suspicion on their faces. When they recognized Sabir's face through the windscreen, they burst into smiles. 'Damo! Damo!'

Sabir pulled the car up onto the verge of the track and got out. Some of the older men were approaching now, with the women holding back a little, to see what was occurring. Radu, Alexi's cousin, whom Sabir had seen married in Gourdon, was the first to reach him.

'Damo. Damo. It is good to see you. Yola will be overjoyed.'

'Radu. Listen to me. We're in a hurry. This is an emergency. You remember the people who killed Babel? Back in May, in Paris? They are after Yola now. We need to warn her and Alexi. We need to get them away from here as quickly as possible.'

Radu didn't waste any time in questions. He took Sabir's arm and led him and Calque towards Alexi's caravan. Alexi was just stepping out of the door.

'Damo! My brother. You have come to visit us. This is perfect timing, because I was just thinking that I need to ask you for another loan. Just for the short term, you understand. This pregnancy is stretching my resources. Not to mention Yola's stomach. Heh. Heh. Heh.' He leapt down from the caravan and threw his arms around Sabir.

'Alexi. Where is Yola? We have an emergency. The Corpus wants to kill her. It's my fault. We need to get her out of here.'

Alexi took a step backwards. Half of him was still locked onto the thought of the loan. 'They want to kill Yola? But why? She has done nothing.' He shook his head, as if clearing it of sleep. 'Is this revenge for what she did to the eye-man?'

'I'll tell you later. Where is she?'

Alexi shrugged. 'Around the camp, maybe. I don't know where she goes in the morning. She is probably roasting coffee beans. Or making my breakfast. She could be anywhere.'

'Radu, can you get all the kids to go look for her?'

Radu nodded. 'I do that.' He hurried off.

Alexi was frowning at Calque. 'You're the policeman. I remember you. Are your people coming to protect her? Or do we have to do it by ourselves again?'

'Alexi, Calque is no longer a policeman. He is helping me. He is a good friend. I am asking you, please, to trust him.'

'He is a friend of yours?'

'A very good friend.'

'As good a friend as I am?'

'You are my brother, Alexi. He is a friend.'

Alexi nodded. 'That's a good answer, Damo. I will trust him.'

'When did you last see Yola?'

Alexi had to think. 'She woke up. With a migraine. It's been bothering her for days. Something to do with her pregnancy, I think. Before that she was sick.'

'What time did she wake up?'

Alexi shrugged. 'This I do not know. Three. Four. Maybe five. It could even have been six.'

'Alexi. For Christ's sake.'

'Six. I think it was six. The light was starting to come in through the windows. I saw her clearly. She was rummaging around in the caravan.'

'Rummaging? What was she rummaging for?'

Both men were already heading up the steps into the caravan.

'This I do not know. But she found whatever she was looking for in that drawer.'

'What do you usually keep in there?' Sabir already had the drawer open, and was rifling through its contents.

'I don't know. Yola does all that sort of thing.'

'Come on Alexi. Try harder.'

'Well. We keep the Bulibasha's telephone number in there. And some other things.'

'The Bulibasha's number is still there. What else would she be looking for?'

'Well, your number maybe. That would be in there too. At least I think so. I can't read, Damo. You remember that, don't you?'

'My number?' Sabir skimmed through the drawers contents. 'It's not here.'

'Then she must have taken it with her.'

'Where's the nearest phone?'

'Well, one or two of us have cell phones.'

'At six in the morning?'

'Okay, maybe not. Maybe she wouldn't have woken people up. Maybe she would have walked to the village. People do that a lot when they want to phone. It's cheaper than using a cell. There's a communal card we all use. All the heads of family contribute to it according to how much they use it. We've got one for abroad and one for France. Yola keeps them in that drawer too.'

Radu came hurrying back inside the caravan. 'She is nowhere. The children made a large circle around the camp. But Bera and Koiné found fresh tracks leading towards the village. They are fresh from today.'

'I remember Bera and Koiné. They are the ones who found Achor Bale's hiding place under the bush, aren't they?'

'Yes. They are your cousins. They are very observant. If they say this, it is true.'

'Let's go to the village, Alexi. She might still be there. Have you got any weapons here?'

'Only my throwing knives. The ones I use in the fairgrounds. When I am giving demonstrations for the *payos*.'

'Are they sharp?'

'Very sharp.'

'Then bring them.'

9

Lamia picked up on the fact that she and Yola were being followed when they were barely half a kilometre out of the village.

'Yola. Look behind you.'

Yola swivelled in her seat.

'It's the Corpus. I know it. I recognize the driver. He was the one who overheard Sabir in the hut.'

'But he looks like a woman.'

'That's what he is. Half man, half woman.'

Yola crossed herself. 'And who is that beside him? She is tiny. Like a child.'

'She is not a child. They are both murderers. They will kill us if they catch us.' Lamia pressed her foot down on the accelerator. The car behind followed suit.

'They are speeding up.'

'We can't risk going to the camp now. We are going to have to make a run for it.'

Yola was still staring uncertainly at the car behind. 'Are you sure of this?'

'Are they still following us?'

'Most definitely.'

'Do they look like police, Yola?'

'No. The police don't use *Diables*. They don't use snails.'

'*Diables*? Snails? What are you talking about?'

'The *Diable* is the hermaphrodite card in the Tarot pack – it corresponds to gold, and so to the union of opposites. All Gypsies know this. The snail, too, is neither one thing nor the other.'

Lamia flashed a look at Yola. 'Adam said you had an exceptional mind. I see what he means.'

Yola shook her head. 'I am full of superstition. My mind is nothing.'

'I don't think so, somehow.' Lamia glanced up at the mirror. 'Is there anywhere we can turn off this road? They have a faster car than us. We are going to have to outwit them, because we can't possibly outrace them.'

'You mean go through the forest?'

'Do you know all the forest tracks?'

'Yes. I have lived here all my life. But you are in danger of bogging down if you use them. There are sudden areas that turn into mud. There has been rain. This car is not designed for that.'

'We'll have to risk it. They'll catch us in no time on the main roads.'

'Then turn here.'

Lamia slewed the Peugeot off the main road. Immediately, she could feel the texture beneath the vehicle change and become more treacherous. When she reached the first corner the car broke away from beneath her and threatened to slide into the ditch. She had to manhandle the steering wheel to regain traction.

'Oh God. They will catch us.'

Yola had twisted around in her seat. 'No. They are having the same problems as we do.'

'Where shall I go now?'

Yola's face seemed to close down on itself. Her eyes turned dead. One hand instinctively strayed to her stomach. 'There is an open mine-shaft. About two kilometres from here. Samois was a mining and quarrying town in the nineteenth century. If you let them get very close, you could lead them to the shaft. Then turn at the last moment, when they still can't see it. They will fall down with their car. It is maybe a hundred metres deep. As children, we thought that *O Beng* – the Devil – lived down there.'

'But that would kill them.'

501

'They want to kill us.'

Lamia glanced at Yola. There was a curious expression on her face. 'Yes. You are right. I am not used to this.'

'Take the next turning on your left. Then slow a little and let them begin to catch up. Make it so that they are sitting directly on your tail. They will not be able to overtake. The track is narrow. You will be quite safe until it opens out either side of the mine shaft. But you will only have one chance. If you don't turn in time we will be dead also. Can you do this?'

Lamia shook her head in wonder. 'Adam said you were a cool customer. Now I believe him.'

'I will not lie down for the lion. That much is true. It happened to me once. With the brother of those people back in the car. Never again.'

Lamia threw the Peugeot into a sharp left turn. Aldinach followed her, six seconds behind. Once on the straight, Aldinach was able to pick up speed, and within twenty seconds he was hard on Lamia's tail.

10

'What the hell was that about?'

Sabir was driving the rental car, with Alexi on the seat beside him. Calque and Radu were hunched forward in the back. Sabir had just seen two cars veer off the main road from Samois village onto a forest track fifty metres ahead of them. For one heart-stopping moment, the three cars had seemed to be heading straight for one another.

'It's them. I recognized Lamia's face. She had someone in the car with her.'

'Are you sure?'

Calque slapped Sabir on the shoulder. 'Of course I'm sure. Lamia's face is unmistakeable, man. I'm not blind.'

'Did you see who was following her?'

'No I didn't. But I'll give you three guesses who it was.'

Sabir floored the gas pedal, then threw the rental into a tight left-hand turn.

'What do you think has happened? Why are Aldinach and Athame chasing Lamia? I thought they were on the same fucking side?'

Alexi turned to Sabir. 'That was Yola inside the first car. I know it. I saw her face in profile. If they hurt her I will kill them all. I will make them eat their own entrails. I will . . .'

'Okay, Alexi. Calm down. We'll catch them.' Sabir was having difficulty keeping the car within the confines of the track. There had been a considerable amount of rain two days before, and the thin November sun had not yet succeeded in drying it off. The top of the dirt track was like a skating rink, therefore, with the very worst potholes reserved for the corners.

'Do you think they've seen us?'

'If they haven't yet, they will soon.'

'You don't think Lamia is trying to protect Yola, do you? That we've got it all wrong? Why would they be chasing her otherwise?'

'Why indeed?' Sabir swung the vehicle through a wide arc, mud and gravel spraying out beside him. 'Where does this go to, Alexi?'

'If you keep straight on, it goes back to the main Fontainebleau road. If you take a left turn about five hundred metres in front of you, it goes towards the old mines.'

'The old mines?'

'This was a quarry area a long time ago.'

As if on cue, both the cars Sabir was following curled left, down the old mine road.

'Tell me about these mines, Alexi.'

'They are very deep. Very dangerous.'

'And Yola knows about them?'

'Of course. *O Beng* lives down there – all Gypsies know that. We are taught it as children, to keep us away from the shafts.'

'*O Beng*?' Calque was leaning forwards in his seat.

'The Devil, Calque. They are going to see the Devil.'

11

___

Lamia threw the wheel over at the last possible moment before striking the fragile fence surrounding the open mine-shaft. The Peugeot almost coped with the unexpected centrifugal strain, but then it struck a hidden rock with one of its back wheels and flipped over onto its side. It continued on, ploughing through some seedlings, and ended up canted against a fir tree at the edge of the surrounding forest.

Aldinach saw the mine shaft at the last possible moment and attempted a handbrake turn. The rental Ford spun around twice, smashed through the wood palings, and came to rest with its tail partially down the mine shaft, and with its two front wheels caught up in the barbed wire that had interleaved the fence stakes.

Sabir was two hundred metres behind the other cars at this stage, and he had ample time to measure his braking. He pulled up beside Lamia's Peugeot while the car was still settling.

He ran towards Lamia's car, followed closely by the others. Grabbing what remained of one of the seedlings, he began smashing in the Peugeot's back window. Alexi wrapped his jacket around both his hands and pulled the glass bodily out of its frame. Then he ducked in through the smashed window and began wriggling across the seats towards Yola.

Sabir ran around to the front of the car. He could see someone trying to open the sunshine roof from the inside.

'Come on, Calque. Help me. Someone is trying to get out. Radu. You go and grab Alexi's legs. I can smell petrol. We've got to get both women out of this car before it goes up.'

A hand emerged from the sunshine roof. Sabir manoeuvred his own hand inside and began to turn the handle. Soon, Lamia's bloodied face emerged from the gap. 'Okay. Hold on. I think we can get you through.'

Calque took one of her arms and Sabir the other. Together they manhandled her slender frame through the half-opened sunshine roof.

'All right. We've got you. Alexi? How are you and Radu doing with Yola?'

'She's fine. She's fine. She's talking to me. We get her out in a minute.'

Lamia got shakily to her feet. She was leaning against Sabir. There was blood all the way down the front of her dress from a gash in her skull. But when Sabir looked closely at it, he saw that, although bleeding copiously, it was only surface deep.

'You were saving her, weren't you? I knew you wouldn't harm her. It would have been impossible. Not after what we said to each other.'

Lamia looked up at him. Then her expression changed. Sabir twisted in the direction of her gaze.

Aldinach was running towards them. His hair was flowing free. He looked like a Mohican brave from one of James Fenimore Cooper's Leatherstocking Tales. A scalpel flashed in his hand. Sabir turned to face him. Both Alexi and Radu were still busy inside the car with Yola. Sabir reached down and picked up the sapling branch he had used to break through the Peugeot's back window and brought it to bear.

Aldinach was heading straight for him. He skipped over the mud and the scattered objects between them like a dancer.

A figure ran past Sabir's left shoulder. It was Lamia. She headed straight for Aldinach, her arms held wide.

Aldinach scarcely hesitated. One hand flashed out and the scalpel entered and exited Lamia's breast like a rapier. She did not even fall, but stood there, her arms cradling her chest, while Aldinach continued on towards Sabir.

A violent rage overcame Sabir – a rage unlike any he had ever known in his life. He, too, ran at Aldinach, so that the two men were sprinting towards each other like rival stags. At the very last moment Sabir raised the sapling branch and sliced it in arc ahead of him. The head of the sapling took Aldinach on the side of the neck, just as he was launching himself, scalpel to the fore, at Sabir. He stumbled and fell to one knee, the scalpel tinging off a rock. He made a lunge for the knife, but Sabir caught him a second blow on the side of the head.

Then Sabir lost all reason. He beat Aldinach again and again with the branch, cursing at him all the while. When he was done, he threw the branch to one side and stumbled over to where Lamia was standing. As he approached she drifted slowly to her knees. It was an elegant movement, almost as if she were curtseying, and only at the very last moment had she decided to kneel.

Her head hung forwards. It nodded once or twice, and then, just as Sabir reached her, she pitched forwards onto her face.

He knelt beside her and swept her up into his arms. She was still alive, but her eyelids were already fluttering.

'I love you. I love you.' Sabir was weeping. His face was grimed with mud and with the blood from the cut in Lamia's scalp.

Her lips moved once but no word came out of them. Then she died. Sabir could feel the life leaving her body like the final fluttering of a curtain in the wind before it once again falls still.

He looked up. Athame was standing a few feet away from him. She was looking at Lamia. Her face seemed sad. She held no weapon.

She took a step towards Sabir and held out one hand.

Something flashed past Sabir's head. He turned quickly to one side to see what it was, but he was far too slow. When he turned back, Athame was clutching at the haft of Alexi's throwing knife, which was protruding from her neck. As he watched, blood gushed out either side of the blade and over Athame's hands. She was so small that she didn't have far to fall.

Sabir looked down at Lamia's face. It was partially turned away from him, so that the damaged side was hidden. He bent down and kissed her mouth, and then the skin around her eyes. Then he lay down beside her and drew her to him, just as he had done in the motel at Ticul.

The two of them lay there, in the clearing, one dead, the other oblivious.

A little later, when Calque attempted, with the greatest gentleness, to prise them both apart, he found it impossible.